RENEWAL

AN AIMEE MACHADO MYSTERY

SHARON ST. GEORGE

CAMEL
PRESS

Kenmore, WA

CAMEL
PRESS

A Camel Press book published by Epicenter Press

Epicenter Press
6524 NE 181st St.
Suite 2
Kenmore, WA 98028

For more information go to:
www.Camelpress.com
www.Coffeetownpress.com
www.Epicenterpress.com
www.sharonstgeorge.com

Photo Credits:
Cover image photo by Harvey Spector
Cover models: Aimee Santone and Michael Osa
Series photo of "Aimee Machado" by Lowell Martinson

Design by Scott Book and Melissa Vail Coffman

ISBN: 978-1-94207-862-3 (Trade Paper)
ISBN: 978-1-94207-863-0 (eBook)

Printed in the United States of America

*This book is dedicated to all individuals who serve in
a health care profession or in any other occupation
that requires dedication to the ideal of serving and
protecting their fellow man.*

ALSO BY THE AUTHOR

Acknowledgments

———•———

THANKS TO MY FELLOW Buckeye Critique Group members Laura Hernandez, Ellen Jellison, Vickie Linnet, and Kelley Sewell for their thoughtful suggestions as they have journeyed with me through every page of Aimee Machado's adventures, and for their constant friendship and support. Thanks to Jennifer Michele for her keen eye for proofreading, and to Jane Jeffers for sharing her knowledge of the world of youth swim team competitions. Thanks to George Souza for keeping me straight about law enforcement and prisons, and to Susan Feamster for providing accurate detail about hospital security protocols. As always, I'm grateful to Jennifer McCord for her guidance and skill in the editing process, and to everyone at Epicenter/Camel Press who contributes to the success of their authors.

Chapter 1

THE FIRST HINT OF DELTA SAWYER'S FATE came before dawn on a rainy Monday morning in March while I was in the barn chopping hay for Old Doolittle. My grandparents' elderly llama had broken another tooth and was having trouble chewing with a total of three missing molars. The vet who treated his dental issues recommended I cut his hay into four-inch lengths and feed him separately from the rest of the herd.

I enjoyed doing the chore myself instead of turning it over to Nick Alexander, the man in my life. Describing each other as "boyfriend" and "girlfriend" felt too much like high school, since Nick was thirty and I was not far behind. Our relationship was exclusive and serious, but "significant other" was too awkward, so we avoided labels.

I had almost finished with the hay when I spotted Nick running toward me from the house, the glow of his headlamp bouncing in the dark. At five o'clock in the morning that could only mean bad news. My heart rate shot up, and a hollow place opened in my chest. I locked Old Doolittle in a sheltered section of the barnyard and jogged up the lane toward Nick.

"What's wrong? Is someone hurt?"

"I don't know, Aimee, Buck just texted asking me to meet him at Timbergate Medical Center."

"Why? Is he ill?"

"No idea. He didn't explain."

We hurried up the lane toward the house. "Should I come with you?"

"Thanks for asking, but I have a feeling I should go alone. You might as well go to work. I'll be in touch as soon as I know what's going on."

"Nick, this might have something to do with Delta. Wasn't she having a medical procedure at TMC over the weekend?"

He shook his head, the beam of his lamp tracing an arc across a curtain of falling rain. "Not likely. Last I heard she was scheduled for cosmetic injections as an outpatient on Saturday. This is Monday. She wouldn't still be at the hospital."

"Did he mention botulinum toxin?" Several brands of the neurotoxin were used for reducing facial wrinkles.

"No, he just said it was a simple procedure with almost no recovery time. Something she's had done before."

As a hospital librarian, I knew that patients could develop severe headaches with neurotoxin injections. I also knew there could be more serious complications. If Delta had run into trouble, I hoped it was only a headache. There was no point worrying Nick with a list of things that could go wrong with a "simple" procedure, especially if it concerned Delta Sawyer, his boss's wife.

We reached the house, where I paused at the mudroom door and caught my breath. "Go. Buck needs you. Get back to me when you can."

Nick gave me a quick kiss and left to drive the eight miles west to Timbergate from our ranching community of Coyote Creek. A welcome aroma in the kitchen told me he'd started the coffee maker while I was in the llama barn. He would have fixed our breakfast too, if not for Buck's cryptic text. I filled a cup and sat at the table listening to rain pelt our windows while I tried to guess the reason for that urgent message.

I considered calling Jared Quinn, Timbergate Medical Center's administrator. My boss would know if there was a medical crisis involving either Buck or Delta Sawyer, but there were confidentiality limits to what he could tell me if either of the high-profile Sawyers was a patient. Better to wait for Nick's call.

"High-profile" was inadequate to describe how prominent the Sawyers were in a rural Northern California city like Timbergate, the county seat of Sawyer County. Buck was a multi-billionaire, and newcomers often assumed he was descended from the county's founders—an understandable mistake. The truth was that Buck's Greek ancestors had come to America with an impossible-to-pronounce Greek surname which they decided to Americanize. They simply changed it to Sawyer.

It was Buck's second and much younger wife, Delta Dearborn Sawyer, who was local royalty. Her ancestor, Elias Dearborn, had been one of the founders of Timbergate, a fact Delta emphasized regularly in her current campaign for mayor. I suspected her cosmetic procedure had something to do with her dive into politics. She had always struck me as fastidious about her appearance. Speaking in front of crowds and having her face plastered all over town would likely reinforce that tendency.

After a trip back to the barn to release Old Doolittle into the main pasture, I warmed myself with a hot shower. I hoped to hear from Nick before leaving for work. I missed our morning time together comparing plans for the day. Missed the sight of him shaving, standing shirtless at the bathroom mirror in his PJ bottoms looking all masculine and sexy, with his fair, sleep-tousled hair. Leave it to a levelheaded half-Chinese librarian to fall for a blue-eyed, blond hunk of a pilot. Amah, my Portuguese grandmother, says I prove the theory that opposites attract.

I shook off my Nick-induced musing and dressed myself in slacks and a blazer, choosing a turtle-neck sweater to fend off the chilly day. My cell phone rang as I was reaching into the closet for a pair of boots. I grabbed the phone from my nightstand. It was Jared Quinn calling from his direct line at the hospital. *Not good.*

"Machado?"

"Yes, what's going on?"

He spit it out. "Delta Sawyer's dead." The phone dropped from my hand and slid under the bed while Quinn continued talking. I groped through dust bunnies on hands and knees and grabbed it in time to hear him say, ". . . be in my office this morning at seven and keep this to yourself. That woman's inflammatory campaign for mayor will have newshounds from miles around storming TMC for details."

Quinn did not elaborate on Delta's cause of death. All he told me was that she died in TMC's Intensive Care Unit.

"From a minor cosmetic procedure?"

"There's only so much I can say about her case, but there are other things we need to talk about. Can you be in my office at seven?"

"Of course."

"Good. Meanwhile, keep in mind Delta Sawyer's death could involve liability issues that would result in a significant conflict of interest for you. Obviously, you feel a sense of loyalty toward Nick, and by extension to his boss, but your primary loyalty must be to this hospital if you're going to do your job."

"I understand. Nick will, too."

Quinn's news came with a sting of guilt. I was fond of Buck and relieved he was all right, but I had never been close to Delta and felt no sense of personal loss about her death. She and I rarely exchanged more than obligatory comments. Her interests and mine had diverged almost completely. My sadness was for Buck. He would turn to Nick, his corporate pilot, sometimes bodyguard, and surrogate son, for comfort and support.

Through Nick, I knew that Buck had married Delta in an effort to blunt the painful losses of his teenaged daughter, Sammy, and her mother. Buck's wealth had not saved him from losing his only child to a drug overdose a decade ago. In her memory, the Sawyers had formed a nonprofit foundation to wage war against addiction and drug trafficking. Sammy's mother died only two years after their daughter; her diagnosis was congestive heart failure. Buck believed the real cause was a broken heart and had vowed to devote the rest of his life to the Sawyer Foundation's mission.

My observations of Delta led me to wonder if grief and loneliness had clouded Buck's judgment at the time of their marriage. I was no psychiatrist, but from the time we first met, I was leery of interacting with her on more than a superficial level. My instincts had warned me she was a complicated, devious woman who could not be trusted. She spent Buck's money freely, mostly on herself, and hung on her prominent husband's arm only when there was a spotlight to share. I noticed she often made decisions without considering his feelings, like refusing to go on vacation with him and instead jetting off to exotic locations with her freewheeling girlfriends. I had tried to give her the benefit of the doubt, but it was difficult. I thought Buck deserved better.

The news from Quinn justified a quick call to Nick. He answered right away.

"You heard about Delta?" he said.

"Yes. I talked to Quinn. How is Buck?"

"Shocked, but staying calm, trying to make sense of what happened."

"I'm glad you're with him. He always seems in control no matter the situation, but this is no time for him to be alone. What's going on now? Are you at his house?"

"We are, but we have to leave in a few minutes, so let's make this quick."

"Okay, here goes. I'm meeting with Quinn at seven. He sees a potential conflict of interest and reminded me where my loyalties lie if TMC is somehow implicated in her death."

"You know what this means, Aimee. We're in opposite camps until it's sorted out."

"We can handle that. We've had to keep our jobs separate before."

"Not like this. Buck is already wondering if Delta's doctor screwed up somehow. Either that, or some TMC employee. I told him you can't get involved, can't take his side about the overdose."

"Is that what Buck was told? Delta's cause of death was an overdose?"

"Quinn didn't tell you?"

"No. Patient confidentiality. But you can tell me."

"Opioid and anxiety meds. Alcohol, too."

"Do you know if she had prescriptions for the meds?"

"Buck says no prescription for the opioid. He said the only pill bottles on her nightstand were her prescription anxiety pills and generic Tylenol in five hundred milligram tablets. He said there was wine, too. Anyway, he took both pill bottles along to the hospital. The TMC pharmacist verified that the anxiety pills checked out, but the pills in the acetaminophen bottle were not generic Tylenol. They were identified as oxycodone."

"In an acetaminophen bottle? Where's that bottle now?"

"It's in Buck's briefcase. Why?"

"Put it in a paper bag, not plastic, but use tongs and make sure no one handles it."

"Forensic librarian speaking?"

"Can't help it, Nick. It's my specialty."

"It comes in handy. I'll tell Buck about the bottle with the wrong pills, but his prints and mine are already on it. And I'm assuming it was handled by whoever checked the pills at the hospital pharmacy. Who knows how many others?"

"Why yours?"

"Buck gave the bottles to me to put in his briefcase after he got them back from the hospital."

"Wish he hadn't done that, but I'm glad you told me about the overdose and the pills. It'll help when I meet with Quinn. Right now, we both need to go. Update me when you can. Let me know how Buck's doing."

I wondered if anyone at the hospital had filed an incident report about the switched pills. That would be something to ask Quinn.

Chapter 2

BY SIX O'CLOCK MY EARLY-MORNING ROAMING from room to room had stirred Nick's Chesapeake Bay Retriever from her bed in a corner of the kitchen. Ginger padded over to me with a puzzled look, as if I might explain what was going on. I did the next best thing. I gave her an extra-large dog biscuit, and while she gnawed on her treat I topped off my coffee cup. My thoughts returned to Nick's loyalty to his boss and his need to help Buck cope with sudden tragedy. I recalled how, early on, I had tried to develop a sociable relationship with Delta, but she had rebuffed my attempts. The truth was, we had almost nothing in common.

Delta had grown up with wealth and privilege, attending an elite East Coast university. She had managed to insert that fact into every campaign speech, interview, and press release from the day she declared her candidacy for mayor. That, and her founding father ancestor.

By contrast, I was a child of the working class. A half-Chinese, half-Portuguese descendant of immigrants, who earned my Library Science degree at a State University in Connecticut.

Comparisons aside, Delta was dead, and concern for Buck Sawyer led me back to the warning from my boss. Whatever was discussed at my morning meeting with Jared Quinn was not to be shared with Nick.

There were strict confidentiality requirements attached to my work as a health sciences librarian. I was required to keep my patrons' research requests confidential. I also coordinated the medical staff's Continuing Medical Education program and the Ethics Committee meetings. Both were confidential. In addition, the Federal HIPAA patient privacy law covered anything pertaining to patient care.

Nick had confidentiality issues of his own, with a boss whose foundation was dedicated to fighting drug trafficking. Still, I believed Nick and I could navigate this situation the way we'd done in the past when we had to be guarded with our conversations. I drained my coffee cup and set it aside. My pulse was already clicking away. No more caffeine for me.

Preoccupied by the mix-up in Delta's pills, I made quick work of grooming by sweeping on a hint of blush and a trace of lipstick. Thanks to my Asian mom and Portuguese dad, I had dark brown eyes and naturally thick lashes, so I skipped mascara and eye liner and clipped my straight black hair at the back of my neck. *Done.*

Ginger watched me from her spot on a throw rug at the foot of the bed. I envied how she had adapted to living in my grandparents' rambling house. After nearly three months, I still missed the cozy barn-top apartment in their llama pasture. The change had come because my little hummingbird of a grandmother and her robust, long-limbed husband, Jack Highland, were spending a few months on the island of Faial in the Azores.

My parents had been living there for a few years, and after visiting them several times, Amah and Jack were considering splitting their time between Coyote Creek and a condo in Faial's port city of Horta. They decided to spend a few months there while making up their minds and had convinced Nick and me to move out of our apartment over the barn and into their house until they made a final decision.

Less than an hour before my scheduled meeting with Quinn the rain had dwindled to a fine mist. I let Ginger out to take care of business and called my colleague and mentor, Cleo Cominoli, Director of Medical Affairs at TMC. I was sure she would be in her office. Quinn would have contacted her before calling me about Delta. Cleo was a step above me in the hospital administration's food chain, and always one of the first to know the most. She answered on the first ring.

"I'm short on facts, Aimee, and Quinn's already warned me about sharing with you."

"I get that, but I've already heard about the drug overdose from Nick. Is there anything else you can tell me?"

"I can tell you Delta wasn't DOA. A noise woke her husband in the night. He got up to check it out and discovered that the wind and rain had caused a tree branch to fall on their deck. They slept in separate rooms, so he looked in to see if it had awakened her. He found her unresponsive in her bed and called 9-1-1. Between the EMTs on the Life Support Unit and our Emergency Department personnel, Delta was kept alive long enough to be admitted to the ICU. You said you already know about the drugs?"

"Yes. Opioid, anti-anxiety med, and alcohol. Was Dr. Beardsley on hand when she was admitted?"

"He was called in, but he didn't arrive until after her death was pronounced in ICU around two in the morning. Have you talked to Quinn?"

"He called. Wants me to meet with him this morning."

"I assume he'll emphasize how sensitive this is, with Buck Sawyer being Nick's boss."

"He made that point on the phone."

"Don't forget the other potential conflict. Your loyalty to TMC is separate from your special relationship with Dr. Beardsley."

"My special relationship with Vane Beardsley? What does that mean?"

"Come on, Aimee. Everyone knows he used his influence with the governing board to get you hired. Between that and your relationship with Nick, your loyalties could be divided three ways once lawyers get involved."

"I get it. Because Beardsley administered Delta's injections in

TMC's outpatient department, our corporate lawyers are looking to defend against error by the hospital staff while also proving TMC blameless of possible malpractice by Beardsley."

"That's a good summation."

"But if Beardsley discharged her Saturday in good condition, and the overdose happened a day and a half after she left the hospital, who knows where she might have been in the meantime? If she was carrying that bottle around in her purse, maybe someone else tampered with those pills."

"Not likely, Aimee. What you don't know is that she was discharged yesterday, not Saturday."

"Why? I thought the injections were done as an outpatient on Saturday."

"Then you haven't heard. She was supposed to be an outpatient, but she got hung up at a candidates' forum and missed her scheduled appointment time. She finally showed up three hours late Saturday afternoon asking if she could be squeezed in. Sounds like 'VIP Syndrome' to me." Cleo's tone told me what she thought of that.

"It worked, obviously."

"It did. She assured Beardsley she had followed his pre-procedure instructions. No alcohol for two days and no blood-thinning meds or anticoagulants like aspirin or ibuprofen for two weeks. Quinn and Beardsley talked it over and agreed to fit her in."

"Why did she end up being admitted overnight?"

"Delta complained of a severe headache and blurred vision after the injections and demanded that Beardsley admit her. Since those are both known complications, he acquiesced and kept her overnight for observation."

"Makes sense he'd opt for an abundance of caution," I said. "So Beardsley discharged her on Sunday, not Saturday."

"Correct. Her headache was gone and her vision was fine. She went home in good condition late Sunday afternoon."

"Again, sounds like both Beardsley and TMC are in the clear."

"Probably, but Beardsley wrote her discharge instructions, so he's not off the hook if something went wrong there." Cleo sighed.

"Let's not go any deeper into this. Much as I dislike it, you and I should stay at arm's length until it's sorted out, and that won't be easy." Her voice softened. "Sorry, gotta go."

Losing access to two allies in the space of an hour was a double sucker punch. Nick and Cleo were always my confidants when there was trouble to sort out. There was only one person left that I could count on for support—my brother, Harry.

As his older sister by almost three years, I had looked out for him when we were young. As adults, we looked out for each other. Our bond had grown even stronger since our parents and grand-parents were living thousands of miles away. I was tempted to call him, but Harry didn't need me interrupting his morning. He was a busy architect and building contractor putting the finishing touches on a three-story shopping mall in Timbergate.

With Nick gone to help Buck, and me with what amounted to a gag order from my boss, I was stymied. I checked the online ver-sions of our local newspaper and television station to see if Delta's death had been picked up. I found nothing; it was probably too soon. As I put down my phone, Amah's peevish Maine Coon cat, Fanny, strutted into the kitchen and sat near her food bowl blink-ing at me in kitty Morse code: *F-E-E-D-M-E!*

That reminded me to check on Ginger, who was waiting at the door. I toweled her off, filled her kibble bowl, and texted Nick, reminding him that the dog would be home alone all day if he didn't come back to the ranch.

My cell pinged as I was opening a can of seafood pâté for Fanny. I glanced at the message from Nick.

Will take care of Ginger soon. At Timbergate PD with Buck.

I replied with shaky fingers. *Why?*

Will explain later.

Chapter 3

I REACHED TIMBERGATE MEDICAL CENTER at six thirty with no word from Nick, likely because he and Buck were still at the police department in the aftermath of Delta's fatal overdose.

I wasn't due in Quinn's office for another thirty minutes, so I parked in the small lot next to the library building and went inside to leave a note for my octogenarian volunteer. Lola Rampley would arrive at nine o'clock. I hoped to be back in the library before then, but considering the potential fallout from Delta Sawyer's case, my appointment with Quinn could take a while.

I locked the library and jogged across the hospital grounds to the main tower, hugging myself against the cold dawn. Though the rain had tapered to mist, the rising sun was making no headway in breaking through a sky draped in gray.

With several minutes to kill before meeting Quinn, I stopped by Cleo Cominoli's office. My tap on her door brought a muffled response.

"Come in."

Cleo's eyes grew wide over her half-moons as I entered. "Aimee, what are you doing here?"

Almost twice my age, my feisty Italian colleague and mentor looked as fashionable as always, despite being called in to work at a moment's notice. Her dark hair was swept into a classic chignon, and a tailored suit flattered her striking figure, its rich plum color matching her glossy lipstick.

"I'm a little early for my meeting with Quinn. Hoped I could hang out with you. I won't ask a single question about Delta Sawyer. Promise." I crossed my heart like a second grader.

Cleo peered around me. "Shut the door. Did anyone see you?"

"No. Why the cloak and dagger?"

"You know we're supposed to keep arm's length about Delta Sawyer."

"We've already said all we could about that on the phone this morning. But we still have jobs to do. We can't break off communication completely."

"No, but let's keep our talks to a minimum. I've never known a patient's death to rattle Quinn like this one."

"That's not surprising, considering the Sawyers' prominence in the community."

Cleo gestured toward a chair across from her desk. "You might as well sit."

I lowered myself to the edge of the chair. "Quinn called you in as soon as he heard about Delta, didn't he? Was that about Dr. Beardsley?"

"Definitely. He wanted to make sure Beardlsey's credentials file was in order." Cleo placed a hand with plum-colored nails on the folder on her desk. "It is, of course."

"Why would Quinn be concerned about that?"

"Because Vane Beardsley's been back on our medical staff for less than a week. Quinn wanted confirmation that all of his privilege requests had made their way through the required committee approvals and the governing board."

"And had they?"

"Absolutely. Every privilege Beardsley requested was approved by all necessary medical staff committees up the chain of command before being approved by the governing board. Including administering neurotoxin injections. They were the same privileges he held here at TMC before he left town two years ago."

"Then why is Quinn worried? Does he think Beardsley's privileges were rubber-stamped?"

Cleo's expression turned dark. "That would imply that I didn't do my job."

"No, that's not . . . I'm saying the *committees* should have checked—"

"Hold on." Cleo got up and walked over to her file cabinets where she stood with arms crossed. "Here's an aspect of my job you may not fully understand. Beyond facilitating all of TMC's twenty-plus medical staff committees—except your two—I'm also the gatekeeper when docs come to TMC requesting medical staff membership and privileges.

"They submit a curriculum vitae to me documenting everything in their background and training that proves they're qualified for medical staff membership and the privileges they request. That CV is my responsibility, Aimee. Everything in it must be verified before a doctor's application works its way through the committee approval process."

"Aren't the medical staff's committee chairmen responsible for the verification process?"

"Only indirectly," Cleo said. "They leave it to me to contact every reference in the applicant's CV to ask for verification. Only after I receive confirmation in writing from every reference listed does the application start working its way through the committees. I did not cut corners with Beardsley's application. I made certain there were no red flags that might have emerged during the past two years."

"You're basically doing the work of the medical staff, hospital administration, and even the governing board. They're all relying on you to be the gatekeeper?"

"That's right. I finished my verification process before Beardsley's application went through the Surgery Executive Committee for privileges, then to Credentials for approval of his membership on the medical staff. Eventually it worked its way up to the governing board. If Beardsley had gotten his approvals by falsifying something on his CV, guess who would take the blame."

"How unfair. And Quinn knows this could come back on you if Delta's death turns out to be a medical error by Beardsley?"

"Not just on me. The TMC Medical Staff Organization and Governing Board would be in hot water. And if that does happen, if I missed something, it will be the first time in the twelve years I've been doing this job."

"How long does it take for an application to get to the governing board?"

"The committee process takes at least a month from start to finish." Cleo walked back to her desk and sat. "It's not going to look good that Beardsley's membership and privileges were officially approved by the governing board only three days before Delta's procedure."

"I don't understand why he did the injections in TMC's Outpatient Department. Aren't those usually done in doctor's offices?"

"Depends on the doctor. Beardsley said he'd feel more comfortable doing them here because his private office was still in the process of being set up."

"Wait, was her procedure the first he's done at TMC since coming back on staff?"

"Bingo." Cleo held up the credentials folder. "Right now, this is the elephant in the room."

"What are you going to do?"

"What Quinn demanded. Double check everything in Beardsley's CV in case something was missed. I already verified that his license is clear with the Medical Board of California, and he has no red flags with the National Practitioner Data Bank."

"How long will it take you to recheck the CV?"

"Not long." Cleo walked back to her desk. "I've said all I can say to you about Delta's case, Aimee. Maybe more than I should have. I don't like it any more than you do, but for now, let's keep our interactions at a minimum."

"It's not going to be easy. You've been my go-to person since the day I was hired."

"We don't have a choice. You need to go see Quinn. And please don't drop in again without warning until this thing blows over." Cleo's heavy sigh hinted at regret, but her set jaw and resolute eye contact told me she would abide by Quinn's order.

I left without another word, knowing she was trying to protect both of us.

Chapter 4

AT SEVEN SHARP I OPENED THE DOOR to the administrative suite expecting to see Quinn's executive assistant, Varsha Singh, at her reception desk. Instead I was greeted by a plump, middle-aged woman with a cap of gray curls and a gentle demeanor—a striking contrast to Varsha's East Indian beauty and vibrant personality. It was general knowledge at work that Quinn and Varsha had been dating for several months. This substitute threw me for a moment.

"Hello," she said, "you must be Ms. Machado. Tell me, am I pronouncing your name correctly?"

"Almost. We use the Portuguese pronunciation. *Ma-SHAW-doe*. Thank you for asking."

"You're welcome. I believe it's common courtesy to get names right." She waved toward Quinn's door. "Mr. Quinn is expecting you."

I hesitated. "Is Varsha on vacation?"

"I'm afraid I don't know." She rose from her chair, extending her hand. "My name is Enid Whitehorn." Her grip conveyed warmth and self-confidence.

"Nice to meet you."

"You may go in," Enid prodded. "As I said, he is expecting you."

Standing at his window with his back to me, Quinn got right to the point. "What have you said to Nick about Delta Sawyer's death?"

"Nothing, because I didn't know anything until he told me she died of an opioid overdose mixed with alcohol and an anxiety med."

Quinn turned to face me, his dark hair rumpled and his chiseled jaw working overtime. "He told you that?"

"He mentioned it. Assumed I already knew."

"What else?"

"He knows I'm meeting with you, and he's very aware of my confidentiality constraints."

"Do you have any reservations about following those constraints?"

"None at all."

"Then let's talk." Quinn walked to his desk and sat. "You first. Since you already know the cause of death, do you have any questions?"

I sat opposite Quinn. "Before I left for work, Nick texted that he and Buck were at the Timbergate Police Department. Do you know what that's about?"

"I haven't been told, but I can guess."

"Were the police here when Delta was brought in?"

"Not that I'm aware of. One of our Life Support Units brought her in comatose from a combo of oxy, alprazolam, and alcohol, but you already know that." Quinn tapped at the keyboard on his desk. "Can't stand these electronic records. Give me a paper chart any day."

"I know alprazolam is generic for Xanax, and I assume Beardsley knows about the opioid. Have you asked him if he prescribed either of those controlled drugs?"

"I did," Quinn said, "and his answer was no. Beardsley swears all he recommended for pain was five hundred milligram acetaminophen."

"That's Tylenol or a generic equivalent."

"Correct. He insisted he never prescribes opioids for cosmetic procedures, and he didn't prescribe the anxiety med, either."

"What does her medical record show? Beardsley must have made a discharge note about the acetaminophen."

"He did. His discharge note documented that he had seen Delta for a pre-op visit on the Friday before her surgery. That's when he told her that all she'd need for pain was acetaminophen. He told her she could pick it up in five hundred-milligram tablets over the counter. He also noted that no other post-op prescriptions were written. None of the opioid options she asked about and nothing for anxiety."

"That means he's off the hook. She got both the alprazolam and the opioid from some other source."

"Looks that way for the anxiety med. Her husband confirmed she had a prescription from her family physician for alprazolam, but he swears all she had for pain was acetaminophen."

"Did anyone here at the hospital ask Buck Sawyer about the opioid?"

"I did," Quinn said. "He claims the acetaminophen bottle that was on her nightstand was one that she purchased at a big box pharmacy two days before her surgery. It was small, holding only two dozen tablets. The dosage directions were two five hundred-milligram tablets every four to six hours. He said she had the container in her purse when she was admitted, and brought it home with her when she was discharged. The problem is, the pills in the acetaminophen bottle were not acetaminophen. They were oxycodone. I assume Nick told you this."

"He did. Does Beardsley know?"

"Yes. As her admitting physician, he was informed as soon as we knew."

"It's no wonder she overdosed. The combined drugs and alcohol could easily have caused severe respiratory depression."

"And it did. She eventually stopped breathing and died."

I tried to read Quinn's expression. "Do you think this was premeditated?"

"Let's avoid cop talk, Machado. The police and the district attorney will have to determine whether it was foul play before they get to premeditated. That's not our job."

"Do the police know about the oxycodone?"

"I'm certain of it. Buck Sawyer has already confronted me about it. He insisted she had the acetaminophen bottle in her purse when she showed up late for her cosmetic injections on Saturday. He said the switch must have happened while she was in the hospital. Vowed to get to the bottom of it."

"But patients aren't supposed to bring in outside pills when they're admitted, are they?"

Quinn shook his head. "Absolutely not. The intake personnel swear Delta denied having any pills with her. The problem here is that our employees aren't allowed to search patients' purses."

"Wait a minute. Buck claimed Delta had the pill bottle in her purse when she was admitted, and you're saying no one who works at TMC can verify that's true?"

"That's right."

"Then it's only Buck's word that the acetaminophen bottle was in her possession while she was in the hospital?"

"No. Nick Alexander backed him up. They both said they witnessed her putting the bottle in her purse Saturday morning before she was picked up at home by a taxi. She planned to come here straight from an appearance at a candidates' forum. Her outpatient procedure was scheduled for one o'clock in the afternoon."

"But she arrived several hours late," I said, "and according to Cleo, Delta ended up being admitted overnight. Are you sure there's no one at TMC who can verify that she had that bottle with her?"

"Looks that way." Quinn glanced at a sheet of paper on his desk. "The nurse assigned to Delta on Saturday filled out an incident report saying the purse was stored in a safe in the Security Office. Sawyer says he didn't arrive at TMC until after Delta was admitted late Saturday afternoon. Apparently, your boyfriend had flown him over to Arroyo County early that morning on business. They got detained by a flat tire on the landing gear and arrived back later than they expected. Sawyer looked in on her briefly and went on home."

"Do you know who drove Delta to the hospital for her procedure?"

"No. We haven't been able to identify who that was."

"Why did Delta's purse end up in the Security Office?"

"Hospital policy. The person who brought her in declined to take possession of it and didn't stick around once she was admitted, so Security locked it in their safe. It was released to her when Buck came to take her home on Sunday afternoon. He says no one mentioned anything about her purse until then, and he didn't think to ask. I've already interviewed the Security staff. They insist no one ever looked inside it."

"If it was locked in a safe how could anyone at the hospital have tampered with its contents?"

"Good question. That's what Buck Sawyer wants to know."

Quinn sank back, his broad shoulders drooping in a posture unusual for someone so dedicated to fitness. A frown distorted the impact of his fine features. I wondered if there was something more than Delta Sawyer's death weighing on him. Maybe Varsha's unexplained absence? I let that go for the moment.

"It seems like a pretty weak argument for accusing the hospital or Beardsley of any wrongdoing. Buck has no way to prove that pill bottle was ever here."

"Not yet, but I have no doubt he's going to try." Quinn shot me a look. "And that might explain why he and your boyfriend are talking to the police."

I let his reference to Nick pass. "Did the pharmacist file an incident report the morning Delta died?"

"He did, and so did I, but all it does is document that the pills in the acetaminophen bottle Buck brought from home after his wife's overdose didn't match the label on the bottle. It goes nowhere to prove whether the switch happened here at the hospital or not."

"I don't see how I can help with any of this. Unless you want me to research opioid overdose. Or medication errors."

"We'll get back to that. First you need to know my phone lines are being flooded with calls from the media. They'll hype this like Lady Di's death after that car crash in Paris, so if anyone from the media gets through to you, offer no comment and refer them to me."

"You really think it's going to provoke that kind of reaction?"

"The way Delta Sawyer was running her campaign for mayor already had her caught up in controversy. Election day is only a week and a half away. For the next ten days, all the conspiracy nuts will be coming up with theories on social media."

"Because of her threats to expose dirt on the other candidates? You think anyone took her seriously?"

Quinn sighed, crossed his arms. "Never underestimate the power of dirty politics."

"But Delta never followed through with those threats. If the dirt she claimed to have was legit, most voters would wonder why she hadn't used it by now."

"Some would assume she was bluffing, but it might have worked on others."

"Seems like Delta would have been smarter to keep her focus on her legacy. As a direct descendant of one of Timbergate's founding fathers, she could have done a lot with her first campaign slogan: *Vote Delta Sawyer—Timbergate's Favorite Daughter.*"

"Ernest Wright was her closest rival. She must have thought dirty politics was her best chance to take him down. Imply a secret scandal in his past."

"Pity she decided to take the low road," I said.

"It's all moot now. Wright's slogan seems to be working pretty well, particularly among our conservative faction. *Vote Wright – The Right Man for the Job.* With Delta gone and no incumbent, he has only one candidate to beat."

"But Nora Nester's a woman, so there's a chance she'll pick up a good share of Delta's followers."

"I wouldn't count on it. Her campaign doesn't have the kind of sex appeal Delta's had." Quinn held up his hand. "Don't get me wrong. I didn't mean that literally. I mean despite Delta's negative approach, she had charisma—a flair that caught people's attention. Nester's better qualified than either Delta or Wright, but she's not exciting. Even her name is bland. *Nester.* Makes me think of comfy places to fall asleep. If you've heard her speak, you know that nasal monotone isn't helping. Wait until Wright comes up with a joke about that."

"You think he'll sink to a name-calling campaign?"

"It seems to be a trend in politics these days. He was already calling Delta Sawyer Timbergate's 'least-favorite daughter.'"

"Maybe that inspired Delta to start hinting at scandals involving her opponents. Wonder how she planned to taint a reputation as impeccable as Nora Nester's. She runs the most popular daycare business in Timbergate."

"Looks like we'll never know, but we need to get back on topic, Machado. Use your librarian's magic to see what you can pull together on drug overdose and medical errors. It shouldn't be difficult with all the media attention on our national opioid epidemic. Look for any scenario similar to Delta Sawyer's. Anything that could explain how those pills got switched."

"I'll do the search, but it's not going to be easy to find results you can count on. There are so many variables, including a mistake at the manufacturer or some kind of sabotage like the Tylenol drug tampering murders."

"That's going way back, but anything's possible. Find whatever you can, and make sure anything you learn about this case is kept strictly between the two of us."

The back of my neck tensed. "I assure you I won't breach confidentiality by talking out of turn. Especially to Nick and Buck."

"Good. And I'll expect you to inform me if you happen across anything about Delta Sawyer that would shed light on the overdose."

"I'm not sure what you mean."

Quinn shrugged. "I'm not sure either, but we do know about her prescription for anxiety pills."

"If you're suggesting she had a drug problem, I can't speak to that. I barely knew the woman." I walked to his door. "You're putting me in an awkward position, Quinn. Confidentiality is a two-way street. Until this is over, you'll have to trust me."

"I know you're pulled in two directions. I'll try to respect that, but Delta Sawyer's death could mean a multi-million-dollar lawsuit and a black eye for Timbergate Medical Center. You've shown yourself to be a savvy investigator more than once before. I'm asking you to report back to me anything you come across that will help prove TMC and Beardsley are blameless when it comes to the pills that caused her death."

"Why Dr. Beardsley? All he did was recommend acetaminophen."

"Because Delta told her husband she thought she could coax Vane Beardsley into writing her a prescription for opioids. She'd had those neurotoxin injections before and had severe headaches afterwards. She was afraid acetaminophen wouldn't manage her pain."

"Buck Sawyer told you that?"

"He did," Quinn said. "He even hinted that Beardsley might have given her the pills on the sly. You can bet Sawyer's not going to let that go."

"If she knew the injections gave her headaches, why would she even want them?"

Quinn shrugged. "Vanity, I suppose. A quick fix with essentially no recovery time and she'd look like a million bucks come election day."

"That sounds like Delta, but Beardsley wouldn't have given in about the opioid. Even if he did, it wouldn't have ended up in a mislabeled bottle. He'd never do it illegally."

"We know that, but Buck Sawyer doesn't. And neither do the police. For now, we need to arm ourselves with anything that would clear Beardsley and TMC."

And Buck, I thought.

"I'll do what I can, but I'm most likely to find a mountain of stats on medication errors in hospitals." I opened his door, eager to leave, but Quinn stopped me.

"Machado, wait. Before you go, close the door and come back. There's something else I want to discuss with you."

I walked back to his desk, but didn't sit. "What is it?"

"It involves a new position for you, and a promotion." Leave it to Quinn to toss me a bolt out of the blue.

"I already have my hands full with the library and the committees I manage. What would a new position involve?"

"You'd still be in charge of the library and your committees, but your responsibilities would increase and your time would be utilized differently, with more emphasis on forensic resources. Your pay scale would jump to a higher level, and you'd have enough funding to hire a qualified librarian to assist you with day-to-day functions of the library."

"How would *my* time be spent?"

"You'd be—" Quinn's desk phone rang. He answered, paused to listen and hung up. "Bad timing. Enid has a TV reporter in the reception area. I have to do damage control."

"Then I should go."

Quinn closed his eyes, pressed his fingers against his temples for a moment, then glanced at me. "Probably for the best. We'll postpone further discussion of your employment status until the Delta Sawyer case is behind us."

He followed me out to the reception room where a slender, dark-haired young woman sat in a visitor's chair with her head bent over a notepad. The eager reporter, obviously.

I hurried back to the library on a day that had begun at five in the morning in the llama barn, followed by news of a mystifying death and two anxiety-ridden meetings with colleagues. I had to wonder if there was a veiled message in Quinn's last comment. No further discussion of a promotion until we knew the facts surrounding Delta Sawyer's case.

Had he dangled a carrot to ensure my loyalty, or was my imagination working overtime? That was not how he usually operated. He had always been firm but fair in the past, and we had developed a working relationship based on mutual respect. This issue of divided loyalties could be our ultimate test. I hoped it was one that Quinn and I would pass.

Chapter 5

Back in the library eight o'clock in the morning felt more like quitting time than the beginning of my workday. I still had no word from Nick. It helped that my day's task list was light. There were no urgent needs related to the library and nothing pressing for the two committees I coordinated for the medical staff. Ethics Committee only met as needed, and Continuing Education Committee wasn't due to meet for another three weeks. I could start on Quinn's request right away.

Opioid deaths. I did a simple search and came up with a result from the Centers for Disease Control website that stated in the most recent twelve-month period in the United States, there were more than ninety-three thousand overdose deaths reported. The CDC was a reference I could trust to be accurate. I read more, and found that the odds of dying from opioid overdose were higher than those of dying from a car crash.

The CDC site listed various pharmaceutical opioids. It named oxycodone, the one found in Delta's pill bottle. Others were hydrocodone, morphine, and methadone. Heroin was listed too, as an illegal opioid.

My Monday and Wednesday volunteer arrived at nine, so I bookmarked the CDC site. I always tried to spend a few moments chatting with Lola Rampley. In her early eighties with a cloud of white hair topping her diminutive figure, she was spry and sharp, but her osteoarthritis and severe dowager's hump led me to wonder if she suffered pain during the course of her volunteer work in the library. She was a proud woman, so I hesitated to ask for fear I might embarrass her.

Lola usually started the morning with a cheerful greeting, so I was puzzled when she offered only a subdued "Hello." She quickly inserted the earbuds attached to her iPod—her current music genre was big band swing—and went to work shelving medical journals without another word.

I wondered if her mood hinted at a personal problem involving her fiancé, Bernie Kluckert, who volunteered for me on Tuesdays and Thursdays. They had met through their volunteer work in the library, which made me an unwitting matchmaker. Over the past couple of years, I had come to think of them as extended family, but that was no excuse to pry.

I circled back to my opioid research, where I had unearthed lots of statistics but nothing to explain how the fatal dose found its way into Delta's system. If not an error by the pharmacy or the manufacturer, someone must have tampered with the pills.

Foul play would suggest that Delta had an enemy with a motive for homicide. It was a stretch to imagine her self-absorbed behavior leading to murder, but I couldn't rule that out.

My first impression of Delta had been her beauty and charisma. Before long, I noticed how obsessed she was with her looks. It seemed extreme to me, but lots of attractive women panic when they spot the first small crop of lines on their foreheads and around the eyes. A quick check online confirmed that tens of millions have received neurotoxin injections, making it one of the most common cosmetic procedures in the world.

Delta's sudden leap into the race for mayor of Timbergate had surprised everyone close to Buck. He confided to Nick that although it was impulsive and not well thought out, he decided to be supportive, hoping Delta's show of interest in community service was a positive sign. Her need for attention seemed more likely to me, but I recognized that my opinion of Delta was colored by my protective feelings for Buck.

Turning back to my task, I compared images of both acetaminophen and oxycodone until I found each of them in a tablet form that looked similar to the other. If Delta was unfamiliar with what oxycodone tablets looked like, she would have assumed the pills in the vial were acetaminophen and taken them as directed on the label along with one of her anxiety pills and a chaser of alcohol. The literature I found online warned that combination could be deadly.

The recommended acetaminophen dosage directions for five hundred milligram tablets stated two every four to six hours. The recommended dose for a ten milligram opioid tablet was one tablet orally every twelve hours. That site warned that patients who use higher starting doses, and who are not opioid tolerant, could suffer fatal respiratory depression.

That raised a troubling question. Cleo told me Delta had gone home from the hospital late Sunday afternoon. If she had taken two of the opioid tablets earlier than her bedtime, why had the fatal reaction not happened sooner? If she had taken the pills with no adverse effects in the hours between leaving the hospital and going to sleep that night, the blame for her drug overdose seemed to point to Buck. Who else could have switched the pills after he brought her home?

I groped for an explanation that would clear Buck. Maybe the pain meds she received while still in the hospital on Sunday had kept her comfortable until her bedtime and beyond. That was often the case with patients on their day of discharge. She might have been warned to wait until bedtime before taking more. Or maybe she only took the pills from the acetaminophen bottle when she woke up with pain during the night.

There were too many *maybes* and competing scenarios to sort through. I had to believe the police were considering all of them and had not set their sights on Buck. One comfort was his being the first person to demand an investigation. Another was his lack of motive.

A glance at the time, almost eleven, reminded me that I still had not heard from Nick. The mystery involving the switched pills had to be why he and Buck had gone to the Timbergate Police Department. They wanted to know what had happened. So did I.

LOLA FINISHED HER SHIFT AND LEFT AT NOON, still unusually subdued. An hour later I was still busy on the CDC site researching opioids when an unexpected and problematic visitor walked in. Dr. Vane Beardsley strode toward my desk. It was the first time I had seen him since his return to Timbergate Medical Center, and he was as dapper as ever wearing a two-button wool suit tailored in a subtle gray plaid. Still proudly bald, he sported his hallmark Van Dyke beard, rusty red sprinkled with gray. I noticed a few added pounds since I had last seen him more than a year ago. His strong, musky cologne scent drifted toward me from several feet away.

He stopped at my desk. "Miss Machado, good to see you. I'm pleased that your hire has been a success. Makes me proud I had a small part in it."

His comment seemed to affirm Cleo's earlier remark. Beardsley knew he was instrumental in my being hired and felt he had a right to expect my loyalty. *Only up to a point.*

"Thank you." I offered my hand, which he held with his right, then covered with his left and continued to hold several seconds longer than necessary.

"Am I correct in assuming you're still Miss?"

"For now." I pulled my hand away as discreetly as possible. "But that could change very soon."

Let him work that out for himself. In the past, Beardsley had seemed a bit too friendly, and not in a strictly avuncular way. I wanted him to know I was in a solid relationship.

He moved on to the reason for his visit. "I suppose you've been told that I lost a patient in the wee hours of this morning."

"I have, but I know very little about the case."

"Nevertheless, I'd like your assistance—if you have a bit of time."

"How can I help?" I gestured toward a small library table where we could sit across from each other.

"Mrs. Sawyer was a high-profile patient, as you are aware. Jared Quinn is concerned that there will be legal difficulties for the hospital. My malpractice attorney thinks the same for me."

"How would that involve my help?"

"My attorneys are quite capable with regard to malpractice when it relates to performing medical procedures, but this pill mix-up is rather a different wrinkle. I felt they could benefit from your expertise as a health sciences librarian." He took an envelope from the inside pocket of his suit jacket. "They've listed the sort of information they would like you to provide. It would expedite their work. You can understand my sense of urgency."

I picked up the envelope and stood. "I do understand, and ordinarily I would go ahead with your request because you're a member of the medical staff with library privileges, but I've been cautioned to ask Jared Quinn's approval for anything work-related that I do involving this case."

He glanced up at me. "I see. I should have thought of that."

I took a few steps toward the exit, hoping he would take the hint and follow. "I'll run it by him and let you know his answer."

Beardsley rose and followed me to the door. "Miss Machado, you will recall that I, too, have lost a wife under similar circumstances . . . there were drugs involved." He looked beyond me for a moment, searching his memory. "That was a terrible time and not so long ago. I know how Mr. Sawyer must be feeling. I would like to offer him my condolences, but my attorneys have advised against it. I don't suppose you could . . . ?"

"I'm sorry, Dr. Beardsley. I can't."

The doctor went on his way, leaving me to ponder the number of lawyers who were already mustering their ammo. TMC, Vane Beardsley, and Buck Sawyer all had separate law firms preparing to defend their clients. I hoped they were all on the same side, but there were no guarantees.

Under normal circumstances, Beardsley would be eligible for my assistance in providing any information he wanted. I opened the envelope. His attorneys' list requested articles on medication errors of all kinds, from manufacturer to place of sale, to hospitals. It also asked for articles related to oxycodone, heroin, and fentanyl. The list was almost identical to the research I was doing for Quinn, who had told me to keep anything I turned up strictly between the two of us. I would need Quinn's approval before filling Beardsley's request.

I first looked up the infamous Tylenol case that had taken place before I was born. In Chicago in the early eighties, several sealed bottles of the acetaminophen capsules were laced with lethal doses of potassium cyanide, causing the deaths of six people.

It was established that the cyanide lacing occurred after cases of the pills left the factory. The police concluded that someone took the bottles off the shelves of local markets and drugstores, laced the capsules with poison, and then returned the packages to the shelves. The Tylenol murders have never been solved, but conspiracy theories are still being posted on the Internet more than thirty years later.

The article ended on a positive note, pointing out that the victims' deaths inspired moves to make over-the-counter medications safer. Within months of the poisonings, tamper-proof packages became the industry standard, with a caution that they can never be one hundred percent safe.

Those safety measures had not kept Delta Sawyer alive. Someone had tampered with her pills in a very different manner. No potassium cyanide was involved. Even easier, switch out the original pills in the bottle and replace them with something far more deadly.

Tampering by a killer of random victims did not fit my instincts about Delta's case. Her death seemed deliberate, motivated by someone either very angry about something she had done, or very afraid of something she might do. Possibly both.

The other category of medication errors on Beardsley's list was known as LASA, which was shorthand for *look-alike, sound-alike*. Those were cases when one medication was prescribed, and a different one was dispensed to the patient because the pills were similar in shape and color, and in their generic or brand name. Things as simple as sloppy handwriting on a prescription pad might cause the error.

From there, I found a variety of other articles, and numerous reasons behind the excessive number of victims of medication errors. The more research I did, the less I wanted to ever swallow another pill.

The most frustrating piece of information I took away was the awareness that a motivated killer could disguise his crime, or hers, as another troubling example of the many mistakes that are made in dispensing medication.

Beardsley's desire to have the information he had asked for seemed to work against the idea that he could be guilty of malpractice. His attorneys had asked for this information to help exonerate him.

I stored the articles in a special file folder on my computer and immediately sent a copy of the entire folder to Quinn. I put off forwarding the same information to Beardsley. I first wanted to follow up with Cleo, who was double checking Beardsley's credentials. If she gave me an all clear, I would touch base with Quinn for an okay to give Beardsley what he requested.

When it was time for an afternoon break, I called Cleo to ask if I could drop by her office.

"What's up?"

"A question I'd rather not ask on the phone. Or in writing."

"Is it work related? We don't want Jared Quinn accusing us of inappropriate communication."

"I need your advice about a member of our medical staff. And Quinn will be informed, so we're not flouting his order."

"Then meet me at Margie's in ten. I could use a break."

I reached Margie's Bean Pot, the diner down the block from TMC, in time to spot Cleo entering. I followed her to our usual table at the back of the room.

Margie Sacchi, a full-figured earth mother with curly salt and pepper hair, came by to take our orders with pen and pad at the ready. "Nice to see you, ladies, what'll it be? The special's three-bean salad with avocado."

We both declined. Cleo wanted hot tea. I asked for coffee.

"Coming right up." Margie hesitated, tapping her order pad with her pencil. "Guess the game's afoot at your workplace, huh?"

Cleo shot me a glance. I let her respond. "Not sure what you mean, Margie."

"Poor Delta Sawyer. Who would have thought?"

"Thought what?" Cleo said.

Margie took a step back. "Oh, I guess you haven't heard the rumors?"

"Already?" Cleo stiffened. So did I.

Margie nodded. "Hit the TV news around nine this morning. Special bulletin. Close to home for my lunch crowd. Anybody know what happened to her?"

"We're not at liberty to discuss patients," Cleo said.

"Then the husband is innocent? And his pilot, too?"

My stomach flipped a somersault. "What have you heard, Margie?" I ignored Cleo's warning frown.

"It's been the hot topic on Facebook and Twitter most of the day. She was fairly young and apparently healthy. Looks like the news folks are being stonewalled about how she died. People are guessing maybe foul play. Saying husbands are always a suspect. Even looking at the pilot. Not the woman pilot, but the other one." Her eyes suddenly widened, and I knew why. Margie remembered too late that the "pilot" was my boyfriend, Nick Alexander. If her face got any redder, she would have needed a blood pressure check. "Naturally, I don't believe a word of that, and I said so." She spun around and hurried toward the kitchen.

Cleo patted my hand. "Hey, take a breath and tell me what you wanted to ask."

"It's about Vane Beardsley. He requested a search on medication errors and opioids. Before I send him the results, I wanted to know if you've finished re-checking his credentials."

"That's a yes. I devoted the morning to it and finished just before you called. He's squeaky clean. Absolutely nothing problematic about his reappointment to the medical staff or his privilege requests."

"Quinn is satisfied?"

"He is. Told me our corporate attorneys are confident TMC's employees and the medical staff organization are in the clear. Everyone followed the appropriate protocols. And speaking of protocol, Delta's case will be reviewed in more than one committee to document that." She put a five-dollar bill on the table and stood up. "And that's as much as you and I should say about it. Sorry, but I have to get back to work."

"Before you go, I have a question about Beardsley that isn't off limits."

"What is it?"

"Quinn asked me for a medication error search this morning that's essentially identical to Beardsley's. He told me to keep what I found between the two of us. I know he was referring to outsiders like Nick or Buck, but I have no legitimate reason to withhold the same search results from Beardsley. He's a member of our medical staff and entitled to library privileges."

"Then that's your answer. If you're in doubt, run it by Quinn, but I'm betting he'll tell you to give Beardsley what he asked for."

I watched Cleo exit and took a few sips of my coffee while her tea cooled across the table from me. It seemed rude for both of us to leave abruptly. Margie dropped by again and eyed the full teacup and Cleo's empty chair.

"What's this?"

"Cleo had to get back to work."

"I know she has an important job." Margie lifted Cleo's cup. "I hope my asking about Mrs. Sawyer didn't offend her." Her face flushed again. "Or you."

"People tend to speculate all kinds of wild things, Margie. We try to ignore them."

BACK IN THE LIBRARY I CALLED QUINN, and with his okay, I sent Beardsley's attorneys the materials they had requested. By then it was nearing four o'clock, and my hectic Monday had gone so far off the rails that I was mentally fatigued and running on fumes when another unexpected visitor dropped in: my Tuesday morning volunteer, Bernie Kluckert.

His showing up on a Monday afternoon was so unusual that I panicked for a second, worrying that something had happened to Lola.

"Bernie, what brings you here?"

"Just got off an extra shift working floater. Covering for a buddy. He's laid up with bunions, don't you know? Stopped by to chat a moment, if that's all right."

"It's fine. Come and sit. You must be tired."

In his early nineties, he was short in stature but solid, sporting an abundant crop of snow-white hair. His gait was stiff and his hands were arthritic, but his brain was in good shape, and his blue eyes twinkled behind wire-rimmed glasses. He shuffled over to my desk and plopped down in a chair across from me.

Whatever had been troubling Lola that morning seemed not to be affecting him. I was debating whether to ask him about it when he saved me the trouble.

"Miz Machado, is the rumor true?"

"I'm sorry, what rumor?" Delta's unexplained death came to mind. Surprising, because all of the volunteers were warned that gossiping about patients, or anything else related to the hospital, would get them dismissed.

"The skinny in the auxiliary lounge is you're gonna be leaving the library." Bernie rubbed his finger against a leaf of the small aloe plant on the corner of my desk. He checked it for dust, careful not to catch his finger on its barbs. "Kinda upset Lola. She likes working for you." He waited for me to reply.

So that was the cause of Lola's unusual behavior. The promotion Quinn had alluded to. If it was already being discussed by the volunteers, chances were it was all over the hospital.

"Bernie, I assure you, I'm not going anywhere. Please tell Lola not to give this another thought."

"A promotion might mean more money, don't ya know? Can't turn it down for the likes of Lola and me."

"Even if I accept a new position, it won't affect you and Lola. I'll still be stationed here in the library, and I'll need both of you."

Bernie's timeworn features lit up. "That's the ticket, then. I'll pass it on to Lola."

"One more thing, Bernie. How did this information get spread around so quickly?"

"You'd be surprised what we see and hear, Miz Machado. In the navy we used to say, 'Loose lips sink ships.' Goes the same for TMC's volunteers. We all know to keep things to ourselves, but this was a special case. Lola gets joy from coming here. She thinks the world and all of you. I didn't like to see her upset thinking things might change, so I felt obliged to speak up, don't ya know?" He left with a promise to reassure Lola that I would not be abandoning the library.

Amazing. I knew the TMC employees' rumor mill was always humming, but I had no idea the volunteers had such an active grapevine of their own. I hoped none of them had picked up the details of Delta's death.

That led me to wonder if there was any mention of it posted on her campaign website. I took a look and found nothing to indicate that she was deceased. Her campaign manager, listed in a sidebar along with other members of the campaign staff, was a man named Fletcher Tremont, who would no doubt post something soon. Either that or he would take the site down, but not before contacting Buck about any decisions involving Delta's campaign.

I had first met Tremont a couple of months earlier when he was introduced to me as the executive director of the Sawyer Foundation. A genial man in his fifties, he was fit for his age, with brown eyes and dark hair that I suspected had been augmented by skillful use of hair plugs. Most likely handsome in his younger years, he had matured into an image best described as distinguished. Well-known in Timbergate as a "community" person, he was someone Delta and Buck already knew and trusted, so her choice to have him run her campaign made sense.

Delta's decision to have neurotoxin injections so close to election day was a different story, but her history of cosmetic touch-ups explained why I had never noticed signs of aging on her face.

Curious for more information about the injections, I visited the National Library of Medicine where I found at least three different manufacturers with FDA approval to use neurotoxin for cosmetic purposes like crow's feet. From there I visited the American Board of Cosmetic Surgery. Their recommendation was to choose a provider with an extensive knowledge of facial anatomy, preferably a board-certified cosmetic surgeon. That would explain why Delta chose Beardsley for her procedure.

I was particularly interested in possible complications and quickly found a site that mentioned severe post-injection headaches in a small percentage of patients. Hence, Delta's request for the opioid pain prescription.

I switched back to the campaign website where Delta's headshot displayed a combination of glamour and professionalism. In the photo, her features were enhanced by a professional make-up artist and the skillful lighting of an expert photographer. She had great cheekbones, a well-formed nose, and a toothpaste model's brilliant white smile. The face looked perfect, and her light brown shoulder-length hair gleamed with expertly applied blond highlights that masked any random strands of gray. Maybe she had been so taken with the striking retouched photo that she wanted the live version to match.

Whatever her reason, there no longer was a live version of Delta Sawyer. A fatal mistake—or something more sinister—had not only taken her out of the race for mayor. It had taken her life.

Chapter 6

MY VISIT TO DELTA'S CAMPAIGN WEBSITE triggered an impulse to do the same for her two opponents: the man and woman whose secrets she had threatened to expose. Maybe not at the top of my job description, but it would fill the waning moments of my seemingly endless workday.

Both of their sites were disappointments, revealing nothing more than the content of their ads that had been airing in the media for the past two months and instructions on how to contribute financial support to their campaigns. Neither offered a window into the past lives of the candidates—just the puffed-up achievements their campaign managers deemed fit for public consumption, like the foamy whipped cream that coats a latte.

I wanted more. Curiosity is a demanding taskmaster, especially for librarians, and even more so for forensic librarians. With all sorts of research options at my fingertips, a peek into the pasts of Ernest Wright and Nora Nester seemed perfectly justified. They were community news. It was possible that a patron would request an in-depth search about either or both of them, so why not be prepared?

At my desk with the last dregs of reheated coffee from the break room, a little digging online told me Wright had grown up in Alabama, the fifth son of a protestant preacher and a church organist. He joined the U.S. Army at age eighteen, but before completing boot camp he received a medical discharge due to a back injury during a training exercise. He then enrolled in a private college in Alabama, where he majored in Public Relations but dropped out after achieving below-average grades in his second semester. His next thirty years were spent dabbling in a variety of franchises, including a fast-food chain, a house cleaning business and a fitness club. Eventually, he relocated to Timbergate where he opened a senior living facility.

Wright's campaign stump speeches routinely emphasized his compassion for the aging population, while his middle-aged wife and elderly mother stood proudly behind him on the podium. His saintly physical appearance suited his message of a kindly caretaker and protector: a full head of white hair, a neatly trimmed beard, and a paunch, but not quite a bowl full of jelly.

A search of Nora Nester indicated she had grown up in Vermont and held dual degrees in Early Childhood Education and Organizational Leadership, which explained her owning the most popular daycare center in Timbergate. Interested that she used her maiden name, I found no evidence of a marriage, and I'd heard no mention of a husband since she declared her run for mayor— something to pursue when I had more time.

I had to admit Quinn was right about Nester's lack of charisma. In interviews her speech was straightforward, but without animation or inflection. Her light brown hair was laced with gray, cut short and straight. She used no makeup, dressed modestly, and wore sensible shoes. Her speaking and appearance aside, Nester's educational qualifications held a definite edge over Delta Sawyer or Ernest Wright.

It seemed an odd twist that Wright was in the business of advocating for seniors and Nester looked after children—equally worthy endeavors that were likely to balance each other out in the eyes of the voting public.

After a very long day, my energy level was sinking fast when quitting time finally came. It was time to go home. The llamas would be hungry.

I STILL FELT STRANGE PARKING in Amah and Jack's driveway instead of continuing down the lane to their barn-top apartment. I was surprised that Nick's truck was not in the driveway. The remaining minutes of my workday had passed with no word from him in spite of my texting at least three times. He was usually in the kitchen preparing dinner when I got home from work. The only sign he had been back to the house since leaving before dawn was Ginger's absence.

Fanny's kibble bowl was empty, which explained why the cat was weaving herself in and out between my legs and yowling for her dinner. Good thing Amah and Jack had found a home for their pet cockatiel before they left. Boscoe would not have survived a day alone in the house with the hungry feline.

It seemed useless to text Nick again. His lack of response was so unlike him that I tried calling instead. He answered on the first ring.

"Aimee, I'm still with Buck. Sorry I didn't get back to you."

"What's going on? When will you be home?"

"I can't talk right now. And I won't be home tonight. Buck asked me to stay with him, Aimee. I couldn't say no."

"Of course not. Is Ginger with you?"

"No, I had to board her at the Coyote Creek Pet Motel for a few days."

"A few days? Why?"

"I'll explain when I can. Buck is going to be out of his house for a while, and I couldn't invite him to stay with us, so he and I are in a hotel. It's a nice suite. Plenty of room."

"Why couldn't he come here . . . oh, because I work at TMC, right?"

"'Fraid so. This has become complicated in a hurry."

"Anything I can do to help?"

"Yes, but it's the last thing I want. You and I should spend as little time together as possible for a while. Buck's lawyer says we should be careful with texting, too. Nothing about the case that could be construed as improper contact."

I recalled my meeting with Quinn. "I'm sure TMC's lawyers would agree."

I heard Nick pull a breath. "I'll try to get out to the ranch and take care of some of the chores tomorrow while you're at work. If you need anything else, contact Harry. He knows our situation with the conflict of interest."

"Is there anything you can tell me? You texted about going to the police."

"I probably shouldn't have, but I don't think I'm out of line by telling you Walter Kass is in charge of the investigation."

"That's a relief." Kass was a TPD detective we both knew and trusted.

When Buck is allowed back in his house, I'll let you know. I'd better stay with him at least until then."

"I understand. He shouldn't be alone right now."

"Thanks." He paused for a moment. "I miss you."

"Miss you, too."

I welcomed ranch chores as a distraction, but even tramping in a muddy pasture to feed llamas and clean watering troughs did nothing to stop my bouts of conjecture and confusion. The police must be considering Buck's house a potential crime scene. Either Buck suspected a killer had somehow poisoned Delta with the overdose, or the police suspected Buck of killing his wife. The latter theory stopped my breath. *Not possible.* But everything I knew about forensics told me Timbergate PD had to consider Buck a suspect. That was their job.

Back in the house with too many hours to kill before bedtime, my speculating about worst-case scenarios had demolished my appetite. After a couple mouthfuls of cold cereal, I gave up and texted Harry multiple times without an answer. Eventually I remembered Monday was one of the nights he volunteered to teach jujitsu. I considered driving into Timbergate and waiting around for him to finish up at the dojo, but I dropped the idea. That was selfish, and not fair to Harry. He had his girlfriend, Rella, to go home to. As Buck's other corporate pilot, she also would be affected by Delta's death, although not as directly as Nick.

The idea of going to the dojo had been a lame excuse to get out of Jack and Amah's house. It was so much larger than our cozy apartment over the barn that it still didn't feel like home. Some of the rooms were closed off and unused, conveying a sense of loneliness that was magnified with Nick and Ginger gone.

I turned on the local television news, but that made matters worse. The commentators were all over the breaking story about the death of Delta Sawyer, "Timbergate's Favorite Daughter." Another newscast from a town seventy miles away on a rival network had picked up the story as its lead.

I compared the coverage on the two stations and found both reporters avoiding speculation about Delta's cause of death. Instead, they focused on her socialite status and her campaign for mayor. They made a point to mention that she was the wife of well-known North State billionaire philanthropist Samuel "Buck" Sawyer, a dedicated warrior in the fight against drug trafficking.

Once word about the overdose became public, the temptation to contrast Delta's cause of death with Buck's crusade would be irresistible. He was mentally sharp and in good health for a man in his seventies, but coping with the unwanted notoriety surrounding his high-profile wife's sudden death would be difficult. The coincidence that his daughter had died of an overdose would add another layer to the trauma. Topping that, the knowledge that he might be a suspect in Delta's death could bring even the strongest man to his knees. Until the mystery of the lethal pills was solved, Buck would need Nick close at hand.

The reporter ended the segment by announcing that a debate among mayoral candidates previously planned for the evening would go on as scheduled with the two remaining candidates participating. Fletcher Tremont, the executive director of Buck Sawyer's foundation who doubled as Delta Sawyer's campaign manager, would appear to make a statement about how donations to her campaign would be refunded or reallocated. The debate was scheduled to begin at seven p.m. at the Timbergate Civic Center.

I had already researched Delta's opponents online. The debate would be a perfect opportunity to observe them in the flesh. I glanced at my phone. Six thirty. Nothing better to do with my evening. I could get there in time if I left right away. The clothes I'd shed after work were still lying on my bed, so I did a quick change and headed to town.

The glut of vehicles in the civic center parking lot told me the crowd size had more to do with Delta Sawyer's death than with the other two candidates. I found a space at the outer edge of the parking lot and ran for the entrance, dodging rain puddles. A security guard politely asked to take a look in my purse before allowing me to enter the building. The precaution had become routine for events in Timbergate as a result of the ever-increasing number of shootings taking place throughout the country. The security check offered some small comfort, while also reminding me never to assume I was safe in a large gathering.

The seats closest to the stage were already taken, except for a few in the area roped off for members of the press. I was scanning the room for an empty seat when someone tapped my shoulder. I turned and saw Lola Rampley wearing an usher's vest and peering up at me.

"Hello dear, do you need help?"

"Lola, I didn't know you volunteered here."

"Oh yes. I pick and choose which events, and once people are seated, I'm allowed to watch for free. It's what they call a win-win." She leaned toward me, dropping her voice to a whisper. "Like your win-win at work. Bernie told me we won't be losing you. We're very happy."

I glanced around the lobby. "Is Bernie here, too?"

"Goodness, no. He doesn't like to miss his quiz show."

"Couldn't he record it?"

"Bernie's TV isn't set up for that, and besides, he's not that interested in local politics."

"And you are?"

"I confess I'm more curious than usual because of that poor Sawyer woman's death. Her campaign manager is going to speak, you know."

"Yes, I heard that. I'd better hurry and find a place to sit. There's quite a crowd, except for the seats roped off for press."

Lola winked at me. "I see a press pass on your jacket. Let me usher you to your seat."

I glanced down. "No, this is my hospital ID badge. I forgot to take it off."

Lola examined my badge with her pen light. "Looks like a press pass to me. Besides, a few of those reserved seats always go empty."

I followed her and picked an empty seat next to the aisle, hoping none of the legit reporters would notice me. Lola gave me a discreet "thumbs up" and returned to her station near the lobby.

Chapter 7

T HE MODERATOR FOR THE EVENT was Wendall Vickers, Timbergate's first openly gay mayor. He had set off the current race for mayor when he announced his wish to retire from politics and open an independent bookstore. A fit man of medium height in his late thirties with striking blue eyes and thinning brown hair, he wore a navy suit accented with a tie that matched his eyes.

Vickers explained that the election board would certify the results a day after the April first election. The swearing in ceremony would take place a week later. While most of the legitimate reporters seated near me were taking notes on electronic devices, I took mine the old-fashioned way, with a pad and pen.

Mayor Vickers thanked the audience for turning out and followed by announcing that Fletcher Tremont, Delta Sawyer's campaign manager, had requested an opportunity to make a statement due to the candidate's sudden, tragic death.

The graying, middle-aged woman next to me sat at attention, her tablet on her lap and her plump fingers poised on its keyboard. I recognized her as a veteran reporter from our daily newspaper. This was the man she had come to hear because she had a job to do—provide her readers with any necessary details about Delta's terminated campaign.

I wondered how many others in the audience had come to hear Tremont. Some were likely Delta's supporters. Simple curiosity might have brought out many of the others. It isn't often that a candidate for public office dies in the final days of a campaign. The people in the crowd were not aware of my reason for curiosity— the switched pills that caused the overdose.

My knowledge of the oxycodone in the bottle labeled for acetaminophen had already led me to a crossroads where one path pointed toward an accident, and the other path pointed toward foul play. As I leaned in to listen to Fletcher Tremont, I suspected the police had already started down the path marked *MURDER*.

Tremont walked on from the wings, the image of prosperity in a gray pin-striped suit and paisley-patterned tie. He might have stepped out of a Brooks Brothers display window on Madison Avenue. He shook hands with Vickers, thanking him for granting time to speak. Vickers exited and Tremont made a show of adjusting the microphone to his height of more than six feet.

He cleared his throat, took a pair of reading glasses from one pocket and a notecard from another and announced that all donations would either be refunded, directed toward another candidate, or given to a charity of the donor's choice. As he spoke, ushers walked the aisles handing out forms to be filled out and deposited into a receptacle in the lobby.

I took one of the forms. It was basic: a place for name, contact information, and boxes to mark either *refund, donate to alternate candidate,* or *donate to charity.* There were spaces provided for the name of a candidate or a charity.

With that business finished, Tremont invited questions. All of the reporters' hands shot up. The woman seated next to me began waving both of her arms. When Tremont pointed to her, she reached across me to grip the mic handed to her by an usher standing in the aisle. I was the obstacle between them that caught Tremont's eye. He smiled at me as if we shared a joke. Just the kind of attention I had hoped to avoid.

The reporter tucked a wayward strand of graying hair behind her ear and spoke up. "Is there anything you can tell us about Delta Sawyer's cause of death?" Murmurs from the crowd suggested it was the question on everyone's mind.

Tremont shook his head. "I'm sorry. I hope everyone here understands that there are reasons why that question cannot be addressed at this time."

The murmuring grew louder. The reporter started to speak again, but Tremont held up his hand. "Let's give someone else a turn." He pointed to a young man at the other end of the row who announced he was with a local weekly news magazine.

"Do you know if there was a medical error? Will her doctor or Timbergate Medical Center be sued, either for malpractice or negligence?" I took off my TMC name badge and dropped it in my purse while Tremont answered.

"Again, that is not a question for this occasion." More stirring from the crowd in the auditorium.

A third reporter, seated directly in front of me, raised her hand. Tremont nodded to her.

"Miss, do you have a question regarding the Sawyer campaign's reimbursement of contributions?"

She stood, took the mic from the usher and announced she was with the local TV station. I recognized her as the reporter I had seen in Quinn's office. "We know the police are involved," she said. "They were seen at the Sawyer home. That suggests foul play. Is her husband a suspect?"

Tremont flushed crimson, glancing toward the wings to telegraph his plea for an escape. Mayor Wendell Vickers walked briskly to center stage and announced that there would be no further questions for Mr. Tremont. It was time for the remaining candidates' debate to begin.

My first reaction was to head home. The questions lobbed at Tremont had killed my desire to spend two hours listening to political talking points. The candidates were not likely to say anything that would implicate them in Delta's death—especially after hearing the reporters' questions. I made it as far as the lobby, where tables were set up on opposite ends of the space, one for Ernest Wright and the other for Nora Nester. I passed the Nester table on my way to the women's room.

When I came out, I changed my mind. What else did I have to do? Go back to a house without Nick, where my only companion was a peevish cat that seemed to despise all members of the human race except Amah? Why not stick around and listen? Nick and Buck were not on my suspect list. Neither was Beardsley. These candidates were all I had.

If the police arrested one of them before election day, the other would win by default. There would be no reason to go to the polls. But there was so little time, and I had seen nothing to indicate either Wright or Nester was being considered a suspect. If that did not change, Timbergate's residents could end up electing a killer.

I stopped by Nester's table to pick up a brochure but declined the campaign pin and the bumper sticker. I crossed the lobby to Wright's table where I did the same. As I was heading back to the auditorium entrance, Fletcher Tremont came out to the lobby, walking toward me.

"Pardon me, Miss. I saw you in the press pool, didn't I?"

"Yes, but I'm not with the media. I was seated there because an usher insisted there were extra seats."

"May I ask why you're here?" His question held no challenge, only polite curiosity.

"I'm a concerned citizen." No way would I divulge that I worked at TMC. Or that I was a close acquaintance of Buck Sawyer.

"Your face is familiar," Tremont said, "but I must admit I don't recall your name. I believe we've met, haven't we?" I hoped he had forgotten our brief introduction two months earlier.

"I'm afraid not."

Tremont smiled. "Well, you have a memorable face. I must say it's gratifying that you feel a sense of civic duty. Did you happen to contribute to Delta Sawyer's campaign? If so, do you have any questions about reimbursement?"

"No. I wasn't a donor, but thank you for asking." No reason to explain that I lived outside Timbergate's city limits and was not eligible to vote.

His expression turned somber. "Considering the circumstances, I suppose that's for the best."

"It must be very difficult for you and all of Mrs. Sawyer's campaign staff."

"We're struggling with the shock of it, but we're helping each other cope."

"I'm sorry for your loss," I said. "It was nice meeting you in spite of the circumstances." I walked quickly back to the auditorium entrance while he called after me.

"Nice meeting you, too, Miss . . ." Only then did I realize that I had not told him my name. I pretended not to hear and made my way back to my seat.

Neither of the remaining candidates started strong. Wright, looking like Santa in church clothes, stressed care of elders. Nester emphasized her dedication to the care of children. In a plain beige pant suit, she reminded me of the drab female house finches that visited Amah's backyard bird feeder.

During Q&A both were asked about their stance on abortion, most likely because of the recent rise in states where abortion rights were being challenged. Nester leaned toward freedom of choice with some caveats, and Wright sat on the fence.

The issue of gun control was raised by an audience member. Nester was in favor of banning all automatic and semi-automatic weapons. Wright quipped that gun control was a loaded question, then pointed out that hunting and sport shooting were popular in our part of the state. He mentioned the right to bear arms, protect our homes, property and lives, but he did concede that more could be done about background checks.

Climate change gave the candidates a chance to find common ground. They agreed that it was not a hoax. The fires that had raged throughout much of the west during recent summers had convinced all but the most hardened skeptics that global warming was real. Both Wright and Nester declared that the problem was worldwide and could not be fixed by one small town in rural

Northern California, but nevertheless, they would support any possible efforts to help mitigate the crisis.

Reporters and audience members tossed out questions about immigration, crime, and terrorism. I felt a twinge of pity for each candidate. The mayor of Timbergate was unlikely to solve problems that had vexed U.S. presidents for decades. When one cub reporter questioned them about potential interference in the mayoral election, Vickers emerged from the wings and announced that the question period had ended, and that each candidate would finish by explaining his or her vision for the town of Timbergate.

Wright claimed that health care and high prescription drug and medical costs were a burden in a city with a struggling economy. He stressed how those issues impacted the elderly, and proposed a study to identify sources of funding for free health clinics for financially insolvent seniors.

Nester spoke about the homeless problem, relating it directly to drug misuse and expressing her concern that some of the children in her care had been placed there because their parents were struggling with addiction. She proposed the city budget include an extensive and ongoing program to eradicate the use of illicit drugs. Both candidates' proposed goals were worthy, although expensive and difficult to accomplish.

HOME CLOSE TO TEN O'CLOCK, I was met by Fanny's demanding yowl accusing me of starving her. She would have gladly eaten my face given the chance, so I lost no time opening a can of salmon pâté. She scarfed her meal while I reviewed my notes from Wright and Nester's war of words. I found myself hoping neither of them would be pulled out of the race and jailed for the murder of their rival, Delta Sawyer.

The problem with that hope was that it left me with unacceptable alternatives: a cover-up at the hospital, which did not bode well for Beardsley or TMC, or worse, either Buck Sawyer had deliberately switched his wife's pills, or whoever had done it would never be identified and Buck would be blamed.

With that thought, Detective Walter Kass came to mind. The

TPD detective had been a valuable ally before when I found myself caught up in mysteries involving the hospital. It was some consolation that he was working the case, because I knew he would follow the evidence and play fair. Trouble was, the evidence so far pointed toward Buck Sawyer.

MY RESTLESS NIGHT WITHOUT NICK ENDED at five thirty on a dry but overcast Tuesday morning when I dragged myself out of bed to silence Fanny's relentless demands for breakfast. The llamas were next. My cell rang just as I returned from the barn. Nick, letting me know he and Buck had to stay away from Buck's home for at least another day.

"How's Buck?"

"Not good. He wonders if he made a mistake by asking the police to investigate."

"Does he think they suspect him?"

"It's beginning to look that way. I've tried to reassure him, but it's not easy when I'm getting the same impression."

"Are his attorneys concerned? Or is it okay to ask that? I don't know if you're supposed to be talking to me about this."

"It's not like I'm giving away secrets. His attorneys are in constant communication, but most of it's to reassure Buck that they're protecting his rights."

I leaned against the kitchen counter. "That doesn't sound encouraging to me."

"Have to agree. It would help a lot if TPD was scouting around for a few other suspects, but if they are, they're not telling us about it."

"Speaking of other suspects, I went to the candidates' debate last night."

"Why?"

"It sounds like a stretch, but they're both potential suspects. Delta claimed she was going to reveal nasty secrets about each of them before election day."

"I remember, but my guess is she was faking that. I hope you're not on one of your sleuthing missions, Aimee. We have to assume there's a killer out there until we know otherwise."

"All I'm doing is wondering and worrying, and I can't help that. I'm not doing anything risky."

"I hope not, but I've heard that before. I have my hands full dealing with Buck. I can't handle the thought of you in jeopardy."

I couldn't accept the thought of Nick in jeopardy either, but I knew his loyalty to Buck could come with unintended consequences—like a trial or even a prison sentence.

"There's no reason to worry about me. Just do what you can for Buck."

"I'm trying. How are things at the ranch?"

"The usual. Feed the cat. Feed the llamas. Feed myself. That's about it. Have you checked on Ginger? I feel bad for her being stashed away at that kennel."

"Some good news there. Harry and Rella have taken her in. If it works out okay, they'll keep her at their condo for now."

Good news for Ginger, but not for me. Nick would not ask Harry and Rella to take her in unless he was unsure about his immediate future.

"I'm glad. She gets along with both of them." I ended the call with a quick, "Love you."

He replied with the same.

A check of morning news on the local station gave a repeat of the account from the night before with no mention of Delta's cause of death and an appeal to tune in later for updates.

A wave of loneliness swept over me as I turned off the television.

This separation felt different from the times when Nick's job took
him away. I was at ease with being by myself for a few days while he
was flying, because we maintained a feeling of closeness with video
chats and texting.

We had always been mutually respectful of the areas of each
other's work that were off limits, but that was different from this
new situation. I hadn't even told Nick about my promotion offer,
although there was little point, since Quinn had shelved the topic
before explaining it in detail.

I considered calling Harry for moral support, but it was almost
time to leave for work. Harry must have picked up a vibe, because
he texted moments later while I was cleaning Fanny's litter box.

Heard about Delta. U ok Sis?

Been better.

Need me?

Come to ranch tonight. Will explain.

K see u six-ish.

BERNIE KLUCKERT ARRIVED IN THE LIBRARY at nine sharp for his
Tuesday morning shift wearing his bright orange volunteer blazer
over khakis and a navy plaid shirt. With a proud smile, he held up
what looked like a new watering can made of green plastic and
embossed with a tulip design.

"You bought that for the library?" I asked.

"You betcha. Spiffy, isn't it?"

"It's very nice. If you brought a receipt, I'll see that you're
reimbursed."

Bernie shook his head. "Not worth the bother for five bucks,
don't you know, but thanks for offering. That old one sprung a leak,
so I threw it out." He placed his new purchase on the volunteers'
desk and clipped off the price tag. "Ship shape, that's how I like
things, Miss Aimee."

"Thank you, Bernie. I appreciate that. Did Lola tell you I saw
her at the debate last night?"

"Sure did. Said she got you a good seat. How'd it go?"

"It was interesting. How was your quiz show?"

"I woulda won a lot of money if I'd been there. The big question was easy."

"Good for you. What was the answer?"

"Loose lips sink ships. Like I told you a couple days ago. How 'bout that for a coincidence?" He picked up his new watering can. "Can't wait to try this baby out. Those plants of yours need some lookin' after, don't you know?" I envied Bernie's ability to focus on his task.

Thinking back to the campaign debate, I had to accept that Wright and Nester were better candidates for mayor than for murderer. There had to be another suspect. Someone had switched those pills, but who else had a motive for wanting Delta dead? Every personal thing that I knew about her was linked to her marriage to Buck, and that was precious little. Maybe there were secrets in their marriage, but why go there? If there were secrets, they would only cast more suspicion on Buck—the opposite of what I hoped for.

The best way to establish Buck's innocence was to discover exactly how the pills were switched. Vane Beardsley's lawyers seemed concerned that he could somehow be blamed for a medical error, but I was at a loss as to how that could happen. Beardsley had refused her request for opioids and instructed her to use acetaminophen for pain. The day she was admitted, that pill bottle in her purse had been locked in a safe where no one could access it, including Beardsley.

Either the pills were switched before she reached the hospital or before she purchased them. If there was an error, it had to involve the manufacturer or the pharmacy where the bottle was purchased, but the idea that a sealed, tamper-proof bottle of acetaminophen purchased at a big box pharmacy would accidentally contain oxycodone tablets was so remote that it was impossible to believe.

A deviant factory or pharmacy employee doing the switch deliberately was such a long shot, I doubted the TPD had even considered it. Why would they, when they had a convenient spouse in their sights who had every opportunity to tamper with that bottle? All they needed was a motive, but I knew with certainty that no motive would compel Buck to kill his wife.

After Bernie's three-hour shift tending plants and dusting shelves, he performed his usual quitting time ritual: dustpan and gardening implements stored in the utility closet, coffee cup rinsed, dried and put away in the break room cupboard. I was surprised when he headed in my direction instead of going toward the exit with his usual farewell wave.

"Miss Aimee, can I trouble you for a minute of your time?"

"No problem. I was about to shut down for lunch. What is it?"

He pulled out his kerchief to wipe at a smudge on the corner of my desk. "It's okay if you nix what I'm asking."

"We won't know until you ask." I encouraged him with a smile.

"Here goes, then." Bernie sucked in a deep breath and blew it out. "Lola and I are thinking of a new living arrangement, and we'd like your help."

Not the kind of help I had imagined. "You'll need to tell me more."

"Here's how it is." Bernie cleared his throat. "We're spending most all our time together and paying for two apartments. That's double the bills we'd have if we shared a place. We thought we might look into an apartment in one of those senior living outfits." He was having trouble meeting my eyes. I suspected it was because this arrangement would not include marriage, and he was afraid I would be shocked.

"Bernie, if that's what the two of you want, it sounds like you've made a sensible decision."

"It's what we want." He grinned. "We get along fine, don't you know?"

"I'm happy for you, but I don't understand how your decision involves me."

"We don't have any kin close by to come along with us while we check out some accommodations. Lola heard Mr. Wright speak last night at the campaign debate. She thinks we could start by looking at his senior living place, but sometimes older folks get bamboozled with a lot of fast talk when it comes to this sort of thing. Lola thinks he's on the up-and-up, seein' as he's likely gonna be our next mayor, but I need a little more convincing. We kinda hoped you'd see your way to help us out."

"I'm willing to help, but I can't be responsible for any financial decision you and Lola might make."

"No, 'course not, we would have our legal folks and tax people take care of that. We'd only ask you to show up with us for the first look around so those people at the facility think we have a relative watching out for us is all."

"A relative?" I started to protest that my being half Asian might make that story hard to sell.

He grinned. "You could be my adopted granddaughter, don't you know?"

He and Lola had apparently put a lot of thought into this proposition. I had to give them credit for wanting backup. If they signed a contract, it would involve a substantial financial commitment. That would be a problem for them if Wright turned out to be Delta's killer. Surely his business would shut down. He might well go into bankruptcy and leave his residents with no way to be refunded.

Restrained from mentioning any of that to Bernie, the least I could do was go with them to look at the place. It might help me convince them to postpone their move until Delta's case was solved.

"How soon do you want to visit Mr. Wright's facility?" I asked.

"Sooner the better, if you're up for it."

"It'll have to be on my lunch hour if we do it on a workday."

"Gotcha. I'll tell Lola to make an appointment right away."

Rain had started up by the time Bernie left, and I didn't relish a dash across the hospital grounds to the main tower for lunch in the cafeteria. I went to check for snacks in the break room where a fishy odor hung in the air. Bernie had apparently mixed a batch of his potent plant food concoction before leaving for the day. That took the edge off my appetite, but I still needed sustenance.

I found no yogurt or fruit cups in the fridge, and the small overhead cupboard was bare—not a single nutrition bar, no microwave popcorn. I finally found half a roll of mints tucked away in one of my desk drawers. I popped two of them into my mouth and promised myself that if the rain stopped, I'd go get real food during my afternoon break.

Bernie called half an hour later. "Lola says we can go tomorrow at noon if that works for you."

"That works."

I had misgivings about the deception, but Bernie's plan to pass me off as his granddaughter at the senior living complex was my chance to investigate Delta's most combative rival. Wright was more than a candidate for mayor. He was also a potential candidate for a prison cell.

Nothing risky about it, so not the kind of sleuthing that would worry Nick. In fact, it seemed so simple that I felt compelled to pull off a similar mission by touring Nora Nester's daycare facility. Although to do that, I needed a baby or a small child on short notice.

I thought of one possibility. My nurse friend Laurie Littletree had recently given birth to a baby girl. I knew Laurie planned to come back to work at TMC part time. She was likely to be researching daycare options. Why not give her a call and ask how she was enjoying motherhood? I got her voicemail and left a message.

The last minutes of my lunch hour were spent deciding what I was free to tell Harry when he dropped by that evening. Only that Nick and I were not to compare notes about Delta's death, and that Nick and Buck were staying in a hotel, which suggested the police were treating the Sawyer home as a crime scene. My real motive in talking to Harry was to find out whether he knew anything he might pass on to me.

My growling stomach sent me across the complex to the cafeteria during a mid-afternoon break in the rain. I returned to the library with a vending machine sandwich just in time to pick up a call from Laurie Littletree, sounding weary.

"You don't know how I miss talking to a grownup," she said. "No one ever warned me about that part of being a mom. I catch myself talking baby talk to Daniel when he comes home from work."

"Be glad you're living in the same house and he can come home at night. Nick and I've been separated for two days, and I'm not sure when it will end."

"You're separated? Oh, Aimee, I'm so sorry. I thought the two of you were such a perfect couple."

"Not that kind of separation." I explained about Delta Sawyer's death and my conflict of interest.

"I heard about Delta. Sorry about you and Nick, but if that's why you called, I'm not sure how I can help."

"No, it's something else. I need a reason to visit Nora Nester's daycare center, and I don't have a baby."

"Want mine?" She laughed. "You can have her, but only if you keep her for a week so Daniel and I can get some sleep."

"Seriously, aren't you considering coming back to work sometime soon?"

"As it happens, Daniel and I were talking about that this morning. We don't have any family here to watch Kiona. Both sets of grandparents still live in Idaho, so we will need daycare."

"Then why don't we visit Nester's facility together?"

"Not a bad idea, but what's your deal? You're not pregnant, are you?"

"Nothing like that. I happened to hear Nester speak at the campaign debate last night and got curious. She might be a candidate to join our TMC Library Consortium, but first I'd like to have a look around her facility."

"Come on, Aimee, this is me you're talking to. It sounds like you're planning a reconnaissance mission. You know Daniel would raise a colossal fit if I got mixed up in another one of your investigations."

"Then we're back to your original offer. Can I borrow your baby? Or rent her by the hour?"

Laurie sighed. "No. She's not for hire. But I am going to need daycare or a nanny soon, so you caught me at a good time."

"Then you'll go? Maybe let Nester think I'm Kiona's auntie?" Laurie was black and Daniel was Native American. I had occasionally been mistaken for Native American. I thought we could pull that off.

"How about godmother?" Laurie said. "We were thinking of asking you."

"For real?"

"Yes, for real. Daniel and I thought of you and Nick, but we didn't know if it would be too much to ask. Do you think he'd be willing to be Kiona's godfather?"

"I think he'd love it, but he's already godfather to his little nephew, so I'll have to ask."

"Thanks, but there's no hurry. Make sure he's okay with double duty and let me know. The point is, you and I now have our bases covered for our immediate purpose. I want to check out this *Nora's Nest* place because I'm going to need childcare. You're going with me because you're Kiona's godmother-to-be. That's all anyone, including me, needs to know."

I glanced at my calendar. "Can we schedule the daycare visit for Thursday around noon?"

"Thursday works. My days are all the same. We'd better meet there, because I'll need a head start. You wouldn't believe how complicated it is to drive with a baby in the car."

After our call I had second thoughts about the Littletree's request. I loved the thought of sharing godparenting duty with Nick, but was it fair to ask him to take on a second godchild? Until I was sure he and I could be an enduring backup team for little Kiona, it would be awkward to raise the issue with him. Meanwhile, I could only speak for myself.

Chapter 9

Harry showed up Tuesday evening with a pizza box in one hand and a six-pack in the other. He must have rung the doorbell with his elbow.

"Hi, Sis. Grab some paper plates. I'm starving." I took the pizza box, inhaling the tantalizing aroma of a sausage medley. I was starving, too.

"How many slices do you want?"

"Three for starters." Harry opened two bottles. "Still seems strange to see you in Amah and Jack's house instead of in the barn."

"Tell me about it. Nick and I keep reminding ourselves to park here when we get home instead of driving down the lane to the barnyard."

We took our dinner to the glass-topped table in the family room. Harry wolfed down half a slice before I asked my first question.

"How's Rella reacting to the news about Delta?"

"She's too levelheaded to let it throw her. She wasn't chummy with Delta any more than you were. She's more worried about how Buck's doing."

Harry and Rella lived together in his condo on the river. They surprised all of us when they started dating a year ago. I was even more surprised when she moved in with him. He usually shied away from anything serious in favor of someone looking for a good time—which was not hard to find, since Harry kept his body in great shape working out at a gym and teaching jujitsu a couple times a week at our local dojo. Like me, he inherited black hair and deep brown eyes from our parents. Some women described the hint of Asian in his features as intriguing. Others came right out and quizzed me, "Your brother's so hot. Is he seeing anyone?"

His dating history had earned him a reputation as one of Timbergate's most eligible bachelors, but that was before Buck hired Rella as a corporate pilot. She and Nick shared the job of flying their boss wherever his business took him. Rella was different from my brother's previous girlfriends. Her Nordic beauty, coupled with her past as a Marine Corp fighter pilot, gave her an aura of confidence that Harry obviously found irresistible. We were happy for him, but privately we wondered if their romance would last.

Harry cocked an eyebrow at me. "Come on, you have more on your mind than asking about Rella. You want to tell me about it?"

I took a breath. "Okay. First, Nick and Buck were at the police department right after Delta died, and so far, Nick hasn't told me why. Second, he's staying in a hotel somewhere in Timbergate with Buck because Buck has been asked to stay away from his house, which I can only guess is because there's a crime scene unit checking it out." I took another breath. "Third, I'm stuck out here in this big empty house in Coyote Creek with orders from my boss to keep quiet about anything going on at the hospital that's related to Delta." Harry opened his mouth to speak, but I held up my hand to stop him. "Fourth, Delta's death has thrown all of us—you, me, Nick, Rella and Buck—into conflicts of interest with each other until I feel I have no one to talk to except Amah's freakin' demented cat."

Harry had the bad manners to laugh. "Are you finished?"

"I guess."

"Good. Give me a minute." He tapped at his phone. "Texting Rella. I might be here a little longer than I planned."

"You don't have to stay."

"No problem." He put his phone on the table and glanced around. "Kinda nice having leg room. Beats crowding around your skimpy little table in the apartment over the barn, doesn't it?"

"I guess. Although I'd enjoy it a lot more if Nick were here. All the extra space in this house makes me feel even lonelier without him."

"Any idea how much longer Nick will be staying with Buck?"

"That depends on the police investigation. For now, Buck's lawyers don't think Nick should be home with me. But that's not the only reason. Nick believes Buck needs him."

"Your text said you had something to explain. What's that about?"

I asked the question that had done away with my appetite. "Have you seen anything about Delta's case on social media?"

Harry looked puzzled. "It's been a few days since I've logged on. Too busy finishing up the mall and bidding jobs. Why?"

"People are speculating online about whether Buck and/or Nick could have murdered Delta."

"Seriously?" His shoulders slumped. "That's the Internet. We all live with it because we can't live without it."

"Any ideas how to counter it?"

"Find the real killer," he said. "It won't stop any other way."

"How do we find the real killer?"

"We don't. We leave that job for the police."

"How can we do that when this is hitting so close to home?"

He pierced me with a frown. "You sure you want to dive into this? How many scars are you already wearing from your other attempts at crime solving?"

"Only two. One on my scalp, the other on the bottom of my foot." I tried for a grin. "Neither of them shows."

Harry winced. "Not funny, Sis."

"Come on, Bro, admit it. You smell a mystery here. Nick and Buck at the TPD. Buck told to leave his house."

"Okay, I admit it. Want to tell me what else you know?"

"I can't be more specific. Not with all the conflicts of interest. I can't tell you anything that comes from my job at the hospital."

Harry's eyes narrowed. "But there is something, right? Something you know about how Delta died? Something suspicious?"

I knew she died of an overdose, but as far as I knew, it was not public knowledge, so Harry couldn't hear it from me.

"Come on," I said. "The police are investigating. Doesn't that tell you they're suspicious?"

"Sure. But let me stop you for a minute. I know what caused her death. Buck told Nick and Rella right away, and Rella told me. I assume you know, too."

"I do. The switched pills."

"Okay, so we don't have to tiptoe around that piece of information, but the pills don't necessarily indicate foul play. It could be a simple mistake. Will you be satisfied if that's what the police decide?"

"It's Buck who needs to be satisfied. He's the one who wants answers about the pills. Wouldn't you? If it were Rella?"

Harry leaned back in his chair, arms crossed. "Obviously, but this isn't about Rella. From what I've heard, she and Delta Sawyer are about as different as two women can get. Delta's been trading on her ancestry and her looks all her life, and she's an heiress to boot, isn't she?"

"That's the common assumption in Timbergate," I said. "According to Nick, that's one reason Buck Sawyer married her in spite of the difference in their ages. He thought it proved she wasn't after him for his money."

"You say it's an assumption. You think she was projecting a false image of wealth before they were married?"

"Who knows? She wouldn't be the first heiress to blow a fortune."

"Seems like Buck would have checked her financials before their wedding."

"I agree. For all we know, they had an iron-clad prenup."

Harry finished making his point. "Either way, Delta grew up rich and pampered, married a rich guy, and the pampering continued. Rella, on the other hand, is a self-made woman with the guts to serve as a fighter pilot in the military and the backbone to make her own way financially."

"So we agree that both of their lives are outside the norm, but in vastly different ways. All I meant was if Rella died under the same circumstances, you wouldn't rest until you got to the truth."

"Can we stop talking about Rella as a victim? You're creeping me out."

Harry's reaction told me their relationship ran deeper than I knew. Something to think about when the Delta Sawyer situation was no longer front and center.

"Sorry. All I need right now is to know you're here for me while Nick is staying away. He's the one who suggested I ask you for help."

"I'll help if I can. The mall job is almost complete. They'll be announcing a grand opening any day. I'm spending most of my time bidding other jobs, so if it's ranch chores, or something you need repaired, text me or call. My schedule is flexible."

"Good to know. And thanks for coming out."

"Welcome, but there's something we need to get straight before I leave. I'm caught in the middle when it comes to keeping confidences. You and I are family, but I'm also best friends with Nick. There might be times when he needs to talk."

"And you might hear something you can't pass on to me. Even if you think it's important. Is that where you're going?"

Harry nodded. "Are you okay with that?"

"I have to be. It works both ways. I may hear things I can't share with you. And remember the conflict of interest extends to Rella, too."

"Understood." Harry got up from the table, fishing his car keys out of his pocket. "I guess you have people at your work that you can talk to."

"Up to a point, sure." Harry didn't need to know that my relationship with Nick had forced my usual allies at work to keep their distance from me. "One more thing I almost forgot to ask. Nick said you were taking care of Ginger, so where is she?"

"Home with Rella. They're bonding."

"Are you okay with having a dog in your condo? I'd have kept her here at the ranch, but I didn't want to leave her home alone all day while I'm at work."

"It's great. We might get one of our own someday. This is practice."

"Do you think Ginger's missing Nick?"

"Hard to tell. She seems okay most of the time, except when she sees one of us on the phone. Then she gets kind of antsy. We're not sure what that's about."

I smiled. "I think I know. She wants to hear Nick's voice. If you happen to be talking to him, let him speak to her for a moment. It should calm her down."

"Ah, thanks. I'll try that."

Before I could respond, a muffled ping sounded from Harry's back pocket. He pulled out his phone. I watched his brow furrow as he read the text message.

"Bad news?" I asked.

"Aimee, in spite of what I just said about keeping confidences, there's something you should know." He leveled a look at me. "Buck was arrested this morning."

I froze. "What? How long have you known about this?"

"A few hours, but before you start yelling at me for not telling you sooner, I promised Nick I'd wait until I heard more from him." Harry held up his phone. "His text says TPD has already released Buck. They thought they had a solid lead from a Secret Witness, but it turned out to have some holes in it."

"What kind of lead?"

"Nick didn't say. All I know is he's been in contact with Abe Edelman."

"The lawyer who helped us back when you were in trouble? Why? Doesn't Buck have a stable of defense lawyers he can call on if the time comes?"

"He does, but this isn't about Buck."

My face went hot and my knees went cold. "It's about Nick?"

"It's a precaution, Aimee, because Nick knows his prints are on that pill bottle."

"The police should consider that as proof he didn't tamper with the pills. Whoever did it would have been careful not to leave prints behind."

"That logic works only if you assume every killer is smart enough to think the way you do. Cops don't give most criminals that much credit. They like dumb crooks and they like hard evidence."

"I get that, but I don't like it. Is Nick going to retain Abe?"

"No, Abe's only doing real estate law these days. Nick asked him to recommend a defense attorney." Harry held up his hands. "Hold on, though, don't get ahead of this. So far, no one is making any noises about Nick being involved in a crime. It's a matter of being prepared in the off chance he becomes—"

"A suspect," I said. "But he has no motive."

"He's been closely involved in Buck and Delta's lives for several years. Who knows what could turn up?"

"What are you saying? The police might suspect Nick had a problematic relationship with Delta? That's crazy."

"We know that, because we know Nick, but impartial investigators might see it differently."

"I hate hearing this, but I'm glad you told me."

"Whatever you do, don't let on to Nick that I told you. It's the last thing he wanted you to be worrying about. But you're my sister . . . I thought you should know."

"Thank you. I won't let on. What about Rella? Does she know?"

"She does. That's another reason I thought it was only fair to tell you."

"I appreciate that." I handed him the pizza box. "You want to take this home? And the rest of the beer?"

"You don't want it?"

"No, take it. I'd keep it if Nick were here, but. . . ."

"I get it." Harry took the box. "Thanks, Sis. And try not to worry. This thing's likely to blow over. Medical mistakes happen, and sometimes people die. Buck will get through this, and Nick will be back before you know it. Keep in touch—whatever you need." He surprised me with a rare hug.

Left alone, I was still processing Harry's news when Fanny wandered into the room. Grateful to have another living presence in the house, I reached down to pet her. She hung back out of reach, staring at me as if making up her mind. Then she turned and trotted away with her tail in the air.

Chapter 10

M Y HEADLAMP LIT THE PATH and my breath clouded with each exhale as I walked to the barn Wednesday morning under a star-filled sky. A freezing rain the night before had left an icy crust on the pasture, making my steps crunch and my footing insecure.

I tossed generous portions of hay to the animals with normal chewing capacity and began chopping breakfast for Old Doolittle, who waited in a separate enclosure. The chore freed my mind to ruminate about Delta Sawyer's death and its ripple effect. Harry's news about Buck's arrest had triggered a variety of nightmares. On waking, my imagination plunged down a dark path where the police would continue to consider Buck their prime suspect and Nick as first runner up. The compulsion to prove their innocence had grown overnight from determination to desperation.

Harry had said the police look for hard evidence—like the fact that both Nick's and Buck's prints were on that pill bottle. The pills had already been identified by the hospital, but TPD's crime lab would do their own analysis and check the bottle for fingerprints. Buck's would not necessarily be incriminating. He could easily have an innocent explanation for handling the bottle. Nick's would be harder to explain.

I told myself not to borrow trouble. Heed Harry's advice and let TPD do its job. Chances were they would close the case as medication error. Except that halfway through cutting the hay, I was compiling a mental list of alternative suspects if the switched pills *were* foul play and not a tragic accident.

Setting Buck and Nick aside, the two mayoral candidates running against Delta were the most obvious. She had threatened to expose both of them with scandals from their pasts, but neither seemed crazy enough to kill in order to win the race for mayor in a town the size of Timbergate. Whatever dirt Delta had on them would have to be damning stuff to provoke homicide—damning enough to result in lengthy prison time.

That thought sent a shudder trembling through me. With the election only a week and a day away, Timbergate's voters could unwittingly put a killer in the mayor's office. It seemed unlikely, but you never knew about people's secrets. I had to know.

There was no denying my specialty in forensic research had spurred an impulse to solve mysteries. Especially if they involved anything to do with hospitals or medicine. Digging into the pasts of Ernest Wright and Nora Nester could do no harm. If I turned up something the police might use, I would call Detective Kass. If I turned up nothing, I had a backup plan. Harry had a skill level far superior to mine when it came to diving deep and dark into the web. The question was whether I could convince him to make that dive.

Doolittle's pile of hay was ready as dawn cast first light in the clear morning sky. It was time to stop musing and get ready for work.

I checked my phone before stepping into the shower. No voicemail or text from Nick. Nothing but a void in the pit of my stomach. While I lathered and rinsed, the thought of him seeking out a defense lawyer made me catch my breath. I could understand the police looking at Buck because he was the spouse. But why Nick? The answer had to be his proximity to Delta, as her bodyguard and occasional stand-in escort if she had a social obligation and Buck was unavailable.

Dried off and dressed, I texted Nick saying I missed him and asking if we could meet somewhere. We had been warned not to share information about Delta's case, but it wasn't as if we were forbidden to occupy the same space. And police reports were public record, so asking Nick about Buck's arrest was technically fair game. He could decide whether to offer the details. What I wanted most was to be with the man I loved long enough to reassure myself that we would make it through this turmoil.

I was toasting a bagel when my cell phone rang. Nick. I answered with the first words that tumbled from my mouth.

"What's happening?"

He laughed. "I miss you, too."

"Sorry, this communication vacuum is taking a toll. How is Buck? Is there anything you can tell me?

"Buck's coping, but he's not sleeping well."

"Understandable. Are the police letting him back in his house yet?"

"He thinks maybe today, but that's not confirmed yet. Let's get back to the reason for your text. I don't have much time."

"Are you saying we can meet?"

"How about tonight at nine?"

"Where?"

"The Sawyer Foundation office."

"I'll be there."

"Good. Can't wait."

I heard another voice in the background, and then Nick's intake of breath. "Aimee, I have to go. Buck has an appointment to make plans for Delta's memorial. I'm going with him."

"Has he picked a date?"

"Looks like this Sunday."

"This is Wednesday. He wants it that soon?"

"He'd like to get it over with. Can't say I blame him."

"No matter when, it's going to be tough. Go, Nick. We'll talk tonight."

I FORCED DOWN A BAGEL WITH CREAM cheese on my drive to work, hoping the blue sky was a sign that the fallout from Delta Sawyer's death would soon pass. The anticipation of seeing Nick was a welcome relief from the constant tension of the past two days.

As I drove around the hospital's main tower, I spotted several TMC employees avoiding the more aggressive reporters who continued to hang out at the entrances seeking a headline-worthy quote. The entrenched newshounds refused to believe that TMC's Public Relations Officer had resigned and left town at least two weeks earlier. They thought they were being stone-walled and were demanding a statement. Quinn had made it clear no one was to talk to the press. All we were allowed to say was "no comment."

I expected to avoid the onslaught, because I routinely used a small employee lot next to the library building. I parked and walked toward the entrance with the day's task list running through my mind. Fill requests for articles, either online or in print. Deal with requests for a medical text or journal to be added to our collection. They were things my future assistant librarian would be handling if I were to accept Quinn's offer of a promotion—an offer he would spell out only after Delta Sawyer's case was behind us. So far, all he had accomplished by bringing it up was to underscore what I had to lose if he, or corporate, lost confidence in my loyalty to TMC.

I reached the library's entrance doors just as a young woman in a tailored blue suit materialized from nowhere. I recognized her dark brown hair styled in a fifties-era pageboy. I had seen the Lois Lane wannabe in Jared Quinn's office and again at the candidates' debate when she asked Fletcher Tremont if Delta's husband was a suspect. A red-haired man wielding a video camera followed her. He looked barely past his teens in dress slacks too large for his thin frame, a rumpled white shirt, and a black tie. He stood behind Superman's girlfriend with camera at the ready as she thrust a mic in my direction and called out, "Are you anyone important?"

My first impulse was to laugh, but I caught myself in time and kept a straight face. "I'm sorry, are you speaking to me?"

"Yes. I'm Oriana Wynn from Timbergate's local television station. We're attempting to update our viewers about the death of Delta Sawyer. We'd appreciate a comment from a TMC spokesperson, but so far, we're receiving no information. I've been told your Public Relations Officer position is vacant. Is that true, or is it an evasive tactic?"

In the face of her rapid-fire delivery, I heeded Quinn's orders and said, "I'm sorry, but I have no comment." Just as the man aimed his camera at my face, the glare of the sun behind him stung my eyes and made me squint.

Wynn took a long look at the name badge on the lapel of my blazer and said, "I see your name is Aimee Machado and you're Director of Library, Continuing Education and Ethical Affairs. All of that certainly sounds important."

My guard went up. I repeated, "I'm sorry, but I have no comment," and made a hurried stab with my key at the library's door. I fumbled, cursed silently to myself, and promised a quarter to my swear jar. The cameraman kept recording.

"You're going on the record with that?" Wynn asked.

"With what?" I put my shoulder to the door.

"You're refusing to say whether the press is being stonewalled?"

"No comment." I tried the key again.

She smiled. "Sorry to bother you Ms. Machado. You must have more important *ethical* matters to tend to than the death of Timbergate's Favorite Daughter."

My fumbling fingers finally got the door unlocked. I stepped inside without another word. The reporter made a move toward the entrance, but I closed the door firmly and locked it. She stood peering in for a moment while the cameraman focused his lens through the glass door. I walked into the break room where I was out of sight and started a pot of coffee. When I stepped warily out into the common area, they were gone.

I hoped when Oriana Wynn returned to her studio the better instincts of her news director would prevail, but I couldn't count on it. I expected my name and my job description to be splashed all over the first airing of the local news at five o'clock, along with a nasty account of my refusal to comment on the Delta Sawyer case. The thought left a bitter taste in my mouth.

I checked my morning emails and found a message from Laurie

Littletree confirming our planned trip to Nora Nester's daycare facility during lunch hour the next day.

The warmth inside the library was welcome as I fired up my computer and the half dozen others provided for patrons. I poured a cup of coffee, and without much success, tried to shake off the aggressive reporter incident.

With the aroma from my steaming cup bolstering my mood, I took a welcome sip and put in a call to Quinn to warn him about my encounter with the reporter. He was out, so I left a message with Enid Whitehorn.

LOLA RAMPLEY ARRIVED FOR HER NINE TO NOON volunteer shift in her usual good spirits. Her steps were brisk in spite of the severe bend in her upper back.

"'Good morning, Miss Machado, what lovely chores do we have today?"

"Your favorite," I said. "Requests for journal articles."

"Goody. I'll get to it, but first, may we talk?"

"Would you like to sit a minute?" I wondered if she was having second thoughts about our lunch hour visit to Ernest Wright's facility . . . or about moving in with Bernie.

She lowered herself onto a chair next to my desk. "I have a concern." I waited. Lola swiveled to glance around the room. Satisfied we were alone, she continued. "I do sometimes take shifts in other departments, you know."

"I didn't know that, but it's certainly fine for you to help in any capacity you like, as long as it isn't too tiring for you."

She smiled, reached out and patted my arm. "You're a dear, but don't worry about that. I have lots of energy."

"Then what is it that you want to ask me?"

She put an age-spotted, but still dainty hand to her cheek. "I sometimes hear things I shouldn't, but there's more. Sometimes I've even *seen* things I shouldn't." Her brows went up and she made a sweeping gesture of the library. "But never here in your area."

"Lola, is there something you've seen or heard in another department that has you worried?"

"That's the problem. I don't always know if it's important." Her powdered cheeks bloomed pink. "I'm not a prude. I've seen employees flirting, and I've accidentally walked in on heated discussions and the like. I know people are complicated, so I make myself scarce when that sort of thing happens."

"Is that how you knew I might be offered a promotion? Did you happen to overhear someone talking about it?"

Her cheeks turned a darker shade. I caught a faint hint of lavender. "Yes. But that's what confused me. I hadn't heard any specifics, so I thought you were being offered Varsha Singh's position until Bernie explained that you were staying with the library."

"I'm glad we cleared that up, Lola." I was mighty curious to know what was going on with Varsha, but my conscience kicked in. *Do not quiz your volunteer for details.*

"But that doesn't solve the other problem," she said.

"Your concern about witnessing something that troubles you? I'm sure we have an employee here at TMC who oversees Volunteer Services. That's the person to report to."

"Yes, we're under the wing of the Public Relations Department, but that's the thing." She hesitated a moment and then pushed on. "At our last auxiliary meeting, we were told the PR director has resigned and has already taken a position elsewhere. We're waiting to hear about her replacement." Lola stood and took in a deep breath. "In the meantime, may I come to you if I feel a need for advice? And Bernie, too?"

"That would be fine with me, but to be sure, I'll ask for Mr. Quinn's approval."

Lola thanked me, plugged in her earbuds and went to work. I watched her shoulders sway to whatever big band was playing on her iPod, likely stirring romantic memories from long ago. Or since she was officially engaged to Bernie Kluckert, maybe they were memories from not so long ago.

Our conversation turned my thoughts in a new direction. What was going on with our administrative employees? Varsha Singh had disappeared, and our PR director was gone—both at the worst possible time, with Delta Sawyer's death hitting the headlines.

I put in a call to Enid Whitehorn asking if I could catch a few minutes with Quinn. Lola and Bernie needed a go-to person until a new Public Relations Officer was hired. Lola had asked if I would be that person, but I needed Quinn's approval to take that on.

While I was at it, I would look for an opening to ask about Varsha Singh. I could remark on the coincidence of two administrative positions currently in transition and turn the conversation from the absent PR director to Quinn's absent executive assistant. There was a chance I could find out why Varsha was missing and why Enid Whitehorn was acting as gatekeeper in the Administration Office.

Quinn carved ten minutes out of his schedule to meet with me, but pointedly did not ask me to have a seat. He had recently added an oversized wrought-iron wall clock to his office décor—an apparent reminder to anyone meeting with him that he had no time to waste. Its loud ticking sounded positively rude.

"What's on your mind, Machado? I told you we'd discuss your promotion after the Sawyer case is settled. You still okay with that?"

"Yes, I'm fine with it."

"Good. And I got your message about the reporter. Don't let that throw you. They're a pack of jackals."

"Thanks, but that's not why I came. I have a question about my volunteers." I explained Lola's concern that she and Bernie needed someone to report to until a new PR director came on board. "She asked if they could come to me. I told her I'd clear it with you."

"Works for me," Quinn said. "I trust your judgment. Bring their concerns to me only if you think it's a safety issue or a procedural matter above your pay grade."

"Thanks. How long do you think it'll be?"

"Do I think *what* will be?" Quinn said.

"Until you hire a new Public Relations Director."

"Couple weeks, maybe."

"Are you interviewing candidates for any other positions?" *Varsha's perhaps?*

Quinn glanced at his annoying wall clock. "Why all the questions?"

"I'm thinking with Delta Sawyer's death and the ongoing news coverage, it's a bad time to be without Varsha or our PR person."

"We'll manage. Home office will pitch in with a temp for PR if I need it, meanwhile Ms. Whitehorn is doing a competent job fielding calls from media."

"Speaking of temps, what's *her* status? And why is she working Varsha's desk?"

"That's a conversation for another time. I have to be somewhere." He walked me to his door. "Let me know how it goes with your volunteers."

He was shutting me out. I didn't like it, but I understood. He had always treated me fairly. If he wanted to withhold information, he had his reasons. I exited his office, walking past Enid's desk on my way out. She hailed me as I reached the door to the exterior corridor.

"Miss Machado?"

I turned back. "Yes?"

"Ms. Cominoli called here looking for you. She asked if you would drop by."

I reached Cleo's office wondering what was on her mind. Another reminder to keep our distance? Her door was closed, so I stood for a moment to take in a calming breath. Just as I inhaled deeply, a man from Housekeeping passed by pushing a cart filled with dirty linens and rags reeking of cleaning solvent. I drew in a lungful of toxic odors that triggered a coughing fit and watering eyes.

Cleo's door opened. "What's going on—good grief, Aimee, are you crying?"

"No . . . housekeeping cart . . . just. . . ." I coughed.

"Come on in." She circled back to her desk, nodded at the door.

I closed it behind me. "The temp in Quinn's office said you were looking for me."

Cleo's lips twisted in a half grin. "You mean Enid? You think she's a temp?"

"I assumed. Why? Do you know something I don't?"

"Not a clue." She handed me a box of tissues from her desk drawer. "Relax. Have a seat."

I sat and dabbed at the corners of my eyes. "Why did you want to see me? Is there a problem?"

"Not at all, but I don't blame you for asking. When we got the news about Delta, Quinn gave me the impression I should keep you at arm's length until the investigation is over, but after seeing your reaction to Margie's comments at the diner on Monday, I decided to have a talk with him."

"And now?"

"I told him you needed a friend here at your workplace. I assured him that we wouldn't discuss any details of Delta's manner or cause of death. Only our normal committee work. He agreed we can go back to business as usual. What do you say?"

"Thank you." I took another tissue from the box. "You're more than a work friend to me."

Cleo smiled. "I feel the same. So as long as we avoid the topic of Delta Sawyer, we're good."

"We can do that." I tossed my crumpled tissues into her wastebasket. "If that's all, I should get back to work."

"Not quite." Cleo peered at me over her half-moons. "There is something else."

"Something you're at liberty to tell me?"

"It's a gray area, but I can justify it. You deserve to know, because it concerns you."

Her ominous tone set my scalp tingling. "Then I'd better hear it."

"The reason Delta Sawyer's death has Jared Quinn rattled goes beyond the Sawyers' prominence in the community. There's been a collaborative project in the works for a while now between the TMC Foundation and the Sawyer Foundation to establish a state-of-the-art drug rehab facility here in Timbergate."

"That sounds like a wonderful idea. How would it concern me?"

"There's more. Vane Beardsley has taken on the role of president of the TMC Foundation, so he and Buck Sawyer are the two men who will make or break the project."

I let that sink in. "The same two men—"

"Yes. They're the same two men most at risk because of the mix-up in Delta Sawyer's pills and the same two men who have reasons to expect your loyalty. I thought you should know."

"Why haven't I heard about the rehab project?"

"It's not just you. Almost no one has. All the parties involved wanted to wait until after the mayoral election before making the announcement." Cleo pulled off her glasses and dropped them on her desk. "It's a good thing they did, because the project has been tabled until further notice."

"How do you know about it?"

"I take the minutes at the TMC Foundation meetings."

I leaned forward. "Cleo, I realize you took a chance telling me about this. Thank you for trusting me."

"I do trust you or I wouldn't have taken the chance. I knew Quinn hadn't told you, and I assumed you hadn't heard about it from Mr. Sawyer or Dr. Beardsley. Everyone involved is keeping it close because of the temporary delay. I doubt even Nick knows."

"You're right. I've heard nothing about it from any of them, so until it becomes public, I'm going to forget you told me."

"Good." In a gentler tone she said, "Do you mind if I ask how you and Nick are doing?"

My throat tightened. "It hasn't been easy. With a tinge of guilt, I held back from telling her Nick and I planned to meet that night. "We're staying in touch, but not able to speak freely."

Cleo shook her head. "Like the situation you and I are in, only worse."

"It is. I keep hoping someone will come up with answers and it'll all be over."

"I hope so, too. Just remember that I'm here for you as much as I can be."

"Thanks, but before I head back to the library, I have a question."

"So do I, but you go first."

"Do you know where Varsha Singh is?"

"Funny," Cleo said, "I was going to ask you the same thing."

LOLA LEFT HER LIBRARY SHIFT EARLY so she and Bernie could have lunch together before meeting me at Ernest Wright's facility at noon. He stopped by to pick her up at eleven, which gave me an hour before our tour to learn as much about the place as I could. I recalled seeing the name of the complex on the campaign brochure I picked up at the Monday night debate. I entered it into my browser and the website popped up immediately.

THE WRIGHT TIME OF LIFE: *Senior Living for the Young at Heart.*

The photos displayed well-manicured grounds, happy, active residents, and delicious meals. There were spacious, handicap accessible apartments with convenient floor plans, a pool and spa, a workout room, and even a small movie theater. I hoped that our visit would live up to the dozens of glowing testimonials singing the praises of the facility and Ernest Wright, but I planned to scout for any hint of motive or evidence that might tend to incriminate him.

Thinking ahead to my tour with Laurie Littletree the next day, I moved on to Nora Nester's daycare site, where her almost-too-precious business name was set against a backdrop of puppies, kittens, ducklings, bunnies and lambs frolicking in various shades of pink and blue. *Nora's Nest: Daycare at its Best*. She offered a combination daycare and preschool where parents could enroll their children as young as two months in daycare and then graduate them up to preschool at age three. The site claimed the facility was state of the art in every way. There were the usual positive testimonials and certifications of excellence.

Despite Delta's claim about dirt on her opponents, nothing about Wright or Nester whiffed of shame or wrongdoing. If Delta had been bluffing, it would have backfired if she promised to deliver and then reversed course. Assuming she *had* found secrets that would put them out of the running for mayor, that information could be found if the right person went looking.

Harry insisted he would not betray his loyalty to Nick, and I had agreed. That meant keeping any further knowledge about the status of the TPD investigation to himself. But digging into the pasts of a couple of murder suspects was a different matter. He knew his way around the hidden depths of the web a lot better than I did. That level of research was not part of my training, where resources were legit and above-board. Anything deeper was more likely taught at places like the FBI Academy at Quantico, Virginia. I sent Harry a text.

Need help can u call?

U in trouble?

No need a favor

My cell rang. "What's up, Sis. Everything okay at the ranch?"

"It's all good."

"Then what's the favor?" I heard reluctance in his tone. He was already primed to say no if I asked him to nose around for me.

"It's a web combing thing."

"Deep or dark?"

"Could be either."

He responded with an exasperated sigh. "Not liking this already. Are you up to something that involves the Sawyer case?"

I tried an evasive tactic. "It's about my library volunteers. They're exploring a move to a senior facility, and they have no family close by to help them, so they came to me. They're elderly and concerned about making a risky financial decision. We have an appointment to visit the facility at noon today. I'm pretty sure they're both on fixed incomes, and I don't want anyone to take advantage of them. I'd like to know more about the place."

"Got it, but I don't have time to talk now. Expecting a call about a bid. Can you come and help teach peewee class at the dojo tonight? We can talk then."

"What time?"

"Six to eight. Will that work?"

"I can do that." Perfect, I could still meet Nick at the Sawyer Foundation by nine.

"Then go ahead and visit the place with your volunteers, but don't let them sign anything. If something dodgy jumps out at you, make notes."

"I will. Thanks."

A sigh escaped as I ended the call. Harry was on board—but only for my volunteers. I still had to convince him to dig for the secrets Delta had promised. I closed the library a few minutes early and headed over to Ernest Wright's facility to meet Lola and Bernie.

THE WRIGHT TIME OF LIFE WAS A SPRAWLING, white two-story structure on a property easily accessible from Timbergate's main thoroughfare—a perfect location in case a quick ambulance ride became necessary. Its well-maintained landscaping featured numerous shrubs and shade trees. When I stepped inside the reception area, I spotted Bernie and Lola seated on a floral loveseat holding hands. They raised themselves up as I approached.

"Miss Aimee, glad to see you," Bernie said. "We were a tad early. The reception lady let us wait here for our granddaughter." He and Lola exchanged excited glances, eager to get on with it.

"Thank you for waiting. Before we start, I have good news. Mr. Quinn approved our request. Until a new PR Director is hired, both of you may come to me with any concerns about your volunteer work at TMC."

Lola reached out to take my hand. "Thank you, dear. You do feel like family, you know."

I hoped Bernie's granddaughter fib would not come back to bite me later if they decided they actually wanted to move in to Wright's complex. I had no idea what the sentence was for impersonating a grandchild. The three of us approached the receptionist, who checked us off her list and called for our tour guide.

My original idea had been to ask if we could meet Mr. Wright. I wanted a closer look at him to try to judge his character. Was he capable of murder? I was no psychiatrist, but my work had exposed me to numerous forensic psychiatry articles on the criminal mind. There were a few telling traits I thought I might recognize.

Concern for Bernie and Lola, and for my own safety, put that plan to rest. Better if we did not meet Mr. Wright, in case things turned sour later on. I cautioned Bernie and Lola not to use my real name since we were only pretending I was a relative.

A thirty-something woman with auburn hair and glittery designer glasses arrived to start our tour. She introduced herself as Glory. No last name was offered from her or from the badge pinned to the lapel of her white jacket.

"We're pleased to meet ya, Glory," Bernie said. "This here's Lola. She's my lady. And we brought our granddaughter along to see to it we don't forget anything."

Glory reached out her hand to me. "And your name?"

I said the first thing that came to mind. "Call me Ginger. My last name is difficult to pronounce." I felt a pinch of guilt about the lie, but it seemed justified. In my mind, Wright was a murder suspect until proven innocent.

Lola's lips started to twitch. I groped in my pocket for my roll of mints. "Here you go, Nana. Have one." She popped it into her mouth.

A trace of frown crossed Glory's face. "You are the granddaughter, though?"

Bernie reached an arm around my shoulders. "You bet," he said. "She's our little angel."

Lola's eyes grew wide. For a moment, I was afraid she would either burst out laughing, or choke on her candy. She managed to keep her cool and we were escorted through the facility in record time. I tried to speed up our visit by telling Glory I had to be back to work in less than an hour. That prompted the usual question.

"Where do you work?"

"I'm a librarian."

Not everyone knows there are libraries in hospitals. I hoped Glory would assume that I worked in one of the branches of the Sawyer County Library.

She started our tour with three versions of model apartments, followed by the recreation room, the dining room, the hairdressing facility that groomed men, women and pets, the small-scale movie screening room, and the well-stocked reading room/library.

We passed another room where the open door revealed a woman sitting behind a desk, pen in hand, concentrating on a document. I recognized Ernest Wright's wife from the campaign debate where she had stood proudly on stage behind her husband and next to her mother-in-law. A platform scale in the room looked like the kind used in doctors' offices. I spotted an exam table toward the back and a blood pressure monitor on a mobile stand. There were glass cannisters filled with cotton balls and Q-tips on the counter-top, and the walls were lined with cupboards that I assumed held other medical supplies.

Glory ushered us past without remarking about the room. Wright's campaign speeches had emphasized the active lifestyle of his facility. He had not described it as a nursing facility, which led me to wonder what level of medical services were available. Did they employ a family nurse practitioner or a physician assistant licensed to dispense prescription medications? I wondered if Wright's wife had medical training.

Glory took us outside for a walk around the grounds, where we viewed the swimming pool, the bocce ball court, and the miniature golf course. There was even a garden area for residents who enjoyed working with plants and flowers.

At the end of our tour, Glory left to fetch someone she called the intake coordinator. As soon as she was out of sight, I asked the receptionist for a brochure and whether the facility produced an annual report. She pulled open a desk drawer and handed me two copies of each document. I gave Bernie and Lola one set and kept the other, saying we needed to leave so I could get back to work. I walked with them to the parking lot, urging them to be sure they looked into the financial health of the facility.

As I drove back to work, I noticed them following me and wondered why until I remembered that Lola had left her car at the library when Bernie picked her up to go to lunch. I was unlocking the entrance door when Bernie pulled up and helped Lola out of his car.

"Would you like to come in?" I asked, hoping for a chance to debrief them.

"Thank ya," Bernie said, "but I got to go get my car serviced."

"I'd like to stop in for a moment," Lola said.

It turned out she needed a pit stop before heading home. When she reappeared from the restroom, I took the opportunity to ask her what she thought of the tour. She told me she and Bernie were eager to move to *The Wright Time of Life,* but she wanted to know my reason for telling them to wait. Full disclosure was not an option. I had to keep my thoughts to myself about Wright as a possible murder suspect.

"Let's sit for a moment, Lola. I have a couple of questions." I walked with her to one of the small tables provided for patrons.

"What would you like to know?" Lola perched on the edge of her chair.

"How much will it cost to make the move? If you don't mind my asking."

She toyed with the clasp of her purse. "No, I don't mind. That's part of why we need all the advice we can get. There will be the cost of two moves, mine and Bernie's, the cost of the first month at the facility, and the security deposit. We're each going to come up with almost ten thousand dollars."

"And what about where you're each living now?"

"We're both living in apartments. My lease is due for renewal at the end of the month. Bernie's is next month. That's why we thought this would be a good time if we're going to make this change. Don't you think it's a good idea, Miss Machado?"

I did not think so. Not until I was sure Ernest Wright was innocent of Delta's murder. I wanted to tell her not to move into a facility that might go belly-up in the very near future. If that happened,
who knew if they would ever get their money back?

"Have you talked this over with your families? You both have
grown children, don't you?"

"Oh, yes," Lola said. "Even our grandchildren are grown." She
laughed softly. "We're counting great-grands now. I have seven,
Bernie has four. I've started college savings accounts for all of mine.
Bernie has done the same for his." She scooted her chair close,
leaning toward me. "That's why we want to be careful about our
finances. We might be able to save more from social security and
our pension benefits by pooling our resources. There'll be more for
the young ones."

All the more reason for this elderly couple to avoid a financial
commitment to Ernest Wright. Who knew what might be hidden in the fine print of his contracts? If they were living on pen-
sions and social security, they could not afford to tie themselves to
anything too long term. In spite of his facility's name and slogan,
Wright's residents were not getting any younger.

"Lola, what do your children think of your idea?"

"They tell us to have an attorney review the contract before we
sign." The trouble was, that attorney would not know the whole
story.

"That's a good idea," I said, "but I'm wondering if one of your
adult children could make a visit to Timbergate to talk this over
with the two of you. I recall Bernie saying you don't have family
nearby, but is there someone who could come?"

"Oh, that would be asking too much. Mine are in Florida, and
Bernie's son and daughter-in-law live in Toronto."

"How about grown grandkids nearby?"

"I'm afraid not. They're scattered to the winds and so busy with
jobs and raising children. Besides, Bernie and I are adults with
sound minds and good judgment," Lola reached out and patted
my hand, "and best of all, we have you. You're a master librarian
and the smartest person we know."

I almost quipped that they must not know a lot of people. "Lola, I'm glad to help, and my best advice is that you wait for at least a month, maybe two, before making any decisions or signing anything. Are you and Bernie willing to do that?"

Her face registered disappointment. "Oh, do you really think that's necessary? There's the problem of renewing my lease. If I don't make a decision soon, I'll be forced out of my apartment. The manager tells me there's a waiting list."

"How long do you have?"

"He's already pressing me, but I have until the end of the month."

One week. "Lola, I'm sorry I don't have time right now to explain further. Can we talk about this again?"

Lola rose quickly. "Yes, dear. I'm sorry, you mustn't let me be a bother."

"You're not a bother. I want to help, but I think it's important that you and Bernie hold off making a decision over the weekend. We can talk about this again on Monday morning. Will that work for you?"

"I suppose," she said, "and I'll talk to Bernie. He values your advice."

Her answer was evasive, but it was the best I was going to get.

After she left I spent a few minutes jotting notes about Wright's complex. What stood out for me was the nursing office where I had seen Wright's wife working. Their brochure confirmed that they employed a nurse practitioner—no name given.

A bit of research confirmed that nurse practitioners can prescribe medication, including controlled substances, in all fifty states and Washington DC without physician supervision, even highly regulated Schedule II substances like oxycodone.

I tried to stop my mind running away with that bit of information. It proved Earnest Wright might have had access to the drug that had killed Delta, but a nurse's office in his facility also demonstrated a higher than usual standard of care for his residents.

There had been no mention of a nurse practitioner on Nora Nester's daycare website. I made a mental note to look for a similar set-up when Laurie and I visited there on Thursday.

A high standard of care by either of them was more endorsement than indictment, but Delta had threatened to reveal damning secrets about both candidates. Quinn and Nick had suspected she was bluffing, but I wanted to be sure. Besides, Delta's opponents were the only suspects I had to work with, unless I could come up with someone else with a killer's motive.

My goal in visiting Wright's facility had been to rule him in or out as a suspect, but failing that, my immediate goal was to keep Bernie and Lola from signing a contract until I was sure Ernest Wright was innocent and that he was, in Bernie's words, "on the up-and-up." I recalled the glances Lola and Bernie kept sharing during their tour. With each feature Glory presented, they seemed more excited. By the end, they were behaving like a couple who had already made up their minds.

I hoped lending a hand with Harry's judo class would earn me the sibling points I needed. I had to convince him to do his magic before it was too late. If he came up with nothing on Wright or Nester, I would be back to square one, which led me to wonder what other suspects were waiting in the wings. Who else might have benefited by eliminating Delta from the race for mayor?

The candidates' supporters came to mind. Elections of all kinds had become so polarizing over the past few years that I had to consider every possibility. Did Wright or Nester have a fanatical supporter willing to bump off Delta just because she was the front-runner? As far-fetched as that idea was, it led me to wonder where I could find a list of campaign donors.

The answer was the Sawyer County Clerk's office. A quick check told me that campaign donations of more than two hundred dollars were required to be recorded and were available as public record. Donors' names and amounts were listed. All other personal donor information was redacted. I also discovered that generally, it was the candidate's hard-nosed, uncompromising supporters who were most likely to donate to political campaigns. A bit of forensic psychology to keep in mind.

Pinpointing the donors for the two remaining candidates gave me something to hope for, since politics could ignite great passion in an unstable zealot capable of murder. If nothing jumped out at me there, I would scrutinize Delta Sawyer's donor list. There was the remote chance that she had ticked off one of her more ardent followers.

I hoped to investigate the candidates' donors at home that night if I still had time after working with Harry's students and keeping my date with Nick, but I knew better than to pull an all-nighter. The three days since Delta's death had demanded excessive mental and physical energy. Those demands would persist until the mystery of the switched pills was solved. Cheating myself on sleep would only make matters worse.

With that plan in mind, I followed my conscience and put my energy back on the job I was being paid to do.

Chapter 12

T HE REMAINDER OF WEDNESDAY AFTERNOON was spent jug-gling legitimate library work with random thoughts about Delta Sawyer's pills. My opioid research had confirmed that the problem was a world-wide scourge raging out of control with America's level of total overdose deaths climbing beyond ninety thousand in one year—far beyond the norm among other wealthy nations. No wonder Buck Sawyer was so devoted to his founda-tion's work. His daughter's overdose had branded his soul with a hatred for drug dealers of any kind, from murderous cartels to the sneaky teenager who steals a few pills from the family medicine cabinet and sells them to classmates.

I wondered if the loss of his only child and his first wife had influenced Buck's decision to marry Delta. He must have expected a younger wife would survive him, allowing him to avoid another personal loss. If so, he had been wrong. Nick was the nearest thing to family that Buck had left—and the only person he could turn to for comfort.

Delta's compulsion to erase those barely visible lines on her face still puzzled me. Unless her obsession with her looks was another symptom of her keen appetite for attention. The last-minute cosmetic procedure seemed another hasty decision similar to her sudden run for mayor when she had never shown an interest in local government. Not even Buck could explain that unlikely move on her part. Whatever the reason for her leap into politics, she apparently thought the faint lines spanning her forehead would have to go. As the front-runner, she must have expected to win and wanted to be picture perfect by election day.

Quitting time finally came, but before I ventured outside I went to the break room window where I could peek out into the parking lot. The last thing I wanted was another ambush by TV reporter Oriana Wynn and her camera-toting sidekick. My luck held. The coast was clear.

AT HOME I THREW ON JEANS AND A SWEATSHIRT, fed the cat and the llamas, and fixed myself a turkey and avocado sandwich on pita bread. Fuel for an evening workout on the mat with Harry's students. Between bites I glanced at the front page of our local paper. Delta Sawyer's death was above the fold with a glaring headline:

MAYORAL CANDIDATE'S
DEATH INVESTIGATION ONGOING

The reporter cited an unnamed source who had seen police at the home of Buck and Delta Sawyer. The piece reported that a TPD spokesperson offered no comment when asked if there was suspicion of foul play. All the more reason to convince Harry to dig deep into the backgrounds of Ernest Wright and Nora Nester for the kind of secrets either of them might kill to conceal.

THE TEACHING SESSION AT THE DOJO WENT WELL. Harry's students were preparing for a junior tournament that would take place in a few weeks. The approaching competition kept them focused and made my job easier. When the session was over and the dojo was empty, Harry and I changed into street clothes and met in the sensei's office.

He pulled two bottles of iced tea from the fridge and handed one to me. "Grab a seat and let's talk."

"Thanks. The kids did good work tonight."

"I noticed. They like working with you." He twisted the cap off his tea. "But you're not here to talk about my students."

"No. I'm paying in advance for a favor."

"Before we get to that, have you had any word from Nick?"

"We're meeting tonight. He didn't tell you?"

"No, we haven't talked in a while. If you're getting together, that's a good thing, right?"

"Up to a point, but it's not the same as before, when we could work together to solve a mystery and share everything with each other."

"Yeah, that's tough. Looks like you're stuck on opposite sides of a whodunit."

"And you're stuck in the middle," I said. "Sorry about that."

"Not your fault." Harry swigged from his tea bottle. "At least I got the benefit of your help tonight. You going to tell me about the old folks' home you want me to look into?"

"It's actually a little more complicated than that."

Harry's eyes narrowed. "How complicated? In case you've forgotten, I have better things to do with my nights these days."

"Better than clearing your girlfriend's boss of a murder charge?"

Harry slumped in his chair. "I thought this was about your elderly volunteers wanting to move to a senior facility."

"That's only part of it. I want you to look into the pasts of Ernest Wright and Nora Nester right away. We need to find the secrets that Delta Sawyer was threatening to expose. She claimed she uncovered scandals that would disqualify both of them from the race, but she never made them public."

"You're suggesting one of them decided to silence her?"

"It's a possibility that should be checked out, but I doubt the City of Timbergate, and by extension, the Timbergate PD, is going to be thrilled about investigating its two remaining candidates for mayor on such short notice. The election is barely a week and a day away. Think of the damaging consequences to the city's image if it got out that the police suspect either candidate is a cold-blooded killer."

"You think that's an even trade? You teach one class and I sit up half the night staring at my screen and developing carpal tunnel?"

"I'm desperate. Buck's prints are on the pill bottle that's potential evidence of premeditated murder. So are Nick's. That bottle is the *only* hard evidence in this case. We need to counter that with something that will convince the police to cast a wider net."

"You're thinking Wright or Nester had a motive? Since when does motive outdo hard evidence?"

"If we find a strong enough motive, maybe evidence will follow. We can at least try."

"Wait." Harry signaled a time out. "If we find something persuasive, we take it to your friend the police detective, right?"

"That's my plan. Nick said Kass is leading the investigation."

"All right," Harry said. "I'll do this on one condition. If I find nothing, you take my word for it."

"Agreed." I filled him in on what I had observed at Wright's facility and told him about my plan to visit Nora Nester's daycare with Laurie Littletree.

Harry got to his feet. "Okay then, here's the deal. I'll start crawling around the web to see what I can find about Wright and Nester. I get that you want something worth killing for. Something you think will convince the police to shift their focus off Buck and Nick."

"Thank you. How long do you think it will take?"

"I might need a day or two. As soon as you give me what you already have on them I'll take it from there."

I jumped up. "I printed off everything I could find about their backgrounds."

"Of course you did."

"It's in my car."

"Of course it is." Harry turned out the dojo's interior lights and we stepped outside. He locked the building and we walked to where our cars were parked side by side.

I reached into my backseat for an envelope. "Here you go. Nothing incriminating, so far."

He took it, opened his car door and tossed it on the front seat. "I'll see what I can do."

With that done, Harry headed home to Rella and I drove across town to the Sawyer Foundation. It was a substantial two-story brick in a business district made up of several similar buildings that lined a bluff overlooking the river. Buck's foundation occupied the entire structure, although the only interior space I'd seen was an expansive, professionally decorated reception area. Its plush royal blue carpets and framed prints of masterpieces had served as a backdrop for Delta's campaign kick-off celebration.

Nick and I arrived within minutes of each other. We parked behind the building in a secluded lot reserved for employees. As soon as we were out of our vehicles, we were in each other's arms as if we'd been apart for months instead of three days. Our first kiss led to a second, and then a third before we finally got a grip on ourselves. I managed to speak first.

"How long before you have to go back to Buck?"

"Not long. He asked me to pick up some files he wants to look over. He says as long as the police haven't raided the foundation, he might as well tend to business."

"He can concentrate on grants now, with Delta's death so recent? Doesn't he have Fletcher Tremont to look after those things?"

"He does, but Tremont is on leave along with the other employees. He probably needs a break. He put in a lot of time and energy managing Delta's campaign, and now the rug's been pulled out from under him. He lost his candidate and a fellow foundation board member in one unexpected tragedy."

"I met Fletcher Tremont at the debate the night he announced how Delta's campaign donations would be handled. He seemed to be holding up all right."

"Buck says he rose to the occasion that night, but apparently he's taking it pretty hard."

"What about Buck? How's he doing?"

"He's having a tough time processing what's happened—still happening. I haven't had a chance to tell you, but we're back in his house. We got permission this morning."

"Is that helping?"

"Not much, with the police still investigating and telling him next to nothing. Plus all the extra attention because of who Delta was—the 'favorite daughter' thing and her run for mayor."

"Not to mention who Buck is," I said. "He has his own claim to fame. Not many towns the size of Timbergate are home to a prominent billionaire."

"In spite of all that, he seems to be getting over the initial shock. He's already survived the deaths of his daughter and his first wife. Maybe he's learned over the years about accepting loss. Or maybe he's coping by sending me here to bring work home for him. His foundation is the engine that drives him. He won't let Delta's death get in the way of his mission. It might even strengthen his resolve."

"I hope you're right." No mention of Buck's arrest.

"Want to come inside with me? Buck told me the files he wants are in a briefcase in his office. It'll only take a minute to find it."

Nick unlocked the rear door and punched in the code for the alarm. I waited in the reception area while he went to Buck's office for the briefcase.

He reappeared right away. "Got it."

"Should we go?"

"In a moment. There's a favor I have to ask you first."

We stood inside the door to the back exit. "What kind of favor?"

"Buck wants me to give you these." He held out a keychain and pointed to one of the keys. "This one opens the building." He pointed out another. "This is a master to all of the offices. The smaller keys are for the file cabinets. He wants you to have access to everything."

Alarm took my breath. I could think of no good reason why Buck would want me to have those keys. Only bad ones. Buck's aborted arrest had obviously spooked him, but I did not mention that, or Nick's seeking a defense lawyer.

"But why me? What about Tremont and the other employees? There must be quite a few."

"Buck's asked all of his employees to turn in their keys while they're on leave. Even me. He told me to give this set to you. He trusts you as much as I do."

"Who else will have a set?"

"Only you and Buck." Nick handed me one of Buck's business cards. "The security alarm code is written on the back of this, although I doubt you'll ever need it."

"Nick, you have to tell me what's going on."

He nodded. "It's more than just giving the employees time off. Buck's lawyers have advised him to close the foundation offices until further notice. He'll handle any pressing business from home until the investigation is over and Delta's case is wrapped up one way or another. The only exception will be for Delta's memorial on Sunday evening."

"What do you mean? Is it going to take place here?"

"It is. Seven o'clock. Buck got the okay from TPD. He invited them to look around inside and they gave him an all clear. It's Buck's attorneys who want the employees to stay away until Delta's manner of death is confirmed."

"Won't the employees be attending the memorial?"

"Some will, but it's going to be a small gathering. Invitation only."

"Who's helping prepare for the memorial?"

"Buck's doing most of it himself. He'll hire outside help if necessary."

"What about you?"

"No keys, remember? I'll run errands. I won't be helping set up the room."

"Nick, what am I supposed to do with this set of keys?"

"Buck said you would use them only in an emergency. If that happens, one of us will let you know."

With a sick sensation, I understood that "emergency" meant if Buck was arrested again. His lawyers obviously believed that could happen, and soon. They had to consider that Nick could be jailed as well.

"If that's what he wants, tell him I'll keep them safe." I slipped them into my purse.

Nick still had made no mention of Buck's arrest. As he walked me to my car, I asked if there was anything else he wanted to tell me.

He took my arm and stopped me. "There is one more thing,

Aimee. I would have told you sooner, but I didn't want it to worry you." Here it comes.

"Can't promise I won't worry. What is it?"

"Buck was taken into custody yesterday morning, but he was released right away."

I took a beat, pretending his news was a surprise. "Can you tell me why he was arrested?"

"I will, since it amounts to nothing. Do you remember when Buck had hernia surgery six months ago?"

"Yes, but I don't—"

"Hold on, I'll explain. He was prescribed an opioid for pain back then. It was the exact same drug that was found in Delta's acetaminophen bottle. An anonymous tipster called it in. The police decided to bring Buck in while they checked it out because he's a billionaire with a fleet of airplanes."

"They think he's a flight risk?"

"They had to consider it."

"Does that mean you're a flight risk too, because you're his primary pilot?"

"Let's not overthink it. The point is the police discovered almost immediately that Buck had never picked up that prescription from the pharmacy."

"That's why they released him?"

"Correct. The overzealous tipster, whoever it was, had reason to know about the mix-up in Delta's pills in spite of the police keeping it out of the news."

"Are they going to try to discover that tipster's identity?"

"Doubt it. The whole point of Secret Witness is anonymity. It would be useless if it got out that those callers could be identified."

"It must have been an employee either at Buck's doctor's office or at the pharmacy that filled the prescription. But the same person knew about Delta's switched pills. Maybe it was someone with a connection to TMC."

"Good guess, but we'll probably never know. I'm sorry I didn't tell you sooner, but I wanted to wait, since Buck was sure it would come to nothing and he was right."

"If there's a next time, please don't try to spare my feelings."

"I won't. The good thing is that TPD will be extra cautious about arresting Buck again, so there won't be a next time."

"Unless they suspect that he got the opioids from some other source."

"But he didn't, so that's not going to happen."

"I hope you're right." I reached to open my car door. "I should get home."

"Not yet." Nick took me in his arms for a lingering kiss. "God, if you knew how much I miss being at the ranch with you."

"It's the same for me." I kept a grip on my emotions. No whining allowed. "Any idea when you might come home?"

"No, but I keep asking. So does Buck. He insists he doesn't need me spending nights with him, but that's not the problem."

"The problem is my job, right?"

He sighed. "'Fraid so, but I'm going to talk to the attorneys again tomorrow. See if we can work something out."

With a final hug, he said, "We'll get through this, Aimee, please try not to worry. Buck's attorneys are the best."

He made no mention of his search for an attorney of his own. I let it go, keeping my word to Harry. And I held off mentioning both my promotion and our potential role as godparents to the Littletrees' daughter. Those topics could wait until the mystery of Delta Sawyer's death was solved.

Chapter 13

B ACK HOME AT TEN THIRTY, I had just opened the Sawyer County Clerk's site to take a look at donors to the remaining candidates' campaigns when my phone pinged with a text from Rella Olstad—something that had never happened since the first day we met. It jerked me to my feet with a burst of adrenaline coursing through my body. I read the text.

Can we meet?
I replied, *When and where?*
FDN office tonight 11?
Urgent?
Think so
Okay. Harry too?
Just me
On my way.

This was big. Rella had played a role before in cases Nick and I had been involved in, but she and I had not developed a personal friendship. At first I thought it was because she and Nick had been friends before I met him. When she and Harry began dating, I let go of that theory. My brother had explained that Rella was a private person who took her time forming new bonds. In spite of that, I knew I could trust her. If she was asking to meet, especially without Harry, my donor search would have to wait.

I drove into the employee parking lot behind Buck's building for the second time that Wednesday night at five minutes to eleven. Rella pulled in and parked next to me. I got out and walked to her driver's side door. When she rolled her window down, Ginger shoved her head out, edging Rella aside.

"You brought Nick's dog. Is she all right?"

"She's fine, but I had to bring her," Rella said. "She was my excuse. She'd been acting restless all evening, which I took as a sign she was missing Nick. I told Harry to go ahead and get some sleep, that I'd take Ginger for a drive to try and calm her down. I didn't tell him I was meeting you."

"You needed an excuse?" My pulse kicked up a notch.

"I'll explain. Thanks for coming."

"Had to. This must be important."

"I believe it is. I don't like doing anything behind Harry's back, but I thought we should talk." Rella leaned over and opened her passenger door. "Want to get in? We can't go inside the building. Buck asked all of us to turn in our keys."

When I slipped in, Ginger nuzzled the back of my head. After I stroked her and crooned a few reassuring words, she seemed content to curl up on the backseat.

"Nick told me about the keys." I kept quiet about the set in my purse. The secrets were piling up.

Rella checked her cell for the time. "We should get this done. It's going to take a little while, and Harry will worry if he decides to wait up and I'm gone too long."

The overhead lights illuminating the private parking area washed Rella's complexion with a blue tinge, but instead of looking ghoulish, she looked like a supermodel with her blond hair pulled back from her flawless face. Her shadowy features added to the mystery of why she wanted this meeting.

"Rella, your text has me worried." I rubbed my chilled hands together to warm them. "What's this about?"

"It's something I came across a few weeks ago. It involves Buck and Delta, and I wanted your opinion. I haven't told anyone else. Not even Harry."

"Why not?"

"If I had, he would have asked me not to tell you. You'll understand when you hear what I have to say." She took a breath. "Because of Delta's death, I think it's something the police should know, but first I wanted the advice of at least one other person. For reasons that will become obvious, I chose you." She turned to me, her eyes locking on mine even in the dim light of the car's interior. "But first, please give me your word that you won't repeat it."

"How can I promise that?"

"I know what I'm asking. All I can say is it affects Buck, and by extension, Nick. You'll have to trust me on that. When I explain, you'll understand why I chose to talk to you."

My shoulders stiffened. "All right. Go ahead."

"Buck called me the morning Delta died and told me her death was caused by a mix-up in her pain pills. That incident affects her doctor and Timbergate Medical Center, which puts your colleagues and your workplace in an awkward position."

"The information about the pills wasn't supposed to get out."

"When Buck told me, he hadn't yet been warned that the police didn't want it made public."

"And I'm aware that you told Harry about this."

"Yes. At this point, several people already know. We should make a count."

"We know that Quinn, Beardsley, the TMC pharmacist, and my co-worker, Cleo Cominoli know about the pills," I said. "And the police. In addition, there are six more who know. You, me, Buck, Nick, Harry, and the Secret Witness who caused Buck's aborted arrest."

"Let's not forget the person who switched the pills," Rella said.

"Right, although we may never know who that was. Meanwhile, the police are still looking at Buck."

"And that's why I wanted to confide in you . . . if you're willing to keep this between the two of us and not let on to Nick that I've told you." *Another secret.*

Rella was no drama queen. This behavior was completely out of character for her. "You have my word. Please tell me."

"Buck was looking into a legal separation. Nick knew, but no one else did."

That bombshell punched the air from my lungs leaving me dizzy, struggling to breathe. Rella reached over and shook my shoulder. "Aimee, are you all right?"

I managed a breath. "I'm okay, but I don't understand. How long have you known? How long has Nick known?"

"I've known since a couple of weeks before Delta died. I'm sure Nick has, too. I suspect he's known even longer. I haven't let on to him that I know."

"And you haven't told Harry?"

"No. Except for Nick and me, I'm fairly certain no one knows except the lawyers Buck had been consulting with in San Francisco."

"Do you think Delta knew?"

"I can't be sure. As far as I know, he hadn't filed. It's all so confusing. Maybe she learned that he'd been seeking legal separation advice and she contrived the overdose to bring on sympathy and make him change his mind. What if she botched it and killed herself accidentally? Or did she actually plan a suicide that she could blame on Buck?"

"That doesn't sound like something she would do. My guess is she'd try to change Buck's mind."

"I get what you're saying, Aimee, but putting it mildly, Delta was a complicated woman. We all knew that. What we don't know is the extent of the forces that drove her."

"You said something about Buck consulting with lawyers in San Francisco. Did he confide in you about this?"

"Heavens no. He wouldn't confide that in me. He doesn't know that I know, but I'm pretty sure Buck took Nick into his confidence from the start. Their relationship is much closer."

"You're right. Nick is the one person Buck would confide in, and the one who would do almost anything to help him. How did you find out about this?"

"I stumbled on it by accident when I flew Buck to San Francisco a

couple of weeks ago. He described the purpose of the trip as following up on a grant request. I drove him into the city from the airport,
dropped him at his destination and arranged to pick him up when
he called. Then I killed some time having lunch and shopping."

"Tough job," I said, "but someone's got to do it."

Rella nodded. "True. Most of the time I get the easier flights,
Nick takes the brunt of the tough ones."

"So far, I don't see how—"

"I'll hurry so we can both get home. Have a look at this."

She took a sheet of paper from her purse, unfolded it and aimed
the beam of a penlight at the handwritten notes. They detailed
Buck's in-person meeting with the San Francisco lawyers, including his suspicion that Delta was having an affair. An assumption
based on her secretive behavior over an extended period of time.

"An affair? Do you think Buck knew who the man was?"

Rella answered with a slight shake of her head. "I doubt it. If he
did, it would have been more than a suspicion."

"Good point. I wonder why a separation instead of divorce."

"I've thought about that. Maybe he wasn't sure he wanted a
divorce. Wouldn't a legal separation have protected him from
Delta's financial decisions while he made up his mind?"

"Pretty sure that's right," I said. "He wouldn't have been responsible for any debt she incurred during the separation. Quite a blow
for Delta if she was cut off with no income or assets of her own."

"Maybe that was Buck's plan. An incentive for her to do some
serious thinking about their marriage and her future. Especially
after seeing how meager her financial situation was before she and
Buck married." Rella aimed her light on the next line. "Look at this."

The figure revealed Delta's net worth at the time of their marriage to be far less than anyone would have guessed.

The note that followed showed their prenuptial agreement to be
a lump sum for Delta of one million dollars if there was a divorce—
a modest amount, considering Buck's wealth, but a wise move on
his part, and perhaps his way to ensure at the time of their marriage that she didn't have designs on a much larger community
property settlement down the road.

"Wow, Rella, you may be right. Delta would have burned through that million in a year trying to maintain the lifestyle she enjoyed as Buck's wife. That consultation in San Francisco might have been Buck's last-ditch effort to bring her around."

"Do you think Buck believed Delta *could* come around?"

"Maybe. He is an exceptional man with a big heart. He might have felt he owed her a chance. He obviously went to great lengths to keep the whole thing a secret from everyone but Nick. And maybe it worked, if that's what inspired her to run for mayor."

Rella faced me in the darkened front seat of her car. "I confess I've never been a fan of Delta's, so I'm just going say this. I think her run for mayor was a power grab of some kind."

"Not sure I follow."

"If Buck did bring up a separation, I wouldn't put it past her to respond by threatening some sort of action that would put his foundation in peril. I just don't know how much damage she could do as mayor. Any ideas?"

"Who knows? But we're treading on dangerous ground. His foundation is his life. She was on the board. As mayor, and his wife, she would have had some credibility if she accused Buck of doing something fishy with the foundation's assets."

"So you think the Feds would have taken her seriously if she decided to go to them as a whistle blower?"

"I'm afraid so. I think the IRS would be all over it. And I think we should drop this theory for now, Rella. It's pure speculation, and none of it proves what triggered Delta's unexpected decision to run for mayor. All we're doing is putting Buck a notch higher on the suspect list."

"I get it. A threat of that kind by Delta could be seen as a motive for her murder."

"Then let's get back to your original question. I'm not convinced it's up to you to take Buck's consult in San Francisco to the police, but that decision is up to you. Just keep in mind Buck may have already done that himself, and it would look a lot better coming from him than from you. Either way, I'm guessing he's at least talked to his defense lawyers about it."

"I hadn't thought of that, but it's exactly what he would have done." I heard some of the tension fade from her voice. She clicked off her penlight and leaned back on the head rest.

"Rella? One more thing. Who wrote those notes, and how do you happen to have them?"

She raised her head, rotated her neck. "The notes are mine. The best I could recall from an incident that happened the day of our flight to the city. When Buck and I returned to Timbergate Municipal, I taxied to the hangar. Buck got out and when he reached into the backseat to get his car keys out of his briefcase, it fell open. He gathered everything up, stuffed it back in and left the briefcase on the seat while he made a trip to the men's room. While he was gone, I secured the plane and took one more look around inside it to see if we'd left anything behind. That's when I found a sheet of paper from a legal pad on the floor. I wasn't sure what it was, so I skimmed it quickly. When I read what was on it, I hurried to put it into his briefcase before he got back to the plane."

"You wrote these notes? When?"

"The morning Delta died I wrote down everything I could recall seeing on that sheet of paper. Including the note at the bottom."

I read the note. "It says, *Talk to Nick.*"

Rella folded the sheet of paper. "That's why I think Nick knew from the start. What I don't know is how long Buck had been exploring the idea before our flight to the city. The other piece of information I don't have is the name of the lawyers Buck consulted. I dropped him off near Union Square, but a simple taxi ride could have taken him anywhere in the city during the two hours he and I spent apart."

"Rella, why ask for my opinion about this?"

"Because I know you respect confidentiality and I know you're involved with both forensics and ethics at your work. Plus you're trained to do research. Those are not my areas of expertise. All I know to do is to lift airplanes off the ground and take them from one place to another."

"That's a lot to know," I said.

"Not as difficult as most people think, but that's beside the point. I need you to give me your opinion. From your reaction, it's obvious you and I have the same concern. I have no way of knowing whether Buck has told the police about his separation consult in San Francisco. If not, and if *I* take it to the police, they'll have to consider it as motive."

"And they're already suspicious of Buck." *That first arrest.*

"You see my dilemma. I don't know where to go with it. Or *if*."

"What if Delta hadn't died? What would you have done about this?"

"Nothing, Aimee. I assure you I would have respected Buck's privacy. To tell anyone would have been nothing more than gossip. Something I abhor."

"Are you worried that you'll be in trouble if you *don't* tell the police about this?"

"Somewhat. Am I guilty of withholding evidence? That's one of the things I was hoping you could tell me. You're the one with a library full of information about forensics and the law."

"Rella, I'm no lawyer, but I don't believe you're withholding evidence. You have every reason to expect Buck to tell the police himself if he had filed for a separation, but as far as we know, that's not the case. He might have already changed his mind before she died. On the other hand, you *would* be withholding evidence if you had witnessed Buck or someone else switching Delta's pills."

"Do you think the attorneys Buck had been consulting with will tell the police? By now he must have communicated with them about Delta's death. Obviously, there's no need to pursue a separation."

"All of Buck's attorneys know what the law requires. If the police need to be told, it's up to them to advise Buck. We have to trust that he's getting good counsel."

Rella leaned forward, looked out the windshield at the rear wall of the Sawyer Foundation building. "I hope this is over soon. Buck deserves a better life than these past few years have given him."

That show of empathy was a side of Rella I had not seen before. Maybe because I'd kept her at arm's length from the time Buck hired her. Back then, I had an occasional pang of jealousy knowing she and Nick had a past of sorts, but when she and Harry got together, it became abundantly clear that Rella had found her man. It was not my boyfriend, it was my brother.

Ginger stirred in the backseat, emitting a soft whine. "It's getting late," I said. "I'd better let you get home."

"Yes, but one more thing. Delta's possible affair. If Buck's suspicions were correct, I have mixed feelings about that. It's something the police might need to know in case . . . could her other man be a suspect?"

"I suppose, but what motive?" Then I followed her thinking. "You think he's someone prominent and married? That an affair with Delta would create a public scandal?"

"Maybe. If he does exist, and the police become aware of that, they'll want to interview him, won't they?"

She had a point. "Yes, but telling the police about the consult and Buck's suspicions about another man is bound to backfire. It gives Buck another plausible motive. I still think it's best to let his lawyers make that decision."

Chapter 14

BACK AT HOME A QUARTER AFTER MIDNIGHT, I was grateful
Rella had confided in me and asked my advice, but Buck's
looking into the possibility of a legal separation definitely raised
the stakes. He and Nick would look even more suspicious in the
eyes of the police if they were to hear about it first from anyone
other than Buck.

Worn out by the long, demanding night and distracted by
Rella's news, I postponed my plan to go online and explore the list
of donors to Wright and Nester's campaigns. I still had to deal with
the keys to Buck's foundation building. Hiding them somewhere
in the house seemed like a better idea than carrying them around
in my purse.

I decided on an antique piece of furniture in the master bedroom. Amah called it a secretary, saying it had belonged to her
grandmother. Its left side was a series of shelves behind a curved
glass door. On the right was a mirror above a drop-front writing
surface. Below that was a drawer, and at the bottom, a small cupboard. I opened the drop-front and put the foundation keys and
the alarm code in a tiny drawer surrounded by cubbyholes. I locked
the cabinet and clipped its key onto the chain that held my car keys.

Settled in bed, I used my phone to check the local TV news. I cringed when I spotted a segment featuring Oriana Wynn reporting from Timbergate Medical Center. There I was at the library entrance being badgered by the relentless woman. The cameraman had zoomed in just as I caught the sun in my eyes. The result was my face filling the entire screen with what looked like an angry scowl.

The edited version consisted of Oriana Wynn saying, "*You're refusing to say whether the press is being stonewalled?*"

When I replied saying, "*I have no comment,*" I looked mean and sounded worse.

That was followed by Wynn's snide response: "*You must have more important matters to tend to than the death of Timbergate's Favorite Daughter.*"

Wynn finished by identifying me. "*That was Aimee Machado, Timbergate Medical Center's Director of Library, Continuing Education and* Ethical *Affairs.* I scooted deep under my covers, hiding from five minutes of fame I could have done without.

I had finally managed to put Oriana Wynn out of my mind when a new thought chased the Sandman away. It occurred to me that Delta's case brought the past together with the present. Three women with ties to either Buck or Beardsley had grown up in Timbergate and attended the same high school. Tragically, all of them had died of overdoses: Sammy Sawyer in her teens, and Bonnie Belcher Beardsley in her late twenties. Delta Dearborn Sawyer had survived the longest.

When Buck's daughter died, a rumor had circulated that it was Bonnie who had pressured Sammy into experimenting with methamphetamine. But Sammy's reputation had also been the subject of local gossip back then. There were some who believed that her parents' wealth had resulted in a spoiled teenager with a drug problem.

Bonnie Beardsley's fatal overdose happened eight years after Sammy's death. Her manner of death was documented as an accidental self-inflicted cocaine overdose. Now Bonnie's widower, Dr. Vane Beardsley, was caught up in speculation surrounding Delta Sawyer's death by yet another drug: oxycodone.

Buck Sawyer claimed that before Delta's cosmetic procedure, she had demanded Vane Beardsley prescribe an opioid for post-procedure pain. Beardsley admitted that was true, but he insisted he had not prescribed any controlled substance. He simply recommended five hundred milligram acetaminophen tablets.

In a complicating twist, Cleo Cominoli confided that Buck Sawyer and Vane Beardsley were joining the forces of two foundations to create a drug rehab center in Timbergate. Though the two men were in opposite camps over Delta's switched pills, they had that worthwhile project in common. Another thing they had in common was second marriages to much younger wives. A quick search on the subject revealed various theories about rich older men who marry younger women and why those marriages might not end well. None mentioned death by drug overdose.

As I lay awake, I mulled over what I had learned from Nick and Rella in the space of one evening. I wondered how Quinn would react if he were to discover that I was keeping two secrets from him: Buck Sawyer consulting about a separation from Delta, and my holding the keys to Buck's foundation building. My promotion might vanish, along with my job. But that was a minor problem compared to my real concern—that Buck was still TPD's prime suspect, with Nick a close second.

IN THURSDAY MORNING'S PREDAWN CHILL, I chopped Old Doolittle's hay with my phone in my pocket on the chance that someone might call with an update about Delta's case. My worst fear was Buck behind bars again.

No bad news had cropped up by the time I showered and finished off a breakfast of high-protein cereal supplemented with Greek yogurt and extra almonds. Three nutrition bars in my purse would get me through a lunch hour spent at Nora's Nest with Laurie Littletree.

While I was dressing for work, my cell pinged a message from Nick, which produced a flash of anxiety. I told myself to stop imagining the worst and read his message about Timbergate's dogged reporter, Oriana Wynn.

Saw u on TV news. Why didn't u tell me last night?

Hoped you wouldn't see. Ambushed yesterday. Embarrassed.

We signed off and I turned on the TV in time to catch Wynn pointing out that TMC was still offering no comment. The station wrapped her segment by replaying the odious clip of me. I must have been the only TMC employee her cameraman had captured speaking on video. Heaven knew how many more times my sun-blinded face would be seen glaring at Sawyer County's viewers.

On my work commute I tuned to the local radio station where the announcer reported a flood of requests for updates on the Delta Sawyer investigation. Nothing like the mysterious demise of a candidate to boost interest in the race for mayor.

Relieved to enter the library without being buttonholed by Wynn, I started the coffee maker and fired up the computers. My online calendar popped up, but I didn't need it to tell me we were entering day four of the mystery surrounding Delta's death, or that election day was only a week away. Based on the flurry of new campaign ads being aired, Wright and Nester were pulling out all the stops now that the front-runner was out of the picture—no more worry about dark secrets being revealed.

I was tempted to text Harry for a progress report about his search for Delta's secrets but figured it was too soon to expect results—unless his curiosity had kicked in and kept him at it into the night. The mystery affected him, too, because of Rella. At quarter to nine, I gave in and sent him a text.

Anything to report? Need info asap.

He replied a few minutes later.

Can u call me?

Now?

Yes

"What do you have?"

"No guarantees, Sis, but I managed to dig up a couple of incidents that were buried pretty deep. They might be what Delta found if she used the right kind of help."

"How bad?"

"Problematic, but nothing that would put either Wright or Nester behind bars."

"You think Delta was bluffing?"

"More or less. But each of her opponents does have a past incident that could be awkward. If Delta played dirty and exaggerated the circumstances, she could have caused them some damage during the last few days of the race."

I glanced at the library entrance. Bernie would arrive soon. "Can you give me a quick run-down? I don't have much time."

"Sure. Nora Nester first. You're in a hurry, so I won't bother to explain how I dug it up. She was twenty, pregnant and traveling in Mexico with her husband when her fetus died early in the pregnancy. I think there's a medical term for that."

"Yes, it's called *intrauterine fetal death*."

"So she had an emergency procedure that her medical record in Mexico referred to as an *abortion*. It's easy to imagine what Delta would have made of that. Nester, the owner of a daycare center who professes her love of children, has an abortion in her past."

"So unfair," I said. "A hospital in the States would have used the term *surgical evacuation for early pregnancy loss*."

"So that's one for Nora Nester. I didn't find anything else on her."

"Anything about the husband? My search didn't find a marriage, and she still uses her maiden name."

"That's easy," Harry said. "They got an annulment not long after she lost the baby. Didn't know that was possible, since their marriage was obviously consummated."

"It is possible, but right now I don't have time to explain."

"So she was a pregnant, married woman who lost her baby through no fault of her own. No scandal there," Harry said.

"Not unless Delta could twist it into one. All she needed was the word *abortion* on that medical record from Mexico. You found it. I'm betting she did, too." Out the front window I spotted Bernie pulling into the parking lot. "I'm running out of time. What about Ernest Wright?"

"Here goes. Ernest Wright briefly managed a senior living

facility in Alabama where a civil suit by the families of several residents accused the facility of mismanagement."

"What was the basis of the claim?"

"Bed bugs."

"That's it? Bed bugs?" I stifled the urge to laugh.

"That's right." Harry said. "It sounds trivial until you read up on it, but a lot of elderly residents where he worked got pretty sick from rashes and infections. After the owners lost the suit, they closed down and Wright was out of a job."

"What about Wright? Was he implicated in some kind of cover-up?"

"No, the opposite. It came out during the trial that he had tried to convince the owners to upgrade their infection control protocols. They refused to incur the extra expense, and it was Wright who finally blew the whistle on them."

"You think Delta knew he was the good guy?"

"Who knows?" Harry said. "Either way, all she had to do was put out the word that Wright managed a facility that lost a lawsuit and closed down over bed bugs. Once that came out, the voters would have to make up their own minds."

"An uphill battle for Wright. He could tell his side of the story, but voters would still be turned off by the nasty little insects." I understood why that particular part of his work history was missing from his résumé.

"Depressing, isn't it? We all have to look harder for the truth these days. There could still be something out there, so I'll keep poking around. Just remember what I said: *no guarantees*."

"Thanks, I will. And I owe you."

"True, and I can always use more help at the dojo. But this one isn't just for you. It's for all of us."

I had promised Harry if he discovered any shocking secrets about Wright or Nester that suggested a concrete motive for murder, I would contact Detective Kass. Harry's mining of the web had suggested the opposite. With mixed emotions, I accepted that I had no concrete reason to suspect either of them.

I told Harry I would help out at the dojo again on Saturday

morning. As we ended our call, Bernie arrived with his usual hearty greeting and began his morning routine. I watched him apply his green thumb to a thriving snake plant. He had made a home for it on a bookshelf against the back wall of the library under a bank of fluorescent lights. He wiped the variegated sword-like leaves with a damp cloth and used his fingers to test the soil for moisture, all the while humming a tune under his breath. It took a bit for me to recognize "Lady," the hit song written by Lionel Richie and sung by Kenny Rogers.

I smiled, thinking of Bernie and his lady, Lola, and recalling how Nick used to call me "Lady" when we first became a couple. It meant even more to me after I looked up the lyrics to that song.

My musing was cut short when Bernie ambled over to my desk.

"Miss Aimee, Lola and I had a meeting of the minds about making our move. We talked over what you said about taking our time, not signing anything 'til we're sure it all checks out." His brow wrinkled. "Thought we should pass on the upshot to you."

"What did you decide?"

I hoped they had taken my advice. It could save them from significant financial losses if Ernest Wright turned out to be Delta Sawyer's killer.

"No disrespect to you." Bernie avoided my eyes. "We know you have good intentions, but we'd both like to get on with it. The way it is now, we're living in two different places, don't you know?"

I do know how that feels, I thought. "Couldn't you and Lola wait a little longer? You might ask your current landlords for an extension, maybe another month or two to explore the pros and cons." Delta's death was forcing me to interfere in Lola and Bernie's lives, but I had to look out for them.

Bernie rubbed potting soil off his fingers with his bandana. "You're young, don't you see? Your idea of time is different from ours. Where you measure the future in years, Lola and I . . . well, at our age, we measure it in days. We want to spend those days together."

"How soon do you plan to go ahead? Have you signed anything yet?"

"No so far. Gotta get all our ducks lined up first," Bernie squared his shoulders. "We have an appointment with a financial advisor tomorrow. It's the one day neither of us is busy with volunteering."

"You'll take your financial planner's advice before you go ahead?"

"We'll surely consider it. We're old, but we're not feeble-minded."

"It sounds like you and Lola are doing all the right things. Let me know if I can help."

While Bernie began his morning tasks, a sense of urgency gripped me. He and Lola were seeking professional financial advice, which should have reassured me, but the advice they received would be based on incomplete information. The advisor they were meeting with the next day had no way of knowing Delta Sawyer's death might have been foul play, or that Ernest Wright was a candidate in two races. Time would tell if he became Mayor of Timbergate or a prison inmate. And time was running out. After my volunteers' appointment with their financial advisor, I suspected their decision would be out of my hands.

Lola's next shift with me was the following Monday and Bernie would be back on Tuesday. I had counted on those two chances to talk with them before the election, but they had moved up their timetable. Meanwhile, Harry had turned up nothing in Ernest Wright's past that was heinous enough to result in a prison sentence, or put him out of business.

Timing was important for Laurie Littletree, too, and for the families whose children were already in Nora Nester's care. Although it was hard to imagine prim, soft-spoken Nora capable of a past too shocking to bear the light of day. The loss of her unborn child in Mexico did not seem to rise to that level.

Through the rest of the morning, I visited the county clerk's website to follow up on the plan I had postponed the night before in favor of sleep. I wanted to scout for additional suspects in Delta's case by checking the donor lists for the remaining two candidates for mayor. One of them may have been inflamed by Delta's threats to expose secrets about her opponents.

But Delta's donors would also be suspects, although for different reasons. Maybe she had disappointed one of her supporters or campaign workers. I was reminded that it took only one crazed fanatic to seek revenge for an imagined slight by poisoning her with pills.

The data was easy to access and the lists were not as long as I had expected. I started with Nora Nester. Her campaign donations were mostly small amounts that added up to a modest total. None of the names stood out. I suspected her supporters were mainly parents of the children in her daycare facility—young working people living from paycheck to paycheck. I knew the feeling.

Next I scanned Ernest Wright's donations. The amounts were greater than Nester's, but again, I saw nothing unusual and no familiar names. A few of his senior residents had probably chipped in, but they would be in the same boat as Bernie and Lola, living on Social Security and retirement benefits.

I was about to start on Delta Sawyer's donor list when Bernie approached my desk pushing the carpet sweeper that was part of his Thursday routine.

"Miss Aimee, sorry to be a bother, but I wonder if I could take another minute of your time."

"What is it, Bernie? Something else about your move?"

"No, it's not that. It's about that poor Sawyer woman's widower."

"Buck Sawyer? What about him?"

"I happened across him during one of my shifts in the main tower back at the time his wife died. Reminded me of when I lost my Imogene. It's a tough blow. Leaves a fella lonely. That's why I'm looking forward to spending my remaining time with Lola, don't you know?"

"I'm glad you and Lola found each other, Bernie. Was there something you wanted to ask me about Mr. Sawyer?"

He leaned on the handle of his carpet sweeper. "I don't suppose you'd know how he's holding up?"

I had a general idea, but I couldn't admit it. Bernie had no clue how entangled I was in the Sawyer case. To him I was simply a member of hospital administration who might have inside information. He had no idea how Delta's death had affected my personal life.

"It's nice of you to care, but we employees have been asked not to speak about the case."

"Gotcha." Bernie swiveled the carpet sweeper into position. "Guess I'd better tackle some of the dust on this floor. Not gonna clean itself, don't you know?"

Bernie's sympathy for Buck led me back to my search. Delta Sawyer's donor list was still available online—probably to give Fletcher Tremont time to follow through with transferring the funds according to the donors' instructions.

A quick glance revealed that Delta's supporters were far more generous and numerous than Wright's and Nester's. I scrolled through the first few lines and right away noticed several donations in the hundreds and even a few who gave one or two thousand. I scrolled farther and stopped short where I did a double-take. The number in the amount column was fifty thousand dollars. The donor name was Vane Beardsley.

I stared at the screen, wondering if I had read it wrong. No, it was perfectly clear. Fifty thousand dollars had been donated to Delta Sawyer's campaign by Dr. Vane Beardsley. The transaction date was the same day as her Friday appointment in his office for her pre-op visit—only three days before she died.

Beardsley's fifty thousand dollars added a stunning piece to the growing puzzle. His donation to Delta's campaign far exceeded any other individual donation. I viewed it as a frantically waving red flag. Instead of coming up with a new, previously unknown suspect, I found myself caught in a revolving door. I had circled back to Beardsley, the person who could do TMC the most harm. He claimed he had not prescribed Delta's opioids, but he could have slipped the opioid pills to her illegally. Quinn might have wondered about that himself, but would he come right out and ask Beardsley? Would the police? They most likely would if they were aware of Beardsley's disproportionately large and inexplicable campaign donation.

I contemplated what to do about it. With divided loyalties,

I couldn't take it to Quinn without telling Nick. The only other choice would be the police, but the donation was public record, so they should have discovered it for themselves. I decided to wait over the weekend. If TPD still had Buck in their sights by then, I would call Detective Kass for advice.

When I tried to imagine what had possessed Beardsley to cough up such a large amount, only two possibilities came to mind. Either he truly believed she was the best candidate, or in a bizarre and mindboggling twist, Vane Beardsley was Delta Sawyer's "other man."

Chapter 15

STILL CONTEMPLATING VANE BEARDSLEY's baffling donation, I pulled into Nora Nester's daycare parking lot where I reminded myself that my immediate purpose was to consider whether Nester was a viable suspect in Delta's case.

I spotted Laurie in the process of transferring Kiona from her car seat to a stroller. With her hands full, Laurie raised her chin in greeting as I parked next to her. Motherhood had not dimmed the beauty of her classic cheekbones and her dark, bouncing curls. Once she finished securing Kiona, we headed for the entrance.

The facility resembled a country cottage in a children's book of fairy tales. The single-story residence with a thatched roof and stone façade was surrounded by thriving green foliage, magnolia and crepe myrtle trees, and an astonishing array of rosebushes. It sat within the Timbergate city limits in the middle of a half-acre lot. An old-fashioned wood rail fence surrounded the property. A sign over the entrance gate in antique lettering read: *Nora's Nest*. The path to the front door was lined with daffodils and crocuses already in bloom.

The whiff of air when we stepped inside brought back childhood memories of trips to the Timbergate Bakery with my mother—the aroma of sweet comfort. Laurie and I approached the reception area with little Kiona snugged into her stroller. The baby girl was barely two months old, tiny and adorable, with dark brown eyes, curly black hair and dimples. I wondered how her mother could part with her for even a few hours a week to work at TMC.

We were met by a young blond woman dressed in scrubs decorated with an array of teddy bears. Her name badge read *K.D., Junior Nanny.*

"Welcome to *Nora's Nest.*" She smiled down at Kiona. "This must be baby Littletree."

After Laurie confirmed that she was Kiona's mom and I was her godmother, the junior nanny began our tour of the interior. I had flashbacks of my recent visit to Ernest Wright's establishment, where the layout and services provided for seniors bore an uncanny resemblance. *Nora's Nest* was complete with an activity room, a dining area, and even overnight accommodations where children could be left with a full-time nanny while the parents went on their adults-only vacations. We viewed a securely fenced backyard complete with a variety of outdoor toys: a sandbox with pails and shovels, three swing-and-slide playsets, and several tricycles and pedal cars.

A phone in K.D.'s pocket rang and she excused herself for a moment. While she was gone, Laurie said, "Let's ask our tour guide if we can meet Nora."

While I debated with myself whether that was a good idea, K.D. came back from her brief conversation with a co-worker. "I think we've covered everything. Do you have any questions?"

"I have one," Laurie said. "Is there a chance we can meet Ms. Nester before we go?"

"I'm afraid Nora's out to lunch," she said. "She's very busy with the campaign, as you can imagine." *Just as well,* I thought.

"Is there someone here to talk to about the cost of using her facility?" Laurie asked.

"That would be our bookkeeper, but she's also out to lunch. I'll get you one of her cards on your way out."

I took a turn. "I didn't see anything on the tour about an on-site nurse. What's the arrangement in the event a child becomes ill while in your care? And what about your evacuation procedure if there's a fire or some other emergency?"

K.D. frowned. "I'm sorry, I forgot about our health and safety protocols." She blushed. "This is my first week on the job and you're my first solo tour."

"Can we do that now?" I asked.

"Our nurse is out to . . . sorry." K.D.'s face flushed. "I can get you a brochure."

I hoped no one else was out to lunch. I avoided meeting Laurie's eyes in case she was thinking the same thing. It would not be cool if we burst out laughing. This girl was too nervous to appreciate the humor.

She ushered us into the OTL nurse's office where she took a handout from the desk and held it out to Laurie. "You can read all about our pediatric nurse practitioner's duties in this brochure, and about our safety protocols. We give it to all prospective clients."

Laurie thanked her. I glanced around the small office and noticed what looked like a small safe seated on a sturdy table against the back wall. "Is that safe used to store medicines?"

"Yes," K.D. said. "Our nurse is the only one besides Ms. Nester who knows the combination."

It was time for me to get back to work, so I asked K.D. if I could have one of the brochures she had given to Laurie. She handed one to me and ushered us out to the reception area.

Laurie thanked K.D. for the tour and assured her she would be in touch again after talking to her husband. Outside, I asked her what she thought of the place.

"Seems legit. Well run, except for all the folks who were out to lunch." We both laughed.

"Well, it was lunchtime, and the new girl gave it her best," I said. "But would you feel comfortable leaving Kiona there?"

Laurie drew in a long breath, patted the sleeping baby on her shoulder. "I don't know. It's amazing how attached I am to this little miracle. Motherhood is a powerful and mysterious thing." Her eyes were misty.

"Is that a no?"

"Truthfully? It wouldn't be easy."

BACK IN THE LIBRARY I REFLECTED ON OUR VISIT to Nester's facility. It was clean, appeared well-run, and was used by many of the working women in Timbergate. Their reviews, posted on the *Nora's Nest* website, were full of praise emphasized by five-star ratings.

I perused the handout listing the duties of Nester's pediatric nurse practitioner. Assessing the needs of a sick or injured child seemed most obvious, followed by relaying that information to the appropriate primary health care provider or emergency room—as well as to the parents. Preventing the spread of infectious diseases was also listed as a primary goal.

Less obvious, but equally important, was monitoring the facility for health issues and cleanliness by providing the center's staff with training on sanitary diaper changing and proper hand washing procedures. The nurse was responsible for keeping the center's staff and parents informed about health care with emphasis on preventative care. It occurred to me that in TMC, those procedures came under the duties of our Infection Control Nurse.

The handout stated that the on-site nurse maintained the children's medical records while they were enrolled, including each child's physical development. If there were children in the center with special needs, the nurse supervised any accommodations necessary to serve those children. Including how their medications were dispensed. The last page described their safety protocols in detail.

I wondered if Laurie would be reassured about *Nora's Nest* after reading the brochure. As Kiona's godmother, I would not—until the mystery of Delta Sawyer's switched pills was solved.

I put the handout aside. Was there more to Nester's past than the loss of her unborn child in Mexico? Could she have another buried skeleton that only Delta Sawyer had uncovered? I wondered the same about Ernest Wright's history. With the days passing quickly and the election only a week away, my sense of urgency was on the rise. If there was an innocent explanation for Beardsley's contribution to Delta's campaign, that would leave Nester and Wright the only suspects I had to work with.

I wanted Harry to look deeper into the pasts of both candidates, but I decided against telling him about Beardsley's donation. I needed time to process that and decide whether to take it directly to Walter Kass.

I texted Harry asking if we could get together later at the ranch. He agreed, saying he'd bring dinner.

At home I fetched the mail and paper and set them aside on the kitchen countertop. After feeding the llamas, I climbed the exterior stairs to the apartment over the barn and entered the rooms where Nick and I had spent so much of our time together. Jack had left the water and electricity on in the apartment, anticipating that he and Amah would be using it on their trips back home from the Azores.

My footsteps echoed on the linoleum floor in the kitchen. The interior of the apartment seemed smaller, and the static air held the lonely smell peculiar to deserted places.

Memories came crowding back of my time alone in that space over the barn when I had struggled with starting a new career at TMC and adjusting to life without Nick. Since then, he and I had made our way back from that separation and had faced other challenges together, some involving significant danger. But we still looked forward to our future.

At least I thought so, until Nick said he hoped I wasn't on another sleuthing crusade that would put me in jeopardy. He had made similar comments in the past about my inclination to jump in and help at the first hint of trouble.

My automatic impulse to solve problems had served me well in my profession as a librarian. Hospital patrons came to me for help related to patient health; forensic consortium patrons came for help solving crimes. The information I provided could involve matters of life and death. I was passionate about getting that right, but I sometimes worried that my compulsion to solve mysteries would cause Nick to rethink our relationship. If that was true, we would have to find the right balance if we were going to have a life together.

Thinking of our future reminded me of something Bernie Kluckert had said. He was in his nineties and Lola was in her eighties. They measured their future in days because they knew their years were limited. Nick and I were wasting our days in this forced separation. It was so easy to assume that we still had our whole lives ahead of us, but what if our years together were stolen from us by an accident or illness? Those things happened to patients every day at the hospital.

There were examples all around us. Sammy Sawyer's life had ended when she was a teenager. Bonnie Beardsley and Delta Sawyer had at least survived into adulthood before their lives were cut short. There were no guarantees when it came to longevity.

That thought followed me as I walked into our abandoned bedroom over the barn. I checked the dressers to see if we had left anything behind. They were empty. I opened the closet and found one of Nick's T-shirts forgotten on a shelf. I picked it up, held it to my face and inhaled a trace of his woodsy aftershave. Another more subtle scent brought back delicious memories of him fresh from a soapy shower.

I closed the apartment and stood on the deck in the chilly evening air recalling the times Nick and I had come out to sit together watching as the sunset faded to deep purple. We had witnessed that sight countless times while we enjoyed a glass of wine and quiet conversation. I held the T-shirt to my face again, missing him with a physical ache in my core.

CHORES FINISHED, I WAS BACK IN THE HOUSE when Harry arrived at six thirty with takeout. Mouth-watering aromas of baked chicken and a gourmet potato salad filled the kitchen. I provided chilled bottles of green tea. We loaded paper plates and sat at the dining table in Amah and Jack's family room. I asked how he and Rella were getting along with Ginger.

Harry swallowed a bite of chicken. "Great. Rella's taking her out for a run tonight. But let's cut through the small talk. Your text was pretty vague. Want to tell me why I'm here?"

"I wondered if you've been digging any deeper into Wright and Nester's pasts."

"You mean since this morning when I told you about her miscarriage and his problem with bed bugs?"

"You said you'd keep looking."

"Sorry. No time. I spent all day today dealing with unexpected snags at the mall site. Why this sudden push? Has something new come up?"

"Last night you told me that Nick is looking for a defense lawyer. A 'precaution,' you said. Then Nick gave me the keys to Buck's foundation office. He said Buck wanted me to have them. Another 'precaution.'" I stopped short of mentioning Buck's inquiry into a legal separation.

Harry dropped a half-eaten drumstick and wiped his hands with a paper napkin. "I heard about the keys being gathered up. Didn't know you were given a set."

"Neither does Rella, and I'd rather you didn't mention it to her. She might wonder why Buck chose to trust me with them. I'm still wondering that myself."

"I won't mention it, although I doubt she'd be offended. That's not how her mind works. She knows we're all constrained by divided loyalties."

"I appreciate that, but my point is these precautions are piling up, and rumors are still flying around social media about Nick and Buck as suspects. I don't like where all this is headed, but I do think it rises to the level of a deeper dive."

Harry raised a brow. "You're holding out on me, aren't you?"

"Okay, there is something I haven't told you. You know about my visits to both Nester's daycare and Wright's senior living community. It turns out each of them has an on-site nursing office and a nurse practitioner. That means access to prescription pads, which means access to drugs, including controlled substances like opioids."

Harry pushed back from the table. "I'm beginning to think you cooked up a couple phony excuses to snoop around, didn't you?"

"You already knew about my volunteers' interest in *The Wright Time of Life*, and I told you why I was going with Laurie Littletree to check out *Nora's Nest*. I was asked to help both times. Was I supposed to say no?"

"I know you, Sis. Admit it. You jumped at the chance to scrutinize both of those facilities."

"Okay, I took advantage of a couple opportunities, but I haven't done anything dangerous, and I don't intend to. Just keep in mind that it's possible Ernest Wright or Nora Nester could have found a devious way to get their hands on the drug that killed Delta."

"I will, but you have to keep to our agreement. You'll call your investigator friend Kass even if I *don't* find anything else the police need to know. Go ahead and tell him what we've already dug up on Wright and Nester. TPD knows Delta was threatening them with some kind of secrets. It was public knowledge. They'd probably appreciate the heads-up if they haven't turned up what I found."

"I will, and when I do talk to Kass I'll tell him to keep me out of it if he talks to Buck and Nick or to Quinn. Do you think he'd agree to that?"

"Probably," Harry said. "What we're looking for isn't about Buck or about the hospital. It's about identifying other suspects who might need to be investigated. All we're doing is looking beyond the obvious."

"Exactly. I want to know if Wright and Nester can be ruled out." If so, I could focus on other potential suspects such as Delta's other man. Something I wasn't at liberty to say to Harry.

"All right, Sis. I'll give it another shot. It'll probably go nowhere, but if we do uncover something criminal, you have to let Kass and the TPD decide how to handle it." Harry drained the last of his tea. "I get your concern about Nick. You don't want him to worry about your poking around. But what's the problem about Quinn? He's not likely to fire you over Delta Sawyer's case."

"Not ordinarily, but there's a new element I have to consider. And I haven't told Nick about it, so please keep this to yourself."

Harry lifted an eyebrow. "Okay. Let's hear it."

I told Harry how Quinn had warned me specifically about not sharing information with Nick, and how he had capped that off by bringing up the job promotion without a full explanation, then saying we'd talk again after Delta's case was solved.

"I don't have all the details yet, but I'm certain the promotion won't happen unless I'm a loyal advocate for Timbergate Medical Center."

"No doubt." Harry stood and headed for the front door. "If we're finished, I'd better be getting home." He stepped outside into a chilly night lit with a half-moon and a blanket of stars. I followed.

"Thanks for helping me. I know all of this is complicated for you and Rella, too."

Harry glanced up at the glittering sky, sighed, and turned back to me. "I've agreed to help you one last time, but only because it's not likely to make you a target."

"I appreciate that."

"Understand there are limits to what you can ask me to do."

"Understood."

"Good. See you Saturday morning."

Harry left me bound by my promise to contact Detective Kass. With the secrets in Wright and Nester's pasts, Beardsley's donation, and Buck's separation consult, I had three reasons to do that. My original plan was to wait until after the weekend to decide about contacting Kass, but that plan had changed. If there was no break in the case by then, I would have no choice.

Nick called at bedtime just moments after I had changed into my pajama bottoms and his orphaned T-shirt. He confirmed what I already suspected. He had no idea when he would be able to come home to spend nights with me.

I struggled to keep my response neutral. "Because of my job, right? The conflict of interest that Quinn mentioned?"

"Buck's lawyers see it as divided loyalties. They think it's better if I don't come home for the time being. Unless the police arrest someone other than Buck, or determine that Delta's death was accidental."

"It sounds like this could go on indefinitely."

"I know, but you have to see their point. This is mostly about protecting you. If we're 'cohabiting,' as they put it, you'll be the one who pays the price. You're stuck in the middle between Timbergate Medical Center and Buck Sawyer." He paused for a moment. "I don't want to frighten you, but you have to understand that our relationship could make you a person of interest."

Numbness spread across the back of my neck and down my shoulders. "Why, Nick? Are you a suspect?"

"Not officially, but I'm Buck's closest friend and confidant, and he's Delta's spouse, which automatically makes *him* a prime suspect, even though that first arrest was a false alarm."

"Then I'll stop asking when you can come home. Can we see each other in the meantime?"

"Discreetly, is what the attorneys said."

"Then I hope the police work quickly. At least we know who's leading the investigation."

"You're relieved that it's Walter Kass, aren't you?"

"Obviously. We know we can trust him to look beyond the obvious. Do you think Buck is comfortable with Kass in the lead?"

"So far, but Buck's lawyers are insisting this is the sort of thing you and I need to avoid talking about, Aimee. Anything involving the case."

"It's pretty difficult to find a topic that doesn't circle back to Delta's case. We're all caught up in it." I hoped he would take that opening to volunteer what he knew about Buck's consultation with the attorneys in San Francisco, but he ended the call with the same last words we spoke every night.

"Love you."

"Love you, too."

Hoping to get to sleep early, I made my nightly check of the house: locking doors, turning out lights. Passing through the kitchen, I noticed the mail I had left on the counter earlier. I tossed the junk mail and opened an envelope with Amah's return address in the Azores. In it I found a letter that the post office forwarded to her by mistake. She had sent it back to me.

It was an invitation from the Prairie Valley State Prison in Arroyo County to attend a parole hearing for Mr. Ora Mercer—the last event I would ever want to attend. Orrie Mercer was the creep responsible for a thin scar at my hairline. Every time I arranged my bangs I was reminded of his violent attack almost two years ago.

It turned out the victims of inmates are the only people other than family who can attend parole hearings. Because of the mail delay, I received it almost a month late. I was supposed to call the contact person indicated in the letter by Friday to say whether I planned to attend in person to offer a victim impact statement. I had less than twenty-four hours to make up my mind. If I went, I would lose a day of work. The hearing was Monday at two o'clock, which meant most of the hours in that day would be devoted to the event and the travel time involved.

With Timbergate's mayoral election taking place on Thursday, I would have only Tuesday and Wednesday to convince myself that neither Wright nor Nester had eliminated the competition by switching Delta Sawyer's pills.

Trouble was, their innocence would leave only two other options: Buck with his legal separation consult, and Beardsley with a fifty-thousand-dollar donation to Delta's campaign.

On top of everything else that was happening, a trip to the prison seemed like the fates were pouring it on, but I felt an obligation to see it through, or at least make a phone call in the morning.

I crawled into bed and pulled Nick's T-shirt snug around me. How much longer until I could turn to him in the night and find comfort in his arms?

Chapter 16

FRIDAY MORNING BROUGHT A LATE-MARCH warming trend. Soon the llamas would be able to graze on the first shoots of green grass sprouting in the pasture instead of relying entirely on their two daily meals of hay.

The sun had risen in a brilliant blue sky by the time I started my drive to work. The color calmed me for a moment, reminding me of the aquamarine sea waters that ebbed and flowed in shore-line grottos in the Azores. I held that memory in my mind as I unlocked the library's entrance door. It was likely the most pleasant one I would have on a day that required an extremely unpleasant chore. I had promised myself I would contact the person at the Prairie Valley State Prison in Arroyo County as early as possible. I wanted to get it over with so I could get on with my day.

I placed the call and was connected with a woman named Officer Paglino. My first question, after I explained about the mail mix-up causing a delay, was whether I was *required* to attend.

She responded with a pleasant telephone manner. "You are not required, but victim impact statements are an important part in helping the parole board's decision process."

"I'm not sure what I would say. Does the parole board have a list of questions?"

"No, this is your opportunity to express what the crime meant to you physically, emotionally, financially and spiritually and to speak from the heart about your pain."

"How much time will I be expected to spend speaking?"

"Your statement should take no longer than five to ten minutes," Paglino said. "It's usually best to have it written out so you can read it to the board."

She recommended I appear in person rather than submit a written statement or a video, because I was the only available victim in Mr. Mercer's case who was directly involved in the assault. The other was an elderly woman currently in a facility for patients with dementia. The officer made a point of saying that my travel time should not be problematic, since I was only two counties away from where the hearing would be held. She stressed that my attendance would be very much appreciated.

I got the message. *Please do your duty so we can do ours.* I told her I would see about getting Monday off from work and making travel arrangements. She gave me until the end of the workday to let her know. Before we ended the call, I followed a hunch and asked her if the other victim was someone I might know. She said yes, she could confirm that, since we were both involved in the same incident with Mercer. The woman preferred to go by the name Maybelline Black, but her legal name was Verna Beardsley.

Dr. Vane Beardsley's sister. I had not thought about Maybelline in more than a year, and now she had popped up. Life seemed to be playing a complicated game of leapfrog where the past and present kept hurdling over each other. I felt a moment of sadness for her dementia, but at the same time, it was good to know she was in a facility and being cared for, most likely financed by her brother, the man who might have found an opportunity to switch Delta Sawyer's pills.

Orrie Mercer was Bonnie Beardsley's uncle and had been involved in the circumstances surrounding her death, including the disposal of her body. I wondered if Vane Beardsley had also been asked to appear at the hearing. It seemed logical that as Bonnie's widower, Beardsley might be asked for a statement.

I set that thought aside for the moment. I had a decision to make about whether to appear in person. I found an online website called The National Center for Victims of Crime. After reading their bulletin on victim impact statements, I really had no choice. If I skipped the hearing, I knew I would regret it.

My next problem was the logistical issue of a trip to Arroyo County. By car, the hundred-and-fifty-mile drive on rural two-lane roads would take two and a half hours one way if all went well. That would be tempting fate since my hand-me-down car already had one foot—or two wheels—in the grave.

The woman I had spoken to at the prison thought it would be simple, but she was not aware that I was caretaking a ranch with a small herd of llamas.

Ordinarily, I would have asked Nick to fly me to the prison, but he was not an option. I would not ask him while he was immersed in coping with Buck and the fallout from Delta's death, but it occurred to me that I had another option. I owned an airplane. Several months earlier, Buck had retired a Cessna 182 from his fleet. It was still in good shape, so he gave it to Nick as a bonus. In the hope that I would someday learn to fly, Nick had registered the Cessna Skylane in both of our names.

All I needed was a pilot. Rella came to mind. With Buck hunkered down at home, she was grounded and probably bored. Maybe a quick round-trip flight to Arroyo County would appeal to her. I sent her a text saying if she wanted to go flying on Monday to please let me know *asap*.

RELLA CALLED BACK AN HOUR LATER. "Sorry I didn't get back to you sooner. I was at the vet with Ginger."

"Why? Is she okay?"

"Nothing serious. She was due for her annual shots and Harry is busy bidding a big commercial job, so I volunteered."

"Did the vet put it on Nick's bill? You didn't pay, did you? Those shots are expensive."

"It's all good," she said. "They'll bill Nick. Now tell me what this flying invitation is about."

I gave her a short explanation about the hearing, which still took a few minutes. "What do you think? Can you get away on Monday? And more important, are you okay with flying Nick's plane?"

"You mean *your* plane?" She laughed. "You know I'm a licensed flight instructor, in case you ever get serious."

"We'll talk about that another time. Sorry about the short notice, but I have to get back to the people at the prison before the end of the day. So what do you think?"

"I'm in. Get back to them and set it up. We can work out the flight details this weekend."

"Thanks, I think. I've never done a victim statement before. I'm not looking forward to it."

"You'll be fine. I had to do it once a few years ago. Maybe I'll tell you about it while we're there."

That took me by surprise. Rella had never told me anything personal about herself. We were edging into a new place in our relationship. It felt good.

"We should probably meet in person over the weekend," I said. "When is a good time for you?"

"We'll both be at Delta's memorial on Sunday evening, but I don't think we should wait that long, do you?"

"No, probably not. By the way, do you know who'll be attending on Sunday?"

"Not specifically. Just that Buck wanted it private, with only close family, employees, and a few key people from the community. He didn't want the general public to get wind of it for fear of it leaking to the press."

"Probably a good idea. "There hasn't been a day since Delta died that her name didn't make the news. I hope that plan worked."

"So do I," Rella said, "but back to our flight, it sounds like we'll be gone most of Monday. I'll need to make arrangements for Ginger in case Harry isn't available for dog duty. I do have a general idea of the distance and flight time. If your hearing starts at two, we'll need to lift off from Timbergate no later than noon."

"I'm already planning to take Monday afternoon off."

"Let's meet at the hangar sometime tomorrow so I can check out the plane and see about fuel." I heard a smile in Rella's voice that told me how much she loved to fly.

"I should have thought of that. I'll probably be at the dojo in the morning, but I could meet you at the airport around two."

"That works. When you call the prison, I'll need the location of the nearest airport or landing strip. And ask them if they can shuttle you from there to the prison."

"Okay, and I'll ask if they can arrange somewhere for you to wait for me. I know you won't be allowed in the hearing."

"They'll have a place for me to wait. And don't worry, I'm used to killing time. It's half the job of a pilot. Fortunately, I like to read, and I'm in the middle of a new mystery." I wondered if it was as convoluted as the mystery of Delta Sawyer's switched pills.

WITH RELLA ON BOARD AS PILOT, I called the woman officer at Prairie Valley State Prison to let her know I would attend the hearing. She provided all the details Rella would need. There was a landing strip on the prison property and a shuttle would be available. I was to call when we landed, and someone would pick us up.

While we were still exchanging final bits of information, my contact put me on hold to take another call. While I waited, I thought about Orrie Mercer, who was Bonnie Beardsley's uncle, and how Bonnie had been implicated by rumor in the overdose death of Buck's late daughter, Sammy. With Bonnie and both of her parents deceased, Orrie might be the only source to shed light on how that rumor got started.

When Officer Paglino came back on the line and we had finished our conversation, I asked if there was a chance I could speak to Orrie in private after the hearing ended.

"Are you already on his visitor's list?"

"No."

"Then that won't be possible while you're on site for the hearing, but there are other means to communicate with inmates. You can write him a letter, or set up an account so he can call you collect at a scheduled time. Do you have a landline phone? He can't call a cell collect unless you make special arrangements with your cell phone provider."

"I have a landline. Can we arrange that now?"

"I can transfer you to someone who can help with that, but bear in mind that inmates rarely get more than four or five minutes for a call, so you would have to make it quick."

"I understand. I'd like to do that, please."

"Then I'll transfer you." she said. "I'm sure they'll try to accommodate you, but keep in mind that your phone call will be monitored by one of our officers."

"That's no problem. What's the soonest it could happen? It would be great if it could be done right away."

"Like I said, you're helping us out. If the inmate is agreeable, you might ask to try for the day after the hearing. Does that work for you?"

"Yes, but I'll be at work all day Tuesday. Can the call be done in the evening?"

"That's not my department, but I believe so."

She transferred me to another officer, this time a man who asked for my name and landline number and the day and time I had in mind. After my telling him I would be participating in a parole hearing on Monday, he gave me a tentative window of time between five and ten p.m. on Tuesday. He said I would receive confirmation by Monday that Mercer was willing to call me.

When we finished, the officer wished me a good day. A nice thing to say, although I doubted many people would expect to have a nice day after going through all that red tape to talk to an inmate for five short minutes. I felt sorry for the families and friends of inmates, but the complicated process also reinforced my opinion that a life of crime was not worth the trouble.

But crimes kept cropping up around the people I knew or worked with. The latest being Delta Sawyer's case. If we could solve it, another inmate might spend a significant number of years lining up for five-minute turns at a prison telephone.

Alone in the library, a sense of urgency gripped me when I

remembered that Bernie and Lola's appointment with their financial advisor would take place within the hour. I should have been
reassured by that, but the advice they received would be based on
incomplete information.

Lola would work her shift with me on Monday and Bernie would
be back Tuesday morning. Those were my last chances to persuade
them to delay their move—but only if they had not already signed
a contract with Wright. If they had done that, their decision would
be out of my hands and I could only hope Ernest Wright's past held
no secret heinous enough to send him to prison—or to ruin his
business. If Delta really had found such a secret, it could explain
why she had died.

THROUGH THE REST OF THE MORNING and early afternoon, speculation about Delta's threat to reveal secrets continued to prod
me. I tried to concentrate on forensic science journals, both in
print and online, that I might add to the library's collection. The
astounding wealth of information for forensic librarians always
triggered ideas for innovative ways to serve our TMC patrons and
members of the consortium.

The three o'clock break I had looked forward to ended before
it started when Dr. Vane Beardsley strode into the library and
advanced toward my desk.

"Miss Machado," he said. "I hope my timing is not inconvenient."

Goodbye, break. "What can I do for you, Dr. Beardsley?"

"I've had another thought about the Delta Sawyer situation." He
paused, gazed around.

"We're alone," I said. "Friday afternoons are usually slow in the
library."

"Good to know. I'll get to the point. I recently got wind of the
memorial arrangements for Mrs. Sawyer on Sunday evening—"

"I'm sorry, but I really can't encourage you to attend."

"No, no, I understand. It would be in bad taste, to say the least,
but perhaps you might pass on a message to her campaign manager
for me. Apparently there is an opportunity for donors to request a
refund. I was not aware of that in time to attend the event where

that information was disseminated." So he was acknowledging he had donated to her campaign. I tried for a poker face.

"Have you tried checking the campaign website? There's a form you can fill out and submit online."

"I'm afraid not. I'm still on top of my game in the operating room, but the convoluted menus and instructions on websites leave me wanting. I wondered if you and I could look at it together on one of your computers here."

I had no choice. He was asking me to do my job—to help a library patron.

"We could try, but I'm not sure I'm comfortable with that. It might require my knowing the amount you donated."

His eyebrows rose. "Really? How so?"

It amazed me the sort of things highly educated, even brilliant doctors did not know. I already knew the amount, but explaining why I had looked it up would have been awkward, and maybe dangerous, if he was Delta's other man.

"Campaign donations are public record. Anyone can look them up on our county clerk's office website."

Beardsley cleared his throat. "Well, in that case, we may as well go ahead, since apparently it's no secret."

I walked him over to one of the patron computers where it was a simple matter to access the Sawyer campaign site. I navigated to a page where I found the same form that had been handed out to donors the night I heard Fletcher Tremont speak.

I was surprised when Beardsley balked at the idea of filling out the form. "I'm not a fan of sending my private contact information into cyberspace," he said.

"What about your office email or phone number?"

"My office staff doesn't need to be privy to this matter."

"Then how about this. You can write out your wishes in the form of a letter, including your private contact information so Mr. Tremont can confirm that he received it. Sign and seal it in an envelope marked *personal and confidential* and give it to me. I'll hand deliver it to Mr. Tremont Sunday night. That way no one else will be involved."

Beardsley agreed with my suggestion, I handed him a sheet of paper, and when he had finished writing his letter, I suggested he keep a copy for himself. I gave him two blank envelopes and pointed him toward the copier. After a few minutes he walked back to my desk.

"There. It's done." He handed me the envelope with Tremont's name printed on it along with the *personal and confidential* alert. I put the sealed envelope into my purse, relieved that he was still unaware I knew the amount of his contribution.

By the time we finished, thirty minutes had passed and Beardsley finally started toward the exit. He hesitated halfway there and turned back.

"Is there something else?" I asked.

"Yes, Miss Machado. I would like to express again happy I am that your hire has worked out so well."

"Thank you," I said. "I love my job."

As he finally went on his way, he left me wondering whether it was possible to become any more entangled in the Delta Sawyer mystery.

MY SOLITARY FRIDAY NIGHT USHERED IN a late spring thunderstorm and a power outage. I barely finished feeding the llamas before the downpour began—quite a switch from the morning's dry and sunny weather.

Fanny welcomed me back to the house by rubbing her head across my shins and then trotting to her empty food bowl. That was the nearest she had ever come to a friendly gesture, but it was obviously a calculated attempt to get her dinner served. I dumped an entire can of seafood pâté into her bowl. Watching her eat reminded me that I had forgotten to eat lunch.

I lit a couple of candles and sat down at the dinette table in Amah's kitchen with an avocado and shrimp salad. While I ate, candlelight flickered in the darkening room, casting spooky shadows on the wall.

Too late, I remembered to check my cell phone battery. It was nearly dead, and my landline required electricity. I wanted to save what little charge was left on my cell, so I retrieved a battery-operated radio from Jack's office. It came to life with the only local station I could find. The DJ played country music with intermittent reports on the weather and bulletins about road conditions. He gave updates on downed trees and large branches taking out power lines, but there was little reassurance as to when power would be restored in Coyote Creek.

When George Strait started singing "One Night at a Time," I began to melt. Those lyrics were about falling in love, and they always brought me back to the time when Nick and I started dating. I told him I didn't listen to country because the lyrics were so sad. He introduced me to Strait's music and I soon became a fan, although the jury was still out on my appreciation for the genre as a whole. Strait was one of the few country artists whose songs I recognized, and I was drowning in memories of first kisses and first nights together when Nick called asking if my power had been restored and whether I was okay.

I turned the radio down and replied that I had no power, but I was fine, refusing to admit to intense loneliness made worse by the stormy night.

"How are things with you?" I asked.

"Missing you. I think we should get together again."

"I'd love that, but how about Buck? Is he doing okay when you're not there?"

"He had been coping pretty well until the last couple of days, but there's more going on now than the loss of his wife, and it's taking a toll." Nick's voice held a somber tone. "Aimee, I wish I could explain, but—"

"You don't have to explain." He wasn't the only one withholding information. "Any idea about where and when to meet? I'm guessing Buck's lawyers still don't want you coming to the ranch."

"That's right, but it's probably for the best. It wouldn't be easy being there with you and then leaving again. Let's meet at the foundation building again tomorrow evening."

"Is that discreet enough to satisfy the lawyers?"

"I won't tell them if you don't."

"Will you tell Buck?"

"Sure. He trusts you, Aimee. He won't mind."

"Then I'll see you tomorrow evening. What time?"

"Buck's been going to bed early the last few nights. Takes one of those over-the-counter sleep aids and drops off around eight o'clock. How about eight thirty?"

"I'll be there." I almost asked if he had heard anything from the TPD but caught myself. Buck's legal team would disapprove.

"Don't forget your keys," Nick said.

"Can't you borrow Buck's?"

"I could, but he keeps them locked in his safe along with the others that were turned in. I think this is one of the reasons he wanted you to have a set. It's just easier."

"Easier for you and me to get together?"

"Maybe. He's knows this has been difficult for us."

LYING IN BED LATER RE-PLAYING STRAIT'S LYRICS in my mind, I longed for those stolen hours with Nick but loathed that we were forced to keep secrets from each other. If he knew about Buck's consultation in San Francisco, he also knew Buck suspected Delta was having an affair. Maybe that was what he meant when he told me there was more going on with Buck than Delta's death.

According to the notes Rella had seen, Buck did not know the name of the other man. Apparently, only two people had known: Delta and her lover. Now there was one.

If the police learned about Buck's consultations with the San Francisco lawyers and about Delta's affair, they would see that as more reason to suspect Buck, but they would also view the other man as a potential suspect in her murder. My mind leapt from there to a frightening thought. There were already comments online implying that Nick's job sometimes included acting as Delta's bodyguard or escort when Buck was out of town. It would be a no-brainer for the police to promote Nick from bodyguard to lover.

I had a different idea. Delta was known for going off to vacation with her girlfriends at exotic resorts. Maybe her lover was someone

she had met on one of those getaways. Or it could have been someone right under our noses—someone like Vane Beardsley. Either
way, the police would not be looking for that mystery man unless
Buck had come clean with them about suspecting an affair and
exploring a legal separation.

Chapter 17

I WOKE TO RESTORED POWER and a cloud-speckled but freshly-washed Saturday morning, but instead of enjoying the warmth of Nick's body by my side, I was confronted by an unwelcome feline stand-in. Fanny had decided our *no-cats-on-the-bed* rule no longer applied. She sat on Nick's pillow poking at my face with her paw and emitting her jarring howl. *Feed mee-now!*

After the cat was fed and her litter box cleaned, I checked the local TV station, curious whether Delta was still the lead story. The election was only six days away and time was running out for Timbergate's voters. If I were one of them, the idea of choosing between two candidates with motives to eliminate the front-runner would have dampened my enthusiasm.

The news anchor led off by hinting that there might be more to Delta's death than a simple medical error. He introduced Oriana Wynn, who reported that both TPD and the coroner had declined to comment on Delta's manner of death. After a dramatic pause, Wynn explained that one of the options in determining the manner of death was *homicide*. The station then ran a video clip of her trying to pin down Jared Quinn. She got no more from him than she had dragged out of me: *No comment*. At the end of the clip, Wynn assured viewers that the station's news team would continue following the case. I turned off the TV.

The gathering of hungry llamas at the barn pulled my attention away from hospital intrigue for the moment. I stopped on the way down the lane to breathe in the comforting perfume of Amah's lilac tree. The scent evoked feelings of love and family and loneliness, and reminded me that I had not spoken to Amah and Jack since before Delta's death. I promised myself a Skype session as soon as I could find the time.

Finished with the hay and back in the house, I finally rustled up breakfast for myself. Between sips of coffee and bites of peanut butter toast, I exchanged brief texts with Nick confirming our plan to meet at the foundation building that evening.

The morning passed quickly at the dojo, where I spent most of it helping Harry with beginners. After they left, he and I worked out for half an hour with a few other black belts. The two of us were finally alone when I asked if Rella had told him she was flying me to the parole hearing at Prairie Valley Prison on Monday.

"She did," Harry said. "I have to be on site at the mall all day, so we had to figure out what to do with Nick's dog."

"I forgot about Ginger. Are you taking her back to the Pet Motel?"

"No, Nick's taking her to Buck's place. He's wants to try to make that work." Harry glanced around the dojo's interior. "Looks like no one forgot anything. Want a cold drink before we leave?"

"Sounds good." I followed him into the sensei's office.

He opened the fridge and handed me a bottle of vitamin water. "Pull up a chair, unless you're in a hurry."

"No hurry." I unscrewed the cap and took a sip.

Harry studied me for a moment. "How do you feel about it? Seeing Mercer in person and telling that panel how he impacted your life?"

"Honestly, I've had so many other things on my mind, I've barely thought about it, but I'm trying to keep an open mind. Whatever I say could have an impact on the rest of *his* life."

"Will any other victims be there?"

"You probably remember the other person involved in the incident. He didn't harm her physically, but she must have suffered some emotional and psychological trauma. I was told she wasn't available for the hearing because she has dementia."

"I do remember her. An older woman you knew from the hospital. Didn't she work with you?"

"Not exactly. She was a volunteer already showing signs of mental decline back then. A sad case, really. She's Dr. Beardsley's older sister, so I'm sure he's seeing that she gets good care."

Harry's brows rose. "Another Beardsley incident suddenly surfaces from the past. Mercer was a suspect in Bonnie Beardsley's death, wasn't he?"

"Yes, along with Dr. Beardsley, but both of them were proven innocent. Mercer was sent to prison for his assault on me, which Beardsley's sister witnessed. He even tried to make her an accomplice."

"That's kind of a strange coincidence, isn't it? How both women's deaths involved the doctor."

"You can call it strange," I said, "but we live in a fairly small town where people's lives are more likely to intersect. Although you do have a point. The circumstances may be unrelated, but Vane Beardsley played a significant role in both cases. In the first, he lost his wife, Bonnie, and in the second, he lost his patient, Delta Sawyer."

"And there's another coincidence. Both of those deaths involved drug overdoses." Harry sipped from his drink and put the bottle down. "Sis, while we're on the subject of coincidence, there's something I think you should know." His somber expression put me on guard.

"What is it?"

"It's about how Sammy Sawyer died."

"She overdosed," I said. "I already know that much. Although back when I heard about it, I was away at college. Wasn't she out of town at a swim meet?"

"Right, you were taking summer courses back east. You hadn't met Nick, and you knew very little about the Sawyers back then. I doubt you ever heard the whole story."

"Probably not. It was old news by the time I came home. Why are you bringing it up now?"

Harry held up a hand. "Let me get through this. Back when it happened, I was two years older than Sammy. So was Bonnie Belcher. We had both graduated high school and had finished one year of college. That summer, at the end of Sammy's junior year of high school, she and Bonnie were both on Timbergate's city swim team. The two of them competed in the same categories, and even though they were on the same team, they were fierce contenders for the best times in their events."

Harry's story had already gripped me, because I knew it was not going to end well. "I've known for quite a while that Buck thought Bonnie got Sammy involved with drugs."

Harry shook his head. "That's never been proved. No one from the team believed Sammy was using, but meth was found in her system."

"From what I recall hearing, she didn't die at the swim meet. Wasn't it after? Something happened at a party?"

"That's right," Harry said, "it was an out-of-town meet. I don't recall which town, but it was at least a hundred miles from Timbergate. Sammy nearly drowned during one of the races where she and Bonnie were the favorites. It was a demanding one called the butterfly. After a couple of laps, Sammy slipped to the bottom of the pool.

"Was Buck there?"

"In the stands, watching with his wife, both of them rooting for their daughter."

"They must have been horrified . . . and you're saying Nick knows this story?"

"He does, ever since he began working for Buck."

"But Sammy didn't drown."

"No. She developed a cramp and couldn't swim. The lifeguards got her out in time, but she was taken out of competition for the rest of the meet."

I squirmed in my chair, wanting the end of the story. "Did Bonnie win the butterfly?"

"No. She came in second, but by such a close margin that her trainer challenged the ruling and requested an opinion from the judges. The outcome didn't change."

"How do you know so much about what happened?"

"My summer job. Remember, I was one of the team's lifeguards. I didn't work that meet, but I heard about it from the other lifeguards who were there."

"I'd forgotten you were lifeguarding back then. So did Sammy see a doctor after the meet?"

"No." Harry tossed his empty bottle into a recycle bin. "By the time the meet ended, her cramp was better. She and a few of her teammates were invited to a pizza party at the home of one of the swimmers from the hosting team. After meeting the parents, Buck and his wife decided to let her go. They thought it was only fair since she had been forced out of the meet. They dropped Sammy off and went back to their hotel, planning to pick her up at midnight."

"Then what happened at the party?" I scooted to the edge of my chair.

"She collapsed not long after she got there. The owners of the home where the party was held called an ambulance. Sammy died in the hospital later that night."

"And the hospital discovered the drug in her blood work?"

"It did, and there was an investigation, focused on the party. The kids who attended and the parents who hosted it were all questioned. No one was ever charged. Unfortunately, that started a lot of speculation among Timbergate gossip mongers about the extent of Sammy's involvement with meth."

"No wonder Buck is so driven about drugs. To live through a horror like that. Watching her nearly drown, seeing her rescued, and then losing her all in the space of a few hours."

Harry nodded. "Not to mention tainting her reputation. That had to deepen the hurt even more for Buck and his first wife, Sammy's mom."

"And now Delta's overdose has dealt Buck another blow involving drugs. I agree that's a coincidence, but I already knew about Sammy's death."

"Except for a detail you probably didn't know. The trainer at that swim meet, the one who challenged the result of that race, was Delta Dearborn."

I caught my breath. "Oh my . . . and she ended up married to Buck Sawyer."

"Seems strange, doesn't it?"

"Definitely, but in another way, it almost makes sense, because I've always wondered what brought Buck and Delta together. That poor man. He's already grieved the loss of a daughter and his first wife, and now the spotlight is on this new case. While Buck is dealing with the loss of his second wife, the ghouls on social media are speculating that he might have killed her."

"That's why I decided to tell you the backstory about Buck and Delta. I thought you should be aware of it in case you hadn't heard it from Nick."

"I hadn't. He's never brought it up, but he's pretty discreet when it comes to Buck's private life."

"That's why I decided to clue you in." Harry picked up his gi bag. "Gotta go. Good luck with the prison trip on Monday."

I headed home to Coyote Creek reflecting on what Harry had told me. It occurred to me that asking Orrie Mercer what he knew about Sammy Sawyer's death might be pointless. Even so, if he was willing to call, he might have something to add to Harry's story.

As I pulled into the driveway at the ranch, the local station's announcer came on my car radio with the midday news.

"There has been a new development in the death of Delta Sawyer, Timbergate's favorite daughter and candidate for mayor. According to local television newswoman Oriana Wynn, an unnamed informant has disclosed that Delta Sawyer died from an opioid overdose. So far, there is no word about medical error or foul play. This station has reached out to the hospital and to the police department for further details with no response from either source."

Anger catapulted me from my car on shaky legs. That impulsive reporter had dared to go public with information the police were withholding. If Oriana Wynn was that desperate for a scoop, I hoped she would be fired before the five o'clock news aired.

I tossed my gi bag into the bedroom, stripped, and stepped into a hot shower, where I stayed until the water turned cool. Dressed in sweats, I fixed a tuna sandwich and chased it with a hot cup of green tea. My body had calmed down, but my thoughts were still scrambled. Should I call Quinn? Or should I call Nick to ask if Buck was upset? *No. Take a breath.*

Wynn claimed to have an informant. She had stalked me outside the library a few mornings ago and then splashed my face across the TV screen after she ambushed me. I wondered if people would remember my "no comment," or if they would remember only my name and my face and assume I had fed her confidential information.

I deliberately left my cell phone in the house and walked out to the llama barn to gather my thoughts. There was nothing to be gained by calling Quinn at his home. Even with the Public Information Officer's position vacant, protecting TMC's image was not part of my job description.

If the radio account had upset Buck Sawyer, Nick would let me know. If we had to cancel our plans to meet later that night, I would understand.

I finished chopping hay for Old Doolittle while I reviewed the rest of my Saturday: meet Rella at two o'clock at the airport and meet Nick at eight thirty.

Aggressive reporters and their tactics circled me back to the vacancy in TMC's Public Information Office. This was the time when TMC could use the talents of a good PR person. The sooner Quinn filled that position, the better.

That reminded me of Varsha Singh's unexplained absence. Still nothing on the grapevine at work. At least nothing on the *employee* grapevine. I smiled, thinking of Bernie and Lola and about Bernie's slogan: *Loose lips sink ships.* I was required to be a poster person for confidentiality, so the workplace gossips rarely shared with me. My volunteers heard way more gossip than I did. Too bad I had a conscience, or I might occasionally be tempted to debrief my senior helpers.

Chapter 18

I CHECKED BOTH MY PHONES BEFORE I LEFT to meet Rella at the airport. There was nothing on the cell or the landline about my Tuesday phone date with Orrie Mercer.

I spotted Rella standing outside the hangar when I arrived. I gave her my notes with the information the officer at the prison had given me. She glanced at the page, nodded, and tucked it into her jacket pocket.

"Have you told Nick about our trip?"

"No. Have you?" I unlocked the hangar and we stepped inside.

She laughed. "No, but you should see the look on your face. Don't ever try playing poker."

"I guess I should have told him, but things have been happening so fast, he and I can barely keep up."

"I'd feel a lot better about flying his—excuse me—*your* plane if he knew about it."

"I'm going to see him tonight. I'll make sure he knows."

Rella performed her walkaround of the Skylane, jotting notes and poking at various points on its exterior. When she finished we stepped out of the hangar. Rella put her notepad away.

"Tell you what. When you see Nick tonight and tell him about our flight, ask him to call me for a quick brief on the aircraft. I'll see you tomorrow evening at the memorial."

"I'll probably be the only person there who doesn't work for Buck." Rella smiled. "Not quite, your brother will be there, too."

BY EIGHT O'CLOCK I WAS SHOWERED, dressed and on my way to meet Nick. During the drive to Timbergate, Quinn's backhanded allusion to a promotion came to mind. That had been almost a week ago, but with our entire focus on the upheaval over Delta's death, there had been no good time bring it up to Nick. Even without knowing the details, I decided I would at least mention it, along with the flight to Mercer's hearing.

I pulled into the dark, empty parking lot behind Buck's building. Nick entered the lot minutes later in his black pickup. We both stepped out into the chilly night. He pulled me close and I tried to speak, but a whimper escaped. He wrapped me in his arms and kissed the top of my head.

"Damn, Aimee, you'd better get hold of yourself or you'll have me sniffling, and it won't be pretty."

I laughed. "I'm okay, really." I glanced into the cab of his truck. "Did you bring Ginger?"

"No, she's taken on a new role as Buck's comfort dog. Uncanny how she's been sticking close to him. It's as if she senses his misery. All of his tragic memories have been dredged to the surface, and at the same time, he knows the police are trying to decide whether he's a grieving widower or a murder suspect."

"Then I'm glad Ginger's there for him, but what about you?"

He brushed a strand of hair from my cheek. "I guess you'll have to do."

I laughed. "No one could adore you as much as she does, but I'll do my best."

He tilted my chin. "Let's give it a try."

The kiss that followed flooded me with desire so intense that everything around us faded away. There was no more Buck or Delta, no more Quinn, TMC, or Vane Beardsley—only the physical longing to merge with Nick's breath and his body. When we broke apart, both of us were trembling.

"Oh, Lady," he said.

"A lady wouldn't be feeling what I feel right now."

"Shall we go inside?" I heard the question he asked aloud, and the one unspoken.

I handed the keys to Nick. We entered through the access door from the employee parking area. Nick keyed in the alarm code. Inside, we went into the community room where the memorial for Delta would be held the next evening. Folding chairs were set up, enough for a couple of dozen people, and a lectern stood at the front of the room. An enlarged photo of Delta had been propped on an easel. It was the same glamorous image I had seen earlier on her campaign website.

A chill raced across my shoulders. Delta's ghost had invaded the space, cooling the heat Nick and I had generated in the parking lot. We left the pall of the community room and walked to the expansive reception area.

I looked at Nick. "I feel guilty that I didn't try harder to befriend Delta over the past few years. It's like I barely knew her."

"Don't feel guilty. I don't think anybody really knew her. I always had the feeling she didn't know herself. She reminded me of the paper dolls my sister played with when we were little—a blank shape that could be molded into almost anything. But once the trappings were stripped away, there was nothing there."

"How terribly sad."

"Sad for her and the people around her," Nick said. "I never knew her to show genuine feelings for anyone except herself."

"Not even Buck?"

"She played the part when it suited her, but I wasn't convinced."

"Want to tell me why?"

Nick's jaw hardened. "Simple observation. My job required spending a certain amount of time around her. Enough for me to have my doubts, but I was taught not to speak ill of the dead."

"Then I'll stop asking questions."

"Thanks." He gave me a peck on the cheek. "Do you mind

waiting here for a minute? Buck asked me to return some files he's been working on from home."

"No problem. I'm glad he's keeping busy. It's probably helping him cope."

"It's that, but I'm getting a feeling it's something more. He isn't usually so involved in the details of the grant process. He's even asked Harry to help out."

"Harry? What's he doing? I doubt he knows much about private foundations."

"Are you kidding? He's such a quick study, he could be up to speed in no time, but Buck consulted him originally about computer security. I'm not sure what else they're working on, but I get kind of a kick out of seeing them in Buck's home office with their heads together."

Nick borrowed my set of keys and opened a nearby office door. He returned to the reception area a few moments later and handed me the keys. "Okay, that's done." He patted the back of an overstuffed couch covered in a floral fabric. "This looks comfy. I don't think I've ever sat on it." He reached out to take my hand. "Let's give it a try."

We settled on the couch, where dimmed track lighting high on the walls cast a false twilight. I loved the feel of our hands laced together, but I slipped mine out of his grip. "Nick, there are some things I need to tell you."

"Then this isn't strictly a date?"

"Not the kind of date we started out in the parking lot, I'm afraid. At least not yet."

"All right. I'm listening."

I started with the hearing at the prison, explaining about being asked for a victim impact statement.

"I've asked Rella to fly me there in our plane."

"Good idea," he said. "I'm glad you're going to do it. You should have your say about what that guy did to you. And I have no reservations about Rella flying you. She knows the plane from when it was part of Buck's fleet."

"That's another detail. She wants you to give her a call, because it's been a while since she's flown it."

"Done," Nick said. "Next?"

"There's been so much going on that I keep forgetting to tell you I've been offered a promotion at work."

Even in our dimly lit setting, I saw Nick's eyes light up. "That's fantastic. They obviously know how lucky they are to have you. What's the offer?"

"I wish I could tell you more, but Quinn got distracted before he could provide me with details. For now, all I know is that I'll have additional responsibilities, a higher pay grade, and an assistant librarian."

Nick pulled me into a hug. "Sounds exciting. When would you start?"

"That's still an unknown, but Quinn made it clear he won't be following up with details about the promotion until after the Delta Sawyer case is settled."

"Makes sense. His hands are full, and with our conflict of interest, he's right to wait."

"I agree, but still, I wanted you to know. If I accept more responsibility, it could affect both of us."

Nick seemed oblivious to the idea that a promotion could carve time and attention away from my personal life. I had assumed he would bring that up—maybe even ask how I felt about balancing my professional life if our future involved marriage and children.

"You've never interfered in *my* professional life," he said. "Look at us—where we're sitting and the reason why. How many women would be as understanding as you are about my commitment to Buck? I owe you the same consideration. I would never ask you to turn down a promotion if it's what you want."

"I appreciate that."

I should have been impressed by Nick's words, but I was torn, wondering if the subtext was telling me something more. He had already raised his concerns about my sleuthing several times, but my thoughts shifted to a more disturbing reason why Nick might sidestep a decision about my future. It could relate to uncertainty about his own—because chances were good he was still a person of interest in Delta Sawyer's murder.

We had been sitting silently for a few moments when Nick finally spoke. "While you're in the mood to share, is there anything else you want to tell me?"

"I can't talk about anything related to work, so no, I don't think so." Especially not about Beardsley's donation to Delta's campaign.

"Then you *are* holding out on me?" He leaned back, head cocked and eyes narrowed.

I avoided his gaze. "Let's say I'm staying within the parameters of my job description."

Nick rose from the couch and pulled me up, circling my waist with his arms. "We're no longer in the mood for love, are we?"

"I don't think so," I said. "Too many distractions."

"Too bad." He kissed my forehead and looked at the couch. "That is a really comfy sofa."

Chapter 19

Nick's comment about Delta's lack of feelings for Buck came to mind as I drove home. It made me sad, but it also worried me. Buck obviously had reason to think she was keeping secrets from him. If not an affair, what other kind of secret would she have kept from her husband? If he found out, was it something heinous enough to result in her murder?

I felt my blood pressure bump up. Buck had been questioned almost immediately after Delta's death, and his home had been secured by the police as a possible crime scene. He had already been arrested once and released. TPD was keeping a tight lid on information about their investigation. Something told me it was only a matter of time before Buck was arrested again. And what about Nick, his right-hand man?

I pushed that worry aside and forced my attention on my upcoming phone call with Orrie Mercer. Most of my curiosity about Sammy Sawyer's death had been satisfied by Harry. His story had placed Bonnie and Sammy at the swim meet on that tragic day. He said Delta Dearborn was there, too, as their trainer. A former competitive swimmer herself, she was most likely a mentor the younger girls looked up to.

Harry confirmed that both Bonnie and Sammy were at the after party where Sammy collapsed. The rumor that circulated back then was that Bonnie provided the meth to Sammy while they were at the party. I wondered why Bonnie was blamed, since there were plenty of other young people there who could have slipped the meth to both girls. If any of the teens there knew the truth, they must have kept silent for obvious reasons. In that situation, no kid doing drugs wants to come clean to parents, let alone to the authorities.

BACK AT THE RANCH I TOSSED IN BED until midnight with all of my thoughts racing toward the same goal. Delta had died six days ago, and the police seemed to be getting nowhere—unless they were close to arresting Buck again.

Midnight in California was seven in the morning in the Azores. I needed someone to talk to besides llamas and a cranky cat. I needed face time with my family. I sat up and reached for my laptop.

"Aimee, what a surprise." Mom's dark eyes sparkled and her beautiful smile filled the screen. "Perfect timing, Amah and Jack are here having breakfast with us. Even Uncle Gabe is here. We're celebrating his birthday." She rotated her laptop so I could wave to everyone.

Amah peered at me from the screen, her dark curls threaded with gray and her complexion glowing as if the moist and sunny Azorean climate had erased years from her age. "Is everything okay at the ranch, honey?"

"Everything's fine." *I wish.*

I saw Jack reach into the frame with his strong, leathery hand and give a *thumbs up* gesture. Dad came next, brushing a wayward lock of graying hair from his forehead and slipping his glasses on a face tanned from sailing.

"How about Nick? We've seen some news about his boss's wife dying. Something about a medical mistake at the hospital. Is that true?"

"She died at the hospital, but no one knows the details yet. And I can't talk about it for obvious reasons."

I assured them it was nothing they needed to worry about. The last thing I wanted was for any of them to decide to fly home. I told them not to take the local news from Timbergate too seriously, that I'd keep them updated if there was anything important to report. I changed the subject to more mundane topics like llamas, the lilacs blooming in the garden, and the weather.

Uncle Gabe took his turn last. Several years younger than my dad, with his dark brown hair worn surfer style and showing no sign of gray, it was hard to believe he was forty-five. I wished him a happy birthday and with a repeat of my promise to keep in touch, I signed off.

It was good to see the faces of my family, to feel a connection as they celebrated with Uncle Gabe, but I was troubled to think they might be worried about Nick and me. I made a note to text Harry in the morning and tell him to follow my lead. If they happened to contact him from the Azores, or if he heard from Grandpa Machado and Tanya in New York City, say nothing that would worry any of them.

SUNDAY MORNING GREETED COYOTE CREEK with the tail end of a rain storm. By the time I pulled on jeans and a sweatshirt and made my way to the llama barn, the sweet-smelling air and its lingering moisture had produced a double rainbow.

As usual, the rote action of chopping hay with the hefty guillotine blade of Jack's old paper cutter allowed my mind to wander. It took me back to a bit of my conversation with Nick that I had almost forgotten. He said Harry had been helping Buck with a computer issue. Nick had the impression that it might be more than a simple security matter, and I knew that he had been taking documents home to Buck and later returning them to the foundation office.

Then I recalled Rella's speculation about Delta threatening to put Buck's foundation in peril. What if Buck suspected something was amiss in his grants process and Harry was helping him get to the bottom of it? Simple logic pointed me toward the obvious. Delta had been on the board of the foundation for as long as I had known her and had high-level access to any grant decisions.

Buck told the San Francisco lawyers he suspected she was cheating on him. What if that was a cover story and Buck actually suspected her of something corrupt that involved the foundation's grants? He would have been reluctant to share that suspicion with anyone, including those divorce lawyers. I hoped I was wrong, because nothing was more sacred to Buck than his foundation. If he suspected Delta was putting its mission in jeopardy, he had a powerful motive to be rid of his wife. The implications of that scenario caused a sickening wave of vertigo.

I went back to chopping to help center myself. Surely my imagination was working overtime. When I finished, I had enough hay to feed Old Doolittle at least four more meals—a good thing, since Monday would be a busy day. I planned to go into the library for a few hours in the morning before meeting Rella at the hangar for our flight to the prison. It would be handy to have the old boy's hay already cut when I finally got home that evening.

EARLY SUNDAY AFTERNOON I SEARCHED my closet for a simple black dress to wear to Delta's memorial. While I was at it, I settled on another outfit that would take me from work Monday directly to the airport and the parole hearing. One of the commonsense behaviors I had learned from my pilot boyfriend was how to dress when flying.

Nick had taught me not to obsess about crashing and burning but to think about the possibility of an emergency landing. If you end up tramping across a landscape covered in several inches of snow, or even if you're trudging out of Farmer Brown's stubbly, fresh-cut alfalfa field, you don't want to be wearing a mini-dress and high heels. I pulled out slacks, a sweater and a blazer. I added my low-heeled boots and a warm jacket with a hood. A few granola bars went into the jacket pockets.

WHEN THE TIME CAME TO LEAVE for Delta's memorial, I drove to Timbergate, reaching the foundation office a few minutes before seven. I found a space behind the building in the employees' lot. Nick's pickup was there, and Harry's Jag, along with various other vehicles, which probably belonged to foundation employees.

I headed toward the front entrance just in time to see the last person who should have been there: Oriana Wynn, the TV reporter who had splashed my scowling face across the screens of every home in Timbergate, Coyote Creek, and beyond. Her gangly, red-haired cameraman stood next to her.

I made a quick about-face and slipped back around the corner. The plan to keep the event private had obviously failed. Wynn called out to arrivals, asking them to comment for her viewers. I heard her strident voice confront someone, saying the public deserved to know the status of the investigation. The male voice that answered sounded like Fletcher Tremont, Delta's campaign manager and Executive Director of the Sawyer Foundation.

"You there, Miss, if you are not in your vehicle and driving off this property by the time I count to ten, I will call the police and have you arrested for trespassing." He began counting. "One . . . two . . . "

Wynn attempted to call his bluff. "Sir, the public—"

The rest of her sentence was cut off. I peeked around the building in time to see her sidekick clutching his bulky camera and galloping toward the TV station's van. Wynn ran after him yelling, "Come back here, you little worm!"

I slid back out of sight until I could stifle my laughter. When I got control of myself, I entered the building and made my way to the community room to look for Nick.

He was seated alongside Buck in the front row. He spotted me and pointed to the empty space next to him on the aisle. On Buck's other side were Tremont and his wife, a round-faced, pleasant-looking woman in her fifties wearing thick glasses. Rella and Harry were seated in the row directly behind us, along with several foundation employees.

I noticed some of Timbergate's dignitaries seated across the aisle, including the city manager, members of the city council, and Mayor Vickers. Ernest Wright and Nora Nester, Delta's two opponents in the race for mayor, were present. That surprised me. I wondered whose idea it had been to invite them. They had chosen seats as far away from each other as possible. Wright was accompanied by his wife and his mother. Nester had come solo. It occurred to me that everyone I had identified as a possible suspect in Delta's case was in the room—except Dr. Vane Beardsley.

Obviously, Jared Quinn had not been invited. That would have been awkward, since my boss and Buck were in opposite camps over Delta's death. Both teams of lawyers would have recommended against it.

An organist at the front of the room played tunes best described as Muzak—nothing religious or sentimental. Buck had done the best he could under the circumstances. He had been ready to part ways with Delta before she died, so why be hypocritical about the music?

The easel holding Delta's photo remained in place front and center. It was surrounded by large standing floral wreaths and sprays of white lilies, pink carnations, and mixed hues of roses. High up on the front wall, a continuous slide show presented visuals of every stage of Delta's life. The clips of her competing in swim events as a teen caught my attention. Another photo where she was older showed her wearing her swim team trainer's uniform. She stood between Sammy Sawyer and Bonnie Belcher while the girls held up winning ribbons. Sammy's was blue for first place. Bonnie's was red for second.

I sneaked a glance at Buck while he viewed the photo of his deceased daughter and his deceased second wife. I watched him shake his head and look down at the floor. Whoever prepared the slides must have been ignorant of the circumstances surrounding Sammy Sawyer's death. Nick sat rigid between Buck and me, and I knew he was having the same thought. How would Buck get through this ordeal? His dead daughter posed with his self-absorbed second wife. And each time the slide show repeated, that scene would flash across the room again.

Sammy's death was the heartache that would last for Buck's lifetime, but his second wife's secretive behavior must have been on his mind as well. Did he wonder if Delta's killer was present somewhere in the room? I did.

When the last guests were seated, the organist stopped playing. Fletcher Tremont took his cue and walked to the front of the room to act as master of ceremonies. The role seemed tailor-made for him. I recalled how composed he had been in front of an audience back when he spoke about redirecting contributions to Delta's campaign.

Tremont thanked the city manager and Mayor Vickers for attending and went on to recognize Delta's opponents, Ernest Wright and Nora Nester. He attempted to lighten the mood by saying, "Let me wish you both good luck. May the best man—or woman—win." A few of the assembled mourners managed a polite chuckle. Others, me included, remained silent in what felt like an awkward moment.

Tremont spoke of Delta's legacy as the daughter of one of Timbergate's founding fathers. He painted a picture of a community-minded woman with high hopes for the City of Timbergate. Because Delta had done very little in her adult life in the way of worthy causes, his eulogy was brief. His invitation to guests who might like to share fond memories brought another awkward moment. There was complete silence until Mayor Vickers broke the lull by standing.

"I have a few words." The audience let out a collective sigh of relief. Politician to the rescue.

"Thank you, Mayor." Tremont beckoned Vickers to come forward.

Wendell Vickers walked to the front of the room and stood at the lectern, where he lowered the microphone to his height and began to speak.

"Delta was proud of her heritage and her family ties to Timbergate. She always spoke highly of her husband," Vickers nodded toward Buck, "and she did an excellent job decorating this facility. She had great instincts and no matter what the challenge, she kept her eye on the prize. The Sawyer Foundation meant the world to her. I'm sure her fellow board members would agree."

Obligatory murmurs of ascent issued forth. At that point, Vickers seemed to run out of words. Tremont stepped up and thanked him. Vickers went back to his seat directly across the aisle from where I sat.

Chapter 20

Tremont brought the service to a close, directing people to the spacious reception area where desserts and beverages had been arranged on a banquet table. A few folks escaped right away, and the rest lined up for refreshments. Nick took me aside to tell me he planned to take Buck home soon. The stress of the evening had taken its toll.

If not for my promise to Beardsley, I would have left right then, but it took a while before I had a chance to approach Tremont. His duties as host kept him occupied with polite small talk. The two mayoral candidates would want equal time to do some politicking, telling him about their views for Timbergate's future.

With Delta out of the picture, there was no one left, other than Buck, with more control over the foundation's purse strings than Tremont. Every worthy cause in Sawyer County lobbied the Sawyer Foundation hoping it would expand the scope of its mission.

I observed how Mrs. Tremont kept out of the limelight and nearly disappeared while her husband was occupied. I decided to go over to where she sat alone on the same comfy couch that Nick and I had occupied the night before.

"Mrs. Tremont, I'm Aimee Machado, a friend of Buck's."

"It's nice to meet you. Please call me Faye." As she spoke, she leaned down to massage her calf. "A cramp," she said. "Must have worn the wrong shoes tonight." She patted the couch. "Would you like to sit?"

"I would. Thank you. I'm hoping to have a moment to speak to your husband before I leave."

"You and everyone else." A smile transformed her face behind the glasses from plain to pretty.

"He's in quite a powerful position, isn't he? There must be an endless stream of people coming at him with their hands out."

"And now it'll be even worse." She paused for a moment, seemed to struggle to continue. "Delta served as somewhat of a buffer, but that layer of insulation is gone." Another pause. "As you can see, Fletcher is already hindered by her absence."

"He seems capable of dealing with it. I'll try to keep my turn with him as brief as possible."

She asked with somewhat halting speech, "Is it anything I might help with?"

"I don't think so. It involves instructions about a donation to Delta's campaign."

Tremont had broken away and was walking toward us. I stood and spoke quickly before anyone else could intervene.

"Mr. Tremont, I'm Aimee Machado. Could I have a moment?"

"Miss Machado, we meet again. I see you've met my wife."

"Yes, we made our own introductions."

Faye stayed seated. "Fletch, Miss Machado needs a moment with you."

Tremont gave me his full attention. "By all means, I'm at your disposal."

"It's a favor for an acquaintance who knew I would be here tonight. He's hoping you can confirm receipt of his instructions about his donation to Delta's campaign. I told him I would ask."

He raised his brows. "I see. What is your friend's name?"

"Dr. Vane Beardsley. He would have come himself, but he felt it would be in poor taste, considering the circumstances." I took Beardsley's envelope from my purse.

"Circumstances?" Tremont seemed confused, then the light dawned. "He was . . . Delta's doctor?"

"Yes."

Tremont nodded. "You're in luck. Mr. Sawyer unlocked my office earlier so I could assist any guests who might ask about their donations. All of the final campaign communications are being forwarded here, so we can take a look if you'd like to come with me. I was already headed that way to shut down my computer."

"That won't be necessary, he didn't use the online form. He wrote out his instructions." I followed him into his office and handed him Beardsley's envelope. "He's very concerned about his privacy."

"Not to worry, my computer is the only one here with access to the campaign files. It's quite likely no one on our staff was aware of the doctor's donation."

"Not even Buck Sawyer?"

"Unlikely," Tremont said. "Mr. Sawyer never dealt with mundane matters involving the campaign, or even with grant processing. All of that was my responsibility. Mine and Mrs. Sawyer's, until her untimely death."

It sounded like Tremont was not aware that Buck had been probing into something related to grant funding. If Buck did suspect Delta of any potential mishandling of the foundation's charitable donations, I understood why he was keeping it to himself.

"Dr. Beardsley told me he provided his home address so you could confirm his instructions for the donation," I said. "Will that be done fairly soon?"

"Certainly, but tonight is not the best time. I'd rather not keep Faye waiting. Tell you what, if Dr. Beardsley should ask you about this, tell him I'll make it my first priority this coming week. The foundation is still closed, but that's something I can manage from home. Will that do?"

"That should be fine."

Back in the lobby area the small crowd had thinned and the catering staff was already starting to clear away the remains of the refreshments. I spotted Nick across the room standing in a small group with Harry, Rella and Buck. As I started toward them, I heard Tremont's voice.

"Excuse us. Can you get the door?"

I turned as he came up behind me pushing his wife in a wheelchair. I opened the door and held it until they made their way outside. I followed them and asked if they needed help with the car door.

"Thank you, no." Tremont smiled down toward his wife. "We've had lots of practice, haven't we?"

"We have." Faye reached out and took my hand. Her grip was cool and fragile. "You were sweet to ask, Miss Machado."

Back inside I found Nick still in the same huddle with Buck, Harry and Rella. I joined them, thinking I should say something polite about the evening.

"Buck, I'm glad the memorial went well. I was impressed with our mayor's tribute to Delta."

"Yes, Vickers rather saved the day," he said. "Must have been the politician in him. Nothing worse than an open mic and no speaker."

The look Nick gave me said let it go, and I was more than happy to oblige. He excused himself to walk me to my car.

The overhead lighting in the parking lot cast our shadows larger than life against the back of the building. In the chilly air, we wrapped ourselves in each other's arms. There were times when nothing felt better than a long, deeply satisfying hug.

"Sorry you have to go home alone," Nick finally said. "I keep thinking of you out at the barn every morning and evening chopping hay for Old Doolittle."

"Then you've pretty much got the picture. I'm either there or in the TMC Library churning out life-saving information."

Nick took my hand as we walked to my car. "That's you. The Avenger Librarian."

"You think you made that up, but there's an actual website called *Librarian Avengers*."

Nick laughed. "I'm not surprised, but speaking of your chosen profession, I noticed that Fletcher Tremont's wife is in a wheelchair. You were talking to her for a while. Any idea what that's about?"

"Now that you ask, there were a couple of clues. I would have missed them when we were sitting together, because I had no idea about the wheelchair."

"What kind of clues?"

"She seemed to have a muscle spasm in her leg at one point, and then her husband mentioned wanting to get her home which could mean she's easily fatigued. She wears glasses, but that could be irrelevant. The thing that struck me most was her difficulty with speech."

Nick leaned against my ancient Buick. "What's your curbside diagnosis?"

"My guess would be multiple sclerosis. I remember back in my teens the mother of one of my friends was diagnosed with it. Sometimes I couldn't tell she was ill, but my friend said there were bad days when she hid herself away."

"I noticed Tremont's efforts to check on his wife several times during the evening."

"I'm glad. She seems like a nice person. Imagine how hard her life would be without him."

"On that serious note, we've circled back to Buck, who is now without a spouse." Nick pulled me close. "I have to get him out of there soon, but there's something I need to do first."

His kiss left me teetering between desire and guilt. According to Tremont, Buck most likely had no clue about Beardsley's fifty-thousand-dollar donation. My conscience told me he deserved to know. And so did the police.

I drove home in a quandary about contacting Walter Kass. The secrets Harry had uncovered about Wright and Nester were the least of my worries. TPD needed to know about Beardsley's inexplicable contribution to Delta's campaign. Trouble was, I couldn't take sides. If I told Kass about Beardsley's donation, I had to play fair and tell him that Buck had consulted lawyers about a legal separation. *Stalemate.* My only consolation was the hope that TPD had already discovered both of those potential clues on their own.

Chapter 21

MONDAY DAWNED CLEAR AND FINE, adhering to the centuries-old idiom. With only three days left in the month, March was going out like a lamb. I uttered a "thank you" to the weather gods as I gave the llamas an early breakfast. Flying even a short hop to the prison in Arroyo County would have been rocky if Rella had to skirt around late spring storm clouds. I had great faith in her flying, but why tempt fate?

I planned to drive to the hangar directly from the hospital, so I dressed in the outfit I had decided on the day before. I fed the cat and headed out, pulling into the library parking lot by six thirty. I booted up my computer and shot off a message to Quinn reminding him the library would close for the day at eleven.

A check of my email showed no pressing items. I glanced at my desk calendar and realized that eight days ago, Delta Sawyer had been the front-runner in Timbergate's mayoral campaign. In all of those days since her death, the police had been silent about their investigation. I blamed that on the tenacious Oriana Wynn. TPD obviously wanted no part of her sensationalist reporting.

Vane Beardsley dropped by a few minutes before nine while I

was in the break room pouring a cup of coffee. I heard the entrance door open and his familiar voice speak my name.

"Miss Machado, are you here?"

I called out, "I'll be right with you."

I left the coffee behind and found him standing at my desk with a small bouquet. The fragrance of roses and carnations mingled with his heavy, musky cologne. He held out his offering.

"These are for you. A thank you for your help with my donation."

"You're welcome. They're beautiful, but that wasn't necessary, Dr. Beardsley." I took the flowers, wondering what to do with them. Should I drop them on my desk, excuse myself to look for a vase in the break room, or keep holding them until he left? Too awkward—I dumped the contents of a pencil cup into my desk drawer and propped the flowers in the cup.

Beardsley looked down at the bouquet and reached out to touch a rose petal. "I wonder, were you able to deliver my instructions to Mr. Tremont?"

"Yes. He said to tell you he'll put a confirmation in the mail to you this week."

"Thank you again," Beardsley said. "I hope Mr. Sawyer is holding up. I know from experience that memorials can be difficult."

At that point Lola Rampley came through the entry door with her customary greeting.

"Good morning, Miss Machado. . . ." She stopped in her tracks when she saw Dr. Beardsley standing at my desk. "Oh, dear, excuse me. Did I interrupt?"

"Not at all," I said. "We were finished, weren't we?" I looked to Beardsley.

"Yes." He checked his watch. "I should be on my way. I have a commitment to keep."

As he exited, Lola spotted the flowers in the pencil cup. "You realize Maybelline would never have approved of that?"

At the mention of Maybelline, I thought back to the days when Dr. Beardsley's older sister had been one of my library volunteers and how she had enjoyed retrieving orphaned bouquets from patients' rooms and bringing them to the library.

"I agree, she would not approve. I'll find a proper vase for these."

Lola leaned over to take in the scent of the flowers. "Lucky for us, we have Bernie to keep our library cheerful with his green thumb. He'll watch over these."

"I'm sure he will," I agreed.

Lola settled at the volunteer's desk. "Has Dr. Beardsley mentioned how Maybelline is faring these days?"

"No, he hasn't brought it up, and I'm not sure it would be appropriate to ask. I'm certain the facility where she lives is providing good care. He would choose the best for her."

I explained that I would be closing the library at eleven without going into details about the reason beyond saying it was a personal matter.

"Nothing urgent, I hope?"

When I assured Lola that it was nothing worrisome, she went about her chores, but I sensed she was uncomfortable that she and Bernie were forging ahead with their plans despite my advice that they wait.

At least they had sought help from a professional. Surely they had been advised not to rush into a significant financial commitment. *Leave it alone*, I thought. Their decision was none of my business. Except it was, because their lives could be caught in the ripple effect of Delta Sawyer's death. Lola and Bernie would suffer consequences if Ernest Wright turned out to be guilty of murder.

The same was true of Laurie Littletree if Nora Nester was a killer with a dark secret in her past. Would Laurie's baby be safe in *Nora's Nest*? Everything in my life seemed tainted by Delta's death. My work and the lives of my co-workers, my personal life and the lives of Nick and Buck, Harry and Rella—we were all caught in the current of an unsolved mystery.

RELLA HAD THE SKYLANE OUTSIDE THE hangar and ready to board when I arrived at the airport at noon. She waved and called out as I hurried toward her from the parking lot.

"We're ready for takeoff."

In minutes we were in the air and cruising, both wearing head-phones. In spite of her comment days earlier that she had once given a victim impact statement, she did not bring it up during our flight. That was a subject better left for a setting unimpeded by headphones. I had already read through my prepared statement several times, until I had it nearly memorized. Both of us preferred to keep our attention on the flight.

I always enjoyed a birds-eye view of the varying landscapes fly-ing might offer. Our trip first skimmed over mountainous terrain, followed by stretches of high desert where deer and antelope com-peted for scarce scrub vegetation. On this trip, the sight of vast stretches of forest scorched by the previous summer's devastat-ing fires brought a pang of sadness, not only for the loss of pris-tine wilderness, but for the untold numbers of animals, large and small, who lost their habitat, and in many cases, their lives. I hoped nature's healing process would bring new life to those scarred areas and wondered if that recovery would happen during my lifetime.

We landed at the prison airstrip, where CDCR employees helped tie down the plane. A thickset uniformed woman with dark, short-cropped hair escorted us to a waiting area adjacent to the hearing room. We were twenty minutes early. The escort offi-cer mentioned that the hot beverage dispenser offered a variety of choices. She pointed out that there was direct access to a rest room and suggested I avail myself of that before the hearing began.

Curious whether Rella would elaborate on the experience she had mentioned earlier, I asked if she had any last-minute advice.

"I noticed you've prepared notes," she said.

"Yes. They said I could read my statement to the board."

"That should help. It did for me."

Here was an opening. "How long ago did you have to do this?"

"It's been more than ten years, but it's the kind of thing you don't forget." She went to the beverage dispenser, took her time, and came back with black coffee. "We can talk later. It's best if you center yourself now. Take some breaths. You'll be fine."

She turned out to be right. When I entered the hearing room and spotted Orrie Mercer, my immediate reaction was pity. He had lost so much weight I would not have recognized him in any other setting. His gaunt face and gray skin tone suggested a chronic illness.

The proceedings included Mercer's statement about his remorse for his crime and his recognition of the impact it had on me and my family. My statement told of the physical wound I suffered at his hands and his threats to my life, including holding me at gunpoint. I told the panel that at the time of his attack, I had feared he would cause me injury or even death, but what had bothered me most, and made me angry enough to fight back, was that he had killed one of our family's turkeys and threatened the life of our baby llama.

Stating how the experience impacted my life afterward was the most difficult part. I said I had been assaulted before and had already reconciled myself to the idea that there was no such thing as a perfectly safe way to live.

When I finished, the hearing officers asked me about any ongoing mental health or possible PTSD symptoms. I said once he was convicted and put in prison, I put the event behind me until the request to attend his hearing. I added that I believed his remorse was sincere and that I had no reason to fear Orrie Mercer if he were to be paroled.

My part in the proceedings ended in less than half an hour. The same escort officer ushered me back to the waiting room. She said the wait for the shuttle to the airstrip might be as much as thirty minutes.

We were alone in the room, so Rella asked how I felt about my statement.

"Kind of surreal, I guess. I keep thinking this is his second chance. He has an opportunity to start on a new path if he's released. I don't want his fate to be in my hands."

"From what Harry's told me, your fate was in Mercer's hands back when he assaulted you."

"You know, that was the second time Harry came to my rescue."

"But this is your first hearing?"

"Technically, yes. In the other case, I was across the country finishing my library degree, so I took the option of filling out a form and submitting it."

I thought Rella was going to tell me about her own experience, but as she started to speak, the escort officer brought in two more people.

Recovering from my initial surprise, I introduced Rella to Dr. Vane Beardsley and his older sister, Verna, aka Maybelline Black.

Chapter 22

——•——

"O H, LOOK, VANE, IT'S MISS MACHADO." Maybelline peered at me with protruding eyes magnified behind her thick-lensed glasses. "Dearie, you remember me, don't you?"

"Of course," I said. "You were so helpful with the book cart when you volunteered in the library." She appeared more elderly and frail than I remembered. No doubt her long-standing thyroid condition had resulted in weight loss and other related health issues.

"We came here to speak about Mister Mercer," Maybelline said. "What brings you?"

In her confusion, she remembered who I was but did not remember that she had witnessed Mercer attack me.

"I'm also here to give a statement."

"Good for you," she said. "Delta Dearborn cannot go free. The villains must be punished no matter who they are." She put a hand to the side of her mouth, as if sharing a secret. "Ask Orrie. Orrie knows all about it."

I stood for a moment with my mouth open, uncertain how to respond. Before I could question her, Dr. Beardsley cut in. "Verna, we should let Miss Machado and her friend be on their way."

She whirled on him and shook her finger in his face. "Do not call me Verna. My name is Maybelline." She turned back to me. "Miss Machado knows my name, don't you, Dearie?"

I nodded. "I do. It's a pretty name."

"I'm sorry Maybelline," Beardsley said, "I'll try to remember." He took her arm, steering her toward the door. She swiveled her head around and called out to me.

"Orrie's got the goods. Delta must not go free."

Beardsley glanced at me over her head, making eye contact and shaking his head. "I'll drop by the library tomorrow morning." His expression telegraphed that Maybelline shouldn't be taken seriously.

I got it. He wanted to explain why he brought her to the parole hearing in her deteriorating mental state, and why she thought Delta was alive and in prison. Meanwhile, her outburst left me puzzled. With her level of dementia, she was obviously confused. Still, if the prison phone call I'd requested was confirmed, I intended to ask Orrie Mercer if he knew anything incriminating about Delta Dearborn Sawyer.

THE FLIGHT BACK TO TIMBERGATE WENT SMOOTHLY, except for my curiosity about Rella's victim statement. She had said she would tell me about it during our trip to the prison. That had not happened, and we were almost out of time.

After we landed at Timbergate Municipal and stowed the plane in the hangar, I said the least I could do was treat her to coffee and pie at the airport diner. While we ate, she brought up Mercer's hearing.

"Are you glad you went in person?"

"I am," I said. "It put the experience in a different perspective."

"Which experience? His attacking you, or your statement?"

"Both. The hearing wasn't as unnerving as I expected, and Mercer looked so feeble, it was hard to believe I'd ever been afraid of him."

"Interesting that they call it a *victim* impact statement." Rella scooped a bite of boysenberry pie with her fork. "I refuse to be identified by that word."

"I don't blame you. I don't want to wear that label, either. Which reminds me, you said you might tell me about your statement. Was the inmate in your case paroled?"

Rella smiled. "Let's say his sentence was terminated. He was shanked a few weeks after his hearing."

"Wow . . . that's . . . did he die?"

"Eventually. I think he suffered for a couple of weeks before the end."

Her story sounded like much more than I had bargained for. I weighed whether to ask a follow-up question. Rella saved me the trouble.

"He was a child molester. They don't always do well in prison." She held up a hand, palm out. "And no, he didn't molest me. He didn't get the chance."

"Rella, you don't have to tell me your story if you're not comfortable."

"I don't mind. It's pretty straightforward. My mother entered me in a Miss Teen pageant when I was thirteen. The prize was a thousand dollars. She was sure I would win, because I was constantly compared to a Barbie Doll. It was awful. All I wanted to do was play sports, but she refused to let me because I might get hit in the face with a ball or develop muscles in the wrong places." Rella's lips twisted. "She wanted me beautiful and perfect."

"Most thirteen-year-olds would love to be pretty and perfect," I said.

"Not if it meant being snatched by a pervert." She grimaced at the memory.

"You were kidnapped?"

"Attempted," Rella said. "He came backstage after the other girls and I had paraded around doing our lame imitations of real beauty contestants. I thought he was one of the girls' fathers, so I paid no attention to him until he started talking to me."

"Were you afraid of him?"

"No, I thought he was nice, at first. He asked me if I liked the beauty contest and I told him I hated it. He acted sympathetic, asked me what I would rather be doing. I said playing softball."

"Where was your mother while this was going on?"

"Out in the audience watching my opponents perform. I told the nice man I had to get changed for my talent act. He wished me luck and I went into the dressing room. By then, the other girls were all changed and I was in there alone. I got into my drum majorette costume and started warming up with my baton."

"You had to twirl?" I almost laughed. "That's the last thing I would have guessed."

Rella's mouth twisted. "Last thing my pervert guessed, too. He came into the dressing room intent on overpowering me and sneaking me out the backstage exit. He didn't expect me to have a weapon in my hands."

"The baton?"

"That's right. I managed to land half a dozen good blows, all the while screaming at the top of my lungs. By the time the police arrived, my attacker had been restrained by the stage manager and some of the backstage crew. We found out later that he was a repeat offender who had tried the same thing at other beauty pageants."

"You were only thirteen. I'm impressed."

"I was tall and strong for my age, and I was so angry about being forced to compete in the pageant that I spent all my pent-up rage whaling on the creep."

"I have to ask. Did you win the contest?"

Rella laughed. "No, I refused to finish the show, and I didn't wear a dress again for five years."

"How did you feel when you heard he'd died in prison?"

Rella looked off into the distance for a moment. "That was quite a while ago, but I remember thinking he changed the course of my life. I learned that it isn't only good people and good experiences that affect our lives for the better. The bad ones can also bring clarity and help us focus on who we are and what we want out of life."

"Thanks for telling me your story," I said. "It helps."

"You're welcome." Rella picked up her fork. "Thanks for the pie."

WHEN I ARRIVED AT HOME MONDAY EVENING, I found a message from Prairie Valley Prison. The landline answering machine confirmed that I would receive a call from inmate Ora Mercer between the hours of five and ten p.m. on Tuesday. I let that sink in. A part of me had expected him to refuse—maybe wanted him to refuse. I did not look forward to a personal telephone conversation with a man who had terrorized me in my own home, but Maybelline's strange comment had rekindled my interest. I wanted to know why she had urged me to pursue the "truth" about the Delta Dearborn Sawyer she imagined was still alive.

I ate a gourmet feast of PBJ and chicken noodle soup while I made notes to help me get the most from my five minutes with Orrie Mercer on Tuesday evening. First, I would ask him what he knew about Sammy Sawyer's death. I doubted he would come up with anything new, but it was worth a shot. The missing part was why blame Bonnie? There were lots of kids at the home where that after party was held.

If Bonnie was guiltless, she must have tried to defend herself, but how would she prove her innocence unless she knew the truth? And if she knew who was to blame, why not come forward? Bonnie and both of her parents were deceased, so if there *was* a different story, the truth had likely died with them.

Back when Maybelline had been my volunteer, she and Orrie Mercer had dated for a time. Maybelline told me back then that Orrie Mercer and Bonnie's mother were siblings. Bonnie must have told her mother some version of the events surrounding the swim meet and Sammy's overdose back when it happened. The question was whether Orrie had been around to hear that account.

The other topic to run by Orrie was the strange outburst by Maybelline in the prison waiting room. Did Orrie know why Maybelline was convinced Delta Dearborn Sawyer was incarcerated for some heinous crime? She called Delta a *villain*. and urged me to ask Orrie. What could Orrie possibly know about Delta? It made no sense.

I hoped Dr. Beardsley would stop by the library to explain his sister's puzzling comments. If he did, I wouldn't have to waste time asking Mercer about them.

LATER, SETTLED IN BED ALONE AGAIN and missing Nick, I turned on the TV for the last airing of the local news. Oriana Wynn was on camera, and her topic was the ongoing Delta Sawyer investigation with pointed remarks about no news from the police. She ran the brief video scene outside the memorial at the Sawyer Foundation. A close-up focused on Fletcher Tremont's face as he threatened to call the police and began counting to ten. The video ended abruptly, and I laughed, recalling the cameraman hot-footing it to their van with Wynn chasing him and calling him a little worm. Too bad that wasn't caught on tape.

Wynn progressed to other stories and I turned off the set. Burrowed under my blankets and still using Nick's T-shirt as my pajama top, I was drifting off when my cell rang. *Nick.*

We had said good night an hour earlier. I answered by asking what was wrong.

"An FYI, but nothing for you to worry about."

"Then why call so late?"

"Maybe an excuse to hear your voice again."

"I like that answer, but what's the FYI?"

"It's about Fletcher Tremont's wife. She's been admitted to TMC. It seemed like something you'd want to know. I know you get a list of admissions every morning, and I guessed you'd see her name and wonder about it."

"Good guess. Why's she being admitted?"

"She had a fall at home," Nick said. "Apparently, one of the complications of her illness is problems with balance."

"How did you hear about her admission?"

"Her husband called Buck. They were supposed to get together in the next day or so to talk about the foundation's grant program. Tremont wanted to postpone until his wife is stabilized."

"I don't blame him, Nick. Multiple sclerosis is sounding more and more likely. He's probably been dealing with her symptoms for a long time."

"You made a good guess about that. I mentioned what you suspected to Buck, and he said he thought the same thing. One of his aunts had it, so he recognized the signs."

"Did he ask Tremont about it?"

"No. He said it wasn't his place to bring it up."

"Good for him. Health information is protected by law. Buck's wise to respect that, particularly as an employer."

"He's thinking Faye's injury might prompt Tremont to confide in him about her illness. If that happens, he can look into potential means of offering help."

"I hope so. If Faye has the primary progressive form of MS, it can come with a lot of out-of-pocket expenses over the lifetime of the illness."

"How long does a patient live with that diagnosis?" Nick asked.

"It varies depending on the severity of the case and the age of the patient when the diagnosis was made, but I've seen estimates up to twenty-five years."

"Where do you come up with these statistics?"

"Um, you realize I work in a health sciences library? We subscribe to all of the current medical journals. Here's another statistic I read recently. More than sixty percent of personal bankruptcies in our country are due to medical costs. Especially with a long-term illness."

Nick blew a soft whistle. "That's shocking, but I'm sure Fletcher Tremont is earning a decent salary working for the foundation. And Buck provides health benefits to all of his employees. I imagine the Tremonts are covered, no matter what they're dealing with."

I thanked Nick for the heads-up and said we should try to get some sleep.

"Wish I were there with you," he said.

"So do I."

I almost confessed that I was sleeping in his T-shirt every night.

Chapter 23

TUESDAY MORNING IN THE LIBRARY I spotted Faye Tremont's name on the admissions list. She was in the Orthopedic Wing, which suggested she had suffered either a break or a sprain. I set my curiosity about her diagnosis aside. The Tremonts had a right to their privacy and I had enough on my mind.

Dr. Beardsley had indicated he would stop by the library sometime in the morning to follow up on our chance meeting at the prison. I looked forward to his explanation about Maybelline's appearance at the parole hearing. Considering her mental decline, I wondered how the parole board could take her statement seriously.

Bernie Kluckert arrived promptly at nine o'clock as he did every Tuesday and Thursday morning. After his usual good-natured greeting, he headed for the break room to fill his new watering can. He reappeared a few minutes later, setting the canister carefully on his work cart and rolling it to a stop at my desk.

"Mind if we talk a bit, Miss Aimee? I've got myself a puzzle."

"Not at all, Bernie. Is it something about your move?"

"No, but since you ask, we're still headed in that direction. Working out the details." He rubbed an index finger along the side of his nose. "This is about something different. You might recall me telling you I saw Mr. Sawyer in the hospital back when his wife passed."

"I do recall. It was nice of you to be concerned about him."

Bernie cleared his throat. "That's the thing, you see, it wasn't Mr. Sawyer after all."

That took a moment to process. "I don't understand."

"I don't want to get anyone in trouble, but you said Lola and I could come to you if we had concerns. That being the case 'til a new PR Officer starts work."

"That's right. And by the way, has there been any word about when that will happen?"

"Soon, is what they're telling us, but nothing definite."

"Until then I'm still authorized to help you if there's a problem. Why are you concerned about the mix-up over this man you thought was Mr. Sawyer?"

"Because I almost gave him Mrs. Sawyer's purse."

The purse. An electric shock set my nerves tingling. *The pills.* "Bernie, please take a seat and explain what you mean—very carefully."

"I see by your face I did wrong, didn't I?"

"Not at all, but this could be important. Tell me about the purse, and why you thought the man was Delta Sawyer's husband."

"He brought her to the hospital. Seemed logical. The nurse thought so, too."

I was more confused than ever. "Bernie, I happen to know that it *was* Mr. Sawyer who brought his wife in when she was dying. And he did take her purse home. It's been more than a week since she died. Are you sure you're not confused?"

"I don't believe so. I'm not talking about when she died, don't you see? I'm talking about the Saturday afternoon when she came to have her face perked up."

"That's the day you saw the other man and tried to give him her purse?"

"Now you got it. I was working floater that afternoon, running errands and such. The man who brought her in was hanging around 'cause there was a flap over her being late. They told him to wait, that she might not get her face done, and she'd need a ride home."

That reminded me of the story I had heard from Cleo. "Bernie, when did you realize it wasn't Buck Sawyer who was waiting for Delta that day?"

"I happened to see that feisty woman reporter on TV the other night telling how she got chased off the day of Mrs. Sawyer's memorial. She showed a picture of Mr. Sawyer. 'Til then, I didn't know what he looked like. Some billionaires kinda keep themselves private, don't you know?"

"Yes, Mr. Sawyer definitely guards his privacy. Or he did, until now."

"Soon's I saw the photo, I knew right away the man I met up with in the hospital waiting room wasn't Mr. Sawyer."

"Now I understand. Buck Sawyer was out of town that day. His wife evidently arranged for someone else to give her a ride here. That must have been the man you saw."

"There you go," Bernie said. "I slipped up trying to give that other fella her purse."

"Why did you have her purse?"

"I told you about her being late for her outpatient appointment. Well, they finally decided to go ahead, her being a hometown bigwig and all. They put her in a private room. That's when the nurse who was to get her ready called for a volunteer." Bernie pointed at his chest. "I got the job. When I got there, that poor nurse was kinda flustered 'cause the patient was throwing a hissy fit about how long she would have to wait." He paused, clearing his throat. "Sorry to speak ill of the dead." His words echoed Nick's earlier comment.

"Go on, what happened next?"

"That's when the nurse told me the husband was still waiting to find out if his wife was going to get her wrinkle shots."

"So the man she *assumed* was the husband was waiting, thinking they still might cancel and send her home?"

"That's how it was." Bernie swiped a knobby hand across his brow. "Anyhow, Mrs. Sawyer got settled and kinda groggy with whatever they use to calm folks down. That's when the nurse asked me to give the purse to the husband to take home 'cause his wife would be stayin' in the hospital overnight."

"How did she identify the man as Delta's husband?"

"She peeked out across the hall. Pointed into the waiting room."

"Pointed at the man she thought was the husband?"

"Yep. He was the only one there. That was good enough for me," Bernie said, "but I shoulda been more careful and looked for his name on the visitor ID tag, don't you see?"

"Why didn't you?"

"Truth to tell, I don't think he was wearing one."

"Bernie, if the nurse pointed him out, I don't think you're to blame. Besides, you said you *almost* gave him the purse. What happened next?"

"I told him Mrs. Sawyer was being admitted and he should take her purse home, but he didn't want anything to do with it. Didn't touch it."

"Why not?"

"He didn't say. Once he heard Mrs. Sawyer was gonna stay, he up and left."

"Did he tell you his name?"

"Nope, and I didn't see a reason to ask. I thought he was Mr. Sawyer."

"What did you do after he left?"

"Took the handbag back to the nurse. Told her the husband didn't take it. Told her he vamoosed soon's he knew the Sawyer woman was gonna get her way."

"And what did the nurse do then?"

"She dismissed me," he said. "Told me she'd call Security to come get the purse and put it in their safe."

"Then it sounds like you have nothing to worry about."

"What about my fingerprints?"

With that, I flashed back on Maybelline's irrational rambling and began to wonder if Bernie might be suffering from a bit of dementia himself.

"Why are you worried about fingerprints?"

Bernie looked down at his shoes, then up at me. "It's got to do with loose lips. Right from the get-go, the skinny among our volunteer troops was Mrs. Sawyer died from taking the wrong pills. I'm worried the police might think someone monkeyed with them—if they were in her purse when she came in for her appointment that afternoon."

"You're worried someone will think you tampered with her pills?"

"My fingerprints are on there, don't you see? I should have been smart like the fella that brought her in. He knew not to touch someone else's belongings."

"Bernie, I'm certain you will not be in trouble about this. Will it reassure you if I write up an incident report and submit it? That's the best way to prove your good intentions."

His face lit up. "Would you, Miss Machado? That would be a relief."

"Then it's done. I have one more question that might help. Could you describe the man who wouldn't take the purse?" I thought the unknown man should be interviewed by the police. He was a potential witness who might remember if anyone had access to Delta's purse during the campaign event. He was also a potential suspect.

Bernie frowned. "You know, my eyes aren't the best, and neither is my memory. Like you said, that was over a week ago."

"Whatever you can remember. Was he young? Old? Short or tall? Bald? That sort of thing."

"He was kinda average in every way, far as I can recall."

Bernie's description of the incident set my antennae vibrating. There had to be a way to identify the man who drove Delta, but I did not want to start asking around and draw attention to myself. There was another way—my cousin Hannah, the forensic artist. I explained to Bernie how she could help him create a picture of the man he had seen, and that identifying him might help the police. He was intrigued with the idea.

"You think that fella was up to something shifty?"

"Not necessarily, but he may have witnessed something at the candidates' event that day without realizing its importance. If he can be identified, the police might want to interview him."

"By golly, that's a smart idea." Bernie's chest puffed out with pride. "I'll do what I can. You got my number. Give me a shout when you want to set it up with your artist."

"Thank you, Bernie. And I'd like to wait until we have the sketch before I submit the incident report. For now, I think it's best if we keep this to ourselves."

"Gotcha," he said with a twinkle. "Loose lips."

While Bernie went about his chores, I recalled that on the day Delta died, Quinn had delivered a mixed message. He warned me not to pass on to Nick or Buck anything to do with Delta Sawyer's death that would implicate the hospital or Vane Beardsley. But he also implied that I might come across something that would benefit the hospital's standing in Delta's case.

I had balked at the idea of passing along any information I picked up from Nick or Buck, but Bernie's revelation was not a case of divided loyalties for me. It was a case of mistaken identity that did not directly involve Buck Sawyer.

I wondered what reaction my report of Bernie's story would provoke in Quinn. Bottom line, he had authorized me to hear any problems my volunteers might encounter. This incident certainly qualified. Besides, Bernie's incident was likely to be nothing more than a simple misunderstanding by Delta's nurse. She thought the man who brought Delta to the hospital was her husband, but no harm was done, because the unidentified man did the right thing in refusing to take the purse.

There was a chance the nurse involved in the incident had already written up her own report. In that case, mine would be redundant, but at least it would satisfy my promise to Bernie. And there was an even better chance that the nurse saw no reason to report the misunderstanding. She had done the right thing by having Security take the purse. *End of story.*

Bernie spent the morning making his rounds with the plant cart and wielding his carpet sweeper throughout every exposed inch of the library's floor. He had just finished dusting the bookshelves at noon when Dr. Vane Beardsley entered the library.

As Beardsley strode to my desk, I faced a looming deadline.

I had decided to wait over the weekend to see if TPD would announce any progress in their investigation. If not, I had planned to contact Walter Kass with everything I knew about Wright and Nester's secrets, Beardsley's donation to Delta's campaign, and Buck's visit to the attorneys in San Francisco. Monday had been out of the question because of my trip to the prison. With Tuesday morning come and gone, and no progress reported by the police, I could not drag my feet any longer.

"Miss Machado, I hope I'm not too late," Beardsley said. "Are you about to break for lunch?"

"I can take lunch a little later if this is a good time to talk."

"I appreciate that. I would have been here sooner, but I've had a somewhat trying morning with my sister. I have an attendant with her now, but I will need to get home soon. I'm driving her back to her care facility this afternoon."

I told Bernie he could leave a few minutes early and asked him to put up the *closed* sign on his way out. He nodded, signaled for me to call him, and went on his way.

Dr. Beardsley caught Bernie's signal, and looked at me, obviously curious.

"It's a private matter," I said. I was not about to bring up anything to do with Delta's purse or her pills while Beardsley was on my scant suspect list. I invited him to sit with me at one of the tables provided for patrons.

"Would you like coffee?" I asked.

"No, thank you. I'm well caffeinated." He drummed his fingers on the tabletop. "I suppose we should get to the reason for my visit. You must be aware of my sister's deteriorating mental state."

"I did notice a decline. She seemed confused at the prison yesterday."

"You're probably wondering why I chose to take her to the hearing," Beardsley said.

"It did surprise me. Although I thought it was appropriate for *you* to be there since Mr. Mercer was indirectly involved in your wife's death and with the disposal of her body."

"A sordid situation." He grimaced, took a second to shake off the recollection. "And yes, I did have the opportunity to give a statement. I assume that's why you were there."

"Yes, but I don't think I tipped the scales in either direction. Did Maybelline speak at the hearing yesterday?"

Beardsley nodded. "Only because I contacted the prison ahead of time, explaining her mental deterioration. I told them she had received the invitation, and in her confused state, she believed it was her duty. She insisted that she would face imprisonment if she didn't appear in person. It seemed easier to go through the motions that to try to talk her out of it."

"Is that why you stopped by? To explain why Maybelline was at the hearing?"

"Not quite, I'm afraid." Beardsley glanced at his watch. "I should go and let you have your lunch, but before I do there's something I'd like to discuss with you. I would consider it a favor."

"All right, if I can help."

"I've been troubled since you told me that my contribution was public information. I realize there are people who might be curious about the amount."

Like me.

"Most people never look into that sort of thing," I said.

"Not in a normal situation, but this is different, what with her death and the mysterious circumstances. I'm aware the police are investigating." Beardsley shifted in his chair. "I want to explain my situation to you, since you know the Sawyers through your friend, Mr. Alexander."

"Dr. Beardsley, ordinarily I would say your donation is your business, but I agree with you that in this case, that might not be true."

"Then I hope you'll bear with me until I've finished." He cleared his throat and began. "Delta Sawyer came to my office for a pre-surgery visit the Friday before her death. She wanted a prescription for oxycodone, which I refused to write. I told her acetaminophen would handle her pain, and that she should purchase it over the counter."

I didn't tell him I had already heard this story. "Dr. Beardsley, you don't have to—"

He held up a hand. "A moment longer, please."

"I'm sorry, go ahead." He was determined to elaborate, which deepened my curiosity.

"After I refused to write the prescription, Mrs. Sawyer began a dialogue about how strange it was that our two lives were intertwined." Beardsley traced a whorl in the table top with his index finger before looking up at me. "I asked what she meant, and she said that my late wife, Bonnie, had killed her husband's daughter."

Chapter 24

"**G**OOD HEAVENS," I BLURTED, "what a horrible thing for her to say to you."

"I admit it was quite a shock." Beardsley exhaled a long breath, appearing reluctant to continue. He finally spoke. "I'll understand if you think this is implausible, but I took it as a form of extortion. She said she knew the true story of Sammy Sawyer's death those years ago. Knew that Bonnie was to blame."

"A rumor did surface that both Bonnie and Sammy had used meth at a party the night Sammy died. I believe Buck has been aware of it for quite some time, but it was never proved that Bonnie was the source of the drug or that she had convinced Sammy to try it."

"I was aware of the rumor. Bonnie had told me about how the Sawyer girl collapsed and died the night of that swim meet. She swore she had no part in supplying the meth."

"Then I don't see how Delta was using this to threaten you." And why was he telling me? So far, his story was lifting him higher on my suspect list.

Beardsley straightened his shoulders. "Are you aware that

TMC's governing board appointed me president of the Timbergate Medical Center Foundation when I came back to town?"

"I am, but I only heard of it recently. I was told it hasn't been made public."

"That's so. Quinn had planned to make it known on the very day that Delta died," Beardsley said. "For obvious reasons, he decided to postpone the announcement."

"I understand that, but I'm not clear how this relates to Sammy Sawyer's fatal overdose."

"I hope to explain. On my return to Timbergate I began meeting with Buck Sawyer about a drug rehab facility we hoped to establish here in Timbergate. There was every reason to believe it would be co-sponsored by our own Timbergate Medical Center Foundation and the Sawyer Foundation."

I pretended ignorance about the planned facility, since Cleo had told me in confidence.

"That's a wonderful idea. It's something the North State desperately needs, and Timbergate would be an ideal location. The number of overdoses turning up in the Emergency Department these days is staggering."

"I'm well aware. That's why I approached Mr. Sawyer when I moved back, and even before. We had talked several times, working out many of the fundamental details, including the name: *Firm Foundations Renewal Center*."

Renewal. The very thing that resulted in Delta Sawyer's death: her desire for a newer, younger image. I swept that thought aside.

"I like the name. Two foundations coming together to offer new life to addicted patients. I can hardly wait for it to open its doors."

Beardsley held up a hand. "Unfortunately, there's more to my story. Delta Sawyer threatened to sabotage the project unless I gave her the prescription she wanted. She told me she could either prove to her husband beyond a doubt that Bonnie had provided the meth that caused Sammy Sawyer's death, or she could prove the opposite. It was my choice."

"I see where this is going. Either you provide her with the oxy prescription, or Delta proves to Buck that it was your late wife, Bonnie, who caused his daughter's death."

Beardsley nodded. "The message was clear. She would see to it Buck would want nothing to do with co-sponsoring the rehab center."

"What did you do?"

"I offered an alternative that wouldn't jeopardize my medical license or the drug rehab project."

"Your campaign donation?"

"Yes. And she agreed. Apparently her campaign war chest meant more to her than a prescription for a couple dozen oxycodone tablets."

"Sounds like you found a good solution, but if you don't mind telling me, was the amount your idea or hers?"

Beardsley's face reddened. "It was hers, and it was more than a suggestion."

"You were being extorted and you knew it."

"It was obvious, but I gave in and wrote her a check for fifty thousand dollars. It did leave me puzzled, though."

"How so?"

"I still don't understand why she extorted money from me when her husband could easily have financed any amount her campaign required."

"Did you ask her?" I suspected I knew the answer. Buck's marriage was already in trouble. He must have cut off Delta's campaign cash flow.

"I felt questioning her would make matters worse." Beardsley leaned in. "Now I'm afraid there's more to this story, and it involves Maybelline."

"How much more? I need to open the library in a few minutes."

"Then I'll make this as brief as possible. You must be curious about Maybelline's reference yesterday to Delta Sawyer being a villain."

"Yes. In the prison waiting room. Her demand that I ask Orrie."

Beardsley hurriedly explained that on their drive back to Timbergate, he had managed to glean what Maybelline meant.

"She insisted that Delta was in prison, and that the crime she committed was providing the meth at the swim meet that had killed Sammy Sawyer."

My breath caught for a moment. "She thinks *Delta* was to blame?"

"Maybelline insisted that when Bonnie got home from the meet, she told her parents Delta had given Sammy something she called special vitamin pills just before the final swim event."

"How could Maybelline possibly know about that?"

"You heard her at the prison. She said to ask Orrie. I have to assume Orrie Mercer, who was living with the Belchers at the time, must have overheard Bonnie's story and passed it on to Maybelline when they were spending time together," Beardsley winced. "I suppose you could call it dating."

"I remember when she and Orrie were seeing each other, but this doesn't prove the pills Delta provided at the swim meet were meth. It's fairly likely the pills Delta gave Sammy really were vitamins, and the meth was being circulated at the party."

"That's what I tried to get through to Maybelline yesterday," Beardsley said. "She became quite agitated and repeated over and over that you must ask Orrie for the truth about Delta."

I had every intention of doing that during our phone call. I wanted to hear Orrie's version of Maybelline's story, but I had another question for Beardsley.

"I don't understand why Maybelline would connect me with Delta Sawyer. Is it because she knows I'm in a relationship with one of Buck Sawyer's pilots?"

"No, even simpler. The television news about Mrs. Sawyer has aired in the facility where she is living. She saw a woman news reporter trying to get you make a statement about Delta's death and the investigation. In Maybelline's confused mind, you became the person who should bring Delta to justice."

"Dr. Beardsley, you know your sister. Give me your honest opinion. Are you saying you believe Maybelline? That it was Delta who caused the death of Buck's young daughter and then tried to blame it on your late wife, Bonnie?"

"I admit I'm mired in doubt and intent on learning the truth, but we have only two very unreliable witnesses, neither of whom was present at the swim meet or at the after party."

"Your sister, whose mental state is deteriorating, and Orrie Mercer, who is behind bars. Both are biased in Bonnie's favor: her sister-in-law and her uncle."

"You realize," Beardsley said, "that if Buck Sawyer had recently come to believe his second wife was responsible for his daughter's death those years ago, it would have given him an obvious motive to harm Delta. Think how he would feel, knowing he was married to the woman who had caused the loss of his daughter and perhaps hastened the death of his first wife."

"But we have no corroboration, so the whole story is open to question."

Beardsley nodded. "Unless you follow through and ask Orrie Mercer. Maybelline said 'Orrie's got the goods.' We don't know if that was befuddled rambling, or a lucid moment."

He was right that the truth about Sammy's death might prove Buck Sawyer had a motive for murder. If Buck had somehow discovered that Delta *was* responsible, he would be a prime suspect. But Beardsley also had a plausible motive. With her first extortion attempt, Delta came away with a load of cash for her campaign. Her threats and manipulations to get him to supply her with drugs could have become a recurring threat to his medical practice. She would have been a constant pain in his side.

"Dr. Beardsley, Maybelline's portrayal of Delta Sawyer as the villain in this story would remove the blame for Sammy Sawyer's death from your late wife. I understand why you would want to believe your sister, but you must have some doubt, particularly when you're aware of her worsening dementia."

Beardsley's ruddy complexion took on a deeper hue. "Naturally, and I must say I respect your discernment as well as your integrity, but I confess I'm at a loss as to how to corroborate Maybelline's story, what with Mr. Mercer tucked away in prison."

"There is a way to set up a phone call with an inmate. You might try that."

"Heavens no. I couldn't," Beardsley said. "After I testified at his trial, Mercer made it clear that he wants nothing further to do with me."

"That's unfortunate, but I'm afraid I have no other advice." I was not about to disclose *my* pending phone arrangement with Orrie Mercer while Beardsley was so deeply enmeshed in the mystery of Delta Sawyer's death.

We both heard knocking and glanced toward the exit where someone was waiting outside the locked door.

"I should let you get back to your duties," Beardsley said.

"Yes, but before you go, there's something I have to know. Have you told Jared Quinn about your donation to Delta's campaign?"

Beardsley's color intensified. "I've told no one except you. Why do you ask?"

"The police may know about it and wonder why you haven't come forward before now."

"Ah, I should have grasped that back when you told me it was public record."

"I believe it would be in your best interest, and the hospital's, if you were to tell Mr. Quinn and let him follow up with the police investigators. You should have the opportunity to explain."

Beardsley dabbed at his forehead with a handkerchief. "But doing that now will make me look as if I had something to hide, won't it? If I divulge what I've told you?"

"Possibly, but at this point, I think you have to trust Mr. Quinn."

"If I do tell him about the donation, but without revealing my reasons . . . the extortion . . . can I count on you to keep my confidence?"

"I'm afraid I can't promise that."

"Very well." He rose from his chair. "Then I'll do what I must."

I should have been reassured, but his last words had the opposite effect.

Chapter 25

Beardsley's extortion story derailed my plan to contact Walter Kass—so much so that I left work an hour early Tuesday afternoon. I wanted to finish the ranch chores well before Orrie Mercer's call, which could come any time between five and ten o'clock. Waiting kept me housebound and within hearing distance of Jack and Amah's landline phone.

If Orrie Mercer confirmed that Delta had been the cause of Sammy Sawyer's death, I would have to rethink everything I had ever believed about Buck Sawyer's character.

From there, my thoughts circled back to my talk with Vane Beardsley. When I said I could not keep his confidence about Delta's extortion threat, he had ended our conversation by saying, "I'll do what I must."

The best interpretation of that comment was that he would come clean with Quinn about the donation, including the extortion behind it. The worst interpretation caused a visceral reaction. If Beardsley *was* involved in the mystery of Delta's switched pills, I had become a significant threat to him. I did my best to shake off that notion while I waited for Mercer's call.

On top of that, there was still a chance that Bernie Kluckert's mystery man might become a viable suspect. That could take some of TPD's focus off Buck and Beardsley. I texted Hannah asking if she could make time to do a forensic sketch the next day. I told her I would be unavailable by phone until later but would explain the details as soon as possible.

By eight o'clock I began to doubt Mercer would follow through. Knowing I probably had only five minutes on the phone with him, I kept my list of questions short. I revised it several times until it was as concise as possible.

1. *Do you know first-hand if your niece, Bonnie Belcher, persuaded Sammy Sawyer to use meth at the after party the night she died?*

2. *Did Bonnie ever mention that her trainer, Delta Dearborn, gave Sammy some kind of pills at the swim meet?*

That was as much as I would have time for, and only if Orrie gave me short answers. If our conversation proved beyond a doubt that Delta *was* to blame, there was always a chance that Buck had somehow learned the truth. That would help to explain why he was secretly planning a separation. It would also explain why he might have resorted to a different option.

In spite of the divided loyalties problem, my involvement in the entangled fates of Bonnie Beardsley and both Sammy and Delta Sawyer kept deepening. I opened the contact list in my cell and looked again at Detective Kass's private number.

But first I needed to hear what Orrie Mercer had to say. Depending on his answers, I might have a legitimate reason to contact Kass with information the TPD needed to know. There was Buck, whose daughter may have been poisoned with meth provided by Delta, and there was Beardsley, a victim of Delta's extortion. And I was still uncertain whether Beardsley posed a threat to my own safety.

It pained me to know that if I did make that call to Kass, it would direct more suspicion toward both Buck and Beardsley, two people I hoped were innocent. But it helped that I would also be telling Kass about another promising suspect—the unknown man who shied away from touching Delta's purse at the hospital. I would even offer a copy of Hannah's sketch.

Waiting for the landline phone to ring was excruciating: eight-thirty, then nine o'clock. Fanny stalked into the living room where I sat next to the telephone table staring at a hospital drama on TV that got at least half of its facts right. The relentless cat issued one of her more annoying versions of a meow—more like *feeeedmeeenow!*

I had just gone into the kitchen and opened a new can of kitty salmon when the phone finally rang. As I rushed into the living room, the cat food can slipped from my hand and splattered on the floor. In my stocking feet, I stepped on the mess, nearly slipped and lost my balance, but managed to get to the landline phone before it stopped ringing.

"Hello, I'm here," I gasped. "Is this Mr. Mercer?"

"Yeah. You okay? You sound kinda funny."

I glanced at the cat food smeared across the family room carpet and Fanny doing her best to lick it up. "I'm fine. Hurried to pick up. Thanks for calling."

"Welcome. You did me some good yesterday, being real fair in your statement. Figured I'd return the favor if there's something you need."

"There is. I hope you can help."

"Then we better get to it. A lot of guys are waiting for a turn at the phone."

"All right. I'm trying to confirm something Maybelline Black told her brother yesterday. She said you could verify her story about Sammy Sawyer's death."

"Whoa, you know that woman's a mental case, don't you?"

"Yes. She has dementia, but I have another source who is sound of mind, and he has already told me part of the same story. I'm hoping you can fill in the rest."

"Then shoot," Orrie said. "We've already lost a minute."

"Maybelline insists it was Delta Sawyer, back when she was still Delta Dearborn, who provided the meth that killed Sammy Sawyer the day of the swim meet. She said to ask you."

"Why me?"

"She said 'Orrie's got the goods.'"

Orrie let out a four-letter expletive short for excrement. "Sorry to disappoint, but I don't know anything about where that little gal got the drugs. Maybelline musta been talking about the other Orrie. She's the one who was there at the meet."

"What? I don't understand. What other Orrie is there?"

"The girl on the swim team back then. She and Bonnie and Sammy were all pals. They used to hang out together at my sister's place back when I was living there."

"There was a *girl* named Orrie?" My brain lurched along, trying to catch up.

"Not exactly, but Bonnie and Sammy thought it was a big hoot to give that girl my same nickname. Don't recall ever hearing her real name. Must of started with an *O*. They called us Orrie One and Orrie Too. Get it?" He spelled it out: "Orrie T-O-O."

"How did Maybelline know about this other girl? The one they called Orrie Too?"

"Don't recall, but you know what a nosy parker Maybelline is. I do remember telling her how Bonnie got blamed for getting Sammy hooked on drugs. My sister and her husband never did know how that rumor started. They figured it was all a big lie made up by the swim team folks to cover their you-know-what."

"Did you believe that?"

"Why not? Those girls went out of town all excited about that swim meet and one of them came home dead. The police down in that city where it happened claimed they investigated, but no one got arrested or charged with anything. The case was closed. Like it was kids being kids at that party, and that little Sawyer girl paid the price."

"Do you think Maybelline took it upon herself to do some further investigating? That she found someone who knew what really happened?"

"Wouldn't surprise me. She's as snoopy as they come. Always liked any kind of gossip." I heard him murmur something. "Look,

I gotta go. You want to know what Maybelline was talking about, find that other Orrie. Maybe she really does have the goods on Delta."

The line went dead.

Chapter 26

I SAT STARING AT THE FISHY-SMELLING CAT food stains on the carpet while Fanny narrowed her disapproving yellow headlight eyes at me. Who in the world was Orrie Too? Was anyone around who would still remember her? Bonnie and her parents were gone, Maybelline was mentally challenged. And Buck was the last person I wanted to ask.

Mercer said the girl was on the swim team. Harry had worked as a lifeguard back then. He was my best bet to identify the mystery girl, and it was not too late to text him.

I stopped myself. If I asked for Harry's help, he would know I was about to delve deeper into the Delta Sawyer mystery. He had expressed concern about that when he agreed to research Ernest Wright and Nora Nester.

There had to be another way to identify Orrie Too. If Maybelline did it, so could I, but that had to wait until morning, along with my call to Kass. It was getting late, and I had more pressing business.

I checked my cell to see if Hannah had responded to my text about doing a forensic sketch of the mystery man Bernie had mistaken for Delta's husband. Hannah had replied, asking if I could arrange for her to do it the next morning at the TMC Library.

After calls to both Bernie and Hannah, it was arranged for nine thirty in the library break room, which was designated for employees only, meaning Lola, Bernie, and me. I could easily set it up so that no one would notice the sketch session.

WEDNESDAY MORNING I GEARED UP to embark on a probable wild goose chase thanks to Maybelline Black, who lived in a mind confused by dementia. Following her hazy lead, I had to track down a woman who was once a teenaged girl nicknamed Orrie Too.

A brief, sweet wake-up call from Nick helped me adjust my attitude and start the day in reasonably good spirits. We agreed to find a time to get together after I got off work.

The weatherman on the morning news promised a clear, dry day with a high of seventy-one degrees. I gave spring a nod with black slacks, an ivory shell and my favorite little blazer jacket decorated with bright pastel flowers.

I started coffee in the break room as soon as I reached the library. While it brewed, I moved the small table and chairs into a corner to make room for Hannah's easel. To give them privacy, I blocked the window in the top half of the door with an oversized poster of the skeletal system. By the time I finished, the coffee was ready. I filled my cup and went to my desk, where my email messages were mostly requests for online journal articles from members of our forensic consortium.

Alone in the quiet space, I recalled my prison phone conversation of the night before with Orrie Mercer. If the girl nicknamed Orrie Too did exist, there had to be a way to find her. It surprised me how few names I could think of that would fit. The only women's names starting with O that came to mind were Olivia, Opal and Oprah.

On a whim, I went to a website for baby girl names. I narrowed the search to *female names beginning with O*. A page popped up with four columns, forty-five names in each. I scanned alphabetically, looking for any name beginning with *Or*, and there, listed between *Orein* and *Oriane*, I found *Oriana*.

The room tilted out of balance for a moment. I steadied myself and did a double-take. Was it possible I had been searching for Oriana Wynn, the relentless reporter, or was it some kind of freaky coincidence?

Perplexed, I closed the page. The chance that my nemesis, Oriana Wynn, could hold the key to Sammy Sawyer's death seemed incredibly remote, but her name was uncommon enough that the need to know took over instantly. Maybe that was the reason she was so determined to delve into the circumstances of Delta Sawyer's death. Her age was in the ballpark. Was it personal for her?

I searched the local TV station's website for the page listing bios of their news reporters hoping to find some reference to their hometowns or at least a general statement about where they were from. Oriana Wynn's education and work credits were substantial, including a degree in broadcast journalism from Columbia University in New York City, fluency in the French language, and a stint as an intern at a Paris radio station. Her bio limited her birthplace to a vague reference describing her as a "California native." There was no mention of early participation in competitive sports such as swimming.

If she had been on the swim team with the other girls, Harry might remember her. So much for keeping him in the dark about my probing. I had to ask him, but it would have to wait.

Bernie Kluckert and my cousin Hannah came through the library's entrance door a few minutes before nine. Bernie, always the gentleman, was carrying her art supply case.

"Met this young lady in the parking lot," he said. "This satchel is kind of bulky for a delicate woman to haul around, don't you know?"

Hannah, a slender blonde who appeared delicate at first glance, but spent most of her recreation time rock climbing, smiled and winked at me from behind Bernie's back. I ushered them into the break room, taking a moment to explain to Bernie that anything he could recall would be helpful.

Bernie frowned, tugged on his earlobe. "Not sure how much I noticed."

"I can help you a bit with that," Hannah said.

Bernie beamed at her. "Then I'll do my darndest."

I stepped out, telling Hannah to lock the door and make sure the poster blocked the window. By that time Lola had arrived to begin her nine-to-noon volunteer shift. She and Bernie had decided on separate cars, since they had no idea what time Hannah would finish the sketch. Lola gave me her usual cheerful greeting but could not resist a glance toward the break room door. Obviously, Bernie had told her about his mission. She used her thumb and forefinger to make a zipping motion across her tightly closed mouth.

"Would you like to start with a bit of filing?" I asked.

"Whatever you need, Miss Machado, but first, I want you to know that Bernie and I appreciate all you've done for us, with your advice about our move."

"I'm glad if I helped, Lola, but your decision should be based on your financial advisor's advice and what your families think is best for you."

"Yes, we considered all of that and signed the paperwork yesterday. We thought it would be a good day to get the ball rolling. We'll be moving into our new home in one month." Her eyes were bright with excitement, and her velvety cheeks glowed rosy pink.

It was too late for me to calm my doubts about Ernest Wright. With the election one day away, there was only a snowball's chance that Delta Sawyer's killer would be apprehended before a new mayor was chosen. Maybe the guilty party would never be identified and I would spend the next four to eight years wondering if the City of Timbergate was being run by a killer. Meanwhile, there was still the frightening possibility that Buck Sawyer would be arrested again with Nick roped in as an accessory.

While Lola began her chores, I circled back to the puzzle of Oriana Wynn. With the clock ticking, my best choice was to go straight to Harry and deal with his disapproval rather than do a time-consuming online search of Wynn's past. I didn't even know if her surname was a maiden name, or if she was married. I texted him.

Lunch?

Where?

Margie's Bean Pot?

12:30?

See you then

Lola and I kept the library functioning while Bernie and Hannah remained hidden away in the break room until nearly noon. Hannah finally opened the door and motioned to me. Inside the small space, the scent of coffee lingered, but the pot was empty.

"How did it go?" I asked.

Bernie nodded toward Hannah. "This young lady is a dandy artist. Looks like a spittin' image of that fella I saw in the waiting room."

I glanced at the sketch of the mystery man's face and turned to her with an unspoken question. She gave me a barely perceptible shrug. The face could have been a composite of Hugh Jackman and Mister Rogers from the neighborhood.

Hannah and I both thanked Bernie, telling him he had done well. His face flushed with pride, making me hope that something about the sketch would offer a clue. By then it was noon, so both he and Lola left for the day. Hannah stayed behind. We stood staring at the sketch.

"Will it help?" she asked.

"It's pretty generic."

"Okay, but you know enough about composites to realize we weren't going to get a photo-perfect image. Remember, we only have Bernie's recollection to work with. Plus the questions I've been trained to ask."

"I know you combine separate facial elements into a finished image. That's why it's called a composite."

"Then we eliminate anything that wouldn't apply to the subject." Hannah tilted her head, studying the image. "This sketch doesn't look exactly like the man Bernie saw, but it gives us a general resemblance."

"I know you and Bernie did your best, but I was hoping for more specific detail."

"Sorry. No smoking gun. At least you know he wasn't bald."

"Already knew that. And his approximate age. Mid-to-late forties. Bernie told me."

"Now you know his hair was dark-ish, cut traditional length, no glasses, no facial hair, he was Caucasian, and he was wearing a suit and tie."

I studied the face for a moment. "I guess we did get something useful. If this man is the person who switched Delta's pills, we can eliminate Buck, Beardsley and the two other candidates for mayor as suspects."

"Not necessarily. Any one of them could have paid this guy to do their dirty work."

"Seriously? A hit man seems pretty far-fetched."

"Unlikely," Hannah said, "but you never know."

"Well, Bernie did his best, and so did you. Whoever that man was, he hasn't come forward, which may not mean anything sinister. Probably a campaign volunteer who's spooked by the police investigation and reluctant to get involved."

"Believe me, that happens a lot with potential witnesses." Hannah gave me the sketch and began picking up her supplies.

"Thanks, I appreciate your help, and I owe you a huge favor in return."

"Yes, you do." Hannah looked around the library. "And you have a roomful of information here that I would find interesting."

"Then I'll set you up with an account. You can check out materials from our stacks, and you'll have access to our online resources. You qualify because you work as a consultant with TPD, and they're a consortium member. How's that?"

"Excellent," she said, heading for the exit.

I slipped the sketch into a manila envelope and put it away in my desk, wondering if we had captured on paper the man whose arrest would clear both Buck Sawyer and Dr. Beardsley.

As promised, I wrote up a brief incident report explaining that Bernie had been concerned because he was asked to deliver Delta's purse to the man who drove her to the hospital the day of her procedure, which meant his fingerprints were on the purse. I also included that the unknown man did not want to be responsible for the purse and refused to touch it. I decided to hold off mentioning the sketch for the time being—that could be explained later—and

I did not suggest that Bernie should be questioned by the police. That would be up to Quinn. I hit *send* and left the library with minutes to make it to Margie's by twelve thirty.

Harry sat at the far end of the diner with his back to the wall, facing the door. *Always prepared.* He acknowledged me with a lift of his chin. The mouthwatering aromas of Margie's luncheon menu filled the air. The special of the day was Hoppin' John. I stopped at the self-serve counter and filled a bowl with the delicious combo of black-eyed peas, rice, smoked sausage, and Margie's secret seasonings. Harry spoke as soon as I sat down.

"Are we going to agree to disagree?"

"I hope not. This'll be a simple *yes* or *no* on your part. Thanks for coming, by the way."

"Yes or no." Harry stood. "Can I go now?"

"And leave your Hoppin' John behind?"

"No, I'll take it with me. And you're paying."

"Why did you come if you're going to be a pain in the neck?" Harry sat down. "It's my week to watch you."

"That's a pretty stale joke." I took a bite of sausage.

"It's not a joke," he said. "Nick's watching Buck, I'm watching you. Go ahead, ask one of your *yes* or *no* questions."

I glanced around the diner. Everyone seemed engaged in their own conversations, but I lowered my voice anyway, and leaned across the table toward Harry. "Do you remember a girl nicknamed Orrie being on the swim team back when Sammy Sawyer died?"

He leaned back, crossing his arms. "What's this about?"

"You were a lifeguard back then. You must have known most of the local swimmers. If your answer is yes, I'll explain, but not here. Yes or no?"

"Where to?" he asked.

Yes. "Library?"

Harry stood, held out his hand. "Give me a twenty."

I found a ten and a five in my wallet, and some ones crammed in my pocket. "Here you go."

He paid for our food and brought back two take-out cartons. We walked across the street to TMC's library building where I left the *CLOSED* sign facing out. We ate in the break room where I made a long story as short as possible. I explained how Vane Beardsley's sister, Maybelline, was linked to Bonnie Belcher's family by dating Orrie Mercer, who was Bonnie's uncle. I repeated Beardsley's story about how Maybelline insisted that Delta Dearborn Sawyer had given Sammy Sawyer the drug that killed her, and that I must ask Orrie.

"Huh." Harry cocked his head. "The local rumormongers speculated for years that Bonnie Belcher had given Sammy the meth at that party after the swim meet. Eventually the case was either closed or went cold and everyone moved on."

"That's right. Now Orrie Mercer, a prison inmate, insists that Maybelline had been talking about some other Orrie who knows the true story—a girl on the swim team that her friends, Bonnie and Sammy, jokingly called 'Orrie Too.'"

Harry swallowed down the last bite of his lunch. "Are you finished?"

"No, but for now, you *have* to keep this to yourself." I told him Dr. Beardsley's story about Delta extorting a campaign donation of fifty thousand dollars from him by convincing him it was his late wife, Bonnie, who had supplied Sammy Sawyer with the meth that caused her death.

Harry rubbed his cheeks with his palms. "I have a feeling you're still not finished. When do we get to the part about this Orrie Too?"

"So you're saying you at least recall hearing about her back then?"

"It does ring a bell. Kind of an unusual nickname, but I don't recall the girl it applied to."

"Pull out your phone," I said. "Now go to our local TV website and pull up the bios of all the on-air reporters. Look at their head shots." He did, brow furrowed as he progressed. Suddenly he looked up at me, eyebrows raised.

"Huh, I think that's her. I wasn't sure about her actual first name. Last name was Winterbottom. She looks different. Whenever I saw her back then, she was soaking wet."

"Winterbottom? Not Wynn?"

"That's what I remember. She used to get teased about it. Cold bu—"

"I get it. She probably shortened it to Wynn when she became a TV personality. Or Wynn is a married name. Look again," I said. "Are you sure it's the same person?"

Harry's expression turned wary. "If I say yes, what are you going to do?"

"Beardsley said Maybelline insisted I talk to 'Orrie' to confirm that Delta was responsible for Sammy Sawyer's death. If Oriana Wynn knows the truth, and she's willing to tell me about it, we need to get the real story."

"What makes you think she'll talk to you?"

"I wondered that myself, until I thought back to how ruthless she's been in pursuing the story of Delta's death. It's as if she's on a personal crusade about it."

"You think she's looking for the final chapter in a secret she's been keeping for a decade?"

"Wouldn't you be if you were her? Think about it, Harry. If she's the only person still alive who knew it was Delta who gave Sammy the meth pills, she might be thinking it's time to come out with the truth. Buck is a billionaire whose life is devoted to fighting drug trafficking and drug addiction. I think Oriana is hungry for an award-winning story and suspects she has the scoop of a lifetime. What if she can prove Buck discovered it was Delta, his second wife, who caused his daughter's overdose? I wouldn't put it past her to insinuate that Buck took revenge by poisoning Delta in a similar manner."

"Sis, if you're right about this, Wynn is going to guard her secret rather than go to the TPD and let them derail her exclusive."

Good. Harry was hooked. He was indirectly involved back then himself, as a swim team lifeguard. Even though he was not at the ill-fated swim meet or the after party, the urge to know the truth of Sammy Sawyer's death had only increased when he and Nick became friends. Eventually, Buck Sawyer had become like part of our family, with my boyfriend and Harry's girlfriend both working for him. Delta's proximity had to be a constant reminder to both Buck and Harry of Sammy's death the night of the swim meet.

"Harry, I have to talk to her. If Wynn can prove that Buck had a compelling motive for Delta's murder, Nick needs to know. So does Rella."

"I can't argue with that, but don't forget Detective Kass."

"I won't, but first I *have* to talk to Oriana Wynn."

"And that's something you can do with a phone call, so not a lot of risk."

I walked to the exit door with Harry and changed my sign to *OPEN*. Harry was halfway out when he stopped and turned back to me.

"Almost forgot. He pulled a folded sheet of paper from his back pocket. "Nick asked me to give you this list. He's hoping you can check out the nonprofits on it. They're a handful of international organizations that received funds from Buck's foundation and failed to follow up with their mandatory reports."

"That can be a serious red flag. Why is he asking me about it?"

"Don't know. I guess because Buck still has the foundation closed up. No one's back to work yet. He said something about an auditor." Harry nodded at the list in my hand. "I would have given it a shot, but this is right up your alley. I don't have the kind of research privileges you have here. If you don't want to get involved, let Nick know."

Chapter 27

MINUTES AFTER HARRY LEFT, Enid Whitehorn called to say Quinn wanted me in his office in ten minutes. Probably about my incident report, but it would also be my chance to find out whether Beardsley had told Quinn about his donation to Delta's campaign. If he had, I could stop worrying about what he had meant by saying, "I'll do what I must."

I told Enid I was on my way, but first I pulled the envelope with Hannah's sketch from my drawer and made a copy for Quinn. I slipped the original back in my desk and sprinted to the main tower where he waited in his office with another visitor. They stood as I walked in.

"Hello, Aimee. Nice to see you again," said Detective Walter Kass.

There they were, my dark-haired hunk of a boss looking like a matinee idol, and my blond, clean-cut police detective friend who always looked ready to tee off at a golf tournament.

Still catching my breath, I managed to respond. "I'm glad to see you, Detective. I understand you're working the Sawyer investigation."

Kass nodded. "That's right. We're doing everything we can to sort it out."

"Let's get off our feet," Quinn said. He sat behind his desk. Kass took a chair opposite him. I took the chair next to Kass. "Thanks for coming on short notice, Aimee." Quinn glanced at a sheet of paper on his desk. "I've made a copy of your incident report for Detective Kass."

"Thanks. Do either of you have questions about it?"

"I have one." Kass pointed at the copy he held in his hand. "How did this volunteer know there was reason to be worried about his fingerprints on Delta Sawyer's purse?"

"Oh, sorry, I forgot to include that. He said he'd heard on the volunteers' grapevine about the pills being switched. Whoever started that rumor either knew or assumed the pill bottle was in Delta's purse when she arrived for her procedure."

"Dammit," Quinn slapped his palm on his desk.

I nodded at the swear jar on his desk. "Don't bother."

"I wasn't going to," he said.

Kass seemed to suppress a smile as he set his copy of the report aside. He took out his notepad and pen. "Probably explains how that tenacious reporter got wind of it. While we were trying to keep a lid on it, the cat was already out of the bag."

It also explained why the Secret Witness had called about Buck's opioid prescription.

Kass clicked his pen. "Aimee, did you get the name of the person who told your volunteer about the pills?"

"I didn't ask. I'm sure Mr. Kluckert would tell you if it's necessary to interview him, but I know he'd be upset if he thought it would get someone into trouble. The volunteers are a close group."

"If an interview becomes necessary, I'll make sure he doesn't feel uncomfortable," Kass said.

"I'd appreciate that." I handed Quinn the copy of Hannah's drawing. "I thought this might be helpful. It's a forensic sketch of the man mentioned in my incident report."

"The man who was mistaken for Mr. Sawyer?" Quinn asked.

"Yes. He drove Delta to the hospital the day she was admitted."

"Have a look." Quinn handed the copy to Kass.

Kass studied the sketch. "Your report says this man refused to take Delta's purse when Mr. Kluckert offered it to him. So as far as we know, he never touched it?"

"That's right."

"How do you happen to have this sketch?" Kass asked.

"An artist friend drew it for me as a favor. And before you ask, I didn't explain the circumstances, nor did she ask questions."

Kass glanced at the drawing again before placing it on Quinn's desk. "Your friend works like a pro, Aimee. Want to tell me who she is?"

"Do I have to?"

"No."

"Then sorry, I'd rather not." No point getting Hannah involved.

Quinn picked up the sketch. "Detective, I'll have a copy of this made for you before you go. Thanks for coming over, Aimee."

He stood up, obviously excusing me, but I hesitated. "Before I go, there's something I believe both of you should know—unless you're already aware of it."

Kass turned a page in his notepad. "What is it?"

"It's about Dr. Beardsley."

"Ah, yes," Quinn sat again. "His substantial donation to the Sawyer campaign."

"Then he *has* told you about it?" I exhaled with relief.

"He dropped in this morning. Said he thought I should know. Apparently he felt obligated to contribute to Mrs. Sawyer's campaign out of loyalty to her husband."

"Did he mention the amount?"

"He said five figures, so I assumed it was around ten thousand."

Kass nodded. "Ten thousand is a generous amount, but not unusual for a wealthy man like Beardsley."

Relief turned to discomfort. "The five-figure amount was fifty thousand," I said, "and it was her idea, not his."

"What are you implying?" Quinn asked.

"It wasn't a donation, it was extortion."

"That's a serious charge," Kass said. "Please explain. And take your time."

I repeated everything Beardsley had told me. How Delta threatened to sabotage the anticipated *Firm Foundations Renewal Center* partnership between her husband's foundation and the TMC Foundation. I pointed out that her first demand was that Beardsley prescribe opioids for her post-procedure pain.

"Beardsley insists that he refused," I said. "Instead he offered a campaign contribution. She finally dropped her request for the pills when he agreed to donate the fifty thousand."

Kass looked up from his notes. "So Delta Sawyer claimed Beardsley's late wife, Bonnie, was responsible for the death of Buck Sawyer's daughter? She used that against Beardsley as leverage?"

"Yes. That rumor had circulated years ago. Beardsley said Bonnie had convinced him early in their marriage that it wasn't true. Delta threatened to prove to Buck that it *was* true."

Kass looked to Quinn. "Did he mention this to you when he told you about his donation?"

"Hell, no," Quinn said, "but to be fair, we were interrupted before he had a chance. He was paged to the Emergency Department."

"He might have told you the actual amount if you'd asked. He didn't realize it was public record until I told him anyone could look it up." I explained my reasoning about checking the donors to all three candidates for possible suspects who might have a grudge against Delta.

Kass jotted on his notepad. "If she extorted him once, Beardsley might have feared she'd try again. I'll have a talk with him, but I won't bring you into it, Aimee. I'll let Beardsley think we found the information ourselves."

"I'd appreciate that."

"Smart work on your part, by the way. I don't believe our people thought to explore campaign donor records, but I'll get them on it now to see what else turns up. We can assume the Sawyer campaign knows about the amount, but not about the extortion. And as you said, the doctor's donation is public record, so anyone with your level of tenacity could look it up."

Kass was right on both counts, so there was no need to add that I had hand delivered Beardsley's donation instructions to Fletcher Tremont. That was beside the point.

Kass reached out to shake my hand. "You made the right decision filling us in."

I hoped that was true. Otherwise, I had just made myself a target.

MINUTES LATER I HEARD KASS CALL OUT to me as I began walking back to the library building.

"Aimee, hold up."

I turned, shading my eyes against the glare of the afternoon sun until he reached where I stood. "More questions about Delta's purse or Beardsley's donation?"

"No, I think we have those covered," Kass said, "but there is something else."

"What is it?" Kass knew me from past incidents involving my job and might have sensed I was holding out on him. On the plus side, he was giving me a perfect opportunity to clue him in on the other mayoral candidates' access to opioids and to let him in on what "secrets" Harry had found in their pasts. Things I would not have shared in Quinn's office.

Kass glanced at his watch. "Do you have time to talk?"

"How much time?"

"Up to you. Maybe a few minutes. An hour, tops."

"Then let's go somewhere private."

"Your library?"

"No, we might be interrupted. There's a pocket park just down the hill. It's usually empty this time of day, except for a few ducks paddling in a pond."

"Lead the way."

Kass stayed silent during the short walk to the park. As I guessed, we had the place to ourselves except for the ducks and a couple of squirrels. We chose a bench where sunlight filtered through the boughs of a leafing oak tree.

Kass broke the silence. "Thanks for taking the time."

"No problem, but we should make this as quick as we can. What's the something else you wanted to talk about?"

"Your safety, Aimee. You have a track record for sleuthing, and it's a good one, but it's put you in harm's way in the past. I appreciate what you've discovered in the Sawyer case, but I have an obligation here. I'm asking that you not do any further investigating. Can you give me your word on that?"

The answer that came to mind was *no,* but I offered him an alternative.

"How about a compromise? I'd like your permission to act as a consultant on the things that I'm already curious about. How about I give you my word that I'll keep you informed as often as you want, and I won't expand my efforts by digging into anything new?"

"That might work, but only if you avoid any situation that puts you in the proximity of a potential suspect. Use your brain and your computer skills only, no legwork. And share with no one but me."

"Works for me. Anything else?"

"Yes. Tell me what you're already working on. And don't withhold any future intel from me, no matter who it implicates." Kass locked eyes with me. "Can you do that?"

I blinked. "I guess I'll have to."

"All right. Start talking. I know you, Aimee. There's something on your mind that you kept to yourself in Quinn's office."

"This should work both ways. Is there anything you're willing to share with me?"

"Let's wait and see. You first."

I told him my theory that Wright and Nester were suspects based on Delta's public threats to reveal secrets from their pasts, and what Harry had found so far. I mentioned the possibility that they both had access to opioids at their facilities.

"I asked Harry to dig deeper into their backgrounds, and he's still looking, but there's nothing more so far. He hasn't had much time to work on it."

Kass pulled his little notebook from his shirt pocket, and scratched a few words. "That's not a bad theory, but we can't justify questioning either of them about bed bugs or a miscarriage."

"What about their access to controlled substances?"

"Their nursing offices are legitimate functions of their businesses, but definitely inform me if Harry finds something concrete to link either of them to those switched pills. Even if it's after tomorrow's election. Anything else?"

"There's another possibility that's come to my attention, but I can't offer anything to back it up."

"Let me hear it and I'll decide."

"I just found out there might be a problem with some of the Sawyer Foundation's grants."

Kass rearranged himself on the bench; he seemed to tense up. "What kind of problem?"

"Some of the international grantees haven't submitted their required reports. Proof of how they're spending their funds. That's a pretty big deal. Nonprofits are monitored and are subject to audits by the IRS because of tax exemptions."

"Go on," Kass said.

"If there are serious irregularities, it's possible the Sawyer Foundation could be shut down. Delta was on the board, and this is probably going to sound far-fetched, but what if she discovered some kind of fraud and started looking into it? Maybe she attracted the wrong kind of attention."

"International grants? Someone from abroad coming all the way to Timbergate to switch her pills and silence her? Is that your theory? Or are you afraid she discovered that her husband was behind the irregularities and confronted him about it?"

I caught my breath. "I'm already sorry I mentioned this. It sounds like I've given you a reason to suspect Buck of two crimes. Believe me, he would never have gotten involved in fraud, and under no circumstances would he have killed his wife."

"Aimee, I admire your loyalty to Buck Sawyer, but if you have stumbled onto that kind of fraud, chances are the Federal Trade Commission is already on it. It's what they do."

"I hear you, but you haven't said whether you think my theory is a possibility. Would Delta have been at risk if she *had* stumbled onto a federal crime?"

"Anything's possible. That's all I'm going to say, except to warn you away from the grant fraud question. That's not something for you to delve into. Stick with your theories about campaign donors and about the other candidates' secrets. If you should come up with compelling evidence in those areas, let me know. But whatever you do, keep your distance from anyone you consider a potential suspect."

Something in his demeanor told me Kass was not being up front with me.

"Your turn," I said. "I get the feeling you know more about the potential grant fraud than what I've just told you."

"Do me a favor Aimee. Stay in your lane." Kass got up and walked to the edge of the pond. I followed.

"I'll take that as a yes, but I won't press you about it. Just promise me that you and the rest of your team keep an open mind about Buck Sawyer."

"You can count on it." Kass pulled out his phone, looked at the screen. "I'd better take this." He waved me off, saying, "Keep in touch."

On my solo walk back to the hospital, I tried to reassure myself that Detective Kass would get to the truth about Delta's death.

Chapter 28

I T OCCURRED TO ME AS I REACHED THE LIBRARY that I had not told Kass about Buck's inquiries with the San Francisco attorneys to discuss a legal separation. I could justify that omission, because I was determined to talk to Oriana Wynn before I handed over any further evidence incriminating Buck. I had to know if Delta really was responsible for Sammy Sawyer's death. Orrie Mercer and Maybelline both identified Wynn as my source for that answer. I called the TV station and got her voicemail. I opted to try again later instead of leaving a message that she might not return.

I switched my focus to the handwritten list Harry had given me of Sawyer Foundation grants with overdue periodic reports. In spite of the warning from Kass, I rationalized it as being related to my job. Buck Sawyer was still a potential partner with the TMC Foundation for the drug rehab project. And Harry was right. Thanks to my job, I had access to many resources that private citizens could not use without paying for a subscription. I could check out the organizations on the list and still "stay in my lane."

There were half a dozen grantees on Buck's list with funds being distributed as far back as two years earlier. The payouts ranged from seven hundred thousand to nine hundred thousand dollars. It seemed significant that all of them were international grants. I visited the IRS website where I found that it was not particularly difficult for a private foundation in the U.S. to fund international grantees.

Most of the rules were similar to funds given by private non-profits to grantees located in the States. The grant must be spent only for the purpose for which it is made, the grantor must obtain full and complete periodic reports from the grantee organization on how the funds are spent, and then must make full and detailed reports on the expenditures to the IRS. There was a cautionary statement recommending that international organizations soliciting grant funds should be carefully scrutinized.

Buck's notes indicated that the required periodic reports were overdue for each of the half dozen grants on his list. No wonder he was giving them a closer look. Each grantee was from a different country: Mexico, Columbia, Spain, India, Nigeria, and China. Each nonprofit displayed a website, in both English and the language of the country, except in Nigeria's case where the country's language was English. On first glance, they all looked legit, but in every case, there were misspelled words in English. There had been no new activity or updates of any kind on any of the websites for several months.

Even with my extensive collection of resources and databases, I could not find a list of international charities or other eligible organizations that had been approved by the IRS.

I called the grants coordinator of Timbergate Medical Center's foundation hoping she would save me some time. I asked where to go to check out specific international charities. She said the hospital's foundation did not accept foreign grant requests and gave me the phone number of another private foundation based in Timbergate that was known to fund international charities.

The receptionist who answered my call there directed me to the woman in charge of international programs. I asked if there was a Federal Government website available that listed international charities eligible for grant funding by private nonprofits in the U.S. She said the IRS does not track all international charities and organizations. She explained that it was her responsibility to take a one-to-one approach with any international grant requests in determining their legitimacy. She also explained that the foundation she worked for did not invite or consider unsolicited grant requests from foreign countries.

"The only international charities we fund are the few where we've initiated the contact. Before making that contact, we go through an exhaustive investigation process until we're certain they're qualified according to IRS regulations."

That conversation offered me little help in determining whether the half dozen grantees on Buck's list were authentic or fairly clever scams. It did suggest that the Sawyer Foundation board had placed too much trust in the dubious international grant applicants. In Buck's defense, and that of his board, the fight against illicit drug trafficking and the need for drug rehab funding were issues where the countries in question needed all the help they could get.

A quick tally of the amounts on Buck's list confirmed that almost five million dollars of Sawyer Foundation funds had gone to the half-dozen international grantees that had not complied with their periodic reporting requirements. That was forcing Buck to determine whether to blame incompetence by his staff or criminality by the grantees in case the IRS came calling. That state of affairs was the last thing he needed while he was still a potential suspect in his wife's death.

I made a copy of the list of grants for myself and backed it up with a photo on my phone. I slipped the original and my copy of the list into the envelope that held Hannah's sketch. It occurred to me that I now held evidence of two separate mysteries involving Buck Sawyer. In less than three weeks, a generous and highly regarded man had suddenly become a magnet for serious trouble—unless he had created the trouble himself. I hoped that was not the case, but it struck me that Buck was the common denominator in two mysteries: the suspicious grants and the death of his wife.

What if Kass's theory was reversed? What if it was Buck who had discovered the fraud and suspected Delta? What would he have done?

Propelled by a sense of urgency and a need to find answers, I texted Nick that we needed to meet, preferably at the foundation offices. I added that it would help if I could look at the complete files related to the questionable grants. He responded suggesting six o'clock. I agreed, even though it would be a push to drive out to Coyote Creek, change clothes, feed the llamas and the beastly cat, and drive back to Timbergate in time.

Next I called the Timbergate TV station's newsroom again and asked if Oriana Wynn was available. My luck held. She came on the line.

"I see you're calling from Timbergate Medical Center." She sounded breathless. "To whom am I speaking?"

I gave her my name. "I'd like to meet with you as soon as possible. Are you free this evening?"

"The hospital librarian?" Her voice grew tense. "Aren't you *Ethics* something or other? What's this about?"

"I'd rather we spoke in person. I'm sure you'll understand, *Orrie*, if you're willing to meet with me. And by the way, do you still swim?"

Heavy breathing. No doubt she was thinking I was her Deep Throat. "I can meet you at eight tonight. I'll be finished at the station by then. Our building is next door to a restaurant that overlooks the river. You must know of it. It's extremely popular."

I did. The restaurant she mentioned sat between the TV station and Buck's foundation building. "The Anchor," I said. "That'll be convenient. I have an earlier meeting close by, but I should be finished in plenty of time."

"Good, then I'll see you at eight."

The day had been so full that when I glanced at the time, I was shocked to see that it was only three o'clock. Enough time to make headway on an inventory of the library's print resources. If I ended up taking the promotion Quinn had alluded to, I wanted everything in the collection to be up to date with no items missing when my assistant librarian came on board.

While I worked, my thoughts returned to Oriana Wynn and whether her story would fit into the mystery of Delta Dearborn Sawyer's death. There was no point in second-guessing the brash reporter. I would have to wait until eight o'clock at The Anchor.

A call from Quinn gave me something else think about.

"I have a librarian question."

"What do you need?" I said.

"One of our neurologists wants the latest status on an experimental multiple sclerosis treatment. What's the quickest way for him to get an answer?"

"He should start by contacting the media spokesperson for the National Multiple Sclerosis Society. They keep close track of research and treatments for MS." I jumped online to the NMSS website and gave him the contact information. "The spokesperson will either have the answer or point the physician in the right direction."

"Thanks," Quinn said. "I knew you'd have the info at your fingertips."

"Does the neurologist have an MS patient in house?" I had to wonder if he was calling about Faye Tremont.

"Apparently, but even if I knew who it was, I couldn't say."

"I know. HIPAA. Make sure the neurologist knows to contact me if I can help."

"Thanks. I'd better get off and follow up with him about his patient. I have the feeling her disease is taking a turn for the worse. You may be hearing from him if he needs more help."

"That's why I'm here."

I sat staring at the phone. He had inadvertently confirmed that the patient whose condition was worsening was a woman. I thought back with sadness to Delta Sawyer's memorial, where I had met Faye Tremont—such a nice woman. If she was the patient in question, it was some consolation that she seemed to have a strong marriage with a caring husband.

As the day wore on, I found myself repeatedly glancing at the date: March thirty-first, a week and a half since Delta had died. I kept thinking ahead to April first. Election day. In less than twenty-four hours, the citizens of Timbergate would be voting for their new mayor.

I lived outside the city limits of Timbergate, so I was exempt from the vote. Would the winner be Wright or Nester? If I were faced with voting, what choice would I make? An advocate for children or for the elderly? All I had to go on was the tenor of their campaigns. Wright's had leaned toward snarky slogans aimed at Delta Sawyer, but he dropped that approach after her death and had treated Nora Nester fairly. Nester had kept her campaign focused on her platform all along, with no personal attacks directed at either of her opponents.

In one more day, Timbergate's voters would have a new mayor. Would any of them wonder if they were voting Delta's killer into office? I could not let go of the idea that those pills were in her purse at the campaign forum she attended before arriving at TMC for her injections. Both Wright and Nester were at that event. Both had access to prescription medications through the nursing offices in their facilities, and both had similar motives: guarding the secrets in their pasts and winning the election.

I thought those motives were unlikely to justify murder, but if neither of them was the culprit, Dr. Beardsley was the only known suspect on my list. Delta had tried to convince him that his late wife, Bonnie, was responsible for the death of Buck's daughter ten years earlier. She claimed she could prove to Buck that the rumor about Bonnie was true. But Beardsley had already donated fifty thousand dollars to Delta's campaign to buy her silence. Why then decide to kill her? It made no sense, unless he feared she would become a constant thorn in his side by continuing her extortion with more demands for drugs or cash.

If Kass and his team concluded that Beardsley was above suspicion, I would have to trust their judgment. Not easy to do, since that would put the TPD back at square one with Buck as their prime suspect. *It's usually the spouse.*

Still, there *were* other possible suspects. Granted, they may or may not exist, but why not find out? Maybe Delta had a jealous lover. Maybe one of the candidates actually had a deranged supporter. Maybe there was an international cabal ripping off the foundation with phony grant requests. What if one of those maybes was capable of murder? I had to put my faith in Walter Kass. He was a superb investigator. I resolved that after I met with Oriana Wynn, I would fill Kass in on everything she told me—and on Buck's pursuit of advice about a legal separation.

Chapter 29

———•———

THE DAY HAD TURNED CHILLY by the time I got home from work. I changed into jeans and a turtleneck, pulled on a light jacket, and raced through the ranch chores. By five forty-five I was driving west toward Timbergate with the late afternoon sun in my eyes.

I forced my thoughts about my talk with Kass to the back of my mind. I was not prepared to share that with Nick just yet. Best leave it alone until after my appointment with Oriana Wynn. That was another topic I planned to keep to myself until I heard what she had to say. What Nick wanted was my opinion about the organizations that Buck had discovered with overdue grant reports. I wished I'd found something more helpful to offer him.

I hoped that topic would leave us time for a few personal moments. I needed to feel his arms around me, but there could be no awkward excuses to explain why I had to leave before eight o'clock. I could not keep Oriana Wynn waiting at The Anchor.

Nick pulled in beside me in the employee parking lot behind the foundation building. I gathered my purse and the envelope with Buck's notes about the grants. As we met at the back door, Nick stepped toward me, then pulled back with a smile.

"I'd better not touch you until we're inside."

"Me, too," I said.

"Did you bring the keys?"

I handed them to Nick. He unlocked, handed the keys back to me and silenced the alarm. Inside, we melted together and a rush of longing swept through me. When we finally broke away, Nick caught his breath first.

"We need to end this separation, one way or another."

"I agree, but how? Without an answer about Delta's pills, Buck is going to stay on TPD's list of suspects indefinitely. Do his attorneys still want us to keep our distance?"

"They do, but that's only part of it. Even if I could come home, I don't think it's a good idea to leave Buck alone for more than a couple of hours at a time."

"I thought he was coping fairly well now."

"He was better a week ago, but this situation with the questionable grants has thrown him a major curve ball."

"How bad is he?" We walked across the reception room toward the couch and coffee table.

"If you factor in depression, anxiety, and agitation, he's struggling, Aimee. For starters, Delta's death brought back all the pain of Sammy's fatal overdose and his first wife's death."

"But he's still able to invest energy in the business of the foundation. That seems like a good sign." I dropped on the couch and Nick did the same.

"That's what I thought at first, but with the discovery of millions of dollars in possible fraud, he's worried the foundation will be shut down."

"That would be devastating for him. The foundation is his purpose for living."

"True, but he's a fighter. That's what he's doing now. Did you bring that list Harry gave you?"

I pulled the original sheet with Buck's notes from the manilla envelope, careful not to reveal Hannah's sketch. Definitely not the time to explain that to Nick. He walked over to the wall switch to turn up the track lighting on the ceiling, then settled back on the couch next to me and picked up the list from the coffee table.

"Were you able to pull up anything about these grant recipients?"

"Not so far, but I have a question. Have the physical files that match this list been returned to the building?"

"They have. They've all been filed back where they belong. When I told Buck you wanted to look at them, he said tell you to go ahead. He wants to know if you can determine whether the charities are authentic, or if you know of a source that can verify them."

I told him about the local private foundation that funded foreign grants. "The woman in charge of their international program wasn't able to help too much, because they don't accept unsolicited grant applicants from foreign countries. She did say the IRS doesn't track all international charities and organizations."

"Then how does Buck or any other foundation know if a foreign charity is legitimate?"

"Someone on Buck's staff should have done meticulous investigating. Did he say how these grantees were evaluated?"

"He said Delta was in charge of that part of the operation."

"How long had she been in that position?"

"It's been at least two years." Nick fixed his gaze on the sheet of paper in his hands. "I remember Buck thought it was a good sign that she was taking on more responsibility as a member of the board. She told him she wanted to be more than a socialite or a trophy wife. She attended several seminars in the States and abroad to learn how the international nonprofit grant process works."

"Maybe that explains her decision to run for mayor," I said. "Do you think she was developing a sense of community?" Giving Delta the benefit of the doubt was tough, but I tried to make the effort.

"That's what Buck thought, until he suspected she was involved with another man."

I pretended to be surprised. "That must have been tough for him. Any idea why he suspected that? Or who the man was?"

Nick shook his head. "No idea. When I asked him why he suspected it, he couldn't give me a positive answer. He said there was a change in her personality. She was edgy, like someone who's feeling guilty and afraid they're going to be exposed."

I decided it was time to test my theory about the grants. "You know, I had been thinking Buck was the common denominator in two mysteries, but so was Delta, even though one of them involves her death. What if the secret she was keeping wasn't an affair? Maybe it had something to do with these grants." I tapped my finger on the list in his hand. "What if she'd come up with some kind of scheme to embezzle from the foundation?"

Nick jerked his head back, eyes narrowed. "You think Delta was skimming money? What for? She was married to a billionaire."

I knew that Delta would receive only a million dollars if she and Buck ever divorced, and I was pretty sure Nick knew that too, but Rella had shared that fact with me in confidence. I tried an indirect approach, hoping he might open up about Buck's legal separation consult.

"Maybe she thought being married to a man Buck's age wasn't worth it anymore. We don't know what their private life was like, but we do know they had separate bedrooms."

"You're taking a big leap from frustrated wife to embezzler."

"Think about it, Nick. What if their prenup wasn't enough and she wanted to squirrel away some extra cash and jump ship? I doubt she was the type to settle for a platonic marriage."

"Can't argue with that. And I think there's a chance you're on the right track about the prenup. So where do we go from here?"

I gave up on Nick telling me about the San Francisco attorneys. I understood his reluctance to betray Buck's confidence about a matter so personal.

"It'll help to get my hands on these files. Buck's staff would've had to go through a pretty exhaustive process to determine whether they met IRS requirements. They should have documented their process as part of the grant records."

"Any idea what that process involved?"

"No, but the woman at that other foundation I told you about said she'd help if she could."

"All right, let me check on Buck, then we'll pull the files."

While Nick made his call I walked into the break room, working my shoulders to release tension. My eight o'clock dinner appointment with Oriana Wynn kept me on edge.

Nick came up behind me in the break room. "Let's get you those files. Buck's convinced the fate of the foundation could hinge on what you dig up."

I turned to face him. "Did he tell you where they're stored?"

"They're in the secure file cabinets in the executive director's office where all the grant documents are kept. The keys are on the keychain I gave you."

The file cabinet drawers in Tremont's office were labeled and matched to the tags on the keys. It took some time to find the half dozen files I needed. I snapped photos with my phone of the exact locations where I found them to make sure they were returned without being misfiled.

We re-locked the file cabinets and Tremont's office door and took the files back to the reception area.

"Ready to take a break from this detective work?" Nick asked.

"I'd like that."

Nick folded the original sheet of paper with Buck's list and tucked it into his pocket. "Now about that break." He wrapped his arms around me, but in spite of the signals my body was sending, I tried to keep track of the time. It had to be after seven o'clock.

My attention had been diverted for more than a few minutes when Nick's cell came alive. He groaned, released me from his embrace, and glanced at his phone. I spotted the time on it: 7:40.

"It's Buck." He answered, listened, shot a glance at me, listened some more and finally spoke. "I'm on my way." He stood and slipped his phone into his pocket. "Gotta go."

"What is it?"

"Reporters are calling, asking him for statements about tomorrow's election." Nick twisted a fist into his palm. "Wanting to know if he endorses either candidate."

"That's ridiculous. It's beyond callous to bother him about the election, and it's too late for an endorsement to make any difference."

"Not quite. There's still the local TV news at eleven."

I thought of Oriana Wynn. She should be off the clock, but she might have found time to pester Buck, even if she was on her way to The Anchor to meet with me. Either way, Buck had saved me from being late to meet with her or making up an excuse to break away from Nick.

"You have to go to him." I picked up my purse and the grant files. "Tell Buck I'll get started on these tomorrow. And tell him not to worry about the IRS closing down the foundation. I'm sure whatever happened can be explained."

Nick turned out the interior lights. We closed up and headed out to the parking lot where he waited while I locked the files in the trunk of my car. He leaned in for a quick kiss, hopped into his pickup and headed out. I let him go first, making it less likely he would notice when I pulled into the restaurant down the street.

Parked at The Anchor, I reached for my cell to put it into my purse. It took a moment to realize I did not have my phone. The clock on my dashboard told me I had five minutes. I spun around and drove back to the foundation building, parked in back and went inside, punching in the security code to disarm the alarm.

Half an hour after sunset the interior was quickly losing light. The last place I remembered having my cell was in Fletcher Tremont's office. There was a slim chance the phone had dropped into one of the file drawers after I finished taking photos. It seemed unlikely, but I had to take a look.

I unlocked his office, slipped inside the darkening space and flipped on the light. I checked his desktop and other work surfaces—nothing. I unlocked one of the file drawers and began flipping through the folders when I spotted a prescription vial tucked in the back corner of the drawer.

I pulled a tissue from a box on Tremont's desk and used it to lift the vial out, careful not to disturb any fingerprints or to add mine to the surface. A bold red and white sticker on the lid displayed a warning:

Caution: OPIOID—RISK OF OVERDOSE AND ADDICTION

The patient's name was Faye Tremont. The medication was OXYCODONE. The vial was empty.

I groped for a legitimate reason why the vial was tucked away in the back of that drawer, but only one answer made sense. Tremont had hidden it. While I stood there struggling with indecision, I heard a vehicle pull in behind the building. Most likely Nick, coming back for something he had forgotten. *I had to tell him about the empty vial.*

From Tremont's office window, I peered out through the blinds, expecting to see Nick's pickup reflecting the blue-tinged glow from the parking lot's security lights. The vehicle I saw next to mine was not Nick's. A lone figure of a man stepped out of the car and sprinted toward the back entrance.

When he reached the exterior light over the door, I finally recognized the face that Hannah's forensic sketch had captured. In seconds, Fletcher Tremont would enter the building—and he was holding a gun.

Chapter 30

I SWITCHED OFF TREMONT'S OFFICE LIGHT, though the hitch in my breath told me he had already seen it. How to explain why I was there? I could tell the truth. I was helping Buck investigate some suspicious grants. But that seemed wrong. If Buck had trusted Tremont, he would have asked *him* to investigate, instead of recruiting Harry and me. I heard the back entrance door open and close as I slipped out of Tremont's office and locked his door.

Footsteps in the hallway signaled his approach to the reception area. Logic told me he had a right to arm himself if he suspected a burglar or a vandal had invaded the building. Once he recognized me and understood there was no threat, he would surely put his weapon away. I tried in vain to think of a plausible excuse for going into his office.

The footsteps halted. Tremont called out from the hallway.

"Who's there?"

"It's Aimee Machado. Please put away your gun."

He entered the room, gun in hand. "What the devil? Why are you here? How did you get in?"

I would have asked him the same thing, except that I had left the back door unlocked.

"Please put your gun away and I'll explain."

"You realize how irregular this is." He pointed his gun down toward the floor as he walked toward me. "It will be difficult to accept any explanation you offer."

"I realize that." I stepped around behind the couch, still holding the pill vial in my hand. "Once you hear me out, I'm sure you'll understand why I'm here."

While a tsunami of adrenaline flooded my body, I recalled Harry's standard warning to his martial arts students: *Don't take jujitsu to a gunfight*. I had no choice. It was the only weapon I had—other than a convincing lie.

Tremont stopped his approach with twenty feet between us, the gun still pointed toward the floor. "Please go on, I'm listening."

"I haven't been able to find my phone since last Sunday when I was here with you in your office the day of Delta's memorial. I've searched everywhere else, and I finally began to wonder if it had slipped out of my pocket last Sunday when you helped me with Dr. Beardsley's campaign donation. I'm sure you remember. I met your wife that day."

Tremont's expression softened. He nodded slowly. "Yes. She liked you."

"I liked her, too." I looked at his gun.

He followed my gaze, seemed embarrassed for a moment to see the weapon in his hand. "Please finish your story. Have you found your phone?"

"Not yet. I asked for my boyfriend's help because I knew no one was supposed to be in the building. I thought he could get permission from Buck."

"Who's your boyfriend?"

"Nick Alexander. You probably know him. He's one of Buck's pilots. He's been spending most of his time with Mr. Sawyer since Delta died."

"Yes, I do know him." Tremont gestured with a slight wave of the gun. "Go on."

"Buck gave Nick permission to help me come in and search for the phone."

"Then why isn't Mr. Alexander here with you?"

"Buck called him away. Media people were hounding him and he wanted Nick to get rid of them."

Tremont shook his head in disgust. "Those people are shameless."

My legs began to cramp from standing frozen in place behind the couch. "Nick felt it would be all right for me to stay and continue searching. He said he'd come back unless I texted that I had found it. He'll be back any time now." *If only that were true.*

Tremont lifted an eyebrow. "You're saying your boyfriend left you here alone?"

"Now I realize I should have gone with him, but you must know how it is. I really need my phone. I told Nick I'd lock up and return the keys to Buck as soon as I found it."

Tremont shifted his weight, turned his head for a quick glance at his office door. "Have you finished searching in my office?" While his head was turned, I slipped the pill vial into my jacket pocket.

"No, not really. I'd barely started searching in there when you arrived. I was worried when I heard a car and saw that it wasn't Nick's, so I turned out the light, hoping if it was an intruder, that he would go away."

Tremont's shoulders lowered and he slipped the gun into his jacket pocket. "Let's see if I can help. I'm sure you'd like to be on your way." He walked to the same switch Nick had used earlier and turned up the lights.

"Yes, I would." I did not ask why he was there, or why an empty oxy vial had been tucked away in one of his file cabinets. I prayed that was not what he'd come for.

He walked closer to where I stood and gestured toward the coffee table. "Is that yours?"

I looked where he pointed and saw the envelope that held Hannah's sketch and my copy of Buck's list of grants. In the rush of loading the stack of grant files in my car and hurrying off to meet Oriana, it had been left behind. That envelope's contents were things I would not want to explain to Tremont.

"Yes, it's mine." I maneuvered around the couch and reached for the envelope. When I picked it up, the pages slipped out across the cushions and onto the floor in front of Tremont.

"I'll get those for you." He bent down to retrieve them.

"No, let me. They're personal items." But Tremont had already scooped them up. Brow furrowed, he studied the forensic likeness of his face. Fear seized me, causing my cheeks to burn and my insides to quiver.

Tremont's eyes narrowed. "What is this?"

I tried to keep my voice steady. "Art homework. I've been taking classes."

He dropped the sketch on the coffee table and backed away from me with his right hand dipped into the pocket that held his gun. He spent several moments glancing over the sheet that revealed Buck's list of problematic grants. Finally, he spoke.

"Miss Machado. I'm afraid you will not be leaving here until we have a serious talk." He pulled the gun from his pocket. Pointed it toward the couch. "Please sit."

His tone erased any doubt. I was face to face with the man who refused to touch Delta Sawyer's purse the day he drove her to the hospital.

As I sank down, I heard a *ping* rise from under the couch where I sat. Tremont tilted his head, then his eyes widened. We both knew it was my cell phone. And I knew who was texting me. For the first time since Tremont arrived, I remembered that Oriana Wynn was waiting to have dinner with me at The Anchor.

"I believe we've found your phone," he said. "Please get it out from under there."

I dropped to my knees and swept an arm under the couch, groping for the device. I wondered how heavy a price I would pay for those passionate moments spent with Nick less than an hour ago. I stood up and glanced at the screen. A text from Oriana: *8:30 r u coming?* I immediately turned off the phone.

"It's Nick." I glanced up at Tremont. "Letting me know he's on his way here. Do you want to wait for him so the three of us can talk?"

"We'll talk now." He pointed his gun at the coffee table. "Put your phone down and back away."

"Why? It's turned off."

He sighed. "You're in no position to argue about this. Do it."

Chapter 31

———◆———

I DID AS HE ASKED. He picked up my phone and dropped it into his pocket.

"Now sit down." He nodded at the couch. I sat. He backed away from me and stood with his legs braced apart like a soldier at ease, except the rigid set of his jaw told me he was not. That, and the gun he continued to hold.

"Mr. Tremont, please put your gun away. I've told you why I'm here, and when Nick returns, he'll assure you there is no reason for you to feel threatened."

"I'll decide that after we've had our talk." He gestured toward the sketch with his gun. "We'll begin with that. Tell me about your art class."

"It's a hobby. I'm not particularly good at it." My only chance was to sit still, maintain eye contact, and lie.

"Who is that person you drew?"

"I don't know. There were photographs of a model. Our assignment was to recreate him with a sketch."

Both of Tremont's hands were full. The gun was in his right, and he held the list of suspicious grants in his left, but a disarm attempt was out of the question. There was no way I could safely clear the coffee table and the distance between us.

He held Buck's list toward me, his face ashen. "Why do you have this? It's Sawyer Foundation business. It's nothing to do with an art class . . . nothing to do with you."

"I don't know what that is. It was in the output tray of the photocopier in the break room. I went in there to look for my phone. I thought I should tell Nick about when he gets here. It looks like something that should be filed, not left lying around."

Tremont shifted his weight. "This was written by Buck Sawyer." *Not good.* Of course Tremont would recognize Buck's handwriting.

"Then you must know what should be done with it."

"But this is a copy," he said. "Where's the original?"

I shrugged. "I haven't any idea. It wasn't in the copier."

Tremont stuffed the list into the pocket that held my cell phone. "You're assuming someone wrote the list, made a copy, and then carelessly left the copy behind?"

"Mr. Tremont, I don't know what happened. Maybe that copy was an extra, made by accident and left behind unnoticed. I work in a setting where things like that are not uncommon."

"You work at Timbergate Medical Center, is that correct?"

"Yes. In the library."

He gestured again toward Hannah's sketch lying on the coffee table. "And you say that's yours? An assignment from your art class?"

"Yes."

"It's time to stop lying to me, Miss Machado." He looked down at the gun in his hand. "You may think I'm gullible, but I assure you, you're dealing with a desperate man."

The cat-and-mouse game was ending, and I was definitely the mouse.

"Mr. Tremont, please don't do anything you'll regret. Think of your wife."

"She's all I've thought of for . . . what feels like forever." His voice broke. He coughed, inhaled. "I've protected her health, her very life, and now it appears everything I did was in vain."

"I'm so sorry. That must be terribly difficult for you."

"You can't imagine. She's been ill for so long that our lives are consumed with a search for cures. They rise up, give us a balloon of hope, and then they're punctured and deflated. All the while her illness devours everything we've worked for. Our life savings, our home, the possibility of children."

"I'm so sorry about your wife's illness. I happen to know she's been hospitalized. She needs you now more than ever."

His brows rose. "Do you know about her diagnosis?"

"No one at the hospital told me, but my guess is MS. If you need more help, TMC's Social Services Nurse can work with you. Her name is Mary Barton. She can—"

"Stop. You're too late. There are other matters." He stared at me. "You think you know something about me—about what I've had to do for my wife—but you have no idea." His eyes glistened.

"I understand that any long-term illness is challenging for those who live with it."

I tried to estimate how much time had passed since Oriana's eight thirty text. I guessed nearly half an hour. She must have given up and left the restaurant. All I could do was keep Tremont talking and hope some shred of decency would prevent him from shooting me.

Fletcher Tremont's reaction to Buck's list and to the sketch told me that *he* was the common denominator in the mysteries of the potentially fraudulent grants and of Delta's death. He said I had no idea what he had done for his wife. I wanted to know how Faye Tremont's illness was connected to those grants and to Delta Sawyer, but knowing the truth could make me Tremont's next victim, unless I could somehow gain the upper hand.

Chapter 32

TREMONT PACED THE RECEPTION ROOM, keeping his distance from me while gripping his gun. I stayed on the couch, planning my next move. My only option was to distract him and hope he wouldn't question my lie about Nick returning.

"Mr. Tremont, it's getting late. Is your wife expecting a visit from you tonight?"

He halted in mid-stride, rotating his wrist to glance at his watch. "You're right. She'll be wondering why I haven't been there."

"You should go to her. We can continue this conversation another time."

"Conversation? That's what you call this? I'm holding a gun, for God's sake."

"And I'm still trying to convince you that I'm not a burglar or a vandal. If you'll take my word and put your weapon away, we can both forget this misunderstanding happened and you can go to your wife. She needs you."

"Stop talking about my wife." Tremont tilted his head, listening. "Did you hear that sound?"

"No. What was it?"

"I thought I heard something outside." A bead of perspiration ran from his scalp down to his cheek. He loosened the knot on his necktie.

"Maybe the wind is picking up. It's been breezy all day." He was not alone in stress sweat. My underarms were clammy with moisture.

Tremont walked to the front door and listened again. "You still think your boyfriend is coming back?"

"Yes. I don't know what's keeping him." I leaned forward but made no attempt to get off the couch. "You took my phone. I can't call or text him."

He patted his pocket, reassured that he still had my cell. "Then here's what we're going to do." He pulled out the copy of Buck's list. "We're going to have a look at each of these files. You will walk over to my office door and unlock it. Use the keys your boyfriend left with you."

His demand did not bode well. He was obviously threatened by that list. He would be much more threatened when he discovered those files were missing—still locked in my car. I had to neutralize him before that happened.

I took out the keys. I would have to take jujitsu to a gunfight after all. Since the age of seven, martial arts training had been preparing me for a situation like the one I was facing. My memory cycled through myriad classes and tournaments, searching for the kind of art that was my only weapon. *Gun disarms.*

I stood. "Are you sure you want to do this? What about your wife? She must be wondering where you are."

"It won't take long if you stop stalling." He jerked his head toward his office.

Great. He would be walking behind me with his gun pointed at my back—the worst-case scenario for disarming him. His mention of stalling gave me an idea.

"Mr. Tremont, before we do this, I really wish you would at least call and talk to your wife. She must be feeling terribly stressed that you haven't been to visit her this evening. She's had a difficult day. Don't you want to reassure her?"

"I told you not to talk about my wife." His chin jutted toward his office door. "Open it."

I began trying one key at a time, fumbling with them, hoping he'd be impatient enough to try it himself.

He stayed at a safe distance. "What's wrong?"

"I can't find the right key," I said. "Nick opened it for me before. Do you want to try?"

"No. But I do want to know what you meant about Faye having a difficult day. What do you know about it?"

"I'm aware that she may have taken a turn for the worse."

"She took a spill. That's why she's in the hospital." He waved the gun with a shaky hand. "Now stop stalling and open that door."

I continued to fumble with the keys. Once inside, he would realize those files were missing—along with the pill vial. I would know what that meant to him and what he was willing to do about it. Still behind me, he stepped closer, but not close enough. Aware of his sharp tone, I tried to gauge how far he could be pushed before he snapped.

He came another step closer. "I'm losing patience, Miss Machado."

I kept working the keys. "I've almost got it. Only two more to try."

"Then hurry up." The edge in his voice told me I was running out of time. He took another step closer. "This gun is heavy and my hand is beginning to shake, Miss Machado. Don't make me wait any longer."

I steadied myself, waiting for the moment, committed to my plan of attack. *Avoid the muzzle, grab the weapon, and yank it away from him.* My only advantage would be the element of surprise.

"Hello? Ms. Machado, are you in there?"

A woman's voice called out from the rear entrance, startling both of us. Tremont grabbed me from behind, covering my mouth with his hand. The list he had been holding drifted to the floor. The muzzle of his gun jabbed at my ribs. I froze. A false move by either of us would send a bullet ripping through my torso.

Chapter 33

THE WOMAN CALLED OUT AGAIN. "I know you're in here. I saw your car outside. That green thing you drive." I recognized the voice of Oriana Wynn coming nearer the reception area. Tremont's grip on my mouth and jaw tightened. The muzzle of his gun dug into my ribcage.

We stood in a ghastly embrace. As I tried desperately to think of a way out that would save myself and Oriana, she walked into the room. When she caught sight of us, her eyes widened, her brows shot up, and she froze.

"What the devil is going on in here?"

"None of your business," Tremont snapped.

"For God's sake, is that a gun?" She took a step toward us.

"Stop right there," Tremont said. "Don't come any closer. I don't want to have to harm Miss Machado."

Oriana's face paled. "All right. I'll stay right here. Don't hurt her."

My jaw ached from the pressure of Tremont's grip. I had to act soon, but Oriana's entrance had botched my original plan. I would have to make the distraction work in my favor.

"This is unfortunate," Tremont said. "Until you appeared, I was almost convinced that Miss Machado was not committing some sort of malice against the foundation."

"You're kidding." Oriana's glance took in the elegant reception area. "What did you think she was going to do?"

"How would I know? She's been prowling in my office. I had every right to be suspicious." His hand shook and the muzzle of his weapon raked against me. "Now it seems she has an accomplice."

"I'm no such thing," Oriana said, "and even if she was in your office, don't you think it's excessive to hold her at gunpoint?"

"Not at all. I'm merely protecting myself from an intruder. Make that two, with your arrival."

"Looks extreme to me." Oriana stuffed her hands in the pockets of her blazer.

"I know who you are, Miss Wynn. You may think of yourself as some sort of fearless reporter, but you're in no position to be questioning me. If you're not involved in this, you have even less business being here than Miss Machado does. How did you get in?"

"Well, I didn't come here to help her rob the place, if that's what you're thinking. And I sure didn't break in. The door wasn't locked." Oriana put a hand up to the side of her head. "Oh, no."

"What's the matter?" Tremont said.

"Panic attack . . . sometimes I faint . . . I have to sit down." She took a step toward the couch.

"Stop right there," Tremont ordered.

"Oh . . ." Oriana swooned and collapsed on the floor ten feet from where Tremont and I stood with the gun in his right hand, and his left still clamped to my mouth. His stance became less rigid. He was uncertain, losing control—dangerous.

An urgent voice called out in my head. *Go for it while she's down and less likely to catch a bullet.*

I stood still, letting Tremont's focus shift to Oriana.

"Get up!" he said. She did not respond. "I said get up." He moved the gun from my ribcage, and as he did, his grip on my face loosened. Before he could point the gun at Oriana, I made my move.

All of those tournaments resulted in a disarm effort that almost succeeded. I managed to grip the barrel of the gun and point it away from myself, but Tremont was strong and struggling to hold on.

Oriana scrambled up, rushing toward us. I spotted the pepper spray in her hand and quickly turned my head away, eyes closed. I held my breath while she shot a stream at Tremont's face. He shrieked and dropped to his knees gagging and gasping while I slipped his gun into my jacket pocket. Oriana helped me remove his necktie and secure his hands. I retrieved my phone while we tugged him to the couch and sat him down.

I told Oriana how to find the break room where she could get wet paper towels. She returned and began wiping at Tremont's face while he threatened to report us to the police for breaking and entering and holding him hostage.

"That's going to be pretty hard to prove," Oriana said. "I've been recording everything that's happened since I arrived."

He jerked his head away from her toweling efforts. "You faked that panic attack?"

"I did." She aimed a smile at me. "I didn't want to miss my meeting with Ms. Machado."

"That was risky," I said.

"I know, but I had to do something to get him out of the way. Since I always research my interview subjects, I knew about your black belt. Wanted to give you a chance to use it."

"I don't recommend trying that again."

"I won't, but this time I had my reasons. I'm still looking for a story that will make my career, and I think we have it here. Unless you call the police before we get the information we both want."

"You've blinded me," Tremont rasped, squinting and blinking. "You two are going to be sued for this."

"I don't think so," I said. "I have a feeling you'll be the one facing a judge." I turned to Oriana. "Let's get this sorted out. Then we'll call the police."

I watched Tremont squirm on the couch, wiping at the tears streaming from his eyes with hands still secured by the necktie.

"Mr. Tremont, since your vision is obviously impaired, I want you to be aware that I now have your gun."

Tremont rocked from side to side, seeming stunned. "I can't believe this. All I ever wanted was to take care of her."

Oriana walked over to where I stood across the coffee table from Tremont. "Do you know who he's talking about?"

I answered softly. "His wife."

Chapter 34

———◦———

"WHAT ABOUT HIS WIFE?" Oriana asked. "Is she sick?"

"I'm not at liberty to discuss her," I said. "Certainly not with a member of the news media."

"Even if that member of the media just saved your hide?"

"Even then." My anger seeped through. "And I appreciate your help, but barging in when you did foiled my chance to save my own hide."

Tremont let out a groan. "For Pete's sake, will you two stop bickering and get me some help before I go completely blind?"

Oriana glanced at the label on her pepper spray cannister. "You're not going to go blind. Keep blinking rapidly to flush out your eyes."

Tremont groaned again and resumed blinking.

I turned to Oriana. "We'd better talk fast. I don't like this situation one bit."

"In front of him?" She nodded toward Tremont.

"Where else? And by the way, how did you know where to find me?"

"Simple. You said you had a meeting near The Anchor. Knowing your boyfriend's ties to Buck Sawyer, I figured this was the obvious place, so I drove over and spotted your car."

"I didn't hear you drive up."

"My car's electric," she said. "Nice and quiet. Anyway, the back entrance door was unlocked, so I assumed you were in here and that you'd stood me up. I wanted to know why, since your reference to my nickname and swimming implied you had questions about Delta Dearborn Sawyer—a subject of great interest to me. I was all set to tell you off until I saw what was going on."

Tremont took in a sharp breath. "You two were meeting to talk about Delta?" He opened his eyes for an instant, closed them. Blinked several times. "Why?"

"This is awkward," Oriana said. "I don't want him listening."

"Then we'll have that talk later. Right now, I have some questions for Mr. Tremont."

Buck's list of grants still lay on the floor where Tremont had dropped it. I walked over to pick it up while a prickling sensation needled the back of my neck. If I was right, both Fletcher Tremont and Oriana Wynn had been keeping dark secrets that involved Delta Sawyer. While my back was turned, I followed Oriana's example and set my phone on record.

"My eyes, I'm in pain," Tremont said. "Why aren't you calling someone for help?"

"We'll do that soon, Mr. Tremont." I walked over to where extra chairs were arranged against a wall and brought one back to sit across from Tremont. Oriana followed my lead, her nose for news quivering.

"What is this?" Tremont's eyes had obviously cleared enough to make out the two of us facing him.

"A few questions," I said. "First, what did you mean about trying to help your wife?" I held up the list. "And how does it involve these grants and Delta Sawyer?"

Tremont swayed side to side on the couch. "That despicable woman was extorting me. She had no soul. No conscience. I begged her not to reveal my transgression. I promised to make it good, but she refused." Extorting. Delta's *modus operandi*. I waited to see where he was going.

A wave of energy radiated from Oriana's body. "What do you

mean by extorting?" She was a bloodhound on the scent of a true crime story.

"She roped me into her scheme by threatening to tell Buck I paid a personal expense with my foundation credit card," Tremont said. "Threatened to have me fired." Tears streamed down his cheeks—tears of emotion mixed with the residue of the pepper spray attack.

"What scheme? Was it something about these grants?"

"Yes. I knew as soon as I saw that list that her threat had come to pass. All along she had planned to pin that on me."

Oriana gasped. "Then you had a motive for murder."

"No . . . no." Tremont stammered, his head swaying side to side. "I could never do that."

"Why should we believe you?" I said. "You were holding a gun on me."

"Not really. That gun isn't loaded. You can check it for yourself."

No way would I risk checking an unfamiliar weapon. That could be verified later, when this ordeal was over.

"Let's back up," Oriana said. "Why did you misuse the foundation credit card?"

Tremont inhaled, nearly choking on a sob. "My wife and I were financially ruined by medical bills. I tried to hide it from Faye—didn't want her to know her illness had taken everything we had. Our personal credit cards had maxed out. The foundation's credit card was my only way of paying the copay on one of her most expensive medications. I hoped I could explain it as an accident if anyone noticed, but Delta discovered it and she was relentless." He coughed, cleared his throat. "She demanded that I go along with her fraudulent grant scheme, or else she would see that I lost my job and our health insurance." He dropped his head into hands lashed by the necktie.

I was appalled by what I heard. Delta's lack of empathy for the Tremonts' situation was unconscionable. "Mr. Tremont, why didn't you go to Buck yourself and explain about the credit card?"

He raised his head. "Because I had to use it again. I used it several times over the next few months while I tried to work with my creditors. We were under water with two mortgages on our home. We had used all of our savings on out-of-pocket costs. The medications, canes, crutches, walkers and wheelchairs. We even remodeled our house to accommodate her needs. We required home health care for her so I could continue working, but that was another expense our insurance didn't cover."

"But if you'd gone to Buck, surely he would have tried to modify his employee health insurance plan. He's a kind, generous man. He might have even offered you a loan."

"I couldn't take that chance. What if he had decided to fire me? We would have lost our health insurance. Even worse, what if Buck pressed charges? Had me arrested? Who would take care of my wife if I was jailed or imprisoned? In every outcome I imagined, Faye would be the victim."

He had done it all for his wife. I coughed to clear a painful sadness from my throat. I glanced at the time on my phone.

"Mr. Tremont, it's getting late. Do you want me to call the hospital and ask about your wife?"

His eyes opened wide for a moment, then closed. "Yes, I'd like to talk to her nurse."

"I'm afraid I can't let you do that." He might tell the nurse he was being held hostage. Which he kind of was, except he had already held *me* hostage, so *he said, she said*. "I think the nurse assigned to her might at least tell me whether your wife is resting comfortably."

Tremont agreed. I reached the charge nurse on Faye Tremont's floor and explained that Mr. Tremont was detained in a meeting and had asked me to inquire about his wife. The nurse knew me from her use of the hospital library. She assured me that Mrs. Tremont was stable and sleeping peacefully.

I relayed her update to Tremont, and watched the tension drain from his face. "Thank you, now can we please get this questioning over with?"

"My turn." Oriana's hand had slipped into the pocket that held her cell phone. No doubt to make sure she was recording. "You mentioned Delta's grant scheme. Please explain what it was and what it had to do with you."

With tethered hands, he gestured toward the list of grants I held. "Those. That was her scheme. The woman bragged that she had 'friends in low places.' She wanted out of her marriage. Was building up a private stash. Had been for at least two years."

I glanced at Buck's notes. "You're saying the six of these are all fraudulent?"

"Yes. Delta had managed to get board approval for all but one of them. She wanted to continue the scheme but thought her ruse would work better if I was in on it. We were both on the board of directors. I was executive director, she was Buck's wife. Any grant request the two of us favored would be rubber stamped by the rest of the board."

"And that worked?" Oriana asked.

"It did. It was actually quite simple. Why would any of them suspect the truth? They respected me, and they were afraid of Delta."

"Afraid of her? Why?" I asked.

Tremont shook his head. "She had a way of intimidating almost everyone around her. She found out where they were vulnerable and used it to suit her purposes. I'm no psychiatrist, but there must be a medical term—a diagnosis for people like her."

"There is," Oriana blurted. "I looked it up in the DSM-5 quite a while ago. It's someone without a conscience or empathy. They do what they want no matter who it hurts and they feel no remorse." She turned to me. "You must know the term. It's called antisocial personality disorder. Am I right?" I was impressed with Oriana's research, but she was a reporter, so it made sense.

Tremont nodded. "No remorse. That's it. A perfect description. I tried to appeal to her sense of humanity, but it was like pleading with an executioner."

"People with antisocial personal disorder are deceitful and manipulative," I said. "And you're right, Oriana, they are remorseless, but I think there's more. I'm guessing there was a lot of narcissism in Delta's personality, too."

"How is that different?"

"Narcissists tend to have a sense of entitlement. They exaggerate their talents and see themselves as unique and superior. Delta displayed arrogance, self-importance, and a great need for admiration. Even her sudden decision to run for mayor fits an obsession with fantasies of power. It also explains why she wanted the cosmetic injections so close to election day. An obsession about her looks."

"I tried to talk her out of that," Tremont said, "but it was useless."

Oriana turned to me. "So you think the antisocial disorder fits, too?"

"I'm not qualified to diagnose her, but it seems pretty likely. Her embezzlement scheme and the extortion of Mr. Tremont are examples of disregard for the law and the rights of others. Her lack empathy for Mr. Tremont and his wife is another example of how the two diagnoses overlap." I didn't mention how Delta had extorted fifty thousand dollars from Dr. Beardsley. "Let's get back to your story, Mr. Tremont. Was she planning to continue the embezzling?"

"Yes. She said if I worked with her, she would see that I got a percentage of the funds from each fraudulent grant we pulled off, and no one would be the wiser."

"Weren't you at least tempted to tell Buck what Delta was doing and throw yourself on his mercy?"

"If only I had." Tremont coughed, took a breath. "At the time, I had a choice to make that could mean everything to my wife. There was an experimental treatment for MS being hailed as a medical breakthrough, but the price tag was close to two hundred thousand dollars. If I went along with just one of Delta's false grants, my cut would have covered that cost."

"What about your health insurance?" Oriana asked. "Wouldn't that cover the treatment?"

"The foundation's policy doesn't cover experimental treatments," Tremont said. "I don't know of any health insurance that does."

"So you conspired with her at least that one time," I said. "Did Faye get the treatment?"

Tremont replied in a broken voice. "No, I was still waiting for my share of the money when the window to apply for the treatment closed. The people overseeing the experiment wanted to do more studies. There was no indication when it might reopen."

"What did you do with the money?" Oriana asked.

"I never received it."

"What went wrong?" I wondered if that had been his breaking point.

"Delta's offshore accomplice ditched her and absconded with the funds, leaving her with no way to recoup the money."

I jumped in with the next question. "How long ago did that happen?"

"A month before she filed to run for mayor." Tremont swallowed hard. "I believe she saw it as a chance to make a fresh start. Becoming mayor would offer her prestige and power of sorts. She couldn't resist the idea of celebrity, even at a local level."

"I get that," I said. "It certainly fits what we know of her personality."

"Yes, but I feared what would happen if she won."

Oriana asked the obvious question. "Why would her serving as mayor be a problem for you?"

Tremont sighed and sank deeper into the couch. "The foundation was about to face a routine audit, and Delta's scheme had begun to unravel. The offshore cohort who had skipped out was supposed to write up any of the required reports that were due. Grantees are supposed to provide believable documentation of how the grant funds are spent so we can follow up with the IRS. It's the procedure that proves the foundation is contributing only to legitimate nonprofit charities and organizations."

"I'm familiar with it," I said. "You're saying Delta expected to receive falsified reports for each of the half dozen faked grants, but those reports never came?"

"That's exactly what happened."

"So the fraudulent grants were going to signal problems during the audit. That would carry the risk of exposing you and Delta."

Oriana spoke up. "How much money are we talking about?"

"Close to five million dollars." Tremont shook his head. "God help me. Delta insisted that if it came to an investigation, she would deny any knowledge and that I must do the same. She wanted my word that I wouldn't reveal her embezzlement scheme and upend her campaign for mayor."

"Did you?" Oriana asked. "Give her your word?"

"What else could I do?" He glanced down at his secured hands. "She said if I didn't, she would find a way to blame all of it on me and use the credit card charges I'd made as proof that I was corrupt. The Federal Trade Commission would get involved and the Sawyer Foundation would be in jeopardy."

I dreaded his answer to my next question. "Mr. Tremont, does this story have anything to do with Delta Sawyer's death?"

He stared at me with dull eyes. "I'm afraid it does."

Chapter 35

———◆———

ORIANA SUCKED IN A BREATH. "Mother of God! Are you saying you *did* kill her?"

Tremont's head jerked up. "No. That's not what I—"

"Wait." I motioned to Oriana to let me speak. "Mr. Tremont, you just implied you had something to do with Delta's death. What did you mean?"

"She wanted pain pills for her cosmetic procedure. Her doctor refused, so she came to me. She knew of Faye's illness . . . asked if I had access to opioids."

"Delta was already threatening to ruin you," I said. "Are you saying she added the opioids to her extortion demands?"

Tremont choked out his words. "Yes. I gave her what she wanted. Faye had been started on opioids because her other pain medications were not working well. I brought the vial of oxycodone to the campaign event the day of Delta's procedure. Gave it to Delta in a private moment. She poured the tablets into a pill bottle she had in her purse and handed Faye's empty vial back to me."

"If she was putting you at risk because of the pills, why did you accompany her to the hospital after her campaign event?"

"I wanted nothing more to do with her, but she demanded I give her a ride because her husband was out of town on business. I was afraid to refuse."

"Didn't she have her own car?" Oriana asked.

"No. She was told she couldn't drive herself home after her procedure. She took a taxi to the campaign forum that morning. She thought her husband would be back in time to take her home after her outpatient appointment."

Bernie's story came to mind. Tremont refusing to touch that purse. "Were you afraid you'd be implicated if someone at the hospital discovered that bottle and its contents in her purse?"

Tremont nodded. "I'd be no better than a drug dealer. I was terrified someone would check, but no one did."

No one checked because of what Jared Quinn had told me. Hospital employees were not allowed to search patients' purses. Delta's was locked in the Security Office safe without ever being opened.

"What about your wife?" Oriana asked. "How did you explain the missing pills?"

"I told her I spilled them. That they fell down the bathroom sink. It happens. Her doctor has known us for years. Didn't hesitate to write a new prescription."

"You saved the empty opioid vial." I carefully eased it from my pocket.

Tremont's eyes widened. "You found it?" His arm shot out, pointing. "Be careful. Delta's prints are on that."

"I haven't disturbed them. Why did you keep this?"

"Back when Delta was still alive, I knew I couldn't trust her to keep me out of it if she was ever questioned about where she got those pills. I thought I would have to throw myself on Buck's mercy. Confess the whole sordid account of her extortion and the embezzlement. I thought her fingerprints on the vial would prove my story was true."

"But Delta died," I said, "and then what? You thought you could play dumb about those false grants when the audit happened?"

"That was my only hope about the grants, but that fear was overshadowed by Delta's death. I never dreamed she would be so reckless as to accidentally overdose. She had forced me to give her the pills by threating my career and Faye's very life. I feared someone would eventually discover the switch. That's why I need that empty vial with Delta's fingerprints. They prove that Delta used my wife's illness as leverage to extort me about the grants and the drug."

"Are you still worried someone will suspect you switched the pills without Delta's knowledge?" Oriana asked. "To silence her so you could keep your job and take care of your wife?"

Tremont cast me an apprehensive glance. "Not as long as Delta's prints are still on Faye's prescription vial."

"They should be safe," I said. "Prints are basically oil and they don't evaporate. They'll last for as long as you're going to need them. Even on plastic."

I shifted to a new topic, wanting as much information as I could get from Tremont before I called Walter Kass. "Why did you come here tonight, and how were you planning to get into this building if you didn't have keys?"

Tremont forced his answer, his voice still scratchy from the pepper spray. "After I left Delta at the hospital, I had copies of my keys made. I wanted to be sure I had access to those counterfeit grants if she got me fired."

"You came here for the grant files? Delta's been gone for a week and a half. Why now?"

Tremont replied with a half-hearted shrug. "Buck wanted to meet with me to prepare for the audit of our grants program. We were to get together tomorrow afternoon. I suspected he had somehow discovered the fraud, and I made up my mind to go to the police tomorrow morning instead. Confess everything. I couldn't let Buck Sawyer take the blame for Delta's death, but I needed that prescription bottle and those grant files to back up my story."

"So you canceled your meeting with Buck?"

"Yes. I begged off saying my wife had been hospitalized."

"Then why didn't you tell me this story in the first place instead of threatening me with a gun."

"How could I know you'd believe me? You had reason to be suspicious or you wouldn't have been snooping in my office."

"For Pete's sake," Oriana said, "if your gun isn't loaded, what was the point of threatening Aimee with it?"

"It was foolish, I know, but I panicked." He looked up at me with pleading eyes. "I hope you can forgive me. I'm desperate to get this over with and to see to my wife's care."

I had heard all I needed to hear, but my next words were painful to speak. "Mr. Tremont, I'm going to call the police now. If what you say is true, you didn't cause Delta Sawyer's death. It seems most likely an accident by her own hand. If you explain everything that you've told Miss Wynn and me tonight, Timbergate PD will get it sorted out. I'll keep this pill vial secure until they arrive."

I called Detective Kass's personal phone rather than try to explain the situation to the TPD dispatcher. I told him we had Tremont restrained. When I finished filling Kass in, he asked that Oriana and I wait for him to arrive.

Kass and two officers were there in a matter of minutes, arriving in separate vehicles. Tremont was taken into custody by the officers while Kass remained behind. I told him that Tremont had insisted his weapon was not loaded and asked if he would check the gun. He stepped outside, inviting us to follow, and in two deft motions he checked the chamber and the magazine. He shook his head. "Not loaded."

Kass then did something that seemed odd. He took what looked like a new, unsharpened pencil from his shirt pocket and slipped it down the gun's barrel, eraser first. He pointed the weapon upward in a safe direction and fired. When nothing happened, he nodded. "Yep, that's what I thought. No firing pin. That man wasn't taking a chance of harming anyone with this weapon."

He stayed long enough to ask the two of us to explain our presence at the foundation. I told him about the files I had been asked to review and how I'd found the pill vial when I went back to look for my missing phone. Oriana told him she'd tracked me down because she was on the trail of a scoop, mistakenly thinking Buck had poisoned his wife with opioids. Kass asked why she had that notion and what had changed her mind. Oriana told him that until she heard Tremont's confession about the switched pills, she believed Buck had discovered a truth about Delta that gave him a motive for murder.

Shaking his head in exasperation, Kass halted Oriana's narrative and told both of us to make ourselves available for in-depth interviews at the police department on Friday morning. He said his immediate priority was a visit to Buck Sawyer to fill him in on our confrontation with Tremont. He took possession of the pill vial and told us to lock the building and leave. He wanted nothing disturbed until he could clear it as a crime scene.

That meant Nick would hear about Tremont holding me at gunpoint. The fact that the gun was unloaded would be of little help when Nick realized that once again, I had ended up in jeopardy. I texted to let him know I was okay but had to meet with someone before I could go home, and that I would call him as soon as possible. First, I had unfinished business with Oriana.

She and I made a quick exit and met at The Anchor where we were told the restaurant had stopped serving, but the bar was still open. We took a table and ordered coffee. I still wanted to know what Maybelline had meant that day at the prison in Arroyo County when she insisted that *Orrie* had "the goods" on Delta Sawyer.

Before I could ask, Oriana pressed me about Tremont. "Did you believe him about his wife's health and her medical bills?"

"Absolutely, but he's going to need a good lawyer."

"You heard him say he's broke. Who's he going to hire? Some third-rate ambulance chaser?"

"I suppose he'll be assigned a public defender, unless he can get pro bono representation. For now, let's get back to the original reason we planned to meet."

Oriana's lips twisted. "Delta Dearborn Sawyer—the devil incarnate."

"That's pretty harsh," I said. "Particularly since she's dead."

"Not a minute too soon, if you ask me." Oriana ran her thumb down the handle of her cup. "You saw what she did to Tremont. To Buck Sawyer. And I saw what she did to his daughter."

My body stiffened at her last remark. "So what Maybelline said wasn't incoherent rambling?"

"Not at all."

"You really do know something about Sammy Sawyer's death?"

Oriana stared beyond me, into the past. "Yes. As mentally compromised as Maybelline is, she's still managed to out me."

"*Out* you?"

"Nearly everyone who crossed paths with Delta eventually got caught up in a secret. My secret is the truth about the night Sammy Sawyer died." Oriana's face flushed with heat. She pressed her hands against her cheeks. "I was a naïve teenager when I figured out what Delta had done. She gave Sammy methamphetamine tablets at the swim meet and passed them off as vitamins."

I stared at her in surprise. She had confirmed Maybelline's story. "Why would she do that?"

"A short-term boost for Sammy in the competition." Oriana leaned in, forcing eye contact. "How do I make you understand the creature that Delta was? She did whatever it took to get what she wanted, and back then, she wanted a winner. She thought Sammy had Olympic potential. Delta's own Olympic ambitions had flopped. She intended to ride Sammy's coattails and become famous as her trainer."

"What about the story that Sammy got the pills from Bonnie at a party after the meet?"

"That was the rumor, but Bonnie Belcher and I both knew better. Sammy told us about the pills that night. She felt guilty because Delta had given her some special 'vitamins' to boost her chances and told her not to tell us."

"Why only Sammy? Why not all three of you?"

Oriana smirked. "Ageism. Sammy was two years younger than Bonnie and me. In competitive swimming, that was an advantage. Delta needed for Sammy's times to be better than ours."

"So you and Bonnie both knew about the pills. But how did you know they were meth and not vitamins?"

"Sammy had a few with her at the party. She wanted to make it up to us, so she gave one of them to each of us, still thinking they were vitamins. She thought they would give us more energy and make the party more fun."

"I heard she had trouble during the meet. Something about cramps. She didn't connect that with the pill she took?"

Oriana's mouth curled in a sneer. "No. Delta assured her that wasn't the case, and Sammy believed her."

"Did you and Bonnie swallow the pills Sammy gave you?"

"Bonnie did. Gulped hers down right away. I was one of those people you hear about who can't swallow pills. I was embarrassed for them to know, so I pretended to put mine in my mouth. Instead, I dropped it in my purse."

I thought I knew where this was going. "How long before you discovered what the pill was?"

"They called me 'intrepid reporter' back when I worked on my high school newspaper. Always looking for a story. Always digging, curious. It wasn't hard to find what I needed online. I was able to identify the pill as meth."

I took a sip of coffee to moisten my dry mouth. "What did you do?"

"Called Bonnie. We got together, talked it over." Oriana shivered, rubbing at her upper arms. "Remember, you're talking about a couple of kids. Barely eighteen. Delta Dearborn had at least ten years on us and she was from a prominent family. Both of us were already intimidated by her because she was our trainer, but it went deeper than that. We were afraid of her and her parents' power in the community. We made a pact. Keep it to ourselves. We justified it because we knew Sammy's death was an accident. The last thing Delta would have wanted was for her to die."

"None of this explains how on earth Maybelline Black knew about you, or how she knew your secret about Delta."

"She knew because Bonnie got hooked on drugs." Oriana pulled out her cell, checked the time. "They're about to close. Let's get this over with."

"What does Bonnie's drug problem have to do with Maybelline?"

"You know Maybelline is Vane Beardsley's sister?"

"Yes, she and Bonnie were sisters-in-law, but Bonnie's marriage to Vane Beardsley didn't happen until several years after Sammy died, so I don't understand how Maybelline fits in."

"Maybelline found an old journal Bonnie had written. It dealt with her feelings about Sammy Sawyer's death."

"How did she find something like that?"

"After Bonnie died, Maybelline was helping Vane Beardsley sort through her belongings. There was no other family to do it. Both of her parents had died, and her only other relative, her Uncle Orrie, was in jail awaiting trial."

"Then Bonnie broke your pact of secrecy. She wrote about Delta in a journal. Why?"

Oriana nodded. "I couldn't believe it either. It must have been part of her therapy back then. The meth she took at that party started her addiction. She liked it and started using, but she switched to cocaine fairly soon. Her mother discovered her habit and insisted Bonnie get counseling."

"Sounds like Bonnie became another of Delta's victims."

Oriana stared past me. "That was when our friendship ended."

"Because of her drug use, or because of what she wrote in the journal?"

"Both, in a way. Back when her mother found out what had really happened at the swim meet, she banned our friendship and made us swear we wouldn't tell anyone about Delta and the meth. She said if it got out, Delta would know we were responsible and she'd find a way to retaliate. She would ruin Bonnie's family and their almond-growing business."

"She thought Delta had that much power?"

Oriana shuddered. "Like I said, you have no idea what she was capable of."

"Apparently not, but we need to go soon, so let me ask you about something I don't understand. I talked to Vane Beardsley about Maybelline after she babbled that 'Orrie' had the goods on Delta. He didn't mention anything about the journal she found. He assumed she'd heard about Delta from Orrie Mercer, back when they were dating."

Oriana nodded. "She never told Beardsley about the journal."

"How do you know that?"

"Maybelline was more than eccentric and on her way to delusional when she tracked me down and confronted me about the journal."

"What did she want from you?"

"She wanted me to verify the truth about what happened at the swim meet."

"Why? What was her point?"

"She loved gossip and she loved secrets. She showed me the journal and asked me who else knew about the meth that killed Sammy Sawyer." Oriana flashed a cold smile. "I said I would only tell her if she gave me the journal for safekeeping."

"What did you tell her?"

"That except for her and Delta, I was the only living person who knew."

"And Maybelline let you have the journal?"

"Yes. She was afraid if she kept it, Vane might discover it. She was adamant that her brother never hear about it."

"That's odd, I'd think she would want him to know it wasn't his wife who had provided the meth that killed Sammy Sawyer."

"That's because you're sane. Maybelline hated Bonnie because she knew Vane Beardsley was miserable in that marriage. She preferred to let the rumor stand and keep that cloud of suspicion hovering over Bonnie. She never lost hope that they would divorce."

"So only you and Maybelline knew the truth, and you've kept this secret until now. Why? Bonnie died almost two years ago, and both of her parents before that. Delta could no longer hurt them."

"No, but she could still hurt *me*." Oriana continued in a resigned monotone. "Why dredge up old news most people had already forgotten? It would have been her word against mine, and with her married to Buck Sawyer, what are the odds anyone would believe me? It wasn't worth the risk."

"What kind of risk? Did Delta suspect that you knew about the meth she gave Sammy?"

"She must have. She knew I had been close with Bonnie and Sammy. When I was hired by our local TV station Delta got in touch with me. Invited me to lunch and in so many words, made it clear that my career would be over if I ever spoke a word to anyone about that swim meet."

The hour was late and my mind was on overload, but I struggled to keep up. "What did she hold over you?"

"Plagiarism. The one word that would destroy any chance of my making it as a journalist."

"Was it true? Did she have proof you'd plagiarized?"

"No, but she had a slim thread that she could use to cast doubt." Oriana's face flushed. A vein pulsed in her neck.

I thought of Nora Nester's therapeutic abortion and Ernest Wright's bed bug infestation and how Delta could have twisted those incidents to serve her purpose. "Do you want to tell me?"

"Might as well. It doesn't matter now. I co-wrote my master's thesis with another student back when I was earning my degree in Journalism. Without my knowledge, my co-author added a paragraph to the design and methodology chapter using someone else's words without attribution. He turned the final draft in before I found out what he'd done."

"And you took the fall along with your fellow student?"

"Almost. He took the high road. Confessed and swore I didn't know what he had done, but Delta somehow managed to dig up that adverse incident. She insisted she could make it public and cast enough doubt to tarnish my reputation."

"She held that threat over you from the time you were hired?"

"Yes, she did." Oriana produced a deep, gratifying sigh. "And then she died."

Chapter 36

---·---

THE ANCHOR WAS CLOSING, but I had one more question for Oriana.

"Did you go after the story of Delta's death because you truly believed Buck had switched those pills?"

"How could I not?" Oriana met my eyes. "Don't you see? The story had everything. Politics, true crime, irony, poetic justice, and I could tie it all in with the drug crisis taking place throughout the entire country. More than ninety thousand overdose deaths a year. Think about that. Have you heard of the Emmy Award for Investigative Reporting?"

"One of the most prestigious, and with the threat of plagiarism gone, there was no Delta Sawyer to stand in your way."

"I was so certain." Oriana looked away from me, lowering her head. "I was convinced Buck had discovered the woman he married was responsible for his daughter's death."

I worked my stiff shoulders. "You weren't the only one. TPD seemed to be zeroing in on Buck, and they didn't even know about Delta and the swim meet. It's likely they never would have discovered it."

"Kass will hear all about it when we meet on Friday morning." Oriana glanced at me. "On the other hand, we can't be sure Tremont's story is true. He claims Delta threatened to ruin him, maybe even the Sawyer Foundation. You think TPD is going to take his word for it?"

"No, but they'll do a thorough investigation. They have Faye Tremont's pill vial, and with luck, they'll identify Delta's prints. Maybe Tremont will come up with some kind of additional evidence to corroborate his story."

Oriana seemed to catch a second wind. "However it turns out, it's still a prize-winning story. Since Buck is innocent, I'll go at it from another angle. I can keep the mystery, the politics, and even the intrigue about the phony grants, but the payoff will come when Tremont is found guilty of embezzlement and dispensing drugs without a license, and Buck Sawyer is proved to be the unfortunate victim. The man lost his daughter, an only child, to a meth overdose. And in spite of his crusade against drug abuse, he ended up losing his second wife to an opioid overdose. Worse yet, he had ended up marrying the woman who provided the pills that killed his daughter." She gazed across the room with a faraway look in her eyes. *Accepting her Emmy.*

"Before you go ahead with that story, there are some people you should talk to."

"Really? That's great. Do you think they'll help me?"

"I think they will." I hoped that once she heard from all of the people who loved Buck Sawyer and cared about Faye and Fletcher Tremont, she would look elsewhere for her prize-winning story.

I REACHED HOME AT HALF PAST MIDNIGHT. Nick's truck sat in the driveway, and our porch light illuminated my path to the front door. I opened it, wondering what his reaction would be.

Nick pulled me inside and wrapped me in his arms. "Damn, Aimee, are you all right?"

"I'm fine now," I mumbled into his shoulder. "Did you get my text? I was going to call you as soon as I got home. You didn't have to leave Buck and come all the way out here."

"Buck's okay." Nick closed the door and led me to the couch. "Harry and Rella are with him."

"You heard about what happened?"

He nodded. "I was there when Kass talked to Buck. The most important part was that you were okay, but I was still worried. I got your text, but it took you so long to get home I was about to start driving around looking for you."

"I'm sorry you were worried, but I finally had a chance to hear the truth about how Sammy Sawyer died. I didn't want to miss it."

"About Sammy?" Nick's eyes narrowed. "What's that got to do with Tremont?"

"Nothing. It was Oriana Wynn who knew the truth." I told him how I had arranged to meet her at The Anchor and then discovered my phone was missing. "I went back to find it and got intercepted by Tremont. That's why Oriana was there with me at Buck's building. She came looking for me when I didn't show up at the restaurant." I recounted everything Oriana had told me about the swim meet and the after party.

"It was Delta?" Nick said. "She gave Sammy the meth and told her it was vitamins?"

"Yes. Oriana Wynn filled me in tonight. That's why I'm so late. She hasn't told Detective Kass about it yet. He's going to interview both of us in more detail Friday morning, but I'm afraid Wynn will disclose it on television at her first opportunity. She wants to focus on the angle of Buck marrying the woman who caused his daughter's death. Thinks it's worthy of an Emmy."

"Seriously?" Nick huffed a quick breath. "You really think she'd do that? Maybe her station manager will rein her in."

"And maybe not. The point is, Buck needs to hear it first, and soon. He needs to hear it from you."

"I'll talk to him first thing this morning before he sees any TV news." Nick attempted to stifle a yawn. "I should get back there and get some sleep, but I have to ask something first. You told me about your lost phone and why the reporter showed up at the building looking for you, but I don't get how you connected her to Sammy and the swim meet."

I explained about running into Beardsley and his sister at the prison and Maybelline's outburst about Orrie having the goods on Delta.

"I had already arranged a call with Orrie Mercer, thinking he might know something about that swim meet. When he called, I asked him about Maybelline's strange outburst at the prison."

"How did that go?"

"Mercer said she must have been talking about another Orrie, a girl who swam with Sammy. I eventually figured out that he was talking about Oriana Wynn."

Nick started chuckling and shaking his head. "Of all the mysteries you've gotten mixed up in, this one's got to be the most convoluted. I'm afraid to ask if there's anything else you haven't told me."

There was, but I had deliberately postponed telling him about godparenting for the Littletrees. That would imply that Nick and I were committed to a future that involved marriage. We had skirted the subject, but never met it head-on, and I hesitated to open a topic that involved our relationship in the wee hours of the morning. It could wait a little longer.

"I think you're pretty much caught up. Is there anything else you want to talk about?"

"Nothing that can't wait. It's already been a hell of a night." He got up to leave. "I'd better get back to town and relieve Harry and Rella."

ELECTION DAY DAWNED FAR TOO EARLY. I dragged myself out of bed at six thirty Thursday morning to head out to the barn, grateful that I had chopped enough extra hay to make quick work of the llama feeding chore.

After a hot shower and breakfast, I turned on the TV in time to catch one of the local station's reporters checking in from a polling place in downtown Timbergate. Regardless of who won the race for mayor, I knew for the first time since Delta Sawyer's death that I could face my workplace friends without worry. Bernie and Lola would be secure in their move to *The Wright Time of Life,* and Laurie Littletree's baby girl, Kiona, would be safe in *Nora's Nest.*

A second news story mentioned that the TPD had made significant progress in the investigation of Delta Sawyer's death. I texted Nick to ask if he had talked to Buck about Delta giving the meth to Sammy at the swim meet.

Nick texted back a few minutes later.

Call me

I called. "How's he taking it?"

"Better than I expected. He says he's determined to move on from Delta's catastrophic misdeeds and to focus on the good news. The foundation can be saved, and best of all, those old rumors about Sammy and drug addiction have been put to rest."

"Did you tell him about Oriana Wynn and her craving for an Emmy?"

"I did. Told him we're going to do our best to talk her out of it."

We agreed to arrange the meeting for seven p.m. at the ranch. Nick said he would confirm with Rella and Harry. As soon as we ended our call, I texted Oriana.

She responded, thanking me for arranging the meeting and indicating that Kass had withheld permission for her to air anything about Delta until he gave her the go-ahead. I almost felt guilty, knowing she expected something different from our gathering than what I had in mind. She even asked if she could bring a cameraman. I rejected that idea, telling her to come alone and plan to use a pen and notepad—no recording. She agreed and confirmed that she would arrive at the set time.

I texted Nick again letting him know that Oriana was confirmed for seven. I asked if he was okay with leaving Buck home alone for a couple of hours.

He's doing okay. More good news. TPD says he's no longer a person of interest.

You?

Same.

So Nick was off their radar as well. I inhaled the first deep breath I had experienced in almost two weeks and replied.

So glad. Love you.

AT WORK I FOUND AN EMAIL from Quinn announcing an impromptu department head meeting at noon in the conference room. That meant he had some sort of announcement to make. I assumed it would be related to Delta's case and wondered how much he would say. I probably had more firsthand information about it than anyone at TMC.

Bernie arrived in the library at nine o'clock and wasted no time asking if Hannah's sketch had helped to solve the Sawyer case. He had heard an early news report that TPD was making significant progress.

"Yes, it was very helpful," I said. "You should be proud that you came to me with your concern about the purse."

"Lola and I won't need to bother you again, now that we have a new Public Relations Officer. Did Mr. Quinn tell you about it?"

"No, but we have a department head meeting today. Maybe he'll mention it."

"I suspect he will." Bernie chuckled. "Yep, I suspect he will."

Puzzled by his behavior, I asked if he knew who had been hired.

"It's on the grapevine, but I best not spill the beans."

I nodded. "Loose lips?"

He gave me a thumbs up. "There ya go."

Bernie went to work pampering our plants and attacking the floor with his carpet sweeper while I tended to library business. His joshing response about the new PR hire had stirred my curiosity, so I asked him to finish up a few minutes early. As soon as he was gone, I locked up and left for the meeting in the main tower.

All of the department heads were present: Cleo Cominoli, Medical Affairs; Edna Roda, Nursing Director; and Mary Barton, Social Services were among the usual group. There were two others there I had not expected to see. One was Enid Whitehorn. The other, to my surprise, was Varsha Singh. Quinn called the meeting to order and started with his administrator's report.

"Our first item of business is to welcome our newly hired Public Relations Officer, Varsha Singh."

Heads bobbed in surprise around the room, then smiles and applause broke out along with calls of "Welcome," and

"Congratulations." When Varsha stood to thank everyone and commented about how much she looked forward to her new position, I spotted something a few others might have missed: a diamond ring twinkling on her third finger, left hand.

I caught Quinn's eye and felt certain I saw him color up a bit. His reluctance to discuss whether Enid Whitehorn was a temp finally made sense. With his next announcement, he confirmed that Enid had accepted the position of full-time Executive Assistant to the Administrative Office. Enid received the same warm welcome that had greeted Varsha.

After Quinn's update on the Delta Sawyer case, emphasizing that the hospital and Dr. Beardsley had been cleared of any malpractice, various department head reports were read into the record and the meeting came to a close. Quinn asked me to accompany him to his office where he closed the door, sat behind his desk and asked me to take a seat. He got right to the point. "I would have liked to announce a change in your position at today's meeting, but we've had no chance to discuss it. Do you have time for that now?"

"Yes, I have as much time as you need."

"Then I'll start, but I want you to jump in if you have any questions."

"I have one already," I said. "I mentioned to Nick that I might be offered a promotion, and he has encouraged me to accept, if that's what I want. I told him I wouldn't know until I heard more about the offer. I'm wondering how much the added responsibility would affect my personal life."

Quinn cocked an eyebrow. "Family? Marriage and kids? That sort of thing?"

I nodded. "I saw the ring on Varsha's finger. I'm guessing the prospect of shared parenting of her four young children has made you more aware of balancing work and home life."

Quinn smiled. "Definitely, and it's raised my awareness of the personal needs of our employees. If that's the issue that has you hesitating, let me assure you, your responsibilities here will never force you to choose between your work and a family." He grinned. "Assuming you and Nick Alexander are planning a future together."

A warm sensation spread through me. "What you've said definitely takes us another step in that direction."

"Then let's discuss the particulars." He pointed his pen at a sheet of paper on his desk. "You're aware that there are twenty-two medical centers in our corporate chain?"

"I saw that in the last annual report. Twenty facilities spaced around the country's contiguous states, plus one in Alaska and one in Hawaii."

"That's right, I'd forgotten you have the annual reports in the library."

"What does that have to do with me?"

"Our forensic consortium has come to the attention of the CEO of the parent company. I've been asked to offer you a position created specifically to utilize your expertise in duplicating our library model in each facility in the corporate chain. None of the other medical center librarians have your specialized training in forensic collections, or in how to develop a consortium that works like ours." He paused, then sipped from a water glass on his desk. "That's the general idea. What do you think?"

What he described seemed so obvious, I wondered why it had never occurred to me. "I think it's a wonderful idea, but it sounds like it would involve a lot of travel."

"Not necessarily. Decisions about travel would be up to you. There are lots of innovative ways to communicate these days without face-to-face meetings. Video conferencing, webinars, that sort of thing. Corporate will see that you have whatever you need along those lines." He formed his fingers into a steeple. "So again, what do you think?"

"That sounds workable." I smiled. "Actually, it sounds exciting. I can't wait to tell Nick."

Quinn stood. "Is that a yes? Home office is hoping for an answer soon."

"I think so, but I'll run it by Nick and have my answer for you on Monday."

"Good." He walked me to his door. "If you don't mind my saying so, Nick is a lucky man."

I looked at my handsome, charismatic boss, thinking of his strength of character and his integrity and the hard times we had shared protecting the hospital and its patients. I knew I would always feel safe and respected in the environment he had created at Timbergate Medical Center.

"If you don't mind *my* saying so, Varsha is a lucky woman."

Back in the library my thoughts turned repeatedly to the meeting with Oriana set for seven that evening. I felt no guilt about misleading her into thinking the gathering would add substance to her scoop when my hopes lay in the other direction.

Chapter 37

————◆————

NICK CAME OUT TO THE RANCH Thursday afternoon to help me with chores. He brought Ginger, whose tail spun with delight at being back at home. She and Fanny chased each other around the backyard playing a canine-feline game of tag.

Harry and Rella arrived at six thirty, half an hour before Oriana. The four of us filled coffee cups and gathered around the wrought-iron table in the family room to plan our strategy. Ginger plopped down near Nick's feet. Fanny disappeared into one of her many hidey-holes.

I spoke first. "Oriana Wynn is a career-hungry woman who wants to make her mark as a journalist. She thinks a bombshell piece about Buck unwittingly marrying the woman who caused his daughter's death is her springboard to bigger things. She expects us to help her. It'll be a test of her character when she realizes we're going to do the opposite."

Nick leaned back, arms crossed. "Buck has been through enough. It's barely been twelve hours since he learned that it was Delta who gave Sammy the meth at the swim meet."

"How did he find out?" Harry asked.

"I heard it from Aimee last night," Nick said, "and had to break it to Buck this morning. The last thing he needs is to see it flaunted on television news for no reason other than sensationalism."

Rella spoke up. "We have to convince that reporter to let it go, but how do we do that? Is there any chance Wynn has a conscience?"

Harry answered. "That's what we're here to find out." Ginger sidetracked him for a moment, nuzzling his hand. He gave her head a pat, looked up at us and finished his thought. "I knew all three swimmers back when I was lifeguarding for their team. They seemed like friendly competitors, but we all saw how Delta goaded them, pitting them against each other."

"Maybe she thought it would bring out the competitive edge in each of them." Nick said.

Rella cast her eyes down at the table. "Sometimes that sort of bullying backfires." I thought back to what she told me about her overbearing stage mom and the ill-fated beauty pageant.

Nick reached over to touch my hand. "You've had the only direct contact with her, what do you think?"

"She's hell-bent on an Emmy. She plans to emphasize that Delta was the source of the drug that accidentally killed Sammy Sawyer. She'll cap it off by pointing out that Delta accidentally died of a fatal overdose herself. Apparently, she sees that as some sort of bleak irony."

Nick stood up. "So she's going to paint Buck Sawyer as a duped, tragic figure for all to see." He paced the room, eyes blazing. "That's unacceptable. It wouldn't be a prize-winning story if it had happened to someone who isn't rich or famous, or notable in some way. It's Buck's prominence that she's counting on. She's going to exploit the fact that even a billionaire with a foundation dedicated to fighting illicit drugs couldn't save his daughter or his wife from death by overdose." He stopped pacing. Looked at me. "Is that about right?"

I simply nodded.

Rella spoke softly. "Buck has dealt with enough grief and tragedy in his life. He doesn't deserve this."

Harry smiled and his dark eyes took on their inscrutable look.

"If Oriana Wynn can't locate her conscience on her own, we're going to have to help her find it."

Nick came back to sit at the table. He glanced at his phone. "Any ideas? She's going to show up here in about ten minutes."

"There is one thing," I said. "She told me that Delta kept her silent all these years by threatening to reveal that a paper Oriana co-wrote in journalism school contained plagiarism. Her co-author confessed that he had done it without her knowledge, but Oriana still worried. Her journalism career could have been ruined if Delta made good her threat and manipulated that incident successfully. "Any ideas what we could do with that?"

Harry grinned and took out his phone. "I'll give it a shot." His thumbs skipped across the screen.

"Any other ideas?" Nick said.

"She wants an Emmy," I said. "What if we can convince her that the story she has in mind will ruin her reputation as a professional journalist? If it did get into print, her career would be blemished and she'd probably end up writing for sleezy tabloids."

"And that would end her hopes for an Emmy." Rella's bemused smile was mirrored by those of Nick and Harry.

Oriana arrived wearing one of her Lois Lane outfits—a navy skirt and matching blazer over a white blouse. Her page boy was smooth and her makeup flawless. Minutes before, Harry had unearthed an article in the archives of her alma mater's newspaper about the controversy over her master's thesis. We invited her to sit with us at the table. I introduced Nick and Rella. Oriana recognized Harry from their swim team years. I brought her a cup of coffee and took my place beside Nick.

Oriana took a notepad and pen from her purse. "Shall we get started? I can't tell you how much I appreciate this opportunity. I want to be sure I spell all of your names correctly when I quote you for this story."

The four of us glanced around the table, meeting each other's eyes. I got the message. It was up to me to set her straight.

"I'm afraid you won't need that, Oriana. We asked you here because we're all deeply concerned about the piece you intend to write and the impact it will have on Buck Sawyer."

She looked up from her notepad, her face tight, her eyes narrowing. "Come again?"

Nick spoke. "Miss Wynn, there's something we want you to understand. Buck Sawyer has spent the last ten years of his life grieving the loss of his daughter. All that time he believed she was tricked into using meth at a party after that swim meet where she competed along with you and Bonnie Belcher."

"Yes, yes," Oriana said. "Sammy died that night. Eight years later Bonnie Belcher Beardsley also died of a drug overdose, and now their trainer, Delta Dearborn Sawyer—also at that swim meet— has died of a drug overdose. It's all part of what will make this such an intriguing story. The human interest. And the connections to our current drug crisis."

Rella shifted in her chair to make direct eye contact with Oriana. "We're thinking of one human being in particular. A man who deserves compassion and privacy, not public embarrassment and humiliation."

Under Rella's unyielding glare, Oriana shrank in her chair. "So this is a setup? You brought me here to quash my story?"

"I remember you from swimming competitions," Harry said. "You were the most competitive person on the team. Sometimes it worked, but you also made some choices that cost you a race. Do you want to risk a story that will brand you as an unfeeling hack willing to exploit a decent, generous man's grief for the sake of a sensational story?"

"Think about that," I said. "You risk being shunned by any reputable news outlet."

Harry held up his phone. "You already have one strike against you with this plagiarism accusation."

Oriana stiffened. "I was cleared of that."

"The taint never really goes away," he said. "Why risk another blow to your reputation? Your superiors at the TV station will face the wrath of every viewer who cares about Buck Sawyer. You'll be fired and end up writing tabloid stories about Elvis sightings and alien babies."

Oriana stared across the room for a moment as if imagining that future. When she brought herself back, her eyes filled.

"Sammy was a good friend to me back then. A kind, innocent girl. She knew I wasn't a gifted swimmer . . . how hard I had to try. She even gave me pointers when all the other girls were only looking out for themselves. Until her death, no one I cared about had ever died. I was horrified and vowed that I would someday get revenge by exposing Delta to everyone in Sawyer County and beyond."

"It's too late for that," Harry said.

"I guess you're right. Delta's gone. And so is Sammy." Oriana picked up a napkin to dab at her tears. She cleared her throat, inhaled a deep breath. "What's the point if all I accomplish is more pain for Sammy's father?"

The atmosphere in the room shifted. The pressure dropped as Nick, Harry, Rella and I exhaled in relief.

LATER THAT EVENING WHEN NICK AND I were finally alone, we each put on an extra layer against the chilly night, picked up our wine glasses and went out to sit on the veranda.

"You think the reporter will back off?" Nick asked.

"I think so. She's career-oriented and loves her profession. She knows what it would mean to lose the respect of her peers."

"She seemed sincere about her feelings for Sammy and Buck. I was surprised to see that side of her."

"So was I. Shows you never know about people."

"Sounds like she stepped up during your scuffle with Tremont," Nick said. "You have to give her some credit for the pepper spray. Every time I think of Tremont threatening you with a gun, I see red."

"It wasn't loaded, Nick. As desperate as he was, he knew he wasn't going to shoot me. I was never really in danger."

"Kass told me about the gun, but it doesn't matter. You didn't know that at the time. All I can think about is what if it *had* been loaded?"

"I would have disarmed him. In fact, the only reason I didn't was because of Oriana's terrible timing."

"You think you could have taken his gun?"

"I've done it dozens of times in *randori* and in tournaments. And that was against opponents who were aware of my intentions and prepared to stop me. Tremont would have been easier, but you know that."

"I'd like to think so, but there are no guarantees." He reached down to give Ginger's head a gentle pat.

My thoughts turned to his remark from two weeks ago. *"I can't handle the thought of you in jeopardy."* No point hesitating any longer. If there was a stumbling block in our relationship, we needed to face it.

"Nick, I know you've worried about risks I've taken in the past, but this time was different. I avoided putting myself in danger and it happened anyway."

"I know, and what bothers me is that because of me, you were doing Buck a favor. Otherwise, you wouldn't have been in that building alone when Tremont showed up."

"But think about that, Nick. What if I hadn't been there? Tremont said he'd decided to tell the truth about the pills and the embezzling, but what if he'd changed his mind? He was torn between two terrible choices: stay quiet and run the risk of Buck being convicted of killing Delta, or confess and go to jail, leaving his wife to survive alone in some nursing home. It makes me ill to think that's what the Tremont's are facing now."

"Buck might have some influence there. He's going to do whatever he can."

"That sounds like Buck. He's an amazing human being." I sipped my wine.

Nick stayed still for a moment, looking up to the sparkling western sky. "Any chance you've had your fill of crime solving?"

"Not entirely, but if I accept Quinn's promotion offer, I'll be going about it differently. Strictly hands off."

"Care to explain?"

"The offer is even better than I imagined." I told Nick how home office wanted to expand my forensic library consortium model. "I'd be training and mentoring all of the other health science librarians in the corporation."

"That's awesome, Aimee. You'd be fantastic in that role. Are you going to go for it?"

"I haven't decided. I said I'd have an answer for him by Monday."

"Why the wait? You deserve the promotion and the recognition of your skills. Is there a downside?"

"I don't see one, but I wanted your input because it'll involve some traveling. I thought it should be a mutual decision." I hoped Nick understood the subtext of my comment. Either we were headed for a future together, or we weren't. I needed to know.

"We talked about this the other night. I respect your career as much as you do mine, but I do have a question about the traveling."

"Okay. Feel free to ask."

"We've already been apart so much because of my flying that I was hoping to reverse that situation in the future. Is your new job going to mean we'll have even more time apart?"

At the word *future*, a lightness came over me. "I asked Quinn about travel and he assured me the bulk of my work could be done virtually. Any travel decisions would be up to me."

"Good to know." Nick smiled. "I have one more travel-related concern."

"What's that?"

"For those times when you *do* have to travel and I'm home alone, you'll need to show me how to chop the hay for Old Doolittle."

"It's a deal."

"Then let's go inside." He picked up our wine glasses. "I have an idea about how we can celebrate your promotion."

BY THE TIME I WOKE UP FRIDAY MORNING, the local television station had already announced Nora Nester as the new Mayor of Timbergate. Ernest Wright had conceded with dignity, pledging to give her his support.

I took the morning off so I could show up as promised at the Timbergate Police Department to be interviewed by Detective Kass. Oriana and I both insisted that we did not want to press charges against Tremont over the misunderstanding that had taken place at the Sawyer Foundation building. He had been acting on the assumption that we were intruders who had no right to be there. His unloaded weapon with no firing pin confirmed that he had no intention of shooting us.

Without revealing the specific details of her medical status, I advised Kass about the burden Faye Tremont's long-term illness had created for the couple, and the impact it had on Fletcher Tremont's psychological and emotional health. I urged Kass to consider the circumstances and to do whatever he could to see that leniency would be considered.

Oriana agreed. She went further by inviting Kass to be interviewed on the air about the outcome of the Delta Sawyer case, assuring him that she would not insert editorial comment of any kind. With that change of attitude on her part, I thought there was a chance that someday she might have a shot at an Emmy.

When our interview ended, Kass excused Oriana, but asked me to stay on a bit longer. Puzzled, I tried to imagine what he had in mind.

Kass closed the door behind Oriana and came back to his desk.

"Is something wrong?" I asked. "I hope I didn't overstep about Tremont's situation."

He shook his head. "No, but your assessment of his mental and emotional status reminded me of something I've been meaning to ask you for some time."

"What's that?"

"You have a unique perspective on law enforcement due to your forensic specialty combined with being a health sciences librarian. You also have a creative mind. I'd like to propose a way to use your skills to enhance the effectiveness of the investigators on our police force."

"I don't see how that would be necessary. Your officers are well trained, and I know Sawyer County has a law library at your disposal."

"True, but that library has no forensic collection. Neither does any other branch of the Sawyer County Library. Yours is the only forensic collection between here and Seattle."

"But TPD is already a member of our forensic consortium.

You're eligible to request any information you might need. You can go online to the library's catalog to review the contents of our collection."

"There's the problem," Kass said. "We're so stretched for manpower that none of us has time to explore your site and become familiar with all of those resources. I'd like for you to provide sessions for our detectives on a periodic basis—maybe quarterly—to give them an overview of all of the various forensic materials at their disposal and to instruct them on navigating your online catalog."

"That sounds like a great idea. Quarterly would be good. That way we could catch any new hires to your department, and also point out any new additions to our collection."

"Then you'll run it by Mr. Quinn?"

"Absolutely. I think he'll be all for it."

From there I headed to work and dropped by Quinn's office to tell him that I was ready to give him my answer about the promotion.

"So you didn't need the weekend after all." Quinn reached for a file folder on the corner of his desk. "Have a seat. I hope you brought good news."

"I think so. Nick and I talked it over last night, and I think I'm ready to accept."

Quinn popped up and extended his hand. "That's fantastic."

"Before we make this final, though, I do have something to run by you."

Quinn dropped back into his chair. "Okay, let's hear it."

I told him what Detective Kass had proposed, and Quinn was on board immediately.

"Now that we've settled that, Miss Machado, can I have your final answer?"

I accepted the promotion, and we signed the paperwork making it official.

Chapter 38

TWO WEEKS LATER NICK AND I watched Oriana's restrained and respectful interview with Detective Kass, who reported that Timbergate PD was no longer investigating Delta Sawyer's death. The coroner had ruled it an accidental, self-inflicted overdose.

A lot had happened in two weeks. Tremont was able to demonstrate Delta's extortion with her prints on the pill vial and with text messages from her that he had saved on his phone. The fabricated grants were being investigated by the Federal Trade Commission.

We learned privately from Kass that a compassionate judge had taken into consideration Faye Tremont's health and how dependent she was on her husband. Even though I did not press charges against Tremont, he had brandished a weapon. Despite the fact that it was unloaded, he was put on probation and sentenced to community service. He was ordered to work one day a week for six months without pay at the Sawyer County Health and Human Services Agency. His assignment was to assist families looking for help in dealing with the financial burdens of long-term illness.

Finally, Tremont was prohibited from serving on the board of the Sawyer Foundation or participating in its grants program or any other, but Buck was able to keep him employed as the general manager of day-to-day operations unrelated to the grants program.

When Buck discovered the devastating financial burden that had led to Tremont's regretful choices, he immediately began the process of procuring long-term care insurance for all of his employees and their families.

The election outcome had resulted in new possibilities for Buck's mission. Mayor Nora Nester was thrilled about a state-of-the-art drug rehab center in Timbergate and pledged her full support. Buck's partnership with the TMC Foundation was secure. *Firm Foundations Renewal Center* would go ahead as envisioned.

As a result of this new direction for himself, Buck informed Nick and Rella that their services as corporate pilots would no longer be as demanding as they had been in the past, and had invited them, along with Harry and me, to discuss how that might impact their employment.

THE FOUR OF US GATHERED A WEEK LATER on the veranda of the Highland Ranch on a bright Sunday afternoon. The massive oaks towering over the property had leafed out, and the llamas were grazing on tender new field grasses. Buck was due any minute, and in spite of the idyllic weather and scenery, an aura of apprehension existed. None of us knew what he had in mind.

I brought lemonade and a platter of sugar cookies out to the table. Buck arrived looking stronger and more relaxed than I had seen him in months. He poured himself a glass of lemonade and took two cookies, which he placed carefully on a napkin.

"I suppose you're all wondering why I wanted this get-together." There was a murmur of agreement. He nodded. "Thought so. Sorry to keep you in suspense, but I had to give this some serious thought before bringing it up."

Nick swallowed a sip of lemonade and set his glass down. "Whatever it is you have in mind, we'll understand."

Buck smiled. "That's good to know, because what I have in mind will depend on that."

The four of us exchanged puzzled glances. Rella spoke first. "Buck, if you no longer need two pilots, I should be the one to go. It's only fair."

"No, no." Buck waved his hand. "That's generous of you, but what I have in mind is quite the opposite."

"You definitely have our attention," Nick said.

"All right, this first question is for Harry. You may have heard by now that the Sawyer Foundation is partnering with the TMC Foundation to open a multi-dimensional drug rehab center that will serve patients from anywhere in the country. We could use your help."

"I have heard about it," Harry said. "Not sure what you have in mind, but I could put together some martial arts classes for the patients."

Buck grinned. "That's not a bad idea, but what we need right now is an architect and general contractor to erect a building. It'll be large, at least three stories. That's going to require a heap of work, both in the planning phase and the execution." Buck locked eyes with Harry. "Are you available to spearhead the project?"

All heads turned toward Harry, whose jaw had dropped.

I nudged my brother. "Hey, he's talking to you."

Harry blinked. "Yes, of course I'm available."

"Then it's done. You're hired." Buck reached out and shook Harry's hand. "We'll make it official tomorrow in my office."

Buck next looked my way. "Aimee, I'm hoping we can find a way for you to be involved, although Nick tells me you're going to have your hands full with an important new position at TMC."

"I will, but there is a way I can help. Once the *Renewal Center* is up and running, you'll need the services of TMC's Health Sciences Library. As a partner with the TMC Foundation, you'll have access to every available resource that relates to your mission. I'll still be in a position to make sure of that."

"That's a true blessing. You're the very person I'd want to count on for something so critical to our success."

I mumbled a "thank you," feeling humbled by his trust.

Buck took a bite of cookie and a sip of lemonade. He wiped his mouth with a napkin and gave a satisfied sigh.

"Now let's talk about my pilots."

Nick glanced at Rella. She nodded. "We're ready."

Buck straightened in his chair. "You'll both be doing less flying for the Sawyer Foundation in the future, what with the emphasis on the rehab center, but before you start looking to pick up work elsewhere, I have a favor to ask." He swallowed hard and hesitated for a moment. "My late daughter, Sammy, always talked about wanting to fly. She even had a few lessons. Her dream was to be a flight instructor, and I think it's time to do something about that. What would the two of you think about operating a flight school and charter service?"

Close to tears, I held my breath waiting for their answer.

"I would love that," Rella said.

Nick rubbed his hands together. "Count me in."

"Then we'll start that ball rolling," Buck said. "Any ideas what we should call the business? I'd like to come up with something inclusive, that shows you're more than employees, you're going to be partners."

I took a shot. "How about an acronym made up of your last names? Sawyer, Alexander, and Olstad? Maybe SAO Flight School and Charter?"

Rella raised her hand. "That might not work." She looked at Harry and blushed.

"You'd better make that SAM," my brother said. "She won't be Olstad much longer."

"Oh my gosh," I stammered. "Do you mean what I think you mean?" They both nodded.

"Then let's go with Sawyer, Alexander and Machado." Nick said. "What name could be more perfect for the business than SAM'S FLIGHT SCHOOL AND CHARTER SERVICE?"

Buck choked up with emotion for a moment before he managed to speak. "That would mean the world to me." There were handshakes all around before Buck took his leave.

The four of us who remained had more to talk about, considering the bombshell Rella and Harry had dropped.

Nick tilted his chin at Harry. "When did you pop the question, Buddy?"

"It's been on our minds for a while, but we didn't want to steal your thunder." Harry and Rella exchanged glances. He took her hand and they walked inside, leaving us alone.

I looked at Nick. "What was that about?"

"Harry knows I've been trying to work up the nerve to do this." He reached into his pocket and pulled out a piece of baling wire twisted into the shape of a ring. "I'm ready, Aimee, and I hope you are, too. I can barely remember what my life was like before I met you. I know I didn't understand what love was all about. I can't imagine a future without you."

I burst out laughing and crying at the same time. "Yes, I'm ready, too, but if you think you're going to seal the deal with that goofy ring, you'd better think again."

He slipped it on my finger. "It's a place holder. I thought you deserved to pick out the ring you want, since you'll be wearing it for the rest of your life."

Harry and Rella must have been eavesdropping from the family room, because they reappeared wearing pleased grins. I held up my hand with the makeshift ring.

"So it looks like there'll be two weddings," Harry said. "Who gets to go first?"

"Good question," I said. "We have to think about Mom and Dad and two sets of grandparents. This would mean they'd all have to make the long trip twice."

"Not necessarily," Harry said. "We could plan dates for both weddings close together so they'd only have to travel once."

That sparked an idea. "I have a thought, but it's up to the rest of you." I glanced at each of them. "It's sort of wild, so be very honest with your answer."

"Okay," Harry said, "spill it, Sis."

"How would you feel about a double wedding?" The three of them sat in silence, letting the idea sink in. Then Rella started to cry. A sight I never expected to see. "Oh, Rella, I'm so sorry, I understand if you'd rather have a separate wedding of your own."

Rella shook her head. "No, that's not it at all. My tears are happy. I can't believe you would share your special day with me."

"Do you think it would be okay with your family? I didn't think about that."

Rella took a breath. She looked at Harry and at Nick. "I think they both know what this means to me, Aimee. You're the only one who doesn't know my whole story. I was born to an unwed mother who died in childbirth. She had no relatives, so I've been an orphan all my life."

"But you told me about your mother," I said. "The stage mom at the beauty pageant."

"That was all true, except that she wasn't my real mother. When I told you that story, the details of my birth were beside the point. I'm sorry if I misled you."

"Then who was she?"

"She was one of my foster mothers. Until that incident, she was talking about adopting me, but after I bolted from the pageant, she wanted nothing more to do with me and the feeling was mutual. I spent the rest of my teens in other foster homes, mostly with good people, but I was never adopted. I have no family." She hesitated. "No, that's not right, I *had* no family, but now I do, and it would be amazing to share my wedding day with you."

I glanced at Nick and Harry. Both of them were swallowing and working their jaws in the hopes that I was not about to see two grown men cry. Rella would never be an orphan again.

SLIPPING INTO BED WITH NICK THAT NIGHT, I knew it was time to bring up the Littletrees' request.

"Nick, there's something I've been wanting to tell you for a while now."

"Sounds serious," he said, "should I be worried?"

"I hope not, but it does involve a serious decision. Laurie and Daniel Littletree are hoping we'll agree to be little Kiona's godparents. I told Laurie I'd have to check with you since you're already godfather to your nephew."

"No rule says I can't do both." He leaned over to kiss my cheek. "I'm all for it. Besides, if I ever do have to step in for either one, you'll be right there with me."

"Right, we'd both be doing double duty. I hadn't thought about that."

"How long has it been since Laurie asked about this?"

"It's been a while. I was waiting for the right time to bring it up."

He reached for my hand and touched my sweet, silly baling wire engagement ring. "Until you were sure we'd both be in it for the long haul?"

"Something like that."

"Would you have agreed to be Kiona's godmother with or without me?"

"Probably, but I wanted it to be both of us."

Nick took me in his arms. "Lady, it's going to be both of us from now on.

Chapter 39

SUNDAY AFTERNOON IN MID-JUNE found the four of us standing on a temporary platform in the backyard of the Highland Ranch. The local wedding rental business had transformed the outdoor space with folding chairs, pop-up canopies, and an ivy-covered backdrop of white lattice work. Mayor Nora Nester stood before us, ready to officiate. She wore a floral dress with touches of pink and blue cut in a flattering style that told me she had decided to brighten her image.

Rella and I each wore white knee-length dresses. Hers was slim-lined and accented with blue, in honor of her past service in the military. Mine was flared at the hem and trimmed with red, as a nod to my mother and the Chinese tradition of red for happy occasions like weddings. Harry and Nick wore dress suits with boutonnieres that matched the accent colors in our bouquets.

My father had given me away, and Buck did that honor for Rella, which seemed fitting, since she had become as close to him as a surrogate daughter.

Nick's brother-in-law stood as his best man, and Uncle Gabe was Harry's. I chose Cleo Cominoli to be my matron of honor, and

Rella chose Oriana Wynn, her first flight school student, as her
maid of honor.

After the vows, the four of us stood facing the assembled guests
while Dr. Phyllis Poole sang "At Last," to the accompaniment of
Jared Quinn and TMC's Code Blues combo.

At the outdoor banquet table, guests enjoyed a surf and turf
meal catered by Margie's Bean Pot. Margie provided filet mignon
and lobster along with mashed potatoes and her special recipe for
green beans with butter-toasted almond slices. A separate table
held two multi-tiered wedding cakes, one on each end, both decorated with Margie's special vanilla bean frosting. One of the cakes
was topped with a dark-haired groom and a blond bride. The top-
per on the other cake was a fair-haired groom and a bride with
raven locks.

After food and cake were served, toasts were made, and photos
taken, the children of our guests were each given apple slices and a
few of Amah's homemade llama cookies. The youngsters gleefully
handed out treats to the festively groomed members of the herd
who stood behind the pasture fence watching the celebration with
great curiosity.

WHEN THE GUESTS HAD GONE, members of the Machado and
Alexander families gathered in the family room. There was talk
about honeymoons in the Azores. Harry, Nick, Rella and I all
agreed that while we loved the double wedding, we would not
be following up with a double honeymoon. Theirs would be first,
since Rella had never been to the islands, and we were all eager for
her to have that experience.

When it came time to do kitchen clean up, Amah and Jack and
Grandpa Machado and Tanya took over, insisting we newlyweds
should make better use of our first night as married couples. My
parents and Nick's hung out on the veranda, enjoying a chance to
become better acquainted.

Harry and Rella went on their way, and Nick and I left the main
house to walk down the lane under a clear, starlit sky, moving
slowly and quietly to avoid startling the wooly mounds of kushed,

drowsing llamas. We had agreed the perfect place to spend our wedding night was in the barn-top apartment where we had first come together to work out the challenges to our relationship.

Tucked under cool satin sheets, a wedding gift from Mom and Dad, we snuggled in each other's arms.

Nick kissed the top of my head. "That went well, don't you think?"

"It was perfect." I leaned my head on his shoulder. "Thank you for agreeing to share the day with Harry and Rella."

"I'd have shared it with an army if that's what it took to get us married." He proved his point with a kiss that set off a shiver. I pulled back, needing to break the spell.

"There's something we should talk about."

"Now? Really?"

"Especially now. We have to decide whether we want to continue living in the ranch house."

"Why tonight?"

"Amah and Jack know your job has changed, and about my promotion. They're thinking about putting the property on the market if we're not going to continue living here. They know we'll eventually want to start a family, and they'd love to see us raise our children here at the ranch if we think someday we'll be in a position to buy it. They'd work with us on the terms of a sale, but in the meantime, we can stay and cover all of the costs of maintaining the place in lieu of paying rent."

"Nick sat up. What did you tell them?"

"I said I'd talk to you."

"I love this ranch, Aimee, but it's your call. You have a more demanding job now, and my time is already filling up with students at the flight school and with charters. On top of that, we'd be keeping up the ranch house and the acreage and the livestock—unless you want to give up the llamas."

"No, I can't imagine not having them. Think about the future. We'll need two for ourselves and one for each of our kids when we go packing in the wilderness. More importantly, the ranch house has plenty of bedrooms for when we start making babies."

"So we stay put, keep the llamas and make some babies? Does that mean you're ready? About the babies?"

A memory came back to me of walking with Nick along Horta Marina in the Azores when a young couple passed by with their dimpled baby girl. Nick and I had talked that day about the kind of parents we hoped to be: loving, kind, honest and courageous.

"Yes, I'm ready, and I'd love to see our children grow up right here."

Nick took me in his arms. "Then let's get started."

The End

SHARON ST. GEORGE is the author of the hospital-based Aimee Machado Mystery series set in rural Timbergate, a fictional town in Far Northern California. She is a member of Mystery Writers of America and Sisters in Crime. St. George is the Associate Editor of *FIRST DRAFT*, a quarterly newsletter produced by the Guppy Chapter of Sisters in Crime. Her past writing credits include advertising copy, newspaper feature stories, three produced plays and a book on NASA's Space Food Project. She holds degrees in English and Theatre Arts and enjoys acting in and directing local theatre productions in her Northern California hometown when her writing schedule permits.

Learn more at SharonStGeorge.com

9 781942 078623